# NATURE'S CHILD

# NATURE'S CHILD

*The Guardian*

B O O K   1

D A N I E L   B A R N E S

# PALMETTO

**P U B L I S H I N G**

Charleston, SC

www.PalmettoPublishing.com

Hardcover ISBN: 979-8-8229-2867-1
Paperback ISBN: 979-8-8229-2868-8
eBook ISBN: 979-8-8229-2869-5

*For Glenna*

# AUTHOR'S NOTE

The legend of the great cities that can be seen even to this day, as they lay abandoned and crumbling all over the planet, has lost much in the telling over the last two hundred years. If asked about these last vestiges of a long dead civilization, most people would shrug their shoulders and reply casually: "The sun destroyed them."

For the most part, they would be right. It was the sun—or "sun flares," as my grandfather called them—that was the beginning of the end for these great symbols of wealth and power. I say the beginning of the end because, truth be told, it was a combination of many things that has brought us to where we are today. Drought, famine, plague, and even war all had their part to play in the drama. Someday, maybe, someone will write this history, but you won't find it in these pages.

You see, this is not a story about the fall of a civilization or of the struggles that followed. True, I have attempted to put down some accounts and theories about the "old world," but only when they pertained to the story—even now I am not sure that they are completely accurate. The fact is, people have moved on, and for the most part, they are content to leave those decaying skylines behind them.

As for the rest of this history and its accuracy, you will simply have to take my word for it. I have tried to put it down as accurately as I could. Some of the incidents recorded here are actual legends passed down by the native people of the northland. Other resources include, but are not limited to, my uncle Jacob, my uncle Kitchi, and my grandpa David, all of who were firsthand witnesses; however, the bulk of it I got straight from the horse's mouth, so to speak: my father. He related it to me on his deathbed, and I have no doubt that he was telling the truth, at least as he understood it. Why *he* never wrote it down, and why he kept it to himself for so many years, I can only guess. It could be that he felt it contained thoughts and emotions that belonged only to him…and one other.

I only mention this because in truth, for all its adventure and all its mystery, this is really nothing more than a love story—the tale of one man and one woman who are bound together not only by love, but by a fate that transcends mortal life. You, dear reader, may dismiss this as simple romanticism on my part, and I wouldn't necessarily disagree with you. I have been accused on more than one occasion of being a hopeless romantic, but it doesn't bother me in the least! In fact, I take it as a great compliment, because, as you will see if you continue to read this story, I get that particular trait from my mother.

Becca

# PROLOGUE

Judge Marcas leaned back in his chair and put his feet up on the enormous desk—it wasn't the original, the one that had sat for so many years in that great white house in DC, but it *was* a reasonable facsimile. It had been delivered just this morning, and other than the chair and himself, it was the only thing in the room.

The building that housed this fine new piece of furniture was the old capitol building in what used to be the great state of Missouri. The building itself was crumbling all around him, but that wasn't the point, was it? This was the seat of power; this was the place where decisions were made—decisions that could affect the whole country—and now he held that seat!

It had been hard won and not without a great deal of sacrifice, but he was certain that in the annals of history, he would be vindicated. Leaning forward, he ran his hands along the polished mahogany and smiled. Had anyone been there to witness this action, they would have shivered, because when the judge smiled, he looked every bit as crazy as he really was—to his credit he was vaguely aware of this fact, so he rarely smiled in public.

He was a tall, dark, slender man with hair growing in little tufts at various points on his emaciated face. For years he had been trying to cultivate a full beard to no avail. The hair would grow thick in some places but not at all in others, causing it to look patchy at best. Still, he had never shaved, and he would spend hours in front of the mirror shaping and darkening the facial hair, trying to cover the bald spots.

It wasn't vanity that drove him but obsession: Ever since he could remember, he had idolized Abraham Lincoln and everything he could find regarding the man—is morals, values, and even his appearance had been meticulously scrutinized and closely emulated by the judge. The problem was that after two hundred years of neglect, a lot of the history of Lincoln—as well as the country he served—had been lost, and what remained was more of an enigma.

The result was that Judge Marcas had come away with a somewhat distorted image of the great man; this, coupled with the fact that the judge's own values were somewhat distorted, resulted in a slightly slanted interpretation of Lincoln's ideals.

For example, on the subject of equality, Lincoln said in his great speech in 1863 that it was proposed by God that all men were created equal. Judge Marcas, on the other hand, preferred to interpret it as all men *should* be equal, and although he didn't know it, he had become the most adamant socialist to come into power since Hitler.

However, there was at least one thing that he and Lincoln did agree on and were even of the same mind completely—and it seemed to Marcas to be the most important thing of all: *The nation must be united;* on this subject he was unmovable.

His rise to power had by no means been easy. After the states' war, he had been left almost destitute like everyone else that had survived. Those were dark days; the government had been on its last legs, and lawlessness prevailed.

"If it hadn't been for me," he thought, "there would be no government, no United States. And then what?"

The country had already begun to separate into territories; the government food stores were being raided weekly by outlaws. What would happen to the people that were left in this great nation if they were left without leadership?

He shuddered. "Anarchy, that's what: every man for himself, and what kind of world was that for decent, law-abiding people?"

It never crossed his mind that there was precious little country left for him to govern. The East Coast had been completely evacuated over 150 years ago anyone living west of Kansas may as well have been living on another continent as far as this government was concerned. The part of the country that was once the Great Plains was locked in the worst drought it had seen since the early twentieth century, making it impossible for any settlements or towns to sustain themselves for long. Overall, the population of the good ole USA had dwindled to less than three million, the majority of which lived in and around the Midwest, with more and more of them migrating north to the colonies.

The colonies were a sort of loose-knit group of towns and settlements in what used to be southeastern Canada that had somehow managed to grow and even thrive over the last one hundred years. Marcas had never been there, but he had heard all sorts of wild rumors about the place. One story that had come to his ears recently was that they had begun to trade with Europe, but he seriously doubted the validity of this rumor. For one thing, if the people across the Atlantic had preserved some semblance of civilization, surely, they would have come to him as the leader of the free world before stopping anywhere else.

In reality, Judge Marcas was not only delusional about the actual scope of his power but fairly ignorant of anything going on outside of his own territory, which consisted chiefly of what was once the state of Missouri and parts of southern Illinois. He had no idea that the people across the Atlantic thought of the US as nothing more than a lawless wasteland without any sort of governing body and few resources. They were right, of course, but old ideas die hard, and the judge was just the last in a long line of men who believed they could return to the old ways: Back to before the sun had wiped out the great cities, back to before the sea had all but swallowed the east coast, back to before the plague that had wiped out millions and the states' war that had devastated the government.

His predecessor had been the one to unite the territories that were left and build the government store houses—but he had been a weak man who believed that each territory should be able to choose for themselves if they wished to be part of the new government.

"If it works," he had said, "then eventually they will all come around."

The judge sighed. "For the most part, the old fool was right!"

He had used what little technology they had left and managed to put people to work preserving and canning food and making clothing and other essentials—and even some rail lines had been reopened, running all the way to Kansas City. But for all his progress, he'd had no vision, no foresight. So, when Adam Brooks had refused to join the new government on the grounds that he saw no benefit for him or his people, the president had simply shrugged and said there is plenty of room for both of us. But Marcas, who had seen the effect firsthand of a country divided, knew better. Adam Brooks was a powerful man with a huge territory that covered what used to be northern Missouri and southern Illinois. It was said that his great-great-grandfather had foreseen the beginning of the end and had prepared for the worst by buying up huge plots of farmland and converting a large group of people to his cause even before the tragedies befell the nation. After the states' war, people started to gravitate northward, and more than a few stopped to homestead on the land that Adam's forefather had set aside, the result being that Adam Brooks governed an area nearly half as big as the rest of the union—and his people were loyal.

For a while, peace had reigned, and people prospered. Even the judge's own family had lived on Brooks's land and did pretty well for a time, only to be turned off it at the end of one summer just because the crop production wasn't up to standard. Adam never asked for rent; he only asked that every tenant provide for himself and his family and, in case of conflict, was loyal to the Brooks standard. But when harvest came around, it was always deficient, and his daddy always seemed to be in debt to Adam Brooks. Never mind that Marcas's daddy had been a shiftless man who spent more time in the bottle than he did in the field.

Normally thinking about those dark days made the judge moody, and he would grind his teeth until his jaw ached. But these thoughts only passed through his mind like a cool breeze as he sat caressing his new desk. Nothing could darken his mood today! Yes, he thought, this day had been a long time coming, but at last he could reap the rewards.

Leaning back in his chair, he suddenly wished for a cigar, but tobacco production hadn't been as good this year, and it seemed that this commodity, along with a great deal of canned vegetables, had been bought up by some conglomerate up north  before he realized it had happened. No matter: today he would put the final nail in the coffin of Adam Brooks as well as his accursed son, and the Brooks gang would become nothing more than a bad memory.

He heard footsteps coming up the stairs. He knew this would be Carl bringing his coffee and the daily news.

The newspaper was his pride and joy—really, his baby. Before its inception, there had been independent writers putting out weekly rags about the happenings in their own region, but this was the first national paper that had been printed in over a hundred years, and he along with a few close friends had started it. Now it was delivered through the mail—where there was still mail service—to post offices across the country, and it was free to whoever wanted it. Carl came in with his usual slow, timid step and set the coffee and paper down on the new desk. The judge didn't even acknowledge him but snatched up the paper with the eagerness of a child opening a present on Christmas morning and began to read.

The headline on the front page jumped out at him: "Last of the Brooks Gang to Be Sentenced Today!" Underneath, in smaller type, it said: "The honorable Judge Marcas to preside." He went over the article with a fine-tooth comb, although he knew it almost word for word, and why wouldn't he? After all, he wrote it. When he was done, he took a sip of his coffee, leaned back in his chair, and smiled.

Adam Brooks had been dead nearly thirty-five years now, and his son Jonathan "Jack" Brooks had been hung right out in front of this very building over twelve years ago; however, it had been no small job rounding up the rest of the outlaws that had sided with him, and it had nearly led to another war. If Phillip, Jonathan's brother, had stuck around instead of fleeing out west somewhere like the coward he was, things might have turned out different. Such was fate, however. Now there would be no more resistance and, best of all, no more division among the people. The fact that he really believed this only goes to show how out of touch he had become with the people he sought to rule.

Leaning forward, he took up his cup and was preparing to take his second sip when a small article at the bottom of the paper caught his eye. The tagline was small, as if it had been written as an afterthought. The judge might have missed it entirely if he hadn't set his cup down on top of it, where it formed a brown ring around the five small words. It was only eighteen little letters, but they produced a big effect on the judge that sent his blood boiling. The tag line read simply: "Was Jack our last hope?" Seething, Marcas snatched up the paper, spilling his coffee on the new desk, and stormed out of the room.

Within twenty minutes he was standing in the office of his colleague and the editor of the paper, Byron Little. He had left the capitol building in such a huff that he nearly knocked old Carl down on his way to the stables. The short ride across town had done little to cool his temper. Byron was a short, stout man with mutton chops and a bald head—this style of facial hair that had gone out in the late nineteenth century seemed to be making a comeback in the twenty-third century. The judge couldn't for the life of him understand why. On Byron, with his almost perfectly round face, you sometimes got the impression that his head was upside down, but today he was in no frame of mind to contemplate something as trivial as facial hair. He paced back and forth in the small office like a dog in a cage as Byron tried to calm him down.

"Look here, Marcas, we're not even sure who wrote it!" Byron exclaimed.

The judge, who was in no mood to be coddled, snapped back at him. "You know damn well who wrote it, and so do I!"

The editor took this opportunity to study the graffiti carved in his desk. He hated dealing with the judge under the best of circumstances, but when he was angered, the man was capable of almost anything. Slowly he looked up and said almost timidly: "We can't be sure it was your nephew."

The truth was, Byron knew very well it was the judge's nephew, Andy, who had written the article, because the boy himself had come to him the night before with the story and begged him to print it. At first he had flat out refused—not on the grounds of the story's content (Byron still liked to pretend that the paper was a fair and unbiased publication), but because of the timing of it.

"We can put it in next week," he argued, "maybe on the second page. The people will see it just the same, and your uncle—"

Here Andy interrupted him. "To hell with my uncle! He cares nothing for this paper; it's just a tool to him, a way to sell his own propaganda to the public!"

"We'll be fired!" Byron interjected. "Or worse!" he said, drawing a finger across his thick neck.

But without missing a beat, Andy argued, "You can say I snuck it in. Me and Meg are leaving tomorrow anyway, headed north. I hear a man can write whatever he feels in the colonies, and I'm a pretty fair writer. We'll make it ok."

Byron had always had a soft spot in his heart for the younger man, and in the end, he had given in. Then he pulled an old jar out of the top drawer of his desk, and as he poured the whiskey into two small glasses, he said, "If only I was younger…" But that was as far as he went. They drank to each other's health, and the young man left the story sitting on the desk. Byron read it after his second pull on the jar and then called for his page. The kid appeared almost instantaneously, and Byron said, "See that this makes the morning edition, front page if it will fit." The boy didn't even look at it but darted out of the office toward the press.

Byron's attention was brought back to the present by the judge as he slammed his fist down on the desk.

"Do you hear me?" He was shouting. "I want him run out of town today! I ain't never been one to sacrifice my own flesh and blood, but if I see him again, I can't be responsible for my actions!"

Out loud, the old editor said in a small voice: "All right; ok, Judge; consider it done!" But in his head, he thought, "Oh Andy, I hope you were true to your word and you're already gone."

Three hours later, a much calmer if not happier Judge Marcas sat in his black robes behind an old desk in the courthouse. The anger that had been brought on by the mere sight of the name Jack Brooks had been gradually turning to a feeling of dread that he was at a loss to explain. This feeling of foreboding, however, vanished when he heard the bailiff announce in one long practiced stream: "All rise—this court is in session. The Honorable Judge Marcas presiding."

"Well," he thought as the prisoners were led into the courtroom, "in the grand scheme of things, I guess it's of no matter. Once I deal with these men, these last remnants of a long-dead rebellion, Jack Brooks will cease to exist once and for all!"

The prisoners were brought in single file, and as they approached the bench, they fanned out so as to face only him. They were a ragtag group, most of them past middle age, and Marcus could see the look of sheer hopelessness in each of their faces. They were beaten and tired and, in most cases, ready to leave this world where they had known mostly heartache.

The judge leaned over the desk and looked down on them, and at the same time he felt as if a huge weight had been lifted from his narrow shoulders—this was his real work. Why should he fret over a small piece of newsprint about a man who died a decade ago? Everything he had worked for, all of his personal sacrifices, had brought him to this point. On this historic day, the name Brooks would become insignificant and eventually—he hoped—forgotten altogether; this thought alone brought back most of his good humor, and he almost smiled.

Instead he cleared his throat and said in his most judicial voice, "You men have been found guilty by a jury of your peers on the charge of treason to the United States of America."

Somewhere in the back of the courtroom, a brave soul mumbled, "What America?"

"Never mind," the judge thought. "Dissenters can and will be dealt with later."

He went on, feeling better than he had all morning. "As chief justice of these United States, it falls to me to sentence all crimes committed in a time of war."

He paused. A sound had come to his ears, something barely discernible yet commonplace. He paused so long that the prisoners began to fidget, and the bailiff turned to see what the holdup was. Marcas noticed these things, but he was momentarily unable to continue.

"What was that noise?" he thought.

A second later, his brain connected the sound with a picture—it was a horse at full gallop. Nothing unusual about that; there were horses everywhere in this town. Still, he shivered a little as he looked out at the packed courtroom.

With an effort he got ahold of himself, and clearing his throat, he began again: "In the case of treason, the law is very clear as to the..." he trailed off again.

The gallop had slowed to a walk, but the sound of the hooves was much louder—so loud, in fact, that it sounded as if the horse was inside the building.

All at once there was a commotion at the back of the courtroom, and even as the judge looked up, the doors burst open, sending people in every direction. There were two loud reports, and both bailiffs fell to the floor as if they had suddenly fallen asleep. Everyone, including the prisoners, were turning to run.

The judge heard himself shouting, "Order! There will be order in my court!"

But his voice seemed to come from far away, and he noticed that one word seemed to be on everyone's lips. Just one word spoken in a whisper: "Jack. It's Jack. Jack has returned."

In the front row, an old woman crossed herself, and the crowd, finding there was nowhere to run, pressed back against the walls to the left and right of the bench, leaving the center of the room wide open. It was as if the man on the horse were Moses and the crowd the Red Sea. To Judge Marcas, every set of lips seemed to be muttering the same word. The room began to spin, and for a moment, he thought he might faint.

Through the door at the back of the courtroom came a pale rider, and he rode a pale horse. "Jack! Jack! Jack!" seemed to be the chant that repeated itself over and over inside the small courtroom. Then suddenly. the man and the horse stopped right in the middle of the aisle. The prisoners, --now that the way was clear—were running for the door, and the judge rapped his gavel, but it was to no avail. Men were gathering around the rider, still chanting and touching his boots as if he were Saint Peter himself come back to take them home to Jesus.

Then, almost under his breath, Marcas mumbled, "I saw you hanged." But right on the heels of this, a more coherent thought occurred to him.

"It isn't real. It can't be, for as sure as my name is Judge Marcas McKay, the president of these United States of America, that's Jack Brooks astride that horse!"

Then the apparition—for that's what he seemed to be—slowly lowered the barrel of a large pistol, pointed it at his head, and said these words: "I am Jack Brooks and I have found you guilty of treason against humanity. How do you plead?"

For his part, Marcas still couldn't believe that it was really happening, and he sat completely still, almost frozen on his bench, gripping his gavel. The ghost man turned his head slowly toward the retreating prisoners, but the large barrel of the revolver never wavered and the judge finally found his voice. He stood suddenly and leaned over the bench.

His face was a mask of hatred and defiance as he screamed, *"You're dead! I saw you die!"*

This outburst had some effect, and the whole courtroom became completely still. But instead of looking to him, their leader, all eyes seemed to turn toward the man on the horse, as if he were the one in charge.

The ghost man took no notice of them but, turning back to Judge Marcas, said so quietly that only the one remaining bailiff and himself could hear: "How do you plead?"

For a moment Judge Marcas stared back, his heart jumping like a scared rabbit, then he began to relax. A new thought had formed in his overtaxed brain: it was all just a terrible nightmare, probably brought on by that stupid article in the paper. Shortly he would wake up, and

Carl would come shuffling in with his breakfast—this realization helped him to recover his wits, and he lowered himself back to the chair. For a moment he stared speculatively at the ghost of Jack Brooks, and then as if coming to a sudden decision, rapped his gavel twice on the old desk so hard that it broke in two.

Then smiling his best lunatic smile, he fairly screamed at the top of his lungs, "I sentence you to go straight to hell!"

"'Twas, far away and long ago,
When I was but a dreaming boy,
This fairy tale of love and woe
Entranced my heart with tearful joy;
And while with white Undine I wept,
Your spirit—ah how strange it seems—
Was cradled in some star, and slept,
Unconscious of her coming dreams."
—Henry Van Dyke

# CHAPTER 1

There was a girl in the meadow.

Jack's heart thumped wildly in his chest as he slipped behind a tall spruce, scarcely daring to breathe. How could it be? A girl out here! He took another peek—she was still there all right, but why, and more importantly, how?

For the last three years, Jack had led an almost solitary existence up here at the edge of the Mackenzie Mountains, and since the completion of his cabin just over the ridge, he had come to think of this little clearing, with its tall grass and array of flowers, as his front yard. He had seen all manner of creatures wandering through it. Once he had even seen a momma grizzly with her two cubs as they ambled through the meadow looking for something to eat—not once in all that time had he seen a person.

Cautiously, he glanced around the tree again. It seemed impossible that a girl or young woman could be out here all by herself. Slowly his eyes moved about the forest, taking in every movement. Subconsciously his hand fell to the butt of the Colt that was strapped to his hip. He neither saw nor sensed anything unusual; it was just another beautiful fall morning in the north country, and the small creatures of this vast wilderness were busy getting ready for the long winter that would arrive with a vengeance in just a few weeks.

The leaves on the aspens had turned a beautiful gold and had already started to carpet the forest floor, making all the bustle of the birds and squirrels sound even more urgent. Jack glanced up at the clear blue sky. September was one of his favorite months in northern Canada, for the main reason that the daylight hours mostly resembled those of his home in Colorado. The one thing he had not been able to get used to was the endless days or endless nights, depending on what time of year it was. But in middle to late September, the sun generally rose around 5:30 a.m. and set about 6:00 p.m., and since he owned no watch and nothing to set it by even if he did, there were only a few months out of the year that he could even guess what time it was. Now he guessed it was about 9:00 a.m. He turned his gaze back to the meadow and slowly scanned the surrounding tree line. Everything was as it should be—indeed, how it had been for thousands of years, with the exception of the girl. *She* was the only thing that didn't fit.

Jack's eyes were sharp, and he could see that the small figure had long dark hair and was wearing a light blue jacket. She was walking through the tall grass, as if she had been in this particular setting a thousand times. Then, coming to a flat rock, she sat down. Jack himself had often sat on that very rock before making the short winding climb to his cabin. For a moment his mind wondered at the fact that another human was sitting in his spot. He thought he saw her take something from a pocket in her coat. She then bowed her head so that her dark hair fell over her shoulders, concealing what she was doing. He took advantage of this opportunity to move behind some low scrub so that he could see the whole meadow without having to steal glances around the tree.

For a couple of minutes, she remained in that same position. To Jack, she seemed to be praying.

Then suddenly she straightened and turned her face in his direction. From his vantage point maybe seventy-five yards away, he could make out her form, her clothes, and her hair, but that was all. Her features and expressions were hidden from him. Still, it seemed to Jack that for a brief moment she was looking right at him—and again he forgot to breathe. He knew that there was no danger of her seeing him behind the low scrub at that distance, but it was still a little unnerving the way she had seemed to look directly at him. For another minute or so, she just sat there as if she were waiting for something or someone. Then she got up from the rock and walked casually over to an old, rotted stump. Here, she paused. Her back was to him now, her little dark head cocked slightly to one side as if she were listening intently for the slightest noise. Then swiftly she knelt and seemed to place something inside the stump. Taking one last glance in his direction, she started off into the trees. Jack watched her go, marveling again at the fact that she seemed entirely comfortable in her surroundings, as if she had been here in these woods her whole life. When he could no longer see her, he stood up. Once again his eyes combed over the little meadow and the forest that surrounded it, but he detected no movement. She was gone.

For nearly five minutes, he continued to stare down the hill at the place where she had gone into the trees. He had never been the type of man to hesitate—this was an entirely new feeling for him. Should he follow her or should he go on about his business? For that matter, why would he even be wondering about her at all? He looked up at the clear blue sky again, and suddenly a memory came out of nowhere—a blast from the past, so to speak. "When she smiles, the sun shines." It was part of a nursery rhyme that his mother would recite to him and his sister when they were little. Why it should come into his brain at this particular instant puzzled him momentarily. He shook his head briskly from side to side in an effort to clear it. Slowly, almost reluctantly, the memory left him, and his rational mind took over.

She was probably part of a hunting party that was camped just inside the forest. More and more people had been migrating north, and he had noticed some new faces the last time he had been in town—but her actions had been very mysterious! Perhaps she had been hiding some keepsake, sure that no one would be observing her. Following this brilliant deduction, his first thought was to ignore the whole scene that had just played out and continue about his day, yet as he stood there, his back against the tall spruce, he found he couldn't put the girl out of his mind. If there were a camp this close to his house, surely he would have bumped into someone over the last few days. He continued to argue with himself: "Maybe they just arrived last night." Either way, wasn't it in his best interest to investigate the matter? The last thing he needed was someone startling him on his trapline or surprising him at the cabin. Besides, his curiosity was piqued. So when he had assured himself that the girl wasn't coming back, he slipped from his hiding spot and went down to the meadow to investigate.

At first he found nothing inside the old stump, just the usual dead leaves and insects. Then his eye happened upon a peculiar yellow leaf stuck inside at the very top. For a moment he stared at it, dumbly scratching his head, his rusty mind trying to make sense of the thing. It was paper—that was for sure—and paper was pretty rare these days, especially up here. Then he noticed the writing on the other side. It was a note! At first glance it seemed to be written in a language foreign to him, but as he looked closer, he realized it was written in cursive letters—something he hadn't seen since his mother died. Studying the small letters closely, he was able to puzzle out the first line. It read, "To the man in the woods"! He looked up suddenly, half expecting to see her standing in the shadows, but there was no one there. She seemed to have just vanished, as if the forest had simply swallowed her up.

Once again he was undecided and he didn't like it one bit. The hair on his neck was standing up as if he had just seen a grizzly enter the woods and not a small girl. He took a tentative step toward the edge of the meadow and his feeling of unease increased—something was wrong here. Over the years Jack had developed a sort of sixth sense; it was like an inner voice that warned him of imminent danger—this voice had saved him from many close scrapes, and now it was telling him that under no circumstances should he enter those woods. The day had become completely still: no birds sang, no squirrel chattered, not even a breeze blew through the tall grass. It was as if the entire world had paused momentarily to see what he would do next. Then a lonely howl shattered the stillness, sending a chill down his spine in spite of the warm day. The next instant, everything was back to normal, and Jack had the sensation of waking from a dream. He still held the note in his left hand, but what startled him most was that he held the revolver in his right. This wasn't strange in itself—when threatened, his hand had often moved faster than his brain, but what was there to threaten him here? Returning the .45 to his holster, he heard himself laugh nervously. Then glancing once again at the note, he turned back toward the ridge and his trapline.

As he went about his business, he found himself throughout the course of the day wondering at himself. What had come over him? He wasn't easily spooked, and he had been in these woods alone so often that not even the wild animals startled him anymore. A dozen times he made up his mind to track down the small figure and put an end to the mystery once and for all, but at the end of the day, he headed back to the cabin, telling himself that he should at least do her the courtesy of reading the note before just barging into her camp. He didn't dare admit even to himself that for just a moment he had been scared.

That evening after he had eaten a little something, he loaded his pipe with his last bit of tobacco and spread the note out on the table. It had taken him a good quarter of an hour to decipher the few words she had written, and as he read the finished product out loud to himself, an unexpected chill came over him again. It read:

"To the man in the woods, my name is Annie. You needn't be afraid of me as I am all by myself and could use a friend. I know you're there because I can feel you watching me. I will be back in the meadow in a few days and hope to meet you in person."

Jack shivered. The chill he felt was caused by the line "I can feel you watching me," but what he felt more than that was embarrassment. In those few words, she had made him feel like a small boy afraid of the world or a Peeping Tom looking into some woman's bedroom window. It made him blush to his boots, and he said to the empty cabin: "Afraid? Afraid of what?!"

Suddenly he was angry—not at the girl but at his own foolishness. He would march right back down there, pick up the trail, and follow her back to wherever she had come from. Surely it couldn't be that far. As he reached for his old jacket, a question formed in his mind: "Yes, but why did you hide in the first place?"

Standing in the cabin door, his jacket in his hand, he found that he had no immediate answer to this. He had walked through those woods hundreds of times without a care, and he knew it wasn't fear that held him back now. It was something else. Slowly, he hung his jacket back up on the little peg by the door and sat down at the table, puzzling over his own reaction to this new thing that had suddenly and unexpectedly come into his little world.

Jack was a quiet man, probably stemming from the fact that he had spent so much of his life alone. His uncle, a gregarious man who loved to talk, would sometimes puzzle over the boy that he had taken under his wing.

"You know, Jack," he had said one day when they had been out mending the fence behind the corral. "I don't believe you'd say shit if you had a mouthful of it."

Jack had just smiled. Phillip Brooks had a whole catalog of old sayings and witticisms, and he wasn't afraid to use them. His uncle would have been surprised to know that under Jack's quiet exterior lay a remarkable understanding of people in general; if anything, his ability to really listen and think before speaking made him an exceptional student of human nature. That was why he was so confounded by this girl—no matter how his mind approached the problem, he always came to a dead end. None of it made sense.

For two days he went back to the same spot at the same time, hoping to see her again. More than anything, he wanted to reconcile things in his own mind. He read and reread the note, mainly to assure himself that he hadn't dreamed the whole thing. Finally, on the third day, he made up his mind that he would try to hunt her up if for no other reason than to prove to himself that he hadn't imagined her. This time, he wasn't disappointed: she was there, and she was sitting on the same rock.

Once again he slipped behind the tree and then he caught himself. He had come out here looking for her and here she was. He took a deep breath, straightened his coat, and was getting ready to step out where she would see him when suddenly she stood and walked quickly over to the old stump, dropped in her note, and ran off into the woods.

He paused. Maybe she wasn't ready to meet him face to face; maybe she was afraid of him. After all, she didn't know him from Adam—maybe she needed a little reassurance. But how could he let her know that she needn't fear him? He had no way of leaving her a message. Then he had a thought: maybe she was still there watching for him from her own hiding spot.

Five minutes later he was standing over his newfound mailbox. As he reached down to fish out the note that he knew would be there, it occurred to him why he had hidden that first time. Number one, he had been startled by her mere presence out here in the wilderness all alone. Number two, he hadn't wanted to frighten *her*! These thoughts made him feel better. Slowly he unfolded the little yellow piece of paper; this time it was easy for him to read because it was written in large block letters. He looked toward the trees and a smile came to his face. He had come out this morning with a half-formed plan of finding her and setting her straight about some things. Now, standing in the meadow with this absurd piece of paper in his hand and the sounds of nature all about him, he couldn't help but laugh out loud.

He laughed, and it felt good because he had been entirely too serious the last few days, especially when it came to this girl. But he was also laughing because somehow she had done it again: she had known he was there and she had known that he had set out to find her, so she had made it easy for him. The second note read simply: "MEET ME HERE TOMORROW MORNING."

"I wouldn't miss it for the world," Jack thought, glancing once more at the spot where he had last seen her. Then in a loud, clear voice, he said, "I won't hurt you." And after a pause, he added, "I'll be here tomorrow, same time."

Still smiling, he started back to the cabin, unaware of the two sets of blue eyes that watched him intently from the darkness of the forest.

That evening Jack went through his normal routine, but his mind wasn't really on his tasks. He had made himself something to eat—a small venison steak and fried potatoes—but he hardly tasted it. Then he washed his few dishes in the creek that ran behind the cabin. He found that he was much too restless to remain indoors, so he had actually taken a bath and shaved his face, though he had done both of these things just four days ago. Afterward, as he stood on the bank drying his hair with an old blanket, he thought about the last time he had worried so much about first impressions.

It had been the end of his seventeenth year, and the girl was someone he had known his whole life. He had been sure that she was his soulmate—shoot, he had been *told* she was his soulmate. So, resigning himself to fate, he had set out to impress her, but she had already been impressed by someone else.

"You waited too long," she said. "Nathan loves me!"

When Jack had inquired as to her feelings on the matter, she had shrugged her narrow shoulders and said, "Beggars can't be choosers, Jack."

Two days later he had left for Missouri. He realized now that this had been his plan all along and that he really had never had any idea of settling down and starting a family.

Ever since he could remember, his one goal—or obsession, to be more precise—had been to find the men that had betrayed his father. At first, he had been uncertain about what he would do once he found them. He had only been six-years-old when he had been forced to watch his father's execution in front of the old courthouse in Saint Louis, but he remembered it vividly. For years afterward he had been plagued by nightmares about it. Slowly, as he grew, so did the hate for these unknowns that had taken his daddy away from him. His mother had done her best to make him forget that fateful day, and had she lived, things might have gone differently for him. But in his tenth year, she had died of the plague, so he and his sister had gone to live with his uncle Phillip in southwestern Colorado.

Standing on the bank of the little stream, he stared into the setting sun and chuckled in his silent way.

"Well," he thought as he wrapped the towel around his waist, "that girl had been right about one thing: beggars can't be choosers."

It wasn't as if women had been lining up to meet him over the last few years.

He returned to the cabin and, after dressing, sat down at his small table with a cup of coffee. Inevitably his mind returned to the girl in the meadow and the girl of his childhood.

The thing was, he thought earnestly, he had really never been looking for love. It wasn't that the fairer sex held no interest to him; it was just that he didn't see how a woman would fit into his life. He was a loner, and women tended to complicate things. On the other side of the coin, he had noticed that most women seemed to regard him with mild curiosity when they noticed him at all. He didn't consider himself unattractive, just... average. He was almost six feet tall, not what you would call brawny, but his build was proportionate to his height, and years of hard work had left their mark in sinuous muscle. He had blond hair that seemed to grow too long almost overnight. His eyes were blue, but such a light blue that most people would have called them gray. At first glance you might assume he was a young man, still wet behind the ears, so to speak, but then your eyes would travel to the old Colt slung low on his hip. After that you would be more apt to notice the slight bit of gray at his temples and the cold, confident look in his eyes. He was a man that seemed to regard most of the human race with casual indifference, which tended to make most people nervous. As a result, they usually left him alone.

He looked around the small cabin. "Well," he thought, "this is definitely not what some young lady would call her dream home." He chuckled again. Then for the first time in four years, Jack began to wonder why he was here, so far away from everything he knew. He had left his home and family nearly nine years before. For two of those years, he traveled through parts of Missouri and Illinois and then spent another two wandering aimlessly through the heartland of what was once the United States. By then he had gained a reputation, and it seemed that wherever he went, he brought trouble. So finally, he had started for home, thinking he would stop and see his sister for a while.

His sister Mary lived in a small settlement on the outskirts of what used to be called Denver. She had never taken to ranching, and when an old man and his wife had stopped at his uncle's place on their way east, she had gone with them with the idea of settling in Kansas or Nebraska. But upon reaching Denver, they had decided to stop, and Mary had stopped with them. When the old folks passed away a few years later, Mary had just stayed on and had become a big part of the community. He was ashamed to admit that he had purposely avoided seeing her on his way east—she would have known what he was up to and objected. How she would have known he couldn't say for sure, but she would have said that she had *foreseen* it or some such nonsense, and Jack was in no mood to take up that old argument. So, he had bypassed her little house well to the south because even though he didn't believe in all that psychic mumbo jumbo, it was uncanny how as kids she had always found him out when he was up to something she didn't approve of.

On his way back, he had arrived in the small town of Hyland at sunset and had first gone to the little store/post office, where he had been pleased to find that news of his exploits had not reached this far west. Then he had gone straight to his sister's place, where he found Mary in the first stages of the plague.

At first, he had tried to get her to come back over the mountains with him, but she had refused, saying, "This is my home, and if I am to die, I want to die here." So, he had settled himself in, determined to be there for her to the bitter end. For two weeks she was fine—she even began to gain some weight. During this time, they grew close again. They would spend long evenings sitting in front of the fireplace in Mary's small living room, reminiscing about their childhood and really getting to know each other again after a long separation. Then one night as they sat, cozied up to the fire, he told her the story of the girl that he was supposed to marry, the one that had married his friend Nathan instead. He had meant it to be a humorous story, but as he told it, a strange and far-off look had crept into Mary's eyes, and that was the first of hundreds of times in those last months of her life that she had repeated the old rhyme: "*When she smiles, the sun shines. When she cries, it rains. When she sleeps, the snow flies. When she wakes, it's spring.*"

He remembered asking her what had brought that verse to her mind, but she only smiled at him wanly and said, "Just remembering Mama."

After that, Mary seemed to deteriorate. She would have good days, but they were more and more seldom. The last two days of her life were a waking and sleeping nightmare for Jack. When she was awake, Mary would recite the nursery rhyme over and over again. At night he would have vivid dreams of great forests and huge winding rivers. On his twenty-fifth day in "Denver," he awoke from one of these dreams to find nearly a foot of snow on the ground and Mary weak but lucid.

She called him to her bed, and they talked of their childhood again and how their mother used to bring them things called ICEES when they were sick. Then, as if she realized her time was short, she had asked him to come sit close because there were things he needed to know. She had him get an old, battered box out from under the bed and dump the contents beside her. It had been full of letters and newspaper clippings, some about his father. Since both of them had read these before, she pushed them aside. Then she pulled out an old yellow envelope that was a little larger than the rest. "This is important," she said. "If you keep none of these things, keep this."

He started to open it, but she stopped him, saying, "Not now, Jack. There is other, more important business we need to attend to. Number one, in the living room under the floorboards where the old rug is, you will find another box. There is a little gold in there, and maybe it will be of use to you on your journey."

Jack just nodded; tears suddenly very close.

Then she held his hand and said, "I knew you were coming, Jack."

He stiffened almost imperceptibly at this statement, but Mary noticed it and said apologetically, "Oh, I know you don't go in for all that physic mumbo jumbo. But I'm afraid you will have to listen to it one more time."

She handed him a piece of paper and asked him to read it aloud. He obeyed, and when he was finished, Mary said, "Well, what do you make of it, Jack?"

"That you're not a very good speller," he said, trying to lighten the mood.

"You know what I mean," she replied curtly, and her eyes seemed to be searching his own for an answer that she didn't believe his mouth would make.

Finally she sighed deeply and said, "Jack, I love you, but you have always been so stubborn, so unwilling to accept anything on faith. I am your sister and I have always had patience with this flaw in your character—but I am out of time, and for once I need you to believe, at least in the things I am about to tell you."

Jack leaned back in the chair and stared at her. Then, glancing back at the paper, he said hesitantly, "They're directions, I guess, to a place somewhere in the north."

"Very good, Jack. A-plus." She smiled a little at the old joke. "Now," she said, closing her eyes and leaning back against her pillow, "I don't know much, but I've been told that there is something very valuable up north, Jack, and if you follow those directions, you will find it."

Jack watched her. She didn't seem delirious—actually she seemed quite sane, at least as far as she was concerned.

"Valuable?" he asked. "You mean like gold or guns?"

For a moment her eyes squeezed tight, and her forehead wrinkled as if she were in great pain, and then she said, "More valuable than both. It's a great treasure, and you must protect it with your life!" Then she looked straight at him and her eyes clouded. "Your whole life to this point has been nothing but preparation for what is to come. Oh Jack, I have done things, hidden things—even deceived you so that you might have a fighting chance at what lies up there in the north country. In my defense I will say that I myself was also manipulated to this purpose. By who or what I can't say, and in the end, it doesn't seem to matter much." Then she sighed and her voice began to tremble. "That's all I know, Jack. I'm sorry."

Large tears began to run down her cheeks as she went on. "I know you went east, Jack." she said. "And I hope that in some way you found closure." Then she sobbed audibly, and Jack saw that she was struggling with her words as she continued. "But now it's time that you moved on. Don't you know that all of us are here on this earth for a reason? We all have our own destiny, Jack."

Then, taking his hand, she smiled up at him through tear-filled eyes and said, "I don't know exactly what your destiny is, but I do know that it is much too important to waste on something as petty and unimportant as revenge!"

After a while Mary seemed to fall asleep, and he leaned back in his chair and thought of the dream from the night before. It sure was a beautiful place, this country of his dreams, and somehow, he was sure that if he tried, he could find it. As for the treasure his sister had mentioned, maybe it *was* to be found there.

He sat for a while watching Mary breathe and thinking about what she had told him, then he leaned over and snatched up the yellow envelope that still lay next to her hand. It was addressed to his mother. For a moment he hesitated, wondering what could be so different about this letter from the hundred or more that he had already read. Why had he never seen it? And more importantly, why would his sister give it to him now after all these years? Slowly he opened the envelope and took out its contents; again he hesitated. Suddenly a chill came over him as if another presence had entered the room and was watching over the whole scene with great interest. He glanced at his sister, and she too seemed to feel it. As he watched her, she pulled the bed covers tightly around her and moaned almost imperceptibly in her sleep. "Nonsense," Jack thought, but a shiver ran through him as he opened the letter and began to read.

After reading the note, Jack knew he must wake Mary and ask her where and when she had received it. One glance at the still figure on the bed told him that it was too late—Mary hadn't moved, but her eyes were wide open and staring vacantly across the small space. He instantly checked his emotions. He even had time to wipe his tear-stained eyes before Mary sat straight up in bed and screamed his name. He jumped and almost drew the Colt in his confusion. Then, realizing that she wasn't looking at him but through him, he knelt before her and, placing his hand on her forehead, tried to sooth away her delusions, saying: "I'm here, Mary. I'm right here." But her eyes were wide and unseeing.

"Jack!" she screamed, almost right into his face. "Jack!"

"I'm here, Mary," he said again, trying to comfort her.

Finally she fell back against the pillows as if some great weight had been lifted from her heart and said almost in a whisper: "North, Jack. You must go north."

Those were her last words. She seemed to relax even more, as if her last purpose in life had been fulfilled. For the next few minutes, her breath came in little hitches until finally she just lay still. That was it, the end of a life that, if not remarkable, was at least not wasted. He kissed her lips and slowly pulled the old, tattered blanket over her face.

That night he dreamed again of the huge rivers and snow covered valleys, but this time there were other things—there was a man, and he always seemed to be just ahead of him. He tried to catch up, but this man seemed to have wings and could fly from one point to another. Finally he had stopped on a crag of rock and pointed down. When Jack reached him, he disappeared. But looking out ahead, he saw what the bird man had been pointing at—*paradise!*

A beautiful country with meadows and forests and streams were ahead of him, and there were cabins and people going about their daily chores, just as it was back home. He felt happy—happier than he had ever been in his life, and he thought, "This is where I should get to!" Then a cloud passed over the sun, and he heard one line from the old rhyme: "When she cries, it rains."

And suddenly it *was* raining—not a light rain but a regular frog strangler, as his uncle would have said, and it seemed to be eroding the very rock beneath his feet. Then the huge boulder that had seemed so stable only seconds before began to separate itself from the cliff, and he was falling into a horrible black abyss.

He woke with the scream just behind his lips and sat straight up in bed. A cold sweat dripped from his forehead in spite of the chill that had taken hold of the old house. He threw off the old quilt that covered him. Looking toward the window, he could see the snow falling in huge flakes, and he wondered how much more snow had fallen since he had gone to sleep. "Doesn't matter," he thought and fell back on his pillow, trying to remember every detail of the dream.

He woke again just as the sun began to shine through the small window. He could see that the snow had stopped, and he could feel that it was freezing in the small room. Dressing quickly, he made his way out to the front porch and found that nearly two feet of the white stuff had fallen during the night. It didn't mean that he couldn't make it back to his uncle's ranch, or that it had even snowed at all in the southern mountains, but to Jack's jumbled mind, the snowstorm was almost like a sign that it was time to go—and soon. Thinking back on it now, he realized that the death of his sister, combined with the almost supernatural dreams he had been having on a nightly basis, had probably made him more susceptible to omens.

He had spent the rest of that day preparing for his trip. He found the box that Mary had told him about under the floorboards in the living room, and upon inspection of its contents, he had exclaimed out loud to the empty room: "A little gold!" Truthfully, there was more gold in that little tin box than Jack had seen in his whole life. Most of it was coins, but there was some jewelry also. Jack felt suddenly rich. How had she accumulated all this? Shortly he was able to answer this question.

Further inspection of the small house produced nothing else of monetary value, but he did find several old photos, and these he added to the box of newspaper clippings. One of these fell out and landed on the table, where he examined it. There was a picture of Mary; she was very young, maybe twenty-one or so. The line under the photo read, "Local psychic finds young boy alive." Then he found several more articles referring to his sister. One was a story about prospectors lining up to get her advice. The first line of the story caught his eye. "Silver seekers make soothsayer their first stop." All of the articles were over ten years old, and Jack was surprised at this part of his sister's life that he had known nothing about. Then he came across a more recent article; it was probably only about four years old. It was front-page news, and the headline scrawled over a more recent picture read, "Local Psychic Predicts Dire Future for the Front Range." Jack read the entire article. It started, "Renowned local psychic Mary Brooks has predicted hard times for the people along the front range." It went on to tell about milder and shorter winters that would lead to drought and many other hardships that would befall the region. One line sent a chill up Jack's spine: "I know that I will not live to see most of these changes, but I felt it my duty to warn the people of a community that has treated me so well over the years." Jack of course had known about his sister's talent but had always thought of it as nothing more than common sense or at the very most woman's intuition—obviously there were a lot of people that had believed in her ability and paid good money for it.

That evening, Jack wrapped Mary's body in her bedspread and carried it out back to a wooden bench that had been placed facing west so that one could sit and watch the sun go down behind the mountains. Earlier he had dug the snow out from around it and placed dry cedar and pine logs underneath. He would have rather given her a proper burial, but the snow and frozen ground made that impossible.

Jack touched a match to the kindling and within minutes the whole bench was consumed in fire. For two hours he stood or sat on the back porch, watching the flames and thinking about his sister. Tears ran from his eyes and froze to his reddened cheeks, but he didn't even notice. Finally the fire started to die out, and Jack shoveled snow over the remains. "Ashes to ashes," he whispered, then turned back to the house.

That night he slept badly. His dreams were intense and everyone he knew seemed to make an appearance. He woke about four in the morning with his sister's words echoing in his head: "North, Jack. You must go north."

So, after eating a cold breakfast of deer jerky and leftover corn bread, he packed up his few belongings and Mary's two boxes. He then went down to the old building that served as a store/ post office and pinned a short note to his uncle explaining his sister's death. He added that he had decided to make a trip north and would be gone awhile longer. He concluded by saying that he had finished with his business out east and that they shouldn't worry about him. His uncle would understand—he had always expected that Jack would leave the ranch someday and would probably assume that Jack had met a girl or something. The store clerk informed him that there was no real mail service this far west and that the letter would probably not get out for some days. In the end, he had just left the letter on Mary's kitchen table, reasoning that if his uncle left his home, he would come here first.

He had started out with the vague idea of the colonies in the back of his mind. The colonies were a series of established townships that ranged across southern Canada all the way to Hudson Bay, and at present they were thriving. Jack had even heard stories that these colonies had established trade with Europe, but he wasn't sure he believed it.

Sitting at his little table in the cabin four years later, he remembered feeling excited as he rode out of the city. He had seemed to feel some invisible pull coming from out of the north, but it was more than that—it was a feeling that had come from deep within him, making his heart beat just a little faster; a feeling that he was being drawn into some grand adventure.

As usual he wasn't tired, but he laid down on his bed anyway, still reminiscing about those first days of his trek north. "Some things will never change," he thought, "and I'm one of them." He looked out the small window. The moon had just moved into view; it had always held a certain fascination for him, but tonight it seemed to be right outside his cabin. It was huge and it lit up most of the interior. Feeling a little foolish, he made a child's wish. "Let her be there tomorrow." He longed to see the girl from the meadow once more. Then he drifted off to sleep, and out in the great northern wilderness life went on, with absolutely no concern for him or his newfound obsession.

In the dream, he was with the girl, and they were running. He wanted to pick her up and carry her, as if by that action he could protect her somehow; however, he was too weak. He felt as if someone had stolen all of his strength, and it was all he could do to keep moving at all. Someone or something was chasing them, and he wanted to turn and fight, but the girl kept urging him on. Then she stumbled, falling forward to the forest floor. He was at her side in an instant, kneeling down to scoop her up. Suddenly it seemed more important to look upon her face, to see the expression written there. He looked into her eyes—they were the deepest blue he had ever seen, and they seemed to hypnotize him for a moment. But her features were blurred as if he were looking at her through a dirty window. Then in a small, sweet voice, she said, "What do you see, Jack? What is it?"

# CHAPTER 2

S lowly, he came awake. He noticed that the sun was already streaming through the small window in the cabin and sat bolt upright. What time was it? He started to check his watch that he had sold over seven years ago and then looked out the window instead. He could tell by the sun that it was late in the morning.

He panicked. He would miss her! He got dressed in a rush, not bothering to comb his hair. He stumbled from the cabin and raced up the hill haphazardly. He didn't even stop to think why his missing her would be such a tragedy—after all, he could find her if he really wanted to—yet he was almost in a panic. He was thinking of good old Uncle Phillip, wondering what he would say if he could see him now as he reached the top of the ridge. Panting and feeling as if his heart would leap out of his chest, he looked down.

She wasn't there—he had missed her after all. His first thought was "Of course she's gone. Why would she sit around waiting for you all day?" Then he scanned the meadow and the edge of the forest, hoping against hope he would see her walking away through the woods, but there was no sign of her. He was just making up his mind to walk down and check the old stump for another note when suddenly, as if out of nowhere, she appeared.

She was running at breakneck speed through the tall grass and Jack's blood ran cold when he saw what she was running from. Emerging from the trees not a hundred yards behind her was a massive timber wolf! He watched in horror as the wolf shortened the distance between itself and the girl in two great bounds. More on instinct than anything else, he reacted.

He hadn't taken the time to grab his pistol, which he always brought with him when he was going more than fifty feet from the cabin. Still, even unarmed, he didn't hesitate—it was in his nature to act first and think second, so he went down the slope carelessly, not thinking of himself yet at the same time knowing he could not possibly save her. He tried to call out, but his voice was barely a whisper through his labored breathing. By the time he reached the meadow, he was at a dead sprint. At the same moment, he saw the huge animal leap at the girl.

She went down in the tall grass. The wolf must have caught her by the feet because she seemed to trip and was able to roll before the beast could get over her. Jack ran on, putting all his effort into the last few yards. As he came to within twenty feet of the tragedy, he pulled up panting.

The wolf had noticed him, and to his great relief, the animal turned from its original target and faced him. Jack stared. Never in all his travels had he seen a wolf this big—not even on the sled teams that he had sometimes seen moving north. The animal had lowered its head; its lips were curled back in a snarl, exposing long teeth that could easily rip him to shreds. There was a low rumble coming from its chest, and for a moment Jack stood completely still, panting heavily from his sprint down the hill. When the wolf growled even more menacingly, a crazy thought flashed through his mind: "Why grandma, what big teeth you have!"

To his amazement, Jack realized that he had spoken this thought out loud, and at the sound of his voice, the wolf crouched lower, gathering its powerful legs under it, ready to spring. All he could do was brace himself for the inevitable. His only thought was: "I'll never get to hear her voice."

Then as if she had appeared out of thin air, the girl was between them facing the huge animal, and *he could hear her voice.* It was low and sweet. He couldn't make out what she was saying, but the effect on the enormous wolf was nothing short of amazing. It lowered its belly to the ground, its hind quarters still in the air, and then it crawled toward her as if it were bowing to some wolf queen. Slowly, they approached each other, and she put her face down to within an inch of those huge fangs. He wanted to yell "Watch out!" But he couldn't speak or even move, for that matter. She knelt down and threw her arms around its shaggy neck; at this, the wolf responded by rolling on its back, pulling her down with him and licking her face furiously.

Jack was struck dumb—this wasn't even close to what he had envisioned for their first meeting. He felt as if he were a boy again, watching a sideshow at the town fair. "Well," he thought, trying to regain some composure, "at least she can't surprise me any more than she already has." As it turned out, he was wrong again.

He cleared his throat to politely let her know that he was still there. She let go of the beast, which bounded off in the direction of the woods. Then turning toward him, still breathing hard from own her mad dash through the meadow, she said, "I'm sorry, Jack."

This was the last straw, somehow she knew his name, and although he had always prided himself on not being surprised by anything people might do, he now felt himself literally shocked into silence.

She seemed not to notice as she continued, "You see, I…didn't think you were coming, and I was just getting ready to leave when Wolf showed up. He watches me, kind of like a bodyguard. I wasn't…prepared for you to meet him." She spoke hesitantly, as if she were unsure of herself, which actually made him feel a little bit better; then she extended her hand to him, and automatically he took it. "My name is Annie Fuller," she said, "and it is my pleasure to meet you, Mr. Brooks."

He felt as if someone had hit him over the head with a goofy stick. The only words he could manage were, "Just Jack, please."

"Ok, Jack then," she said.

The way she said his name sent chills down his spine. Her voice had a musical quality and he found himself hoping that she would keep talking. Her eyes were as they were in his dream, but now that he could see her clearly, the word that leapt to his mind was stunning. Her hair was so dark that it reminded Jack of a raven's wing; it shimmered in the sunlight as it fell loosely over her shoulders, almost to her waist. For a moment he found himself wishing he could touch it, which brought the blood to his face. Her features were soft. Her skin, although tanned by the sun, was still a shade lighter than his own. Her face was like that of a statue come to life: there were no signs of wear from worry or weather; it was flawless. She wore a buckskin dress like the Native American girls he had known in his childhood—and if this wasn't strange enough, over her dress she wore a denim jacket that looked almost brand new. It was a warm morning, so she had rolled up her sleeves to her elbows, revealing a gold bracelet on one delicate wrist. A gold cross with a loop at the top hung from a chain around her neck, but he barely had time to recognize the significance of this symbol before her hair fell over it.

She seemed so small even now that he was close to her, but maybe it was just an illusion created by the huge animal that had seemed to cower at her feet. The contrast between the light-blue pools of her eyes and the shimmering black in her hair made her seem almost unreal somehow, and he couldn't drag his eyes away from her. In fact, he felt as if he had been put into some sort of trance.

Then her voice cut through the fog that threatened to make him deaf and dumb. "Mr. Brooks, are you ok?"

"Yes. Fine," he said feebly. "Please, Miss Fuller, call me Jack."

"Then you must call me Annie," she said and turned in the direction the wolf had gone, her long tresses bouncing about her head.

When she turned back to him, he noticed the concern in her face, and she seemed to shiver as she said, "I hope I haven't put you off, Mr. Brooks—I mean Jack. I am normally not so bold. It's just that…" Here she paused, as if thinking how best to proceed. "It's just that I have so little time, you see?" Then she sighed and said, "No, I guess you don't!" Finally she looked him straight in the eye, a flush gathering in her cheeks that seemed to make her even more beautiful—if that was possible—and said, "I hope we will be great friends, Jack, because I have come a long way to find you."

They walked in the direction that the wolf had gone, neither of them speaking, each involved in their own thoughts. Jack had questions of course, but for the moment he was content to watch and wait.

Finally, her silence began to make him uncomfortable, so he blurted out, "I think he's run away."

She looked at him quizzically, as if he had broken her train of thought, and said, "Excuse me?"

"The wolf," he said, and then repeated, "I think he's run away."

She laughed lightly, and to Jack it sounded like silver bells. He looked at her, blushing slightly (why he was blushing he couldn't understand), and saw that she was pointing at the high grass fifty feet away.

"He's right there," she said, smiling up at him.

He followed the direction that she had indicated and could just make out the creature sprawled out at the end of the meadow.

"I told you, Jack, he is always watching me." And she started again toward the huge animal.

"Well," he said, starting after her, trying feebly to make a joke, "I hope he doesn't get the idea that I'm your enemy—or lunch!"

The effect on Annie was immediate. She turned to him, her blue eyes seeking his own. The color had left her cheeks, and she was as white as a ghost. She said, "Oh Jack, I could never hurt you or allow Wolf to hurt you!"

She was so sincere—so serious—that he felt he should offer some explanation, but all he could manage was, "No, I guess not."

"Come on," she said, "I want him to meet you."

Jack trudged on behind her. He had no great urge to meet a wolf as big as a pony, but at this point, he seemed to be completely within her power. As they approached the animal, he seemed not to even notice them. He was lying in the grass, his face between his paws. When Annie said something in a low voice, he looked up as if he were seeing her for the first time. Jack learned later that this was just a ruse, and when it came to the girl, this wolf was always on alert.

He bounded out of the tall grass and sat at her feet as if to say, "Yes, mistress. What do you require of me?" There was no hostility toward Jack—Wolf seemed to regard him with indifference, as if he were just another creature of the forest that the girl had brought home.

She reached out lightly and took hold of Jack's hand. She didn't seem to notice the effect it had on him—as if an electric current had shot up his arm—and he was thankful for that. Still talking to the wolf in that low voice, she brought his hand down near the muzzle of the animal, explaining, "This is how Wolf gets to know people."

It sniffed at him lightly and then she placed his hand on the wolf's massive head. He stroked it a few times; its coat was thick and surprisingly soft. After a moment Jack straightened up, and the wolf sat back on its haunches, looking content and waiting to see what the girl would do next. Jack found himself also waiting to see what she would do next.

After a moments pause she spoke. With her back still to him, and facing the wolf, she said, "Will you walk us home, Jack?"

Somehow he managed to find his tongue enough to say, "Where's home?"

She turned, smiling up at him, and said, "Not far." She then started off in the opposite direction. He walked beside her, the wolf slightly ahead, sniffing the air from time to time.

She didn't speak, so he decided to take the opportunity to ask a question. "Are you really out here all alone?" he inquired, glancing at the tall timber at the edge of the clearing.

She giggled and said, "I am not alone; I have Wolf." Then smiling slightly, because she knew what he meant, she added, "But there are no other people with me. My brother Kitchi was here, but he has gone home." A cloud seemed to come over her features as she said this.

Jack couldn't suppress the astonishment in his voice as he said, "And he just left you here?"

Her smile returned but it she seemed more wistful. "It's not like that," she said. "I sent him away." She then paused for a moment and added slowly, "Now I kind of wished I hadn't."

They had reached the forest and the wolf had disappeared again. He noticed that they weren't keeping to a trail; she seemed to be wandering aimlessly.

He looked around uncertainly and finally said, "Is your camp near here?"

She nodded toward a rock outcropping about fifty yards to their left and then started in that direction. The woods seemed to be teeming with life. Jack had never seen so many birds and small animals in such a concentrated area. He had been this way only a week before, and nothing like this had greeted him. There were rabbits, squirrels, ermine, and fox. Once, when he paused for a moment, a huge marmot stopped right in the trail, regarding him as if he were no more than an intruder, before passing on. He had walked by this very mass of rocks a hundred times and had even been by it just two weeks ago as he had come back from his last trip to the settlement in the south—there had been no camp here then, so she must have come to the area just before he had first seen her in the meadow. They rounded a huge boulder that seemed to grow right out of the ground and came into a small camp; there were the remains of a campfire and a clothesline running from a small sapling to the tent with a few articles of clothing hanging on it.

"Home sweet home," she said, laughing nervously. "Would you like some tea? "

Jack nodded and she ducked into the tent. From inside, she called to him to restart the fire, which he did with little trouble as the coals were still hot. She came out with an old coffee pot and a small leather bag, out of which she carefully selected what she wanted, then she sat down beside him on an old log that had been dragged up near the fire.

"You're not a very talkative person, are you, Jack?" she asked as she placed the pot over the fire.

He smiled slowly and said, "To be honest with you, ma'am, I am not quite sure what to make of you." Then, since he had started, he figured he might as well plow straight in before she could surprise him into silence again. "I mean, here's a young lady out in the forest, miles from the nearest town, just her and her pet werewolf."

At this last comment, she smiled sweetly, and once again Jack was struck dumb by her beauty. "When she smiles, the sun shines," he thought, and he couldn't help but smile back.

She studied him for a moment, as if trying to make up her mind about him,  then she looked up at the sky and said so softly that he could barely hear: "Can I trust you, Jack?"

It wasn't directed at him; she seemed to be asking herself the question. He answered anyway. "I'm mostly harmless," he said, smiling at her sideways, adding, "I would never hurt you, if that's what you mean."

She poured him a cup of tea and stood up, seeming to come to a decision. "What if I were to tell you that I'm from here," she started, then corrected herself. "Well, not exactly here, but about two hundred miles north of here. Would you believe me, Jack?"

He studied her face. She didn't smile or turn away; she just stared at him with those wonderful blue eyes.

"Well," he said, turning away as he felt it impossible to think rationally when he was looking directly at her. Then he thought of some of the legends that he had heard since he had moved up here. "I don't believe you would lie—it's just that I've heard that there is nothing but natives and myself, of course, north of Fort Simpson." He went on quickly before she could interrupt, "My friend Jacob says that there are still tribes of Native people out past the Great Bear Lake, but that no one else has been that far north in over two hundred years."

She crossed her arms over her chest and sighed. "Your friend is right," she said, "About the people, I mean. But it is also true that I am from there. My family has lived in a place called Goodhope since my great-grandfather was a boy. I have lived a happy life there. It was a beautiful place to grow up—even more beautiful than your meadow, Jack." She sighed once again, adding, "I have known nothing else. But now…I can never go back." Before he could interject, she went on. "That's where you come in, Jack. I want to hire you as a sort of guide or escort.

I see he said hesitantly, and where is it that you would like me to "escort" you to?

She paused and stared into the fire. Then she said wistfully, "oh I don't know maybe the colonies, or… and here she here she sighed as her eyes met his. Maybe as far as the United States."

For a moment he was speechless, but Jack was starting to get used to her little surprises, and he recovered quickly. He said the thing that seemed to be foremost in his mind: "How old are you, Annie?"

Now whether she had expected him to jump and say, "Of course, let's leave for the US today," or tell her, "No, I'm fine right here," he didn't know.

However, this particular question seemed to anger her. A flush came to her cheeks, and she took a step toward him.

"I am not just some runaway," she said and stamped her little moccasin in the dirt. "I was twenty-two last November, and I have thought this through. I have made up my mind, Mr. Brooks, and I am going!"

He looked at her warily. He had learned either from his mother or just experience that diplomacy was the best course of action when it came to the opposite sex.

Mentally, he took a deep breath and said, "It's just that I don't understand why you would leave your family and travel to a distant land, when by your own admission you were happy where you were."

He expected her to throw up her hands and walk off into the forest, but she did neither of these things. Slowly she lowered her arms, and Jack thought he caught a slight tremble in them. She seemed to be fighting with her own emotions, and as if to confirm this, a single tear rolled down her cheek. She wiped it away quickly and sat back down next to him.

"I can't tell you," she said simply, "not yet. You will have to trust me when I say that if I went home, it would mean a fate worse than death."

He thought for a moment but decided not to press the issue—at least not at present.

"But why the US?" he said finally.

Suddenly she jumped up and ran into the tent, leaving him to think that he really had offended her. He heard her rummaging around and presently she came out carrying something in both hands. It was a book; a large book.

As she walked toward him, she asked, "Can you read English, Jack?"

"Yes," he replied, trying to read the cover as she thrust it at him; but just as he was reaching out for it, she pulled it back.

"Wait," she said. "Before I show you this, you have to promise me two things." He blinked, and before he could answer, she went on. "First, that you won't laugh at me. And second, that you will invite me to dinner."

# CHAPTER 3

Jack hadn't had company since he had moved up here, not even his friend Jacob had visited him, and as they approached his small cabin, he started to worry about the state in which he had left it that morning as he had run out in a panic. But as they entered the little one room space, her face seemed to light up, and she said, "It's wonderful, Jack! Did you do this yourself?"

At first he thought that she might be making a joke about his housekeeping, but when he turned to look, he realized that she was studying the workmanship of the cabin, not the contents, and he felt a certain pride that he hadn't felt since he had left his home in Colorado.

"Yes. It took me the better part of a summer, and I am still mending things every day, but," and here he used her words, "home sweet home."

She laughed, and once again Jack thought of little silver bells.

As he got dinner together, she wandered through the room, stopping now and then to look at something that would catch her interest. It made Jack nervous, but he said nothing, giving her the benefit of the doubt.

When she came upon his holster and revolver hanging on the headboard, she seemed to pause, then casually she asked: "Are you a good shot, Jack?"

He replied, "Not bad with the rifle," and left it at that.

By the time they sat down to eat, she had explored every inch of the little place and was prepared to keep him talking about himself.

"Who is the photo of?" she asked first.

He told her it was his older sister and that she had died about three years ago down in Colorado.

"What was her name?" she wanted to know.

"Mary," he replied and added, "Aren't you hungry?"

He had cooked two big venison steaks with fried potatoes, cornbread, and the last of his greens, thinking, "If there's gonna be a special occasion, this is it."

But she hadn't even touched it. He was starting to wonder if forest goddesses ever got hungry when she said, "Shouldn't we give thanks first, Jack?"

He literally blushed, right down to his boots. The last time he had heard those words, he had been about seven, and they had had the same effect on him then.

He cleared his throat and said, "Sorry, ma'am," just as he had done all those years ago. Then he bowed his head and mumbled, "God is great," or something to that effect. When he had finished, Annie managed to set him back on his heels again.

The girl looked up at the ceiling and added in a clear voice, "And thanks to the mother for her bounty." What happened next was almost as big of a surprise as their first meeting—the girl dug in. She ate everything on her plate, and when Jack offered her his last bit of cornbread, she took it lightly. Through a mouthful of steak, she said, "Thank you. I'm so hungry."

Up until now, Jack hadn't taken the time to reflect on what it would mean for her to be out here by herself, then he had remembered the tea and realized that although she had served him two cups, she hadn't had any. Why? Because there had only been one little tin cup. She really had nothing except a few pieces of clothing and a tent. Suddenly he felt ashamed, and his pride in the cabin seemed almost vain.

He asked, "How long have you been traveling?"

She paused between bites and said, "Only about four days."

Jack sat back. "You came two hundred miles in four days, on foot?"

She swallowed her last bit of cornbread and said, "No, we came from the settlement down at Fort Simpson."

"You were at Fort Simpson?" he said. "I was just there three weeks ago."

"I know," she said, smiling across the table at him. "That's how I learned you were here. There is a man there with a patch on his eye; he has a store."

"Eddy!" Jack interjected excitedly.

"Yes, Eddy," she continued. "Anyway, I had casually asked him about the United States of America, and he had said that he had never been there and never intended to go there. I guess he saw my disappointment because as we were leaving, he said. 'Little girl, if you really want to know about the US, there is a man from there living upriver.' I asked him if he knew this man and where I might find him. But he wouldn't tell me your name, no matter how much I batted my eyes. Anyway, he finally told me that you had a little cabin up the Mackenzie near Camsell Bend. Then he drew me a little map, but it wasn't very good so we still got lost. Kitchi and I spent several days trying to pick up your trail. I was getting ready to start back to the settlement when we came across the little meadow, and you know the rest. She laughed, and he couldn't help but to laugh with her.

"Even when you found the meadow, you couldn't have seen the cabin from there," he said, still smiling.

She shrugged. "Sometimes I feel things," she said, glancing around the cabin, and then she added, a little hastily, "and sometimes I could see the smoke from your chimney."

Jack stared at her for a moment, a hundred questions on the tip of his tongue, but he could wait. He felt more himself tonight—maybe it was because he was in his own environment, but he was more at ease.

"Do you drink coffee, Annie?" he asked.

"Yes, please," she said and then added, "Where are you from, Jack?"

He poured the coffee and sat down across from her. "I," he began and then paused, not sure how far back he should go with his story. "Well, I was actually born in a place called Missouri," he said finally, thinking that was as good as any place to start.

"Is Missouri a big city?" she asked, pronouncing the word like it was the first time it had crossed her lips.

"Not exactly," he replied, and before he could go on, she asked, "Is there a big city near there?"

Jack sat back, studying her. She seemed so eager for knowledge. Carefully he said, "Well, there used to be big cities there, but they have almost disappeared."

Before she could ask another question, he went on. "When I was very young, I moved with my mother and sister to a place called Colorado."

"Was that after your father died?" she said casually, as if she had known him for years instead of just a few hours.

Now Jack *was* taken aback, but she seemed not to notice his surprise. As she slowly sipped her coffee, he studied her eyes, so wide and innocent as she looked at him over her cup. Feeling no malice in the statement, and at the same time realizing that everyone in North America must have seen the article about his father, he went on.

"Yes, and then after my mother died, I went over the mountains to live with my aunt and uncle. As for the last four years, I have lived here," he concluded.

Suddenly she stood up and went to the table beside the door, where she had placed the giant book. She brought it around the table and set it down in front of him, opening it to the first page. It was a map of the US. She was looking over his shoulder and her hair was in his face It smelled like lilacs, and he briefly fought the urge to reach out to touch it. When she said, "Where is Colorado, Jack?" he snapped his attention back to the book. He pointed, showing her the square block almost in the middle of the country, then slowly he closed the cover to read the title: *The Rise and Fall of North America*. Jack turned a page and noticed the copywrite date and sighed—this book was obviously speculative as it was published a good twenty years before the first sun flare.

He leaned back in his chair and said, "Annie, where did you get this book?"

She had turned back to the map on the inside cover and was studying it, presumably looking at Colorado. Without looking up she said, "It's my father's."

Jack was silent, thinking how best to proceed. Noticing his silence, she turned her face and her eyes met his. "How is it wrong, Jack?" she said earnestly. "I need to know!"

Some internal feeling made him take her small hands in his own. It was the first time that he had initiated physical contact, yet she seemed not to notice. In this moment he felt as if he were talking to a child, then he looked deep into her wonderful blue eyes and a blush rose to his face. He let her hands drop and turned toward the little window. Looking out he could see nothing of the surrounding trees; but the moon, still full, lit up the dooryard.

Finally, he slowly said, "Look, Annie?"

But before he could continue she said: "Oh, I realize this book is old, but I have read other books about the United States, and I've seen pictures. This is just the only book I have with me."

At first Jack wished he could let her keep her dream. But then he thought, "No, she must know before she gets hurt!"

"Let me tell you about myself," he said finally and as cheerfully as he could. She closed the book and silently sat down across from him.

"Where to start?" he thought as he got up and poured them both another cup of coffee. As he sat back down he said, "Like I said before, I was born in a place called Missouri. But after my father died, we moved to Colorado. My mother was a doctor, and because of this she was able to provide for me and my sister. But a few years later, she got the plague, so we went to stay with my uncle Phillip. He had a ranch with cows and horses, and I was taught how to live off the land. My uncle taught me many things, like how to fish the stream and hunt deer, but most importantly he taught me about the world and where I fit in it. He told me of great wars and famine and plague. He told me that at one time there were huge cities where large numbers of people lived and worked. He even told me something about the United States and why it didn't exist anymore." Here he paused for a moment, waiting for her reaction.

She turned back to the book and said, undaunted, "But there must be something left. It was such a great nation."

"Well," he went on, "there are people and towns just as there are here, but the towns get smaller every year, and more and more people are migrating north because of the drought."

"But what of civilization? You have guns. Even where I live, we receive goods once a year, like this jacket that my father gave me for my birthday."

"Well, as for my guns, they were my father's and were passed down to him from his father. But your jacket and goods you refer to must come from the colonies."

Annie set her cup down and her eyes lit up once again.

"Have you ever been to the colonies?" he asked, studying her face.

"Nope," she said shaking her head. "This is the first time in my life that I have been away from home. But I have heard of the colonies—my father used to go there every spring—but Fort Simpson is the first town I have ever visited."

Jack stared at her, astonished, "Surely your father would know more about these things than I do. Hasn't he ever spoken to you about it?"

"No," she said and sighed deeply, sitting back in the chair. "He seldom speaks of the outside world, and when I ask, he just says that there is no place like our home on the whole earth, because there is no other like 'my Annie.' He loves me very much, but he shelters me, Jack."

"Well, my uncle says that there will come a time when we will have to be completely self-sufficient, and take my word for it, he is constantly preparing for that day." Then sighing, he added, "He's been like a father to me. I left the ranch nine years ago and haven't returned, but when I left, he had been stockpiling things like guns and ammo. I worry about him sometimes and have thought often about going back, but something has held me here—something I can't explain."

That was the short version, but Jack didn't feel any urge to tell her the details of his life. She already knew more about him than anyone else he had met up here, and he had only made her acquaintance this morning. There was a short silence, then she said, "How old are you, Jack?"

At that, he smiled—there was such a directness about her, and once again he thought, "In some ways, she is just a child."

"Old enough to know better," he said, quoting his old uncle.

Then, seeing the disappointment in her face, he said, "I turned twenty-six this June, but don't worry about getting me a present."

They both laughed at this then sat in silence, Jack wishing for tobacco and Annie looking down at her hands. Suddenly she looked up and said, "Oh Jack, I almost forgot!" Then going to the dresser beside the door, she picked up her small bag and started rummaging through it as she came back to the table. "Here it is," she said, a smile lighting up her eyes. But before she removed her hand from the bag, she asked, "Do you smoke, Jack? I saw your pipe but wasn't sure…" She trailed off, waiting for him to respond.

At first, he was too startled to respond, feeling like she had just read his mind again.

Then slowly he nodded his head, and she exclaimed, "'Cause I have tobacco," as she produced a small leather pouch. "Happy late birthday," she said, giggling at his surprised look. He stared at her, speechless and slack-jawed. After a moment in which he once again found himself lost in her incredible blue eyes, he said, "How do you do it, girl?"

"Do what?" she asked, as she opened the little bag.

He reached across the table and grabbed both her hands again, asking: "Am I crazy?" She looked back at him questioningly but didn't attempt to take her hands back, so he went on.

"Are you just a figment of my imagination?" He looked seriously troubled, and Annie was a little taken aback when he said most earnestly, "Are you real, Annie? I need to know for sure. I know I sound crazy but listen. When I was a kid, I had a reoccurring dream. It wasn't always exactly the same, but the same person was in all of them. Sometimes we would just sit and talk or just walk together through the forest. But the point is, these dreams were so vivid that they felt real, and when I woke, I would wish I could have stayed in the dream forever.

"Sometimes," he said, looking down at the table, "I feel that way around you, as if you're nothing but a really vivid dream, and that I any minute I'll wake up, and you'll be gone."

They stared at each other across the table, and in that moment Jack realized that at some level, deep in his soul, he already loved her, even though he didn't really know her and even though he couldn't bring himself to say it out loud. Slowly she pulled her hands from his, went to the shelf above his bed, and took down his old pipe.

He thought, "It's like she's been here all along," as she sat back down, loaded the pipe, and handed it to him.

Lighting it, he wondered again if he was dreaming the whole thing, then she came around the table and leaned over him. She smiled, but Jack seemed to see a sadness in her eyes. Softly she said, "Yes, Jack, I'm real, but I understand how I must seem to you. I know you have questions, yet you don't press me, and I thank you for that. There is so much that I can't tell you now because I'm afraid. I don't want to hurt you; you're a nice man." Then, sighing deeply, she sat back down and stared blankly into her empty cup.

He hated to see that look on her face, and he wanted to say something to reassure her that everything would work out. But before he could speak, she reached across the table and touched his hand.

"Jack," she started, still looking into her empty coffee mug. "If I tell you something personal, something of the truth, will you try and have an open mind? Jack nodded thinking, "It's about time!" She went on hesitantly. "The thing is Jack; I didn't come out her to find a guide." Then, taking a deep breath she said, "I came out her to find you, and I knew you grew up in the United States." For a moment, Jack just stared at her blankly, then all at once it hit him like a freight train.

She needed a hired gun! He wasn't angry—this kind of thing had happened before—but he was a little hurt. He was about to say, "I'm not in that business anymore little girl," when he noticed the look on her face. She looked almost defiant, as if she had read his thought and was daring him to speak it out loud. At the same time something deep inside him seemed to cry out: "This is why you've come north: she is what you've been searching for." He dropped his gaze and walked over to the window. When he thought of all the perils this little girl would face alone down there in the good old USA it sent a shiver down his spine. She would be helpless, and her pet wolf couldn't protect her from the kind of dangers that he knew she would face—she seemed so innocent and naive of the world. Finally, his nerve broke, and he blurted out part of what his heart felt.

"Stay here with me, Annie. I will protect you. I…" and he managed to stop himself before he went too far.

Color came into her cheeks and she smiled, then she stood and walked to the door. "Thank you for the wonderful dinner, Jack. I had better find Wolf and make sure he hasn't been up to any mischief."

She opened the door, and Jack realized at once that he couldn't let her do it—not alone. That inner voice spoke up again, nearly shouting: "You can't lose her now that you have finally found her!" So, he reached out and lightly grabbed her by the shoulder.

"Annie," he said, "if you're sure it's what you want, then I will go with you, but you must promise me one thing."

She looked up at him, eyes shining in the moonlight. "What's that, Jack?"

"Don't go off on your own. Understand?"

She put her small hand to his cheek and said, "I knew you were the one, Jack. I always have, and from the first time I felt you watching me from behind the big tree, I knew you could never hurt me."

He wrapped her jacket around her shoulders without so much as a comment on this latest revelation, then they walked up the ridge together. He had no intention of leaving her alone tonight, and Wolf was nowhere in sight. They walked along in silence for awhile, and Jack felt good, as if the gods had smiled down on him. He looked up at the moon, thinking: "Well, if I am crazy, at least it's a good crazy."

Eventually they came into her camp, and he helped to build up the fire. Wolf suddenly appeared out of nowhere and Annie hugged his neck, then she turned to Jack and bid him good night. As she ducked into the tent, she paused and looked back.

"Thanks again for dinner, Jack. Do you think we can leave tomorrow?"

Slowly he shook his head. Smiling, he said, "I'd like to have a few days to prepare. Tomorrow we will move your things to the cabin. I will be here in the morning when you wake up."

"Thanks, Jack," she said. "But I've got Wolf to look after me. Go home and get some sleep. Good night."

"Good night," he said and sat down on the old log. The wolf walked stiffly around the camp, nose sniffing the air. Apparently satisfied, he made his way to the front of the girl's tent and lay down, eyes watchful. Jack looked over at him. "Well, nothing is getting in there," he thought.

There was a lot to do if they were really going to do this, so his mind was racing. He knew he would be unable to sleep. Feeling sure that Annie was safe, at least for the moment, he stood up and turned toward the tent. Wolf tracked him with his eyes, but he didn't move from his post.

"Keep an eye on her, buddy," he said and started back to the cabin.

# CHAPTER 4

Since the completion of his home, Jack had fallen into something of a routine, and he had to admit that it had been a welcome change from his wanderings over the last few years. It's amazing what you can accumulate in such a small time, he thought, as he tried to decide what to take with him and what to leave behind. He was pretty sure that he wouldn't be coming back. He had two guns, the .45 and his uncle's old hunting rifle. The problem was he was running low on ammo. He laid it out on the bunk. His belt held twenty cartridges for his pistol, and he had two boxes of cartridges for the rifle, about forty rounds. As it was late fall, most of what he took would be clothing, but he had to allow room for food.

Suddenly he stopped. What was he doing? Dropping down on the edge of the bed, he thought, "I'm not prepared for this!" He tried to clear his mind. It was early in the morning; maybe 1:00 a.m. He knew that Annie was in a hurry to go, but if he could just get back to the settlement, he could outfit them better. He had plenty of gold and a few fox furs; he might even be able to get a couple of horses. For two more hours, he turned over different scenarios in his head, but he couldn't get past the point that it would be impossible for the two of them to carry everything he thought they would need. If he had been traveling alone, he would have taken the chance that he could live off the land; however, he wasn't willing to take that chance with *her* life. Finally, around five in the morning, he resigned himself to fate and started back toward the girl's camp. It was just as he had left it. Wolf hadn't moved, but his eyes watched him as he approached the tent, and when Jack got to within ten feet, he growled low in his throat.

"Ok," Jack said as he took a couple of steps backward. "I can wait!"

He stoked the fire and leaned back against the log. Slowly he went over his plans in his mind, determined not to miss a trick. Now that he had decided to go, he was excited to get home. He wondered what his uncle would make of Annie. The fire was warm and he found himself starting to nod off.

In the dream, they were again running. It was the same dream, but this time he could see her face clearly, and she was terrified. Once again she fell and he knelt down to pick her up. Then, for the first time, he noticed the blood on her dress—she was hurt. Jack felt the blood run out of his own face as he looked into her eyes.

Then she spoke the same words as before: "What is it, Jack? What do you see?" He woke with a start. The sun was up and Wolf was gone. He could hear Annie rummaging around the tent, and presently she came out carrying a small bundle of clothes.

"Good morning, sleepy head," she said, dropping the bundle on the ground before her. "I'm going to wrap everything in the tent. There isn't a lot, and I think we could carry it as far as the cabin. I'll go through it there; I won't need all of it. Did you sleep here all night, Jack?"

"No," he said, rubbing his eyes. His legs had gone to sleep, and at first he couldn't stand up, so he propped himself up on the log and waited for the pins and needles to pass. As he was doing this, he told her his plan.

"Will we have to come back here after we go to the fort?" she asked.

"Actually," he said, thinking this would be where she protested, "I thought I would go alone, and you could stay here and get things ready."

He didn't add that he would be able to travel faster by himself. She stopped what she was doing and looked around.

"Will you be long?" she asked, still not looking directly at him.

"Four, maybe five days," he said. "And then we can start right away."

Just then, Wolf loped into camp and walked up to her. He nuzzled her hair and licked her face, making her giggle.

Now she looked at him and said, "Ok, Jack, whatever you think is best. But I think you should leave right away—today, if you can."

He had already planned on leaving that morning, but by the time they had moved her stuff to the cabin, and he had finished unpacking, it was midday. So by the time he shouldered his pack and assured Annie for the hundredth time that he would be back in less than a week, it was dusk. As he went out the front door, he took one last look around. She had persuaded him to set up the tent, saying that it would be a familiar thing to Wolf and then he would know it was her new camp. She had been right because no sooner had he got it up than Wolf appeared and plopped down in front of it. He was still there, head up, watching the girl as she came out of the cabin. He turned to say goodbye, and for the first time, he noticed the fear in her eyes; he started to reassure her one more time that he wouldn't be gone long when she did something that startled him into silence.

Quickly, before he realized what was happening, she stood on her toes and kissed him.

Then, with her face still inches from his own, she whispered, "Hurry back, Jack. Please hurry."

Before he could respond, she took a step back, and the fear seemed to leave her. "We'll be waiting," she said, and she gave him her best smile.

In the end he was afraid to speak, afraid he would reveal what his heart was screaming in his chest, so he just nodded and started off up the hill. For half an hour after he left, he had to fight the urge to go back, especially when he passed the spot of her old camp. Why hadn't he said something—anything? He knew his limitations; he knew that he wasn't good at expressing what he felt to anyone, but she had needed reassuring and he had said nothing. It was the kiss, he knew that. It wasn't just that she had caught him off guard. He had felt an electric current, a physical thing that had passed between them. In that fleeting moment, he had smelled her hair; a lock of it had brushed his cheek. He had felt her warm breath as she had spoken so near to him and he had forgotten to breathe himself—never in his whole life had he felt that way. It was as if with that kiss, the world had ceased to move. Everything stood still; the very air seemed to shimmer, and the only living thing in the universe was her. As he reached the spot where her tent had been, he noticed something buried under a small pile of leaves. It was another piece of yellow paper. Jack stared at it for a moment before picking it up—there was something written there in Annie's hand, two words: "GO HOME!!!"

He knew that the note wasn't meant for him—it was probably for her brother—but it felt like an omen, and suddenly he was undecided. He had always been a man of action: when things fell apart, he made decisions; when everyone else gave up, he pushed on as if by his will alone, things would come out right. Yet here he stood, unsure of himself and his plan. *She* had done this to him, made him question himself; made him careful. He shook himself. She had the rifle and Wolf was with her—he was just wasting time. So, after one last glance around, he started off toward the small town at a trot, even though he still couldn't shake that uneasy feeling; after a few minutes, the trot turned into a run.

The rest of the trip to Fort Simpson was uneventful. He managed to make pretty good time, and on the afternoon of the third day, he found himself on the outskirts of the settlement. It was typical of most outposts these days. Small cabins dotted the scene, and a dirt road ran through the center of old dilapidated buildings. Here and there were new structures, one being the store, another the restaurant and hotel, and of course the unavoidable saloon or bar. Jack had been here many times and had eaten in the restaurant. He had even played cards in the bar on nights when the weather had been too bad to journey out. Once in town he went straight to the corral and picked out two horses that looked at least half-tame. He thought at first that he had paid too much for them but was satisfied that they would serve his purpose. Then he had gone to see Eddy over at the store.

The first thing out of the shopkeeper's mouth when he came in was: "Did the girl find you, Jack?"

For no good reason, Jack lied. "Girl?" he said, not looking around.

"Yeah, pretty little thing; black hair. She was asking about the good ole USA. I told her about you and where to find you. She seemed excited to make your acquaintance."

Jack turned and walked toward the counter. "Must have missed her, I guess," he said, looking Eddy in the eye for the first time.

Eddy looked him over, then he looked over his shoulder through the front window, and Jack knew he was studying the horses tied there.

"Got any tobacco?" Jack asked amiably enough, but Eddy was back to staring at him with his one good eye.

Finally he said, "Yeah, sure, just got some in yesterday; good stuff, too."

Jack bought tobacco, a few canned goods that he thought the girl would like, and a small tin of coffee. He paid with two silver fox furs, which made the storekeeper's day. Then he turned to leave, saying, "See ya around, Eddy."

But just as he reached the door, Eddy said, "Planning a trip, Jack?"

He turned once again, another lie on his lips, but Eddy continued. "Not that it's any of my business, but if you do run across that little girl and her brother, be careful."

Now Jack was curious. "Why? Are they dangerous?" he asked casually.

"No, not them, but I happened to overhear some of their conversation out there in front of the store."

Jack smiled. Eddy was the biggest gossip in town and he always had his ear to the ground.

"What did you hear, Ed?" he said, still smiling.

Suddenly the old man seemed nervous, but he went on anyway. "Well, I didn't catch what the girl said—her voice was so soft—but her brother practically yelled, and I realized he was scared. He said, 'They will find you, Annie. They will track you to the end of the earth, and then there will be another man dead!' Made me sorry that I had told them about you, Jack. After that the boy stormed off, but for a moment, the girl just stood there with her head down, and..."

"Yes?" Jack said, studying the old man's face.

"I think she was crying. It gave me the shivers!"

Jack shrugged and once again turned to go when something occurred to him. He paused, the door half open. "Ed," he said, looking back over his shoulder, "you didn't happen to tell her my name, did you?"

"Jack," Ed said, trying to sound indignant, "you know I would never do that. Me and you is old friends!"

Jack smiled at this. They had only known each other for a few years, so he said sarcastically, "Sure, we go way back."

But instead of smiling back at the joke, Eddy looked puzzled, scratching the back of his head. He said, "But you know, now that I think about it, she never asked for it. Seems strange, don't it, Jack?"

Jack started back that afternoon. The horses turned out to be worth the gold he had paid for them. The small black-and-white mare was completely tame, and it was evident that they had both carried riders before. Jack made one more purchase before he left. The corral owner had told him about a man just outside the town limits that had lost his last horse the past winter.

"Probably still has the saddle," he said through a mouthful of tobacco.

In the end Jack had bought two saddles and two bridles from the man. It had taken the rest of his gold, but he felt he had gotten a fair deal. When he had thrown the saddles over the horses' backs, they had barely flinched, but when he had thrown his leg over the big gray stallion, it had reared, and it took Jack a few minutes to get him calmed down. Jack had been around horses his whole life and he knew their ways. If this one sensed fear or weakness, he would take advantage of him. Slowly the big horse settled down, and Jack patted his neck and talked in a low reassuring voice in the animal's ear as he headed him out of town, the small black-and-white following without a lead rope.

That first day he made excellent time; Jack had forgotten the advantages of a horse. He could gallop along at twice the speed that he himself could run and the horses never seemed to tire. As he stopped to rest on the first night, he realized that he would probably be home the next afternoon. He was tempted to ride straight through the night, but he didn't want to risk the horses—the last thing he needed now that he was so close was a broken leg, so he camped for the night in a thicket near a small stream. He built up a huge fire tying the gray to a spruce near a small clearing where he could graze, yet close enough that Jack could still hear him if there was trouble. He let the little black-and-white roam free, knowing she wouldn't go far from her companion. Just as he turned from the horses, a small hare darted from behind a rock maybe twenty feet from where he stood. If anyone had been watching the next few seconds, they would have wondered what they had seen. The rabbit darted from its hiding spot, there was a loud report, and it rolled over three times, coming to a stop not ten feet from the fire. It was dead—almost completely decapitated, as a matter of fact.

The rabbit was small, but Jack took great care with the fur, thinking he would use it to line a pair of gloves for Annie. He ate the rest and then laid back against a boulder. He covered himself with his jacket and stared up at the stars. "It's getting chilly," he thought and silently wished the snow would hold off for a few more weeks. He remembered the first year after he had crossed into the northwest territory. By that time, it had already snowed twice. That winter he had come to within inches of death more than a few times, but he had taken it all in stride. He had known hard winters where he had grown up, so he was used to snow and cold. Where he came from it would sometimes fall below zero, and the snow drifts could reach over ten feet, but that first winter in the north, the temperature had reached thirty below on a few occasions—although Jack didn't know it and the snow had come in waves. If it hadn't been for Jacob, he would have died.

Good old Jacob! They had met on the last day of Jack's life, or it should have been, anyway. Jack had been setting traps near a large beaver dam when the storm hit and he had hastily built a small shelter near what used to be called Willow Lake River, just east of the Mackenzie. It snowed for three days and he was perilously low on provisions. As suddenly as it came, the storm departed and the temperature plummeted. Jack was in the process of starving and/or freezing to death when the sound of a barking dog brought him back from the edge of sleep. He had managed to crawl out of his little shelter and fire his pistol into the air. He was rewarded by the sound of more barking and a man's voice cutting through the stillness. After that, he had fallen into oblivion only to awake a few hours later in a fairly large cabin next to a blazing fire. He raised himself up on his elbow and looked across the room, wondering to himself where he had gotten himself to now when the door had flown open and a figure had stepped through with an armful of firewood. Jack knew right away, even before he could see the stranger's face, that this man was a native. He could tell by the way he was dressed, so he had felt a tinge of anxiety and glanced around for his pistol. But his fears were immediately dispelled when the figure had grabbed his holster off of the back of a small chair and dropped it on the floor in front of him—this was how he had met Jacob.

Later when Jack had inquired as to how he had found him, Jacob had brushed off the question, saying the Great Spirit had led him there, and from that day forward, Jack was eternally grateful to the Great Spirit.

He had spent the rest of that long winter in Jacob's little cabin on Willow Lake; that's where he had completed his wilderness training and a close friendship had developed. Their friendship had been set in stone the night that Jack had killed the ranger, and that was the year that Jack had met Eddy, the storekeeper. It was his second year in the north.

The ranger had been from "New Texas," a place Jack had never heard of, and he hated everything about the north. He was here for one reason: gold. He had hired Jacob as a guide, giving him two gold pieces up front and offering five percent of whatever they found that summer, but he seemed to expect that *Jacob* would find the valuable mineral and *bring* it to him.

Jacob had joked at first, saying: "As long as he's paying me, I will walk all over Canada!"

The ranger was trained in every manner of self-defense and he wasn't afraid to practice on the locals in Fort Simpson. Most people thought that it was just a matter of time before he killed someone, and they all avoided him like the plague. It seemed like the longer he was here, the more violent he became. Jack had been in the bar the night that Eddy lost his eye. It had started innocently enough with a game of cards. It had been Eddy, Jack, Grizzly Bill, and the ranger. They hadn't been playing for "keeps," but Eddy had been having a great stream of luck, and the ranger had accused him of cheating. Bill had tried to calm the ranger with free drinks, but to no avail. What ensued was a pretty good fight, but Jack had seen his fair share of fights and didn't find any real interest in it, so he had gone to the bar and ordered another coffee. Secretly he had been hoping that Eddy, who outweighed the ranger by eighty pounds, would beat him down. Then there came a terrific scream, and Jack whirled around in time to see the ranger standing over the crumpled figure of Eddy on the floor, holding his left eyeball in his hand. Everyone in the place was staring at the ranger incredulously. Then calmly, as if it was the most natural thing in the world, he dropped the eyeball in his shirt pocket and strolled out of the bar. Later that evening, as the doc was tending to Eddy, Grizzly Bill had told him what had happened. Eddy had been on top, chocking the life out of the smaller man when, fast as a snake striking a helpless mouse, the ranger reached out and plucked out the eye. Bill had been shaking as he related the story to Jack, summing his feelings up by saying that it was unnatural how fast the ranger had moved. After that, Mr. Ranger seemed to disappear, and everyone was of the opinion that he had gone back to "New Texas." One night, about two weeks after the incident in the saloon, he had stumbled into the very store where Jack had bought his tobacco just a day ago.

As he looked back on it now, it seemed almost like a dream. He could see himself and Jacob leaning on the counter just shooting the shit with Eddy, his patch already in place. There was a horrible storm raging outside, and both Jack and Jacob had already decided to stay in town that night—that's when the door flew open, and the ranger, covered in sleet and snow, staggered in.

He was almost ghostly, and the first thing that Jack observed was that he wasn't wearing a coat. His clothes were plastered to his body and he was soaked to the bone. Even worse, his exposed skin had a blue tint to it. Jack remembered thinking that it must have taken inhuman strength to hold the door with only his left hand and close it before the storm blew it away, because in his right hand he was holding a shotgun.

He accused Jacob of finding gold and keeping it all to himself, then he had cocked his head as if listening to something only he could hear, and yelled out: *"No!* This will be the last night you drink on my dime!"

Now the only weapon Jacob carried on his person was an old bowie knife, which he used for everything from gutting a caribou to cleaning his nails, but he hadn't even flinched when the ranger had pointed the shotgun at his chest. Jack would never forget the look on Jacob's face as he walked toward the ranger. There was a peace there that Jack couldn't imagine in the face of certain death.

He said, simply: "I have taken nothing from you."

Jack, on the other hand, didn't feel so calm, and he blurted out suddenly: "I am the one that took your gold."

The ranger's eyes narrowed as if he were noticing Jack for the first time and he lowered the gun as he took a step forward. He said, "So the badass can talk!" Jack leaned back against the counter and laughed. It was the first time in his life that anyone had used that word to describe him, and he found it funny coming from this lunatic's mouth. Unfortunately for everyone there, the ranger thought that Jack was laughing *at* him, and he brought the shotgun up in one swift move. Jack was quicker: he had drawn his gun and fired before the ranger got his hand to the trigger. The ranger fell to his knees as Jack holstered the .45, and the ranger died before anyone could make a move toward him.

To this day, Jacob sometimes called him Lightning Jack when they were alone because neither he nor Eddy had seen him draw or holster his gun. The bullet had hit the ranger right between the eyes and Jacob said it was like he had been hit by lightning. Jack could have simply disabled the crazed man at that range, but as usually happened in these situations, his instincts had taken over. He never wondered why he had decided it would be better to kill the man than just wound him, nor did he feel any remorse. For one, Jacob had been between himself and the ranger; had he missed, his friend may have still been in danger, but this wasn't the only reason he had killed him. After the fact, he recalled an incident with an old cattle dog of his uncle's. Jack had developed a strong bond with this particular dog, but it had gotten rabies and needed to be put down before it hurt someone. He had loved that dog, but that hadn't stopped his uncle from shooting it down right in front of him. Jack had burst out crying just like a little girl. Instead of chastising him, his uncle had put his arm around his narrow shoulders and said, "He wasn't himself, Jack. That wasn't Buddy."

As far as Jack being blamed for the ranger's death, it was never an issue. Nobody had heard the shot through the noise of the storm, and as far the town knew, the ranger had never come back. Jacob had bundled the body in an old bearskin and tied it to his sled, and Jack never saw it again.

One night when he and Jacob had been out hunting, he had asked him straight up, "What did you do with that crazy man from Texas?"

Jacob had looked into the fire and said as pertly as you please: "He finally got his gold."

Then he rolled over on his side and pulled his blanket over his head. Puzzled, Jack stared at the back of his companion, but he never mentioned the incident again.

# CHAPTER 5

The next morning, Jack was up before dawn saddling the horses. That anxious feeling had returned, and he had barely slept. He couldn't resist the thought that he needed to hurry, and somehow he had communicated his own nervousness to the horses. They were jittery, and the little black-and-white had tossed her head when he had tried to put a lead rope around her neck. It was still dark when he started, and there was a fine mist in the air, so at first he led the horses instead of riding. The sun finally came up about an hour later but the rain came with it; still, he jumped up on the gray's back and started off at a gallop. The rain came down in huge drops that soaked both him and the horses within minutes, but Jack barely noticed. The closer he got to home, the more he felt the need to hurry, and as a result he pushed the animals more than he would have liked to. About midday he came to Annie's old camp and he dismounted. He looked around for the little note, thinking that he would ask her about it.

By now the rain had nearly stopped, but the clouds were close and a heavy fog set in, blocking out most of the sunlight. He finally found the little scrap of paper, but it was soaked and the writing was smeared. He put it in his pocket anyway, but he still felt uneasy. As he walked into the little meadow, the fog seemed to thicken around him. He couldn't even make out the ridge where the small cabin sat. More by instinct than anything else, he moved slowly in the direction where he thought the path that led up to the cabin would be. Leading the horses behind him, he searched for familiar landmarks until he found the foot of the hill—here he stopped suddenly and the hair stood up on the back of his neck. There was an eerie quiet—not a sound came to his staining ears, not even the normal sounds of the forest. Everything stood perfectly still and he caught a faint smell of smoke in the air.

Jack turned and looked at the horses; they were even more nervous than they had been in the meadow. Moving swiftly and making as little noise as possible, he led the horses back down the slope and tied the gray to a sapling. Patting his nose reassuringly, Jack started back up the hill. The smell of smoke grew stronger the closer he got to the summit, and the stillness seemed to grow as if he, Jack Brooks, were the only living thing left in the world.

The first thing he thought as he topped the ridge was that he had taken a wrong turn and had come up in the wrong direction, then he saw the tent right where he had placed it the day he left. The cabin, however, was gone—it had burned completely to the ground. Jack briefly fought the urge to race toward it, shouting Annie's name. He turned back to the tent. Walking slowly, his very soul wanting to scream her name, he whispered instead: "Annie...you there?"

Jack listened closely, every inch of his body ready for action, and then...a sound, a whimper. Jack drew his revolver and knelt down in front of the tent. He used the muzzle of the gun to part the tent flaps and what he saw made his heart stop.

It was Wolf. He was lying on his side and there was blood everywhere. The animal looked at him but didn't move. Slowly, Jack crept toward him, saying to him in a low voice, "It's ok, boy, I'm here. It's ok." Wolf looked away and Jack started to examine him with his hand. Finally he found a small bullet wound right below the bone in his left hind leg. He looked closely at the wound. The problem wasn't the bullet hole—Wolf had done a good job taking care of that himself. So where else was he hurt? He looked around the tent again—there was too much blood here; someone had been hurt badly. Could it have been Annie? The thought sent a shiver up his spine. He looked directly into Wolf's eyes. Wolf looked back as if he understood the situation exactly and then laid his head back down. Jack licked his lips; he felt paralyzed to the spot. Part of him wanted to race out into the forest blindly calling Annie's name, but another part of him was saying, "Calm down; you've got time." Fortunately for everyone involved, it was this voice that won the day. Once he got ahold of himself, Jack realized that the only way he could possibly find Annie was with this animal's help. Could he even help at this point? He wasn't sure how badly Wolf was hurt. Slowly, he ran his hands alongside Wolf's body, finding nothing until he reached his neck.

Here, buried under the fur, he found a thick rope. It was so tight that Jack couldn't get his finger between it and the skin—it was a wonder that Wolf could breathe at all. He took out his small pocketknife and began to work at the rope slowly. Finally it parted, but to Jack's dismay, he found that part of it was actually embedded in the skin. He would have to pull it out swiftly, which would cause the animal even more suffering. He only hesitated for a moment, then taking hold of one of the ends he had cut loose, he braced himself, sending up a short prayer that Wolf wouldn't turn on him as the cause of this fresh pain.

It was Wolf himself that decided for him—suddenly he yelped like a puppy, as if to say, "What are you waiting for?" and that was enough for Jack. With one swift movement, he pulled up and out. The rope came free of Wolf's neck but snagged on something else, jerking him back and nearly breaking his wrist in the process. During the whole operation, the wolf never made a move to stop him, but now he struggled to his feet and bounded out of the tent. Jack picked up the end of the rope and gave it a gentle tug; it ran underneath the tent. Jack went out. Wolf was nosing around the remains of the cabin and paid him no attention. As he came to where the rope came out from under the tent, he stopped, staring in astonishment. Now he understood why Wolf hadn't tried to move when he entered the tent and why he hadn't followed after Annie even though he had been wounded in the leg. He couldn't—the rope was short, maybe six feet long, but very thick. Jack could see where Wolf had tried to chew through it to no avail. It came out from under the tent and snaked along the ground to where it had been tied to a large fallen tree. Jack knew this tree—he had even sat on it and smoked his pipe, but he could have never moved it by himself, yet Wolf had managed to drag it nearly fifty feet before it had lodged itself between two boulders. Jack puzzled it out. For some reason Annie had tied her loyal companion to this tree, probably to save his life. But when she didn't return, he had tried to escape. Unable to chew through the rope, he had dragged the old tree through the woods, trying to get back to the tent that he had always associated with the girl. He had made it, but she wasn't there. Exhausted he had laid down, and that's where Jack found him. As for the blood in the tent, it couldn't have all come from the wound on Wolf's leg, but farther than that he didn't dare speculate.

The rain had washed away most of the footprints in the dooryard, but Jack found at least one that he knew didn't belong to himself or Annie.

Jack explored what was left of the cabin—there wasn't much. He found a few cooking utensils, including his old cast-iron skillet, but that was about it. The gun was gone, but that wasn't surprising: guns were more valuable than gold these days, so he guessed that whoever had kidnapped Annie had also taken the .30-30. He walked back into the dooryard and noticed something shiny half buried in the soot. He bent down to pick it up between his fingers but instead nudged it with his boot; it was a spent cartridge, one of his—he was sure of it. Looking closer and moving the ashes around with his toe, he found four more in the same spot. He thought about the bullet hole in Wolf's leg, but he knew that had been a smaller caliber, a .22 maybe. What had happened here? Had Annie fired the rifle? The fog was finally lifting and Jack could see across to the woods. He thought that the fire couldn't have started more than four or five hours ago, as it was still smoldering. Even with the heavy rain that had come along and helped put it out before it burned down the surrounding forest, the ashes were still hot. As he was puzzling over the scene, trying to get some idea of what exactly had happened, a lonely howl drifted to him from the direction of the ridge. Wolf had found something! He turned and ran toward the sound, calling the animal's name. He came upon him suddenly. Wolf was digging at the ground a few feet from the spruce that Jack had hidden behind only a few days before. He knew at once it was a shallow grave and his heart jumped in his chest. Kneeling down beside Wolf, he dug at the ground with his bare hands, choking back the emotion that threatened to overtake him. Suddenly Wolf let out a low growl and clasped something in his teeth. Bracing his forepaws he yanked backward, and suddenly the head and shoulders of a small form came up out of the ground. Jack fell back, a small cry escaping through his clenched teeth. The figure was wrapped in his old bedcover, and it was this that Wolf had between his powerful jaws. Even as he watched, it tore away, revealing the face of a young man. The relief that Jack felt was instant and complete—it wasn't Annie! Jack examined the face closely. He was just a kid really, not more than seventeen or eighteen. He was a white man, but his features were sharp.He ripped the bedcover down to his chest, and that's when he noticed that the man's throat had been torn completely out. This was no bullet wound and he knew exactly who's handiwork this was. There were teeth marks on the chest and shoulders and one ear was practically severed. Wolf was trying to get back at the corpse, and Jack had to put himself between him and the body to keep him from tearing it apart. Finally, Jack covered it back up and put a few large rocks on top of it so that Wolf couldn't dig it back up. When he had finished, he started back to where the cabin had been, and Wolf, after nosing around the rocks for a few seconds, followed him.

Jack looked around. What was he waiting for? There was nothing left of his small cabin. Everything he had left was already packed on the horses. He hadn't even taken the time to unsaddle them. He walked over to the tent and stared down at it. Behind him, Wolf whined almost inaudibly. Jack turned to look at him, and the animal half barked at him as if to say: "What are you waiting for, ya big dummy? Let's go get her." That decided it for him. He went to work rolling up the tent, and within a few minutes, they were walking up the hill for the last time. Jack didn't even look back. In the end he had taken the old iron skillet with him; he wasn't sure why—probably because it was the only thing left of the life he was leaving behind forever. As they reached the spot where the shallow grave was, Wolf walked over and sniffed at it. Then, to Jack's amazement, he lifted his leg. Jack laughed. He couldn't help it; it was so comical. Wolf finished his business and trotted off in the direction of the meadow. Jack followed, saying out loud: "I feel the same way, boy."

The horses were right where he left them, and they stared at him accusingly as he approached, but they seemed no worse for the wear. From here he wasn't exactly sure how to proceed. The rain had washed away any tracks that his enemies would have made. He had been hoping that Wolf would pick up a trail and he could just follow him, but the animal was just sitting there as if he were waiting for something. Jack took out his compass. He had never heard of Good Hope, but Annie had said it was about two hundred miles north of here, so he would head north and hope he would come upon some sort of sign. If nothing else, he would eventually just follow the river. They couldn't have made it that far, and the horses gave him an advantage. He could catch up if he could only figure out which direction they had gone.

Then a thought came to him—he had been going on the assumption that there was more than one man with Annie and that they were headed back to Annie's home. He thought that if they had gone south toward Fort Simpson, they would have passed him. Now it occurred to him that with the fog and the rain he might have ridden right past a whole army and not even noticed in his haste to get back to the cabin. Once again he was undecided, and he was wasting precious time. For the tenth time, he cursed his own stupidity, and Wolf whined impatiently.

He looked over at his canine companion and, speaking more to himself than to Wolf, said, "How do we even know that that's where they're headed?" Wolf cocked his head, and for a moment, Jack could have sworn the animal actually understood what he was saying. Then, more because he was out of ideas than for any other reason, he said without much hope, "Find Annie, boy!"

Suddenly, Wolf turned and loped off in the direction of the forest to the north. Jack smiled and shook his head. Was it possible that Wolf had been waiting for him the whole time? It seemed unlikely—more likely he had just assumed that Annie would return or that Jack knew where to find her. Whatever the reason, he was glad to have his company and his nose; with Wolf around he didn't have to worry about anything or anyone sneaking up on him.

Wolf had started out with his nose to the ground, but finally he seemed to decide he knew where he was going and fell in just in front of Jack and the horses. It was funny how all three animals seemed to accept each other's presence—in the wild they were natural enemies, yet here with him, they were walking nearly side by side at times. True, the big gray would get a little skittish if Wolf got too close to him, but Wolf seemed to realize this and kept a little ahead where the horses could see him. He finally decided that it was a combination of two things:

the fact that Wolf had probably been around horses his whole life, and that the horses had been around men with dogs. Still he was pretty sure things would have gone differently if he wasn't here, and he wondered at the effect that man had sometimes over nature.

They had come about twenty miles when Wolf stopped suddenly, causing Jack, who had been leading the horses and looking up at the gray sky, to nearly trip over him. Wolf's ears were cocked forward and the hair on his neck was standing up. Every muscle in his body was tense and Jack was instantly alert. Then Wolf turned and loped off in the direction that they had just come from, leaving him standing there, mouth open. Jack looked around. They had been walking through a sparsely wooded area, mostly scrub brush with a few trees here and there. He sensed nothing, but he knew that Wolf's senses were far more acute, so he was on his guard. He waited, listening, trying to make out the smallest sound, but nothing came to him.

At first Jack waited patiently for Wolf to come back, giving him the benefit of the doubt. But after about an hour had passed, he became impatient and had almost convinced himself that Wolf had sensed some sort of game and had gone off hunting. Finally he decided to continue on cautiously on their original course. So, taking one last glance back in the direction Wolf had gone, he started off, leading the horses behind him. He hadn't gone twenty feet when Wolf reappeared—not from behind, but directly in front of him. He stood sideways as if he were trying to bar the way. Jack studied the animal;

he was trying to tell him something. Jack took a step forward, but Wolf didn't move. "Ok, fine," he said out loud. "Which way, boss?" and as if he actually understood him, Wolf started off to the left, looking back from time to time to make sure Jack was following.

Jack wasn't very hungry, but he was worried about the animals. He knew that Wolf usually found something to eat on his own, but he was still hurting, and Jack hadn't seen him go hunting all day. The sun was starting to go down when they entered a little clearing. He looked around. "Well, at least the horses could probably find something to eat here." And if he was honest with himself, he was exhausted. "Camp here," he said, but Wolf just kept going. "Wolf," he said, a tinge of irritation in his voice. The animal noticed the change and turned to face him. "Camp here," he said and pointed to the ground. Wolf stared at him for a moment and then casually loped off into the woods. "Fine!" he said. "Every man for himself." And he turned to the horses.

He didn't bother to make a fire or set up the tent. He ate some dried venison and a small can of peaches. Wolf came back after a while, and Jack asked him frankly what kind of wild goose chase he was leading them on. Wolf made no reply; instead he plopped himself down in the leaves under a massive tree and immediately went to work on his wounded leg. Jack was uneasy. The skies had been gray all day, and for the last two hours, the air felt heavy; it was going to snow. He didn't think it would be a big storm and it wasn't yet cold enough during the day to stick to the ground for long. Jack wasn't fooling himself, though; he knew the weather could change any time now. He realized he hadn't even thought this through. As a matter of fact, he had done precious little thinking since he had found Annie gone. He had been running on pure adrenaline, and he was also feeling the effects of the stress. His brain seemed foggy. He looked over at Wolf. He actually seemed to be doing pretty well, everything considered. Jack walked over and sat down beside him. Absently he stroked the animal's fur as he looked vacantly across the little clearing. "We're some rescue party," he said at last, and at the sound of his voice, Wolf looked up at him. He looked into the wolf's eyes and said, "We need a plan, boy." Wolf laid his head in his lap, and Jack leaned back against the tree—he really was tired. He looked over at the horses, his eyes heavy, and his last thought before sleep took him was: "Maybe I should turn them lose to graze."

Wolf listened to the man breathe. If he could speak, he would have told the man that he wouldn't have to worry about the coming storm, the horses, or Annie for that matter. He knew exactly where she was, and it wasn't far from here. He could have gone to her right away, but some instinct made him return to wait for Jack. Wolf relied completely upon his senses, and just as he sensed the good in this man, he had sensed the evil in the men that had come to the cabin even before they had hurt him and taken Annie. He didn't understand guns, but he knew their smell and that they were associated with man exclusively. In a way, he regarded them as part of a man; a part that could be dangerous. Just as he used his teeth to maim and kill, men used these extensions of themselves to maim and kill. Therefore, it wasn't the guns that made Wolf leery; it was the men. On some level, Wolf realized that having this man and his gun was to his advantage. In addition to these faint instincts was the fact that Wolf was raised around humans; he was comfortable around them. Mostly he just ignored them unless they directly affected himself or Annie. In short, Wolf was no pet—he came and went as he pleased, his only loyalty being to the girl. The girl had saved him, had raised him, and had kept him from harm, and he loved her.

It would have surprised Jack to know that Wolf had seen her just a few hours before when he had gone off on his little foray. He had caught the slightest whiff of a campfire and had realized immediately that they were going in the wrong direction—they were walking right past the very people they were hunting. So he had fol-lowed his nose, expecting that the man would follow him. Eventually he had come to the big water and there they were, right on the bank. It was then that he noticed the girl. She was sitting off by herself in front of a big tent. A pet, a dog, would have bounded out of the woods right to her side, tail wagging and tongue licking, only to be shot on sight—that was the essential difference between himself and his canine cousins. Wolf sensed the danger, so he would be careful. Wolf knew how to be careful. Slowly, hardly making any sound at all, he had crept around to the back of the tent, and there he waited, every sense on alert. Finally he saw the girl's shadow as she rose and went into the tent, so he had put his nose against the canvas and whined in that almost inaudible way that he had—and she had heard him.

"Wolf!" she said in a tentative little voice, then put her hand against the inside of the tent. Wolf responded by putting his nose to her hand on his side. Then he had heard her crying almost silently, so he had whined again, a little louder this time, and that's when she had told him to go away.

"Go!" she had said in a whisper. "Wolf, run away now!"

This had been followed by another voice, a harsh voice, and although Wolf didn't understand the words, he could sense the menace in them. So he had melted back into the trees just as silently as he had come. He watched from his hiding place for a moment to make sure that no harm would come to the girl, but there was only more talking that Wolf could not possibly understand. Since she didn't seem to be in any danger at the moment, he took one last look around the camp and started back in the direction he had come.

He didn't understand why the man, "his man," as he had come to think of him, hadn't followed. But it wasn't in his power to question such things, so he had just followed his nose back to where he was, only to find him once again going in the wrong direction. Wolf had employed the same tactic that he had always used when Annie had been walking blindly into some dangerous situation: he blocked his way. If this hadn't worked, he would have nipped at him or grabbed at his clothes with his teeth, but the man had understood and followed. He had wanted to take him right away to the girl, but the man had stopped and fallen asleep. So he would wait, because Wolf could be careful, and Wolf could also be patient.

# CHAPTER 6

Before Jack was entirely awake, he was aware of some danger that was menacingly close. All of his senses were screaming for action, but somehow he forced himself to stay still. He was cold, and he could tell even through his closed lids that it was fully dark. His hands were resting in his lap and they were almost completely numb. "Served him right," he thought fleetingly. "Falling asleep like a small boy that had played too hard." He heard a sound almost like a man grunting as he lifted something heavy, just to his left and very close. He opened one eye ever so slightly and caught a glimpse of a huge, dark, shaggy head not three feet away from where he sat with his back against the tree. He immediately realized the situation, and his nerve broke. Living up to the name that Jacob had bestowed on him, his hand moved like lightning to the holster at his side. But his hands were too cold, and even as the gun came free, it fell to the ground between his outstretched legs. Luckily for Jack, the sudden movement had startled the huge creature momentarily, and it reared back, almost falling over. But the animal was at least as swift as he was and regained his composure quickly, bringing down one lethal paw in a giant arc. Jack rolled. He felt the air whoosh through his hair as the long claws came within inches of the top of his head. It was full dark, and the sky was too cloudy for the moon or the stars to offer any light—all Jack could make out were vague shapes. He could see the darker shape of the enormous bear as it stood up on his hind legs and let out an earsplitting roar, shaking its head violently from side to side. Jack took one glance in the direction of the gun, which lay useless on the ground not four feet away, and then rolled again in the opposite direction. He couldn't escape—the bear dropped back down to all fours and charged at him. Suddenly, there was a dark blur to his right and a sharp growl.

Wolf hit the bear at a dead run, knocking it over and rolling with it into the forest. Jack had no time to react. He watched helplessly as the rolling mass of fur and teeth hit the tree and rebounded back toward him. In the darkness he couldn't even tell where one animal ended and the other began. Finally the bear stood up on its hind legs, facing Jack once again. The momentum had thrown Wolf directly behind the bear, but instead of attacking from behind, which was the most logical choice for Wolf's own self-preservation, Wolf did something that Jack would never forget: Like a bullet fired from a gun, he darted straight between the bear's legs, placing himself directly in front of Jack's outstretched body, just as the huge paw that had been meant for him came down. It caught Wolf in the side, flinging him like a rag doll ten feet through the air, where he came to the ground in a bone-rattling heap. Still, the huge wolf struggled to his feet, and Jack had time to marvel at the tenacity of this animal. Wolf growled again, and the bear momentarily turned his attention to his antagonist. Jack saw his opportunity. He still had his buck knife, and when the bear turned its head to look at Wolf, Jack sprang, thrusting the knife with all his strength into the animal's shaggy neck, where it stuck fast. The bear went crazy, clawing at the knife and shaking its great head. Jack hurled himself in the direction of the gun—he knew he would only have one shot, and his hands were still numb; by dumb luck he finally located the pistol right where he had dropped it.

The bear had slowed its attack, still clawing at the knife protruding from its neck. It whirled first on Wolf, who still stood his ground, growling deep in his chest but not moving. Then the bear, getting much more of a fight than it had expected, seemed to resign itself to fate and turned once again to Jack, walking toward him slowly on all fours. From his knees, Jack forced himself to aim the weapon as best he could in the dark and squeezed the trigger. The bear took four more halting steps and then fell with a thud not two feet from Jack's outstretched hand. It was a lucky shot: the bullet had caught the bear just above the eye, and it took most of the brains with it as it exited the back of the skull. Had he been farther away, the result most certainly would have been different. Jack stared at the huge dark shape lying in front of him, half expecting it to rise and resume its attack—but it didn't move. Then Wolf was there, struggling to keep his feet. He sniffed at the body and then, satisfied that the bear was dead, fell in a heap next to it, panting. Jack went to him and put his arms around his shaggy neck.

"You saved my life, boy," he said, panting himself and choking back the emotion that threatened to overtake him. Wolf whined softly and licked his ear.

Amazingly, Jack had come through their scuffle with the bear without a scratch. Wolf, on the other hand, had been mauled pretty bad in the fray, and there wasn't much that Jack could do for him. He built a small fire near where Wolf had laid down, and after examining him as closely as the animal would allow, he was relatively sure that a couple of his ribs were broken. As for internal injuries, Jack wasn't sure. He would just have to wait and see if Wolf would live or die. This would delay his progress, but he found that he couldn't leave the brave animal until he was sure either way. When the sun came up, Jack set up Annie's little tent and managed to get Wolf to move inside with a little coaxing. He then poured some water into his old skillet and placed it near Wolf's head. As he lapped at it, Jack noticed a little dried blood on his jowls, but he wasn't sure if it was Wolf's or the bear's. He stroked the animal's fur for a-while, trying to talk in a low, soothing voice as he had heard Annie do when she was trying to calm him down. Then, not knowing what else to do, he had exited the tent, trying to lay aside the feelings of dread that kept wanting to come.

For a-while he just sat staring into the fire, then he heard a sound that brought him out of his stupor. It was the horses—he had completely forgotten about them, and as he walked in the direction of the sound, he tried to remember if he had tied the lead rope to something. Surely he must have, or they would have bolted at the first sign of the bear. They seemed fine, if a little spooked, but Jack decided that it would be better to let them roam free in the future, relying on their association with him to keep them near. As he untied the gray's lead rope, he galloped off about ten feet and halted, swishing his tail and shaking his head, as if irritated by Jack's neglect of him during the night. The little black-and-white followed him, but as the day wore on, they both seemed content to stay somewhat near Jack and the little camp.

After checking the horses, Jack decided that he had better do something with the bear carcass. So he cleaned and dressed it, stretching the skin between two saplings to dry. He kept very little of the meat, knowing that it would be tough and not very palatable, and hauled everything that was left far back into the forest, burying it under dirt and rocks. That done, he took some of the meat to Wolf and made sure he had fresh water before settling down in front of the fire to make his own supper. By this time it was after noon, and Jack was famished. He decided to brave some of the bear meat himself and set a small piece of it on a spit over the fire. He was just getting up to go to fetch some water for the coffee pot when a voice cut through the silence.

"Hello in the camp."

Jack heard Wolf's low growl coming from the tent and in a whispering but sharp tone said, "Wolf, quiet!"

Then he turned in the direction of the voice and could just make out someone coming through the trees toward him.

"Who's there?" Jack queried, his hand resting on the butt of the Colt.

"Just a fellow traveler," came the reply. "I saw your fire, and it's mighty rare to come across another human being in this neck of the woods."

The man seemed amiable enough, so Jack invited him in for a cup of coffee. It wasn't until they were close enough to shake hands that Jack noticed the stranger's rifle, and the hair stood up on the back of his neck. It wasn't that the stranger seemed menacing in any way—it was the gun itself that made Jack's blood run cold because it wasn't just any old rifle—it was his own .30-30.

Jacks's mind raced; a thousand questions filled his brain but thankfully stopped short of his lips. He must keep a cool head if he was going to have any hope of finding out anything this man may know about Annie. He prayed that Wolf would remain silent, but he knew that there was nothing he could do about it.

The man introduced himself as Jeffery Blake. "But most people just call me Blake," he said as Jack poured the coffee.

"What brings you way out here?" Jack asked, trying to seem jovial and at the same time restraining the urge to wrap his fingers around Blake's neck until he told him where to find Annie.

"Oh, we're on our way home," he said, sipping his coffee.

"Where's home?" Jack asked lightly as he placed the pot back on the fire.

Blake seemed to hesitate at this, and Jack noticed the smile faltered slightly. "North," he said, giving Jack the vaguest of answers. "We're camped just west of here, and last night we heard a gunshot coming from this direction. So this morning I decided to come have a look—just wanted to make sure nobody was in trouble." Blake finished, the smile never leaving his face yet never touching the cold gray eyes.

Jack didn't like that smile—it seemed forced, and there was something else—something in Blake's demeanor that told him this was all some kind of act. What did this man know about him? Had he been to the settlement, talked to Eddy, who happened to mention the man from the US living upriver? No, he didn't think so. Eddy had been genuinely worried the last time they spoke, and he would have known that this man was dangerous. Still, Jack got the feeling that Blake knew exactly who he was and what he was up to.

As if to confirm this, he said, "You out here all by yourself, mister…" and here he paused, waiting for Jack to introduce himself, the smile never leaving his lips.

"Brooks," Jack said. "Jack Brooks." He looked for any indication that Blake had heard the name before.

Blake just sipped his coffee and nodded. "Trying my hand at bear hunting," Jack said as he motioned toward the hide hanging between the two trees. "I'll be starting back to Fort Simpson in the morning."

"You always hunt grizzly in the middle of the night?" Blake asked, smiling even more broadly.

Jack looked into Blake's unsmiling eyes. "He does suspect something," Jack thought, "but he's not sure. He seems to be fishing." Jack felt like the two of them were engaged in some deadly game of chess. He took the coffee from the fire and nodded at Blake's cup.

"Only when they come into my camp," he said calmly. Then laughing lightly, he added, "I think that one was hunting me."

Blake laughed back, but it sounded more like a snort than a laugh. "You got lucky," he said. "That's a big boy! You kill him with that?" he asked, indicating the pistol on Jack's hip.

Here Jack didn't hesitate—it would be strange for a man to be out here hunting without a rifle, and they both knew it. "Nah," Jack replied, replacing the coffee once more. "Got him with my grandpa's old Weatherby—shot him right from the tent. Seems a little unfair, now that I think about it."

It was Blake's move, and Jack was beginning to think he was going to have to kill him after all. But suddenly Blake burst out laughing, as if this were the funniest thing he'd ever heard, and he seemed to relax all at once.

He asked, "You ain't from around here, are you?"

Jack understood at once: Blake had formed a mental picture of him cowering in his tent as a bear ransacked his camp until he finally got up enough nerve to fire a shot into the dark, then being surprised to find he had actually killed it. This was fine with Jack, and he laughed right along with him.

Blake's laughter tapered off, and he said more casually, "Where are you from, Jack?"

"Came up from the States last spring," Jack replied, acting only slightly offended.

"Ah," Blake exclaimed, showing real interest for the first time. "I'm from the States myself; came up about ten years ago out of Kansas."

Jack relaxed and thought, "Checkmate." He could talk about his home country all day. Blake was completely off the scent.

"Things had gotten pretty bad by the time I left; lots of plague around. Nasty stuff, that plague. It's not so bad anymore as long as you stay away from the old cities," Jack told him, which was mostly true.

"Well, I don't know about you, but I don't miss it much except for maybe the women." The fake smile rematerialized suddenly as he said, "I ain't seen a woman in nearly two years. How 'bout you, Jack?" And here Blake leaned forward, looking directly into Jack's eyes.

"Well," Jack said, calmly staring back, "there are some women in the settlement."

For a moment neither of them spoke; each man seemed to be sizing the other up. Then all at once Blake seemed to relax.

Finishing his coffee, he stood slowly. "Well, I guess I ought to be moving along. They're probably wondering where I've gotten off to," he said, gesturing back over his shoulder.

"You camped on the river?" Jack asked, casually wondering if this question would raise some alarm in his visitor's mind.

But he seemed to be totally thrown off the trail now, and he answered casually, "Yeah, we'll be meeting up with some friends from upriver. Faster traveling by boat, ya know?"

He held his free hand out, saying, "Pleasure meeting you, Jack."

Jack shook with him, replying, "Likewise, I'm sure."

Blake turned to go but then paused. "You ain't seen anyone else in your travels north, have ya?"

"No," Jack said, pretending to contemplate the question. "Not since I left the Fort," he answered truthfully. "As you said, human beings are pretty rare this far north."

Blake snorted a kind of laugh and said, "Ain't that the truth?" Then started off in the direction he had come.

Jack watched him go, the whole time restraining the urge to shoot the man in the back. He knew that this was one of Annie's captors, and he made a silent vow that if Blake had hurt her in any way, being shot in the back would be the least of his worries.

He sat where he was for another half an hour. He ate his dinner and had another cup of coffee. He wasn't sure if Blake would stick around to see his reaction to their little visit or not, but he didn't want to betray himself in any way. Blake wasn't the sort of man that you wanted to take for granted. As he sipped his coffee, he began to wonder what this man was to Annie. "Not a relation," he thought. Blake seemed more like a hired gun to Jack.

Had her family hired this man to bring her back? If so, they took an awful chance that he wouldn't harm her in the process. Jack found he had no answers to these questions, and now that he thought about it, Annie herself had told him very little about her family or her situation.

"I can't tell you, not yet," she had said. And for once, Jack wished he hadn't kept his mouth shut—after all, she had needed him; the least she could have done was to let him in on some of the dangers that they would be facing. Then again, he had been so mesmerized by her in such a short time that he had barely given any thought to anything or anyone else.

"Well," Jack thought, "not anymore. From now on we do things my way." And he began to form a plan in his head.

It was fully dark when Jack started. The clouds that had threatened snow for the past few days had suddenly dissipated, leaving the night sky cold and clear. He traveled west using the moon and stars as his guide. He had no real idea where he would find the camp, but he didn't think that Blake had lied when he said that they were camped somewhere on the river, which he figured to be roughly a mile in a westerly direction. He wasn't being particularly careful, running along at a pretty good pace because his plan depended on it still being dark when he and Annie made their escape. Wolf worried him some—before he left he had patted the animal, who didn't seem any better, and told him to stay. He knew that it wouldn't do any good. If Wolf made up his mind to follow, he would follow, but there was nothing else he could do. He had spent the rest of the day after dinner preparing their getaway. He had used the bearskin and saplings to fashion a sort of pole drag. If Wolf was still alive when they returned to camp, he would have to ride in it. It would undoubtedly slow them down, but Jack had an ace up his sleeve, and he was pretty sure that if he could get a couple hours lead on his pursuers, they would never find them.

His whole plan revolved around Annie being isolated with only one or two guards. The last thing he wanted was a full-on gunfight, not knowing how many there were, and him being low on ammunition. So, he would be as stealthy as possible. If it turned out to be too dangerous to Annie herself, he wouldn't attempt it at all, but he had an idea that these men would probably not harm her and had in fact been charged with bringing her back unhurt.

So he ran on, his breath quickening and his blood flowing fast through his veins. Living up here for the past few years had toughened him, and he felt good. He wondered if this was how it felt to be a wolf on the hunt, running with the moon. There was something primeval about being alone in the wilderness after dark—sure there were dangers, but there were also adventures, and Jack felt as if he were on the greatest adventure of his life, trying to save the woman he loved.

He had gone about a mile and a half when he smelled smoke. He stopped and leaned against a huge boulder, catching his breath and sniffing the air as Wolf often did when he was trying to get his bearings. It seemed to him that the smell came from the north. Quietly he moved in that direction, at the same time angling toward the west. After a few moments, a new sound came to his ears. It was a continuous noise like the sound of light rain, and Jack knew that it was the river.

A hundred more yards and he could see the light of the campfire through the trees. Making a circle, he came around in back of a fairly large camp. He didn't know it, but he was standing almost in the very spot that Wolf had stood only a couple of days before. Crouching behind a small bush, he was able to make out the entire camp between the branches. There were two small tents off to the left and closer to the river, and the larger tent just to his right with the woods backing it; between them was the fire with ten or twelve men lying around it in sleeping rolls. He caught a movement from the corner of his eye. From around the side of the large tent came a short, dark-haired man carrying a rifle. He had evidently been relieving his bladder, and he leaned the rifle against a tree in order to fasten his belt, then he took a cursory glance at the woods beyond and walked back to the fire.

"This must be the lone guard," Jack thought, "and Annie must be in the large tent." Taking his time, he moved silently to the back of the canvas structure and paused. He could hear no sound from within and was wondering how he could let Annie know he was there—he mustn't startle her. Just as he was about to place his hand on the tent, he heard his own name spoken in a tiny whisper.

# CHAPTER 7

Annie lay on her side, staring into the darkness. Her worst fear had become reality: Jack was here! She had come awake suddenly and once again could feel him near, just as she had in the meadow below his cabin. She had expected that Jack would try to find her, and had even thought that with Wolf's help he might be successful, but she had never thought that he would try to rescue her single-handedly—it was suicide.

Yet he was here, and there was no denying her feelings. Ever since she was a little girl, she had been able to feel things. Her father had called it "the gift," but it was more like a sixth sense. Most of the time, she didn't even notice it, but on more than one occasion, this ability had startled people and in some cases even frightened them. It wasn't something she tried to do or even worked at; it just happened. She could feel someone's presence, and if it were someone she was particularly close to, could even identify them before they showed themselves. Her father had liked to play a game with her when she was very small—sometimes he would try sneaking up on her in the kitchen by way of the back door or from the secret passage in the library, but she always knew he was there. Other times he would hide either in the house or behind a tree in the backyard, but she would always find him. Still, he never seemed to tire of the games and was always testing her ability in one way or another. When Boris and his men had come to the cabin to get her, she had felt them also and had hidden in the woods, clutching Jack's rifle in both hands. They probably would have never found her if it hadn't been for Wolf. She didn't blame him; he had simply been trying to defend her and his territory. Lying here in the darkness, listening for the slightest movement, the whole terrible scene replayed itself in her mind.

Wolf had been gone all morning, presumably out on a hunt. The gnawing fear in her stomach that would shortly turn to sheer terror made her wish that he would have waited until this evening to go off on his own. Finally, she had decided that she would walk down to the little meadow and see if she could find some late wildflowers for the table. She was planning a nice dinner for her and Jack upon his return, and she had become sure that he would be home the next day. Besides, maybe she would come across Wolf. But she had never made it to the meadow. About halfway down the hill, a feeling of dread had come over her, and suddenly she just knew: There were men in her old camp and they were coming for her. She turned and ran back to the cabin as fast as her feet would take her, only stopping long enough to grab the rifle and a box of cartridges. She had shut the door and looked around the dooryard.

"I should take down the tent," she thought, but there wasn't time. Already she could hear voices coming from the top of the ridge. So she had fled, running into the woods behind the little house and hiding herself between two rocks that might have been some small animal's den at one time. For awhile she listened to the sounds of the men as they ransacked the cabin, but she felt an overwhelming urge to see what was happening. So she had crept on her hands and knees to an overturned tree about twenty-five yards away from her would-be captors—it was a bold move and one to which Wolf owed his life. From her vantage point, she could see the men standing in the yard; most of them had their backs to her and there were two or three in the cabin. Then she saw Wolf for the first time—his gray fur stood out against the background for only a moment. No one else had noticed him. She knew by the stealthy way that he was moving that he was planning some sort of attack. Her heart sank; there was nothing she could do but watch helplessly from behind the tree. As she lost sight of the dark shape in the forest, Annie turned her attention back to the men. One of them was walking toward the tent. The man leaned over and poked his head inside, and she heard him call out something to the others. Then, in a flash, Wolf came around the side of the tent.

The poor man had no chance—the impact sent them both tumbling inside. There was a loud roar followed by a horrific scream that was cut suddenly short. The rest of the men had been taken off guard by this stealthy attack. They had begun to believe that the camp was abandoned and were facing the cabin when Wolf made his move, so they hadn't seen him. At the sound of the scream, all of them turned in the direction of the small tent. The three men inside the cabin had come out on the porch, and Annie recognized two of them immediately. The first man was Boris—he was a short bald man who always insisted on wearing a long black leather coat, even in the warmest weather. The second man she would have known from a mile away. At over six and a half feet tall, he towered over the other two. His long dark-blond hair fell loosely over his shoulders in a tangled mass that had at best only a nodding acquaintance with a comb or brush. He wore buckskins, and the shirt was stained dark in places with sweat and grime. In place of a pistol, he carried a long knife or machete in a sheath that was attached to his belt and tied with a thong around his thigh.

This was Blake, her father's hired man. Annie fancied she could almost smell him from twenty-five yards away; his presence had given her mixed feelings. On one hand his being here meant that her father had found out why she had run away, but on the other it showed that he was still in charge. Her father trusted Blake, and if he learned that Boris and his men were looking for her, he probably sent him along to protect her. But for some reason not even she could explain, she had always mistrusted Blake—he was always watching her, and in some ways she feared him more than Boris and his whole clan. She had no time to dwell on these fears, though. As she watched, the two men closest to the tent had drawn their weapons and were advancing toward it.

Annie was torn. If she fired on the men, she would betray herself, but she couldn't just let them kill Wolf like a dog in a cage. Being careful of any sudden movement, she slowly rested the barrel of the rifle on the trunk of the fallen tree and waited.

The man in front had leaned down and was using his pistol to part the tent flaps. Then, from inside the tent there issued a terrific roar. Wolf sprang—not at the man, but over him—landing on his lower back, his weight forcing him face first into the tent. The other man, who was directly behind his companion, tried to lower his weapon on the giant animal, but Wolf leaped from one man to the other easily, catching the wrist with the gun directly between his great jaws and snapping it like a twig. This unfortunate creature screamed and fell to his knees immediately, his weapon flying from his hand. The remainder of the men had by now gotten over their surprise, and at least six of them aimed their guns at Wolf, the one closest firing almost automatically—this was the bullet that had hit Wolf in the leg. Instinctively, Wolf jumped backward as two more shots came simultaneously. Annie, who had been just as surprised by Wolf's actions as the men in the dooryard, fired the .30-30 almost as a reflex when Wolf had been hit. She hadn't been aiming at anything in particular, and the bullet had struck the ground harmlessly right in front of the men, throwing up dirt and rocks. It did, however, have an effect on them, allowing Wolf a few precious seconds as he bounded off into the woods behind the tent.

None of them seemed to know from what direction the shot had come, and they scrambled, seeking refuge behind various trees and rocks. Their reaction was so comical that Annie had to suppress a nervous giggle as she leaned back against the fallen tree. Unfortunately for her, though, at least one of the men understood the situation at once and had already started slowly circling around behind her.

Meanwhile, Boris's gruff voice cut through the thin air. "Hold your fire! It's just the girl!"

Blake had whispered this fact into his ear just before starting off into the forest, and now Boris spoke directly to her. "Annie!" he shouted to the forest in general. "We are not here to hurt you. We have just come to bring you home. Please come out before someone else gets hurt!"

Annie snuck a peek over the top of the tree. He was walking out into the small yard, apparently unconcerned about what a nice target he was making of himself. Some of the other men followed his example, slowly coming from their hiding spots.

Again he spoke to the forest, since he still had no idea where she was. "Your father is worried about you and it has affected his health."

It was meant to distract her, and it worked admirably. At the mere thought of her poor old father worrying himself to death because of her, she let down her guard—then she heard a new voice, barely a whisper just over her left shoulder. "He lies."

Annie turned, but it was too late. Blake seized the rifle with one hand and her wrist with the other, saying, "Don't fight with me, little girl. I'm on your side."

Then, with absolutely no effort on his part, he picked her up with one arm and started off toward the cabin. As they came to the edge of the trees, Annie, who had resigned herself to fate—at least for the moment—said calmly, "Put me down, Blake. I'll walk from here."

He set her down lightly, warning her not to try to run off.

Annie shrugged. "Where would I run to?" she asked, as she started off in front of him.

Blake snorted a laugh and followed her.

Boris saw them coming out of the forest and smiled broadly. "Ah, there you are," he said. "I was beginning to think we had missed you after all. If it hadn't been for your pet doggy, we might have moved on." His accent was heavy, but Annie had heard him ramble on so many times that she barely noticed it anymore. "Why don't you call him in," he said. "It would be a shame if one of my men shot him by accident."

By now Annie was standing directly before him. Defiantly, she looked him straight in the eye and said, "Wolf can take care of himself, Boris. And as for your men, it doesn't appear that they have fared too well so far. If I were you I would be more worried about Wolf hunting them."

At this comment, some of the men looked around the clearing nervously. Boris laughed, "I have always admired your spark, girlie." Then to Blake he said, "Take her to the cabin and keep an eye on her. We have a little mess to clean up here, so we will wait until morning to start back."

It was then that Wolf darted between two trees behind the tent. Boris reached out and grabbed the .30-30 out of Blake's hand, lowered it in Wolf's direction, and pulled the trigger with a clumsy repetition, firing blindly into the forest. The result was that all of his men hit the ground, covering their heads with their arms. As for Wolf, he had been tracking Annie with his nose in the air, and when Boris started firing, he stood completely still. Then finally, after the barrage was over, he loped silently back into the trees untouched; this seemed to infuriate Boris, who shoved the gun into Blake's chest. Turning to Annie in sudden agitation, he said, "Maybe your new friend will show up today. I would love to meet this American."

Annie suppressed a shudder at the thought but managed to keep her voice even as she said, "I'm sure I don't know what you're talking about. Whoever it is that lives here hasn't been back, and I have been waiting here for almost a week."

Boris studied her for a moment and then, deciding that she was telling the truth, began to bark orders at his men as Blake led her silently toward the cabin.

That night she heard several gunshots. She knew Wolf was out there and trying to reach her; she also knew that he would not give up until he had found her or was killed. It wasn't that she was concerned for her own safety—she knew that these men were under strict orders to bring her back to Andre unharmed, but they wouldn't hesitate to shoot Wolf on sight. For all she knew, they might even actively hunt him down after what had happened this morning, and she had no way of warning him off. By morning she had become so concerned that she had actually confided in Blake, pleaded with him to help her find Wolf and restrain him somehow.

"I know my father sent you to look after me," she said to him when they were left alone for a moment. "You are the only one I can trust."

Blake seemed to stir a little at this statement, but they were interrupted by two men who had come in to pillage what was left in the cabin. After that, Blake made no indication that he planned to help her, and Annie was afraid that she had made a mistake in trusting him. But when Boris and his men had been busy setting fire to the cabin, Blake had casually mentioned that "the girl had to pee," and then he had done something that was strange and totally unnecessary. He took a thick rope and tied it around her waist. She had started to protest, but he had winked at her and said loud enough for Boris to hear: "Wouldn't want you getting lost," and led her off into the forest.

She called to Wolf softly as they walked along, and as they approached the fallen log, he suddenly appeared from behind it, a low growl issuing from his massive chest. Blake stopped in his tracks, his hand going automatically to the handle of the long blade. But Annie quickly diffused the situation—they didn't have much time. Blake untied her and then, to her surprise, cut the rope in half and handed her one of the severed ends. She took it and approached her longtime companion, talking softly, her blue eyes seeming almost to glow in the gloom of the forest. Wolf's long tail thumped uncertainly a few times, and then he became completely still as if he were frozen in place as she tied the rope around his shaggy neck. Not daring to take her eyes from Wolf for a moment, Annie then told Blake to secure the other end to the heavy log.

Blake stood back and said, "Done. Now let's go before someone gets suspicious."

In the end, she hadn't cried. She didn't want to show any sign of emotion in front of Blake. Also she was sure that Jack would be back this afternoon, and he could set Wolf free. So she had simply hugged his neck and whispered, "Stay, Wolf, please stay." Then Blake tied the other half of the rope around her waist, and Annie understood why he had cut it in half even as he whispered his explanation. "Sorry, girl. Boris ain't too bright, but it's best not to take too many chances."

This whole scene had replayed itself within a few moments in Annie's mind as she lay staring into the darkness. Then she heard a noise, a twig breaking or the crunching of leaves under a foot, and she knew that Jack was just outside the tent. Not daring to move a muscle, she whispered his name into the blackness.

"Shhh!" Jack said as he pulled his knife from its sheaf.

Then slowly, trying not to make any sound, he began sawing at the canvas. It took only a few moments, but to Jack it seemed like hours before he had made a big enough hole for Annie to slip through. At first she hesitated, and Jack had to reach through and take hold of her hand to get her moving. Finally she was through, and Jack led her silently back through the forest. For the first quarter of a mile or so, neither of them spoke as Jack carefully picked his way through the brush, occasionally looking back to make sure they hadn't been followed. He was practically pulling Annie along behind him, she seemed to be dragging her feet, almost as if she were hesitant to follow him. Eventually she stopped completely, and Jack turned to face her.

"We have to hurry!" he whispered as he looked down at her dark shape beside him.

"No, Jack," she said in a quiet voice.

Jack stared down at her, wishing he could see her eyes, but the forest canopy had blocked out the moon, which had aided in their escape, but now prevented him from seeing her face.

"What is it?" he whispered.

"Jack," she started, and then a sob escaped her lips, and he realized that she was fighting back tears.

He put his arms around her and kissed the top of her head. He breathed in the sweet smell of her hair and felt her tiny body tremble in his arms.

She didn't push him away but looked up at him and said, "I must go back before they find me gone. You have to leave me, Jack. You must forget about me!"

Jack stood stunned in the darkness, a million thoughts flooding his mind. As usual, he couldn't quite find the words to express them. He loved her—it was as simple as that. He would die for her if that's what it came to, but it was obvious that she had no idea how he felt. In any case, standing there in the darkness with their pursuers less than a mile behind them, he knew that this was no time for discussion or reflection on these subjects, so he did what he had always done when faced with a crisis: he acted. In one swift movement, he scooped Annie up in his arms and started off at a run toward his little camp. Annie was too startled to protest; it was the last thing she had expected. Part of her wanted to give in to this man, let him take care of her, shelter her from the big bad world. But another part of her protested; her spirit cried out against it. She hadn't escaped from one man just to be owned by another—she was not property! She looked up at Jack. He didn't seem to be exerting any effort at all as he ran along; he was as sure footed as any forest animal as he navigated the dark woods, and for the first time she wondered: "Who is Jack Brooks?" She had been so sure that she had figured him out, so sure of her own intuition, but now she wondered. After all, they had only spent a few hours together. She really knew very little about him. He was so quiet, so reserved, that she had thought him timid, yet she had never seen fear in those gray eyes, not even when Wolf was about to rip his throat out. And now he had been bold enough to come after her, alone, one man against twenty. He had run with her in his arms about another half mile when they came out of the dark woods where the moon lit up a small clearing. Jack slowed to a walk, setting Annie back on her feet, yet resumed leading her by the hand.

"We have to talk," she managed finally.

"No time," Jack replied. His pace didn't slow, but he added, "We need to check on Wolf." He hoped that this statement would urge her forward, and it worked, she was beside him in an instant, "Is Wolf hurt?"

"Almost there," he said. They quickened their pace, the moon and stars lighting the way.

Wolf was alive. It seemed that he had tried to follow Jack after all but had only succeeded in dragging himself out of the tent. That's where he lay, his great head resting on his paws, when the two people came into camp. Wolf knew who they were, and at the sound of Annie's voice, his tail thumped weakly on the ground. She went straight to him, and in that same sweet voice that she always used when she addressed the animal, she said, "Oh Wolf, what has happened to you?"

"It's his ribs," Jack said from across the camp. "I think a couple may be broken."

He was already busy. Everything had been packed and ready to go before he had left, with the exception of the tent. He was in the process of leading the horses into camp when Annie turned to look at him.

"Can you ride?" he asked.

Now it was her turn to be startled. She saw the two horses and could just make out the pole drag behind the smaller one. She understood his plan almost at once and was getting ready to shoot holes in it when he spoke again.

"Look, Annie, I don't know what kind of trouble you're in. You told me that you couldn't tell me yet and asked me to trust you. I have—now I'm asking you to trust me. I promise I'll do right by you and Wolf, but at least for now you have to put yourself in my hands."

He had been trying to position the horses so that the pole drag was as close to Wolf as possible as he made this little speech. Annie had time to wonder at the fact that both Wolf and the horses seemed entirely comfortable with each other.

"Ok, Jack" she said at last, "but I want to tell you everything. If you're going to risk your life for me, then there can be no more secrets between us."

He looked down at her. The moon was almost down and there was a bluish tint to the sky in the east. He could just make out her face in the fading starlight. It was turned up to him and her lips were slightly parted. Once again, he seemed to be made speechless by her beauty.

Finally, he said in a voice that seemed forced and not entirely steady: "We can talk while we ride. Help me get this big ole shammer onto the pole drag."

She looked back at Wolf—he had raised his head as if he had been listening to their whole conversation and she could swear he was smiling.

# CHAPTER 8

Blake lay on his back, staring silently up at the stars. From his position on the far side of the camp, he could hear the sounds of the men snoring around the fire. He knew that he could probably sneak over and kill every one of them before they even knew that they had slipped from sleep into hell. Blake was an opportunist—he had no ties and he felt no loyalty to anyone but himself. His employer, Annie's father, had sent him on this circle jerk, trusting him to bring back his headstrong daughter unhurt. He could do this, but it wasn't his first choice. If Andre hadn't double-crossed him, she would already be his, and none of them would be out here. Since the moment he had first set eyes on her, Annie had become his one and only obsession. She had been only seventeen at the time, and that blasted animal was just a pup. But he remembered how it had growled in its little throat and bared its teeth at him when he had tried to pet it. For her part, Annie barely seemed to notice him at all when her father had introduced them. To her, he was just another of her father's hired men. She had shaken his hand lightly and then walked off in the direction of the house, the little wolf pup right at her heel. After that he had taken every opportunity to talk with her, at first just hoping to become her friend, but for some reason that he couldn't understand, she had mistrusted him from the start. He couldn't seem to overcome it, no matter how nice he was to her. It had puzzled him at first, then angered him. Who was she, this little slip of a girl, to judge him? She didn't even know him—not that she would have felt any different if she had. No, she probably would have added fear on top of mere contempt if she had known anything about his past. But the fact that Annie seemed to show no interest in him whatsoever hadn't in any way affected his own feelings toward her. If anything, it seemed to have had the opposite effect. Sometimes at the end of the day when the other men had retired to the clubhouse to play cards or just shoot the shit, he would sit on the porch of the big house, hoping to catch a glimpse of her when she came in. It had never occurred to him that by doing this it had made her even more apt to avoid him.

Whatever Annie's feelings were toward him, her father didn't seem to share them. Almost from the start, the old man had taken him into his confidence, making him his right-hand man, so to speak, even inviting him to supper on occasion. Yet even on these rare occasions, sitting at the same table with her, she would have very little to say. For a while he had been content to wait and watch; he told himself that someday she would need something from him, and he would be there, good ole "Blake, and he would do whatever he had to do to win her over. For five years he watched her grow from a girl into womanhood as his obsession seemed to grow with her—then the strangers had come into the valley.

Blake thought he detected movement in the direction of the girl's tent. It might have been nothing but a slight breeze...or she could be escaping. He had no doubt that at some point, Mr. Jack Brooks would attempt to take her away. In fact, he was counting on it—only he knew the identity of the stranger that had taken Annie in, and such a man might be more use to him alive than dead, at least at present. The frame on the picture in the cabin of the older woman had been his first clue; the name engraved on it had rung back to his early childhood. He had cleverly hidden this picture before anyone could see it. Even then he had an idea about whom it belonged to, and he liked to keep his cards close to his chest.

He had heard many stories about the Brooks gang when he was a boy. At that time, they were considered heroes out east, but this man was too young to be one of them. Although the name could just be a coincidence, Blake didn't think so. Jack Brooks, the elder, had been hunted mercilessly by what was left of the government and hanged in Illinois nearly twenty years ago. When the stranger had boldly given his real name, Blake was almost positive that this was his son. This name had become synonymous with the word outlaw, and no woman in her right mind would have wanted her son tied to that legacy in any way—unless...he had been named for his father. There were news stories and even romances written about the gang. Blake as a young boy had been intensely interested in the group, so he had seen pictures and drawings of all of them. He thought he had noticed a resemblance when he was in Jack's camp this afternoon, but then he had been looking for one, and maybe his mind had just created it. What really convinced him that this was the son of the famous outlaw was the holster with the big Colt inside it. One of the treasures that Blake had as a kid was a Wanted poster of Jack and Phil Brooks. He wasn't sure where the picture had been taken, but it was obvious that they had posed for it. In the photo they were standing close, almost facing each other. Phil was holding a rifle in his left hand, pointed toward the sky. Jack had his arms folded across his chest, but the gun on his hip was clearly visible. Stenciled in black on the holster were the initials JB in stark relief.

This was the same holster he had seen today—a little worn and faded, but the same one, he was sure of it. Still, even if he was who Blake thought he was, it didn't necessarily mean that Jack was anything like his father—but the more he thought about the situation, the more convinced he became that this Jack Brooks, the one in the camp to the east of him, was just as formidable, if not more so, than the man that had led the rebellion down in the States. For one thing, he had to know at least something of the number of their party from the evidence left at the cabin, yet he came after them alone—that either meant he was crazy as a loon or awful sure of his own ability. Secondly, the man he had spoken to just a few hours ago had nerves of steel. Blake had walked into his camp carrying Jack's own rifle out in front of him, yet he hadn't flinched, hadn't even seemed to notice. Blake found himself admiring the man in spite of the fact that he knew that eventually, he would have to kill him.

His mind wandered back to a rainy afternoon when his father had decided to set him straight on the subject of the Brooks brothers once and for all. With a swift backhand to the side of the face, he had torn a news story that Blake had been struggling to read from his hands and stood drunk and furious, shaking it in his face.

"They ain't nothin' but hoods and thugs," he yelled, tearing the paper into little pieces. "Hired guns taking what they want from innocent folks that's just struggling to get by. But if they come by here, they won't find it so easy."

At ten years old, Blake hadn't yet been completely educated in the ways of the world, but he was a genius compared to his daddy. He was pretty sure that if the Brooks gang showed up at their house, his father would hide like a little girl. He secretly wished they would; then, with his father gone, he would join them and become an outlaw himself. Such were the dreams of a ten-year-old Jeffery Blake.

In the long run, he found that he couldn't wait for the Brooks gang or anyone else to put an end to his father's relentless abuse, so at fourteen he had taken the situation into his own hands. It had been easy as pie—he had just waited for his father to pass out on the old chair on the porch. Then, as casually as you please, he had walked out to the barn where he found his father's weed whacker, which was nothing more or less than a long knife. Even at the tender age of fourteen, he had been strong, so it had taken him only one blow to nearly separate his father's head from the rest of his body. The man never knew what had hit him. As for Blake, he hadn't bothered to bury his father; didn't even move him from the porch. He simply made himself something to eat and went up to bed. That night he slept better than he had since his mother left.

The next morning he had set off with the vague intention of finding his mom. However, it hadn't been so easy—he had spent years wandering from town to town, begging at first and then taking what he needed by force. He had never gained the fame of the Brooks gang even though he had killed his fair share of men. Still, by the time he was twenty-three, he found that some people had taken notice of his mischief and actually posted a reward for his arrest, so he had headed west with no real plan other than getting out from under the long arm of the law.

Whether it was fate or just pure luck, he finally found the woman who had abandoned him at such a young age. He had been wandering through the desert for nearly a week and was nearly starved when he came upon an old fallen-down building outside of what had been Las Vegas, Nevada. The place had been some sort of a brothel at one time, but now it seemed to have become a shelter for the aged and insane. The only reason he had stopped there in the first place was the promise of water and food. Upon entering the fallen-down structure, he found little to entice him to stay; still, he had wandered from room to room, hoping to find anything that might help him out of what was turning into a dire situation. He had already been contemplating the benefits of going north; he had heard that anyone could find work in the colonies. His immediate problem was to find enough sustenance to get out of this accursed desert. He hadn't had water in over twenty-four hours, and his last bite of food had been considerably longer than that. So he had searched the whole place, finally finding an old well and a tame goat that the inhabitants had kept right in the front room for the milk. He promptly killed said goat and shared some of the meat with a young boy, even trying to make friends with him over the fire, but he was as feral as a cat and had run away after he received his share of the meal. Blake had wrapped some of the meat in an old tablecloth and filled his water bag, meaning to move on right away, but something drew him back to the old building, and he decided to have one last look inside. In a small room at the end of a long hallway full of doors, he had found her—his dear old mother.

She hadn't even known him. In fact, she thought him to be some angel of mercy sent to end her suffering, and Blake thought it could be she guessed right. But before he could send her home to Jesus, he needed to know certain things. She had the plague, of course, and was in the last stages. He had nursed her for two days, making her as comfortable as he could under the circumstances. The plague, or the walking death as most people called it, was a peculiar thing. He had seen it in varying stages in most of the places he had wandered to after leaving his home in Kansas. From what he had gathered on the subject, he knew that it couldn't be passed from one person to another—you were simply born with it. Some people could live their whole lives and never get sick; some babies were born sick and didn't make it out of the cradle. The one common thing was that once you got sick, you never got better. The different stages could last anywhere from one day to almost a week, and he had heard of some cases where people had lived two months before dying of what looked like utter exhaustion—this was the stage he had found his mother in.

Blake's mind snapped back from its mental wanderings in a flash—this time he was sure he heard something; the breaking of a twig or the rolling of a small stone, maybe. He laid perfectly still and listened, but no other sound reached him. Well, it didn't matter; he was quite sure that their little bird had flown the coop, probably in the company of one Mr. Jack Brooks. That was just fine and dandy because he had a plan. Slowly, his mind turned back to his mother dying in that old broken-down building. At the time he had felt no emotion whatsoever about her; he had just wanted to know why she had left him in the clutches of a madman. Looking back now, he felt cheated somehow. Though she hadn't known him, he had finally gotten a short explanation of her actions.

"Oh mister," she had cried, "how could I take him with me? I wasn't even sure I could take care of myself, and to stay meant certain death at the hands of that madman."

She was right. In this hard old world, self-preservation trumped everything—no one knew this better than Blake himself. The only way he had survived his father and subsequent wanderings through this long-dead country was by always putting himself first with no regard for anything or anyone else. "Hmm," he thought finally, "maybe she did pass something on to me after all."

Out of the east, the sky began to turn a faint blue. The sun was coming up, and he felt himself becoming drowsy. His mind turned back to Annie. How much did she know about Jack, and how would she react if she knew that she had entrusted herself to a man who had probably killed more men than he had? Maybe her friend Blake would have to enlighten her. He found he was too tired to think any more on the subject. One thing was sure in his mind: he would have her. Above all else, this one thought had consumed him for the last six years, and the time had finally come for him to make his play. Smiling to himself, he rolled over on his side. His last thought before sleep took him was: "Don't worry, little bird. Blake will save you from the bad men."

What seemed to be only a minute later, he was being shaken awake by a young boy with a look of sheer panic in his eyes.

"The girl," he said, almost yelling in Blake's face. "She escaped!"

The boy ran off, presumably to yell in someone else's face, and Blake grabbed for his boots. He took his time getting dressed, noticing that it was just after dawn;

he had only been asleep for about an hour. Out of the corner of his eye, he caught a glimpse of Boris walking in his direction and thought, "Oh great; it's too early for this garbage."

The old man was in a huff, and Blake wondered how much abuse his heart would take before it just exploded in his chest. The thought brought a smile to his face, and as usual Boris misinterpreted it.

"You knew about this!" he accused, pointing his stubby little finger at Blake's chest.

"No," Blake said slowly. He was running over his half-formed plan in his head, but he would have to be careful with this man. It would have to look like his idea.

"I don't trust you!" Boris shouted. "I never have! You probably even helped her!"

Blake took one step in Boris's direction, and he was so high strung that he literally jumped backward.

"Calm yourself," he said, turning his attention back to his belt and making sure the knife sheath was fastened securely. "I wasn't in charge of guarding her; besides, she couldn't have gone far."

Then, before Boris could reply to this, he added, "How'd she get loose?"

Blake watched as the fat little man paced back and forth, occasionally rubbing his bald head as he explained that somehow she had gotten hold of something sharp and cut a hole in the back of the tent—apparently the idea that someone else might have had a hand in her escape hadn't even crossed his mind.

"We'll get her back," Blake said. "She's alone and on foot."

This seemed to calm Boris down a little, and he asked, "Do you think she'll go back to the cabin?"

"I'm sure of it." Blake replied, though he was fairly sure this wasn't the case. "There is a small chance that she headed for home, though," he continued, acting as if this thought had just crossed his mind. "Maybe you should send a few men north just in case."

Boris thought this over for a moment, the vein in the side of his neck pulsing at an alarming rate.

Finally Blake could stand it no longer, and in his most congenial voice, he said, "I'll tell you what: Give me a couple of men, and we'll trek north for a few miles. You take the rest and start back the way we came. If I don't find any trace of her by tonight, then we will know she went back to the cabin, and I will meet up with you there by tomorrow evening."

Boris scratched the side of his face. "Maybe I should send Jeane north, and you could come with us."

Blake thought fast—he was almost sure that Jack wouldn't be stupid enough to head back to the cabin and meant to send Boris with most of his men on a wild goose chase; it was the only way his plan could work. Casually he bent down and started rolling up his sleeping bag.

"You're the boss," he said. "But," and here he looked out at the forest behind Annie's tent, "if it was me, I'd want my best tracker along. It could be the girl doesn't know her way and is lost."

# CHAPTER 9

J ack sat with his back against a large boulder, watching Annie as she went about the business of their evening meal. He had offered to do it, but she had insisted, saying, "Whatever your particular talents are, cooking isn't one of them."

"I didn't hear any complaints back in the cabin," he replied, a slight smile coming to his face.

To this she had shrugged and said, "On that particular day, I could have eaten one of Wolf's offerings and not complained." Then she had picked up her little bag and started off into the forest.

"Where are you off to now?" Jack had asked with a tinge of panic in his voice that he didn't like at all.

"Just as far as I need to pick up a few things for dinner. Check on Wolf for me."

Wolf, in fact, was doing a lot better and had even ventured from the tent a few times to sit by the fire. Annie, it seemed, knew a great deal about wild plants and their uses both as food and medicines. Jack had seen this firsthand last night when they had stopped to camp. He was uneasy about making a fire, although he was fairly certain they weren't being tracked, as he had gone to great pains to make it appear that they were headed south. But Annie had persuaded him, saying she needed to heat some water so that she could treat Wolf's wound. So he collected the wood while she sat down beside the animal, digging through her little bag and produced some sort of root. After the fire was going, Jack took the frying pan and went down to a little spring to fill it with water. By the time he returned, he noticed that she had cut about half of the root into little pieces and was using a small stone to grind them into powder, which she then added to the water. When it began to boil, she asked him if he had an old shirt or some kind of cloth that he would be willing to part with. He provided easily enough. She cut it into strips. After soaking them in the water for about twenty minutes, she sat down next to Wolf and talked to him in a low soothing voice, managing to wrap them tight around his middle, tying the ends with a piece of thong from her moccasin. Closing her eyes, she then placed both hands over the bandage and seemed to pray or meditate for a moment. It struck Jack as strange, but he didn't interrupt her.

"Is it some kind of poultice?" Jack had asked when she was done.

"Not exactly. The root has strong medicine in it; it helps with swelling and pain, but mostly it helps to make you feel relaxed—at least that's the effect it has on people," she added, looking down at Wolf. "I'm not sure about animals."

"Are you some sort of medicine woman?" he had asked as she put the rest of the root and the small stone back into her bag. She laughed lightly and stood up, brushing the dirt from her dress. "No, but I've picked up a few things over the years from the native people back home, and of course my father, who knows almost everything."

Jack raised his eyebrows. "Everything?" he asked. It was an attempt to draw her out.

"Sometimes it would seem so," she replied as she walked past him toward the fire. "He has even found a cure for the plague." Jack looked at her, startled, but her back was to him, so he only shrugged, inwardly thinking he would find out soon enough about these things; this was just another piece in the puzzle that was Annie.

She had promised to tell him everything, but every time she seemed about to open up, she would get that sad look in her eyes and then turn the subject back to him. Not that he had told her much, either. It almost seemed as if they were both waiting for the other to make the first move. Back at his little cabin, they had really had no time to get to know each other. As a matter of fact, since meeting her it seemed that they had been doing nothing but running for their lives, and now that they were relatively safe, she was afraid to let him get too close. He tried to put himself in her place. He wondered how she would look at him if she knew about his past. Would she fear him—or worse yet, would she write him off as just another bad man in a world full of bad men? He wasn't sure he could take that chance, so he had been elusive when she had inquired about his past, giving her only a glimpse of his real world.

Now that he thought about it, he was being completely unfair to her because when it came right down to it, she had no idea of what she was getting herself into by following him back to a place where, more often than not, it was kill or be killed. It was obvious to him that her father had sheltered his little girl from the cold, hard world that existed outside their little community, and now, in his own way, he was doing the same. But he was also sheltering her from himself and his own past, which seemed even worse because of the blind faith she seemed to have placed in him. As he watched her now, spreading a blanket on the ground for them to eat on, he resolved to tell her the truth—at least some of it—tonight. Then she could make up her own mind about him once and for all. As for himself, well, he was sure of one thing: He would follow her to the end of the earth. There could be nothing in her past or present that could make him feel otherwise.

They sat side by side on the blanket, staring out at the fading sun. There seemed to be more of a chill in the air than on previous evenings, and Jack asked casually if she wanted the blanket to wrap around her.

"I'm ok," she said without turning her head.

They had said little to each other through dinner, which was one of the finest he'd had in years, and he told her so. This compliment had only brought a ghost of a smile to her face; his own mind was preoccupied with the things that he wished to tell her and how best to start.

Finally, steeling his nerve, he turned to her, but the words that had to come to his lips were cut off by what he saw.

She sat facing the setting sun, its last rays seeming to fall directly on her while a single tear glistened on her pale cheek. Her raven hair fell loosely over her shoulders, and her face was turned up toward the sky in an almost defiant look. Another tear fell, and Jack felt as if his heart would leap from his throat. He wanted to comfort her; he wanted to tell her he loved her, that everything would be all right. Somehow he knew that these words would just make things worse and that he himself was to blame for at least some of those tears.

On impulse, he reached out and took her hand. She seemed to flinch a little at his touch, but she let him do it, and after a moment he felt her fingers wrap around his own.

Then without turning to look at him, in a voice that seemed to come from far away, she said, "I'm married, Jack."

To his credit, Jack didn't flinch. In fact, he felt as if he had been turned to stone.

She then turned to look at him, and in the same small voice that seemed to crack with emotion, she asked: "Do you hate me?"

This seemed to break the spell, and he said the first thing that came to his mind: "I could never hate you, Annie."

Then he leaned over and kissed her lightly on the forehead. At this, the dam broke. Her tears came in great heaving sobs and she buried her face in his chest. He held her, stroking her hair, but could find no more words of comfort. He was too bewildered himself.

"Married," he thought. The thing seemed impossible!

The Annie that he had begun to know and love seemed exempt from such worldly ties. It was true that he himself had loved her from almost the moment he first saw her—this was not strange because it seemed to him that he had always loved her, or at least her spirit. Jack had never been a religious man. It had always seemed to him that God was all around him, in the babble of a small stream or the rustle of the leaves as a summer breeze passed through them. Annie seemed in some strange way to be the physical manifestation of these things—a daughter of nature for men to admire, yet was somehow unattainable. In his heart he hadn't really expected that she could return his love, at least not in the same way. Deep down he knew that there were men who would look at her differently; they would seek to possess her, to have power over her like a prize— not fought for, but stolen. He consoled himself with the thought that marriage, at least in the legal sense, was really a thing of the past, although this just served to make him even more uneasy.

After a while—Jack wasn't sure how long—her tears began to dry up. It was fully dark now, and he left her for a moment to stoke the fire. Annie wrapped herself in the bear skin and faced it.

Slowly at first and then with more urgency, she began to tell Jack her story. "When I told you before that I was born here," she began, "I meant that I was literally born in the forest. You see, my mother was a great lover of all things in nature—at least that is what my father told me. She was also a very good artist who loved to paint pictures, some of which still hang in the great room back home. She would often take trips into the woods and valleys that surround the country where we live. Most times my father would go with her, but occasionally he wouldn't be able to go, and she would take one of the native women that knew the country. The night I was born, this was the case. My father and some of his men had gone off on a hunting expedition to the north. Neither of them expected that I would make my appearance for at least another month, and he was only to be gone about three days. My mother became restless after the first day of his absence and asked a native girl, Adsila by name, to accompany her on a day trip, just a few miles upriver, where she hoped to capture some of the fall colors and be back before dinner time. They took the horse and wagon, and according to Adsila, it wasn't until late afternoon that my mother found a place to stop and set up her easel. Without even realizing it, they had gone almost three miles from home. She felt the first pains of labor just as they were packing up the wagon, so they rode as fast as they could back toward the house. After they had gone about a mile, my mother realized that I wasn't going to wait for a soft bed to be born in, so she had the girl stop the wagon. Still, she wasn't worried.

"'I am strong, and after all,' she said, 'women have been doing this since the beginning of time.'

"So they spread an old blanket on top of the pine needles under a huge tree near the river and prepared themselves the best that they could. But something went wrong that night—nobody, even to this day, is sure what. All the young Adsila could say was that there was too much blood. Anyway, at some point my mother told her to unhook the wagon and ride for help. Even riding as fast as she could and nearly killing the poor horse in the process, it had taken her almost an hour to get back and at least another on the return trip. My mother died shortly after I came into the world, but they found me safe and sound, wrapped in her coat.

"My father was devastated. I don't think he has ever gotten over it. He says I am the spitting image of her, except for the blue in my eyes, which are so much like his. Growing up he was my whole world, and I was his. He has been my teacher as well as my father. I have only told you all this so that you might understand—I love him more than anything and would do anything to protect him."

Here she sighed and looked into the fire. "That is how it is that I am married, Jack." He stared across the fire at her. She looked so tired. "So your father forced you to get married?" he asked.

"Oh no! He would never force me to do anything against my will. He only wants me to be happy. As a matter of fact, I don't even think he knows about it... yet. It happened this way: my father and I, with my brother Kitchi, had been making frequent visits to Andre's camp. Some of his people were very sick and most were suffering from malnutrition. So we were nursing them the best we could, but on the third day my father had to return to our house for more supplies, leaving me and my brother to care for those poor people. To make a long story short, that's when Andre asked me to marry him. When I repeatedly turned him down, he went and got a preacher and even had a marriage license made up for me to sign. That poor preacher," she said, and now the tears came.

She continued: "He had been one of the men that we had brought back from the brink of death. He had been so grateful to me especially, because I had been the one to nurse him. He stood up to Andre, saying that he would not perform the ceremony against my will. Well," she went on, wiping away the tears. "Without a word, Andre just pulled out a pistol and shot him right in front of everyone. Then he pulled in another preacher, a man named Chance, and he said in my ear, 'Now girlie, I have plenty of preacher's but very little patience, so you might want to reconsider your option's.' Oh Jack," she said with a sob. "What else could I have done? I consented to the marriage on the condition that me and my brother be allowed to return home so that I could break the news as gently as possible to my father. Of course, Andre knew as well as I did that if I told my father that he had forced me into it, he would be furious and confront him about it, and I had seen firsthand what happens to people who confront Andre." Jack thought grimly to himself that he wouldn't mind giving it a shot.

Annie sighed and then continued: "Right after the ceremony, he told the whole camp that within a few short days they would all be moving to a better place where they would never be hungry. Then turning to me he whispered, 'Ok little wifey, run on home and tell daddy we are coming.' I was so afraid and ashamed that I didn't even bother going home. I just ran, and my brother came with me. At the time, I thought it was the only thing I could do to save the people I love, and now I feel like I have abandoned them." Then she turned to him, and Jack fancied that her eyes seemed to glow in the firelight.

"Oh Jack," she said, "I've been so selfish! I know now that I must go back, but I'm afraid."

Jack gently took her hand and said, "You needn't be afraid, Annie. Tomorrow morning we will start for your home together, and I promise you I will never let anybody hurt you again."

She tried to smile, but Jack saw that it was forced, and she said, " it's not me I'm worried about."

She buried her face in her hands, and after a moment's contemplation, Jack stood, scooped her up in his arms, and carried her to the tent. She looked up at him questioningly, and he said, "Sleep now, Annie. You're exhausted. There will be time tomorrow if you wish to tell me more; then we can decide what to do next."

He laid her down beside Wolf and turned to go, but she caught his arm. "Thank you, Jack, for not pressing me but mostly for having faith in me."

He winked at her and said, "I'm not going anywhere, Annie; wherever you go, I will follow.

Jack woke shivering under the light blanket just before dawn. A few light flakes of snow fell from the starless sky. He went to build up the fire when he was nearly startled out of his wits by Wolf as he appeared out of the trees. He was glad to see the animal up and about. As the fire started to blaze up, Wolf came over and nuzzled his hand.

Jack patted his head lightly and asked, "Feeling better?"

In answer, Wolf plopped himself down and began to gnaw at the bandage that Annie had wrapped around his ribs. Jack sat down beside him and stared into the fire. "What are we to do with her, boy?" he asked, looking to his companion for an answer. But Wolf simply yawned and laid his head in his paws. The action struck Jack as funny, as if the animal were saying, "Whatcha gonna do?"

Jack suppressed a laugh, not wanting to wake Annie, who was only a few feet away in the tent. He thought of her story from the night before and her marriage to a man she obviously hated. To Jack, this was nothing—it was obvious that she had felt trapped and that only by wedding this man could she save her father. The question that was foremost in his mind was how to best annul this union in the swiftest way possible. Personally, he couldn't wait to meet Annie's husband, and he supposed the only way to do this was to go home with her. His mind wandered back to his meeting with Blake, and he wondered if he knew the man that had blackmailed her. He didn't think so, although he felt that Blake was capable of such treachery. Still, he felt that Blake was more of a loner, like himself. No, Blake's interest in Annie was strictly personal. This other man, the man she had married, must have other motives, and Jack would have given all his remaining gold to know what they were.

The first rays of the sun lit up the horizon. Jack and Wolf watched the sunrise together, like old friends, and it was one of the best sunrises he had ever seen. The clouds were close, but in the east, the sun seemed to slice through them, creating streams of sunlight, one of which fell directly on the little canvas tent. Wolf whined, and Jack stoked his fur, saying, "I know, buddy. I love her too."

An hour later Jack heard movement from the tent, and he hurried to finish the breakfast that he had hastily thrown together.

He kneeled down before the tent and said, "Knock, knock." Pushing the flap aside, he found her sitting up and rubbing the sleep from her eyes.

"I know you said that cooking wasn't my strong point, but Wolf helped."

He handed her the skillet that contained rabbit meat and a biscuit one of the last in his pack.

She looked at the sparse meal and giggled. "Did you cook it or did Wolf?"

"Well, I thought it only fair that since he went hunting, I should do the cooking."

She smiled up at him as he sat the skillet down beside her. She picked lightly at the meat, and Jack told her Wolf seemed almost completely better.

This brought another smile to her lips, and she said, "I haven't lost a patient yet."

He was silent for a moment, thinking how best to proceed. Finally he said, "I think he's ready to go home."

She only hesitated a moment before smiling up at him and saying, "Me too, Jack. I miss my father, and I want him to meet you."

It didn't take them long to break camp. They seemed to be getting into a sort of routine. By midmorning they had already gone about five miles. The snow came and went, and at one point it came in huge flakes. Jack began to worry that they were in for it. By noon, though, it had stopped completely. They were making a course north and west, trying to reach the river before nightfall, when they came to a small clearing with a brook running almost directly in the center. Neither one of them had felt uneasy, but Wolf sniffed the air and suddenly vanished among the scrub.

"Let's stop a moment and see if he comes back," Annie had said, and Jack was more than happy to oblige.

He hadn't spent this much time in the saddle since he came up here, and he was starting to chafe a little in uncomfortable places. They let the horses graze and drink their fill from the brook while they sat in the grass. She began to tell him about her home.

"Oh Jack," she exclaimed, "you will love it! There are meadows and deep woods with deep secrets. The native people call it God's country. There is game everywhere."

Jack listened and was glad that she seemed to have thrown off the sadness of the night before.

When she paused for a moment, he asked her to tell him more about the man she called her husband and was almost immediately sorry. The smile disappeared from her lips and she looked down at her hands.

"I'm sorry," he started, but she interrupted him.

"It's ok, Jack. I feel better today. Andre came into the valley about six months ago. He was leading a big group of people that were starving and sick. He had come to the house one evening with a few of his men, asking if there were any doctors that knew about the plague and if they could have leave to hunt in the area. My father is a generous man and had offered immediately to go with him back to his camp."

Here she paused, and then, turning slowly to him, she said, "Oh Jack, it was awful!"

"He took you with him that first day?" he asked, raising his eyebrows in surprise.

She shrugged. "He always takes me with him when someone is sick. He says that I have a gift for making people feel better just by being there; besides, I wanted to go. I hate to see anything suffer, and he didn't seem dangerous at the time. Andre can be charming and even humble when he needs to be; my father has even had him over for dinner a few times. Anyway, like I said, it was awful! There were about a hundred of them—men, women, and children—and they were all suffering more or less from malnutrition. Some of them had the plague, but not many. Some of the children were so thin that a strong wind would have blown them away. They all had a defeated look in their eyes, as if they would be content to just die right where they sat. We stayed a week, and my father had food and medicine brought over from the house. It took a lot of work, and I was so tired by the time we started for home that my father made me ride with him on his horse."

Jack looked at her, thinking that she seemed to get tired just talking about it. "How many were you able to save?" he asked finally, looking down at his own hands.

She turned to him, smiling. "All of them," she said and then added, "I told you, Jack, I haven't lost a patent yet."

Both of them were quiet for a moment as Jack took this in. Annie picked up a blade of grass and started twisting it nervously between her fingers. Then she said, "Well, we managed to save all of them, but there were about ten that had the plague. My father, who will go anywhere and do just about anything to help someone, for some reason of his own has strict rules about treating that particular ailment. When someone is diagnosed with it, he makes them come to the house and sit in the middle of the front room. The sick person is not allowed to actually touch the medicine, which is in the form of a small pill. The pill is then placed on their tongue. As I said, they are not allowed to touch it. Then they must swallow it dry with no water or anything to wash it down. He says it's because if anything touches the pill, it could make it less potent."

"But what about him? Doesn't he have to touch it to give it to the patient?" Jack asked, perplexed by the whole ceremony.

"Oh no, he never touches it either. I am the only one allowed to touch them."

Now he was more confused than ever—it seemed whenever Annie answered one question, a thousand more would pop into his head.

He was about to ask what difference it made if she touched the pill or her father, when suddenly Annie exclaimed: "Wolf, where have you been?!"

The animal appeared out of the trees at the edge of the meadow, and she sprang up and went to him, kneeling beside him. Jack was about to get up also, but he found himself temporarily frozen to the spot by what he saw—it was like a painting come to life. She knelt with her arm over the animal's shoulders, their heads virtually on the same level. Wolf stood completely still, and they both seemed to be staring into the woods behind him. Annie's long black hair fell loosely over her denim jacket. Her body was tense, as if she had been suddenly turned to stone. Her blue eyes had a far-off, vacant look. The eagle feather in her hair moved slightly in the breeze, and directly behind her, to the right and left, two aspens made a nice frame for the picture.

Then he saw her whisper something in Wolf's ear, causing him to turn quickly and fade back into the trees. At the same time, the hair stood upon Jack's arms, as if the very air had become electrified. Annie rose and slowly started toward him. Something was wrong—it was as if she were in some kind of trance, and as she approached him, he stood up.

"Everything ok?" he asked as she stopped right in front of him. But even being so close, she appeared not to have heard him. Jack looked down into her eyes, which were wide and almost unnaturally blue. He realized that she wasn't seeing him.

Three things happened almost simultaneously. First, Annie closed her eyes, and with a strength that he never would have attributed to her, she shoved him. Second, a sharp pain shot through his brain as if somebody had run a knife through his temple; and third, he heard the loud report of a rifle.

Jack had the reflexes of a cat, and as he hit the ground, he rolled, pulling the pistol at the same time. But Annie was there, and she almost screamed in his face: "*Run!*" He grabbed her hand and they sprinted for the trees. The horses were gone; Wolf was gone. It was only him and Annie left in the world and his head was on fire As they reached the forest, Annie tripped over a large root, and as she fell, Jack realized dimly that this was his dream come to life. He knelt to pick her up, but he was dizzy, and his strength was gone. He looked into those deep-blue eyes, knowing exactly what she would say, yet hanging on every word.

"What is it, Jack? What do you see?!" Then he looked down at the blood on her dress, and he knew it wasn't her that had been hurt…it was him.

Annie looked into Jack's face. It was covered in blood, and he seemed to be staring, not at her but through her.

Her voice seemed to come from far away as she asked, "What is it, Jack? What do you see?"

And then he had collapsed on top of her. She screamed his name, and then Wolf was there, standing over them. Slowly she put her hand against Jack's neck, and there she found the pulse of life. She managed to squirm out from under him and frantically she looked around. Her eyes rested on the pistol that Jack had holstered in their flight, and she knelt down and extracted it from his side. It took both of her thumbs to pull the hammer back on the huge pistol, but she did it. She held it out in front of her, straddling Jack's body with Wolf standing in front of her. From deep in the forest, a voice came, and Annie fired almost on reflex, drowning out the words and making Wolf jump. The huge gun recoiled, and she fell backward over Jack's body.

Then the voice came again. "Tie up the dog, or I will kill him!"

Annie looked down at Jack. He was alive; she could tell that, but his breathing was shallow, and she needed to attend to him right away. She had recognized the high-pitched voice, and suddenly a calm came over her.

"Jeane, is that you?" she said as she knelt down, putting her arm around Wolf's neck.

"Yes, it is me. I won't hurt you if you tie up the dog."

"I have nothing to tie him with, but I will send him away."

There was a pause, and then Jeane's voice came again, a little closer now. "Ok, Annie, but the first time I see him, I will shoot him."

Annie leaned down and whispered in Wolf's ear the one command that he had always obeyed. "Wolf, hide!"

For a second he seemed on the verge of disobeying her, but then he took off in a dead run into the northwest.

She shouted, "He's gone; he won't be back. Please don't hurt us."

She had held onto the gun as she struggled to her knees and trained it on the forest in front of her, but she had no feeling that he was there.

Then from directly behind her, she heard, "Drop the gun, Annie."

It was Jeane all right, Boris's best tracker and best shot. She knew that she was caught.

"Please don't hurt him, Jeane," she pleaded again, letting the gun fall from her hand. Then she felt the man's hands in her hair, and he was dragging her kicking and screaming away from Jack's lifeless body.

Jack's mind was reeling. The pain was exquisite! With a great effort he was able to hold onto the last thread of consciousness. He heard Annie scream as he managed to open one eye. He saw a man with long dark hair standing over him with a rifle pointed to his head.

He heard Annie scream again, "No, Jeane, you promised!"

He saw that the man had pinned her left arm down with his foot and that she was beating at his leg with her right as she struggled to pull free. Jack's anger flared, momentarily bringing him back to full consciousness. He wasn't angry about this man shooting him, but that he was hurting Annie. Summoning all his remaining strength, he managed to raise up on one elbow, meaning to kick the man's legs out from under him if he could.

Then the strangest thing happened: A huge knife blade seemed to grow right out of the young man's chest. He dropped the rifle and stared down at the blade as it slowly retreated back into his body. Jack saw him fall to his knees, already dead. Blackness overtook him again, and the last sound he heard was Annie, screaming his name.

She was still screaming as she pushed past Blake and rolled Jack over on his back. There was blood everywhere. She turned to Blake, who was wiping the long blade of the knife on the shirt of the dead man.

"Get me some water," she said, looking directly into his eyes.

"Annie," he started, but she cut him off.

"Now, Blake!" she screamed and turned back to Jack.

Blake pulled the canteen from around his neck and handed it to her. It was only about half full. She turned to him again, "Find the horses and bring some more water—this won't be enough."

"Annie, he's dead," he said finally.

"No!" she screamed. Then in a calmer voice, she said, "No, he's not—not yet anyway. Please Blake, do what I say."

Blake grunted and started off in the direction that he had last seen the horses. She took off her denim jacket and placed it under Jack's head. Then, taking his Buck knife from its sheaf, she cut off a large strip from his shirt and began to wash the blood from his face. As she worked, she talked to him. "Please, Jack, don't leave me now. Stay with me. I need you, Jack!"

# CHAPTER 10

J ack heard nothing. He seemed to be floating on some peaceful stream. All around him was darkness. He tried to move, but it was as if his body had abandoned him and only his consciousness was left. He tried to yell out for Annie, but he had no mouth to yell with. Then he noticed a pinpoint of light that seemed to grow slowly. The light seemed to take shape, and he thought: "It's her." Still, he could do nothing. The light grew brighter and a figure was definitely forming. Jack recognized it at last. But it was not Annie—it was Mary. The light that surrounded her was much too bright, and if he'd had his eyes open, he would have had to close them.

There was pain that seemed to come directly from the center of his brain, and through it he heard his dead sister's voice. She spoke softly: "Go back to her, Jack. She's gonna need you." Then she was gone, along with the terrible light.

Once again, everything went black. After that, he seemed to float in and out of his own little hell. There were times when all he heard was his sister repeating the old rhyme over and over.

"When she smiles, the sun shines.

"When she cries, it rains.

"When she sleeps, the snow flies.

"When she wakes, it's spring."

Jack wanted to tell her to shut up and leave him alone. There were other images; some were of Annie leaning over him, and some were of his own mother doctoring him when he had the pox. At one point he had even heard the man Blake's voice saying: "He's dead, Annie, and now you belong to me."

This had horrified him, and he tried again to cry out to tell Annie that this man was dangerous. Jack wasn't sure how long this went on—it could have been days or just a few minutes. Then, he was in a dream. It was the scene that had played out just before he had been killed, but it seemed to be playing out in slow motion and with greater clarity. This time he noticed things that he hadn't seen before. He saw Annie walking toward him, and out of the corner of his eye, he saw a flash of light. He knew instinctively that this was sunlight reflecting off the barrel of a rifle. He saw the trancelike look in Annie's eyes, and he felt her whole strength as she pushed him; he even seemed to see the bullet in his peripheral vision as it left the gun. Then he was falling—falling forever into some bottomless abyss.

Jack opened his eyes slowly. He felt his body jerk violently, and it seemed as if his head would explode. He was lying down, although he seemed to be moving. He could see Wolf walking beside him. He tried to speak, but all that came out was a croak. His throat was so dry and the sun seemed to be beating straight into his brain.

He closed his eyes and tried again; this time, he managed to say, "Water!"

He came to a jolting stop. Suddenly Annie was there, looking down on him. Her face was pale, but she was smiling. He heard her call to someone to bring the water, and then the cool liquid was trickling past his lips. To Jack it was the best thing he had ever tasted—he would have drank forever if Annie hadn't taken it from him.

"Easy does it, Jack. A little at a time."

"Where?" he asked, struggling to get a grip on the situation.

"We are almost to the river, where we will camp for the night." She was nervous, and she turned to look behind her. "Try to rest, Jack; we will be there soon."

Then she left him, and he began to move again. He tried to turn his head, but the action almost made him pass out. Finally, it came to him: He was in the litter, the one they had carried Wolf in, and there was Wolf walking beside him. He managed to reach out his hand, which Wolf nuzzled.

"Good boy," he said. Wolf whined in that quiet way he had then trotted off.

The next time Jack woke, it was almost dark. He knew that they had stopped near the river. He could hear it roaring away somewhere off to his right. He still laid on the litter that had been placed next to a blazing fire and his coat had been thrown over him.

His head still hurt, but it wasn't the blinding pain that he had felt earlier in the day. He managed to raise himself on one elbow as he saw Annie coming out of the tent. At the same time, she saw him and ran to him saying, "No, Jack, you mustn't move around."

She looked so concerned with her face still so pale. She produced the canteen, and Jack was able to hold it himself, which seemed to please her.

She reached out to touch his face. "You scared me!" she said and smiled that wonderful smile that lit up her whole face.

She put her hand to his head, and for a brief second, he seemed to be completely cured. Suddenly, Jack felt as if he could jump up and crush her in his arms—all his hurts were chased away by that one little action. He reached to take her hand when he noticed a slight movement behind her.

"Look out!" he said, his hand moving toward the gun that was no longer there. Annie turned her head sharply. She relaxed, putting her small hand back to Jack's face.

"It's ok," she said. "It's just Blake. He's a…" She paused. "He's a friend."

Blake had stopped behind her. He stooped down and looked into Jack's eyes. "Yeah, a friend," he said. "Jeffery Blake. It's nice to meet you, Jack."

Jack understood immediately and he held his tongue. Annie didn't know that they had met before. For some reason, Blake thought it should stay that way.

"Meetcha," he managed, and then lay back on the litter.

"Blake is my father's right-hand man, Jack. He saved your life."

"Well, I'm not sure about that," he heard Blake say from somewhere behind him. "If we don't get up this river before it starts to freeze, we'll all die out here."

Jack looked into Annie's eyes. "How long have I been out of it?" he asked.

"Two days," she said. "The bullet just grazed the side of your head. I feared it may have cracked your skull and injured your brain, but now I think you may just have a bad concussion. The wound is healing well, but too much movement may cause it to start bleeding again, so try not to do too much, ok?"

Jack raised his hand to his head and felt the bandage there. There were so many questions he wanted to ask her, but he dared not say much with Blake standing only a few feet away. He may have saved his life, but Jack still didn't trust him.

Blake's voice broke the silence. "Supper's ready."

"You think you could eat something, Jack?" Annie asked, still smiling down at him.

He smiled back. "Yeah, I could eat a bear," he replied, to which he heard Blake reply, "Well, you'll have to settle for rabbit and partridge—no bears around here." He snorted a laugh, the meaning not being lost on Jack. Annie wanted Jack to sleep in the tent, but he refused this flatly. He didn't wish to be coddled like a child, especially in front of Blake. Besides, he wanted a little time alone with the man, now that he had his wits about him. After eating something and having his fill of water, he felt almost like his old self again. He managed to sit up as Annie removed the bandage and put some kind of paste on his wound.

"I think you're gonna be fine, but no strenuous activity. Doctor's orders," she said. He heard Blake chuckle a little.

Annie flashed him a look that said, "You boys play nice." Then she disappeared into the tent.

Blake stared at him across the fire as they listened to Annie getting ready for bed. Wolf came in and sniffed around the tent before taking up his usual place in front of it. His eyes moved from one man to the other.

Finally Blake asked, "Smoke?"

He produced two cigars from his jacket pocket and handed one to Jack.

Hesitantly, Jack took one. "Thanks."

"These are hard to come by; the old man gets them for me," Blake said. He used a twig from the fire to light his, then passed it to Jack.

They smoked in silence for awhile, and then Blake stood up and went over to a bundle on the ground. He picked up Jack's holster and revolver, then tossed it to him.

"Been missing that, I bet," he said. "A man like you probably sleeps with it on."

"Sometimes," Jack replied. "When I feel there's a need. How 'bout you, Blake? That's a nice old .30-30 you carry."

Blake smiled and glanced toward the tent. Then, lowering his voice, he said, "Let's cut the crap, Jack. I'm not the enemy here. We both know where I got that rifle. I just thought it a shame to let it burn up in the fire. You can have it back; there are still almost thirty cartridges left, minus the one that creased your skull," he said, smiling broadly. Then he added, seeing the glint in Jack's eyes, "No, it wasn't me that shot you."

Jack relaxed a little and took a deep draw on the cigar. He leaned forward and looked straight into Blake's dark eyes. "What's your game, Blake?" he asked frankly. "And why didn't you tell her that we had met before?"

"It's no big mystery," he began. "I work for Annie's father. He thought it would be a good idea if I tagged along with Andre's men to make sure she made it back safe, that's all."

"And where are these men now?" Jack asked.

Blake smiled. "By now they're probably back at your old cabin. I sent them on a wild goose chase hoping to catch up with you before they did. Unfortunately, Boris, the lead man, didn't trust me to go alone, so he sent Jeane with me. I left him in the forest with the idea of sneaking up behind and warning you. Unfortunately, he got the drop on you before I could act. You got lucky, Jack; Jeane was the best shot I ever saw. If Annie hadn't shoved you at that exact moment...well, let's just say we wouldn't be having this conversation."

"And if you hadn't shown up exactly when you did, he would have finished the job. Is that right?" Jack added, watching the other man closely.

Blake shrugged. "Right place at the right time, I guess."

"Seems pretty convenient," Jack said, trying to get a reaction. He got one, but not the one he expected.

The smile left Blake's face and he flicked the butt of the cigar into the fire. "Look, Jack, I didn't come out here to save you. I have one mission and one mission only—to get that little girl safely back to her father. If you get in the way, I'll kill you myself."

Jack smiled and flicked his own cigar into the fire. "Well, I guess that means we have nothing to argue about then, because that's what I was in the process of doing, when you and your friend came along and shot me."

For a moment Blake seemed puzzled. "Why would you want to do that?" he asked. "Boris and his men would kill you on sight, and surely Annie has told you about her husband."

"She told me," Jack replied. "That's why we were going back. You see, I'm very anxious to meet this husband of hers. There's a few things he needs to explain."

For a moment Blake said nothing. He just continued to stare at Jack across the fire. Then he snorted and reached for his blanket. "You really are crazy," he said and rolled on his side, pulling the blanket over his head.

Jack continued to stare into the fire and thought, "Yeah, maybe a little."

Both men lay awake, the smoldering campfire between them. Jack was thinking about Annie. How had she known? Some sort of intuition had led her to push him at exactly the right moment, thereby saving his life. She had told him before that she had premonitions, but Jack had written this off as he did most things that he couldn't explain. He tried to picture her face in that moment before he was shot. She had been in a daze, as if she wasn't really there, like some other spirit had temporarily taken charge of her body. It was spooky. And the push he had felt—he remembered now that he had actually left his feet and flown backward at least three feet. It hadn't felt so much like a shove, but more like a strong wind had passed between them, strong enough to lift him off his feet. He was sure that Annie didn't weigh over a hundred pounds soaking wet, yet in that moment she had blown him over like a feather.

Blake was also thinking about that moment, but he was cursing his bad luck. Unlike Jack, he had witnessed Annie's unusual gifts before and had no problem believing that she had known the exact moment when Jeane would fire. But he hadn't been thinking about Annie's intuition when he told Jeane to take the shot—he had been sure that Jack was dead when he ran his knife through Jeane's heart. It seemed as if his plan had come off perfectly: Jeane kills Jack, and then the hero—namely himself—steps in and kills Jeane, easy peasy.

But Jack wasn't dead, and now he would need to alter his plans again. It was still possible that Jack may meet with an accident before they got home, but he couldn't help thinking about his thinly veiled threat toward Andre. If Jack did manage to kill him, wouldn't that just make his own job so much easier? On the other hand, if Jack was killed in the process, he would be totally innocent of the murder, and Annie would not have any reason to suspect him. He thought that he would just wait and see. Besides, the look on Andre's face when he learned that Annie had come back on her own with a new boyfriend would be worth all the trouble—this thought made him feel better, and still smiling to himself, he finally dozed off.

Wolf followed the girl through the woods, whining sharply at her. He had tried to head her off, but she just turned and went around him. She had left the tent silently; neither man had heard her as she walked slowly toward the river. Wolf's anxiety became worse the closer she got to the water. He thought of going back and waking the man, but he was afraid to leave her alone. She almost seemed to be asleep, even though her little feet kept moving. They were taking her closer and closer to the river. Once again, Wolf stood in her path, but she seemed not to even notice him. Finally, she reached the edge of the great river and stopped. Now Wolf felt another presence; he could see no movement, but he felt it all around them. A low growl started in his chest and the hair stood out on his shoulders.

Then Annie spoke for the first time. "I'm here," she said.

Wolf couldn't understand the words. He whined like a puppy at the sound of her voice. It didn't sound right, and suddenly there was a cold chill in the air. There was no wind; the air was heavy and the presence that Wolf felt was stronger than ever. It scared him more than the giant bear that had almost killed him. At some level, Wolf knew that this wasn't something he could fight—

there was nothing of flesh and blood to it and he was powerless to protect the girl this time.

She then took a step into the river, saying, "You're not my mother."

This was more than Wolf could stand. He bounded to her side and took her hand in his mouth. Just as she was getting ready to take another step that would have taken her into the strong current, he did something he had never done in his life: He bit down on Annie's hand. Suddenly she seemed to come awake, and she staggered as Wolf pulled her toward the shore.

She sat down hard on a protruding root and Wolf released her hand. Annie looked around her, then at Wolf. "What are we doing out here, Wolf? And why are my feet wet?"

She seemed to notice the river for the first time. Suddenly, understanding seemed to dawn on her face, and she scooted back away from the water. Slowly she stood, and she felt a dull throb coming from her right hand. She brought it up to her face and saw two small puncture wounds with blood running from them.

"Wolf," she admonished, looking down at him. "Wolf, you bit me."

Wolf whined his assent and bowed his head, his tail curling between his legs.

She knelt down and hugged him. "No, it's ok. You saved me, Wolf."

Now she looked around her and asked, "Where's camp?"

Wolf started back toward the tent, stopping now and then to make sure that she was following.

By the time Annie slipped back into the tent, she was shivering violently, and it wasn't entirely from the cold. Wolf lay down beside her and she threw the blanket over both of them. She thought, "It was just a dream." She had always had extremely vivid dreams. In this one, she had been walking through the forest with her mother. They were talking and laughing. She dreamed of her mother often, and always they were together in the woods. They would have great talks and her mother would tell her things about herself before Annie was born. In turn, Annie would tell her mother secrets that she shared with no one else. They were good dreams! But this one had been different. In this dream, she could hear her mother calling her, but she couldn't find her. She followed the sound of her voice, and finally, there she was, standing on the edge of a huge meadow.

"I'm here," she said, and her mother turned smiling, but she wasn't the same. Her face seemed to change and then waver back to normal.

"Annie," she said, and again that mysterious change came over her. "This man is dangerous," she warned.

"You mean Jack?" Annie asked.

"Yes," she said, and now her voice sounded funny.

"No, Mother," she pleaded, "Jack is a good man."

Her mother's face changed again, and this time she saw pure hatred in it.

"There is no such thing as a good man, Annie!" she snapped.

Annie hesitated and retorted, "You are not my mother!"

The woman, whoever she was, turned toward Annie, and her features softened. She was her mother again. "Yes, Annie, I am your mother—your real mother."

Then she said, "Come, Annie; come with me. I have something to show you."

She had taken her by the hand and started leading her into the meadow.

That was when she had awakened to find herself at the edge of the river. If it hadn't been for Wolf, she would have walked right to her death. She hugged the animal close, but it was a long time before she could sleep.

Jack looked at the tent and then glanced over at Blake, who just shrugged his shoulders. He felt almost like his old self this morning with the exception of a dizzy feeling if he stood up too fast. It was already midmorning, and Annie still lay asleep in the tent. Twice Jack had gone to the tent flap and quietly called her name. The last time, about fifteen minutes ago, he heard her say sleepily, "I'll be right out."

The two men had been up for over four hours and Wolf was nowhere to be seen. They had packed up the camp with the exception of the tent. Blake had even managed to secure breakfast, consisting of a couple of fish from the river. Jack thought, "She must be sick."

He was just getting ready to go into the tent and check on her when, to both of the men's surprise, Wolf emerged and shook himself all over. Annie came out slowly behind him, still wrapped in her blanket. She looked at the two men questioningly as they both stood staring at her. She looked around the camp and up at the sky. It was a gray, cold morning, but she could see that the sun had been up for awhile.

"I overslept," she stated, her eyes finally coming to rest on what was left of the fish sitting in the skillet. "Jack, you should have woken me."

"He tried," Blake started, but Jack interrupted.

"We aren't on any schedule, and you needed your sleep."

She shuffled over to the fire. "Can I have a cup of tea before we get moving?" she asked and then looked up at Blake. "Would you rinse out the skillet and get some fresh water?" she asked, giving him a wan smile.

"Sure," he said. "You need to eat something, though." He looked through his pack and found an old, battered tin plate and placed what was left of the fish on it. "Thanks," she said and started to nibble on the cold meat.

Jack had been watching her closely. As Blake disappeared into the trees, she turned to Jack and told him about the strange happenings of the night before. Jack listened intently. When she had finished her story, he said, "So, you were sleepwalking?"

"More like dream walking." She sighed. "It was so real, like I was awake but in a different place. Over there, she continued pointing at the river, there was a long green valley, and it was full daylight instead of the middle of the night."

Jack picked up her hand and examined the two small puncture wounds that Wolf had made with his giant fangs. "Are you scared, Annie?" he asked, squeezing her hand lightly.

"A little. If it hadn't been for Wolf…" and she shuddered a little bit, pulling the blanket tighter around her shoulders.

"Well, I will keep a better eye on you from now on," he insisted.

"How, Jack? You have to sleep, too," she implored.

"Blake and I can take turns—"

Annie cut him off in midsentence. "No," she half whispered, "I don't want Blake to know anything about this. Please, Jack, let's just keep this between us."

Jack studied her face. She looked tired, as if she hadn't slept at all. "Don't worry," he said, giving her back her hand and standing as he saw Wolf coming back into camp. "Between me and the amazing giant Wolf, we'll think of something."

He meant to greet Wolf and give him a much-deserved pat on the head when suddenly the animal stopped short, his nose in the air. He turned sharply and loped back into the forest. At the same instant, Blake came back into camp. He tossed the empty frying pan down next to his pack and picked up the .30-30.

"Someone's coming," he said urgently, looking directly into Jack's eyes.

Jack nodded, pulling the Colt from the holster while ducking into the trees behind the tent. Blake came over and sat down next to Annie, placing the rifle across his knees. He pulled out one of his last cigars and struck a match. Looking down at Annie, he said, "Finish your breakfast, girl. Ain't nothin' to worry about. We got the famous Jack Brooks on our side."

He snorted a laugh and turned toward the fire. Annie continued to stare at Blake for a moment. What did he mean by "famous Jack Brooks?"

She was about to ask him what he meant when from out of the trees they heard Jack shouting Wolf's name. Like a shot, Annie was up and running in the direction of Jack's voice. As she entered the trees, she saw the trail they had left the day before with the pole drag, and some intuition told her to follow it. The forest was pretty thick here, and she was forced to zig and zag as she followed the two lines in the dirt. She heard Wolf growl and turned in that direction. In the end, she almost stumbled over him as she came into a small circle of trees.

It was a weird scene. Wolf was standing stiff legged, but she could tell he wasn't in attack mode. She saw Jack leaning over another man, who was staring at Wolf in wide-eyed fear.

"Annie," he said, panting, "call him off."

She knelt beside Wolf, whispering, "It's ok, Wolf."

Wolf had already lost interest when he saw that this new man posed no threat to her or Jack. Now Annie looked back at the man. Jack was in the process of helping him to his feet as the man's eyes fixed on her.

"This is my friend Jacob," Jack was saying, but the man didn't even seem to hear him.

He was still staring at her, with his mouth open, as he took a few hesitating steps toward her. Finally he was within three feet of her when he closed his mouth with a snap and swallowed hard, never taking his eyes off of her face. Mincingly, as if it hurt to speak, he said in a low voice, "It's you!"

Annie stared back. She had a sudden feeling that she had met this man before even though she knew this was impossible. Their eyes met and a shiver ran down her spine. She wasn't afraid of this man, yet she felt funny, as if she had suddenly slipped back into her dream from the night before. With a little effort, she managed to speak, but her own voice seemed to be coming from far away as she said, "Yes…it's me."

By now Jack had come up from behind Jacob and was watching the situation with a questioning look on his face. Finally he asked, "Have you two met?"

Annie dragged her eyes away from Jacob's, and her mind seemed to clear instantly. Looking up at Jack, she said, "No, I don't believe we have."

For a moment longer, Jacob continued to stare. He shook his head slightly and turned to Jack.

By this time Blake had found them, and as he entered their little circle, panting and out of breath, he said, "Jeez, girl, for having such short legs, you can sure run." He leaned over and put his left hand on his knee; in his right he still held the rifle. Looking over at Jack, he asked, "Find yourself an 'Injun,' Jack?"

They returned to camp and the three men sat around the fire smoking. This time Annie had taken the frying pan and gone down to the river for water. As she came back into camp, Jacob's eyes once again fixed on her. The other two men looked at each other questioningly, but Annie seemed to not even notice. She went about the business of making tea. Jack broke the silence.

"So how did you find me this time? Was it the Great Spirit again?"

This seemed to bring Jacob back into the world, and he shook his head. "No, the Great Spirit didn't send me to you this time, Jack."

"Well you're an awful long way from home to have just been out for a walk."

Jacob looked from Jack to Annie and said, "I was on my way to meet a friend coming up on the river."

Jack watched him as Annie handed him a cup of tea. He knew Jacob wasn't being entirely truthful, but he decided not to press him for the moment.

"Well, we are on our way north," he said. "Kind of an escort to make sure Annie gets home safe."

Jacob was watching Annie again and asked her, "And where is your home, Little Mother?"

Jack thought this was an odd way to address her, but Jacob had a habit of renaming people according to his whim, like when he called him "Lightning Jack," so he didn't find it too strange.

Annie, however, stopped in her tracks and turned to him. "I am no one's mother, Jacob. Not yet anyway," she said and blushed to the roots of her hair. "I come from the north," she added almost as an afterthought.

Jacob smiled his best smile and said quietly, "No, not anyone's mother."

Turning to Jack he said, "Well, I've come this far; maybe I'll just tag along."

For the first time, Blake jumped into the conversation. "What about your friend?" he asked, that familiar gleam in his eye.

"Already saw him," Jacob replied, looking at Blake as if this were the first time he had noticed him.

Jack knew this was just an outright lie—Jacob had been walking toward the river when he and Wolf had come upon him, but Blake seemed uninterested and didn't pursue the subject.

By the time they had finished their tea, it was already midafternoon, and everyone agreed that it would be just as well that they camp where they were another night. Jack was almost completely recovered, but he would still get a little dizzy if he stood up too fast. Annie still looked tired after her night of adventure. Blake was the only one who wanted to move on, saying that although they had a good lead on Boris and his men, the weather could break any day, and they all might be here until spring—if they lived that long. Annie put in that she had a feeling that the weather would hold for a few more weeks. Blake mumbled something about "women and their feelings" as he went off to try to hunt up dinner.

Jack and Annie took the opportunity to take a walk down to the river. They walked in silence for awhile, each lost in their own thoughts.

Finally, Annie said, "Your friend Jacob is sort of strange."

"You don't like him?" Jack asked.

"It's not that, it's…well, he makes me uncomfortable. He is always watching me like…like he's seeing a ghost or something."

"Jacob is kind of a mystery," Jack told her. "I know that among his people, he is considered a great medicine man, yet he lives alone miles from his own tribe. I know he saved my life, and I trust him almost as much as I trust you. He would never hurt you, Annie."

"I'm sure you're right," she said, looking up at him. "But for now the only one I trust is you, Jack."

It was moments like this when they were alone and her wonderful blue eyes were focused on only him that he felt he could fall to the ground at her feet and profess his love for her, begging her to love him back. The longer he was around her, the harder it was to hold these feelings in check. How would she react? Possibly he would lose her respect. He knew that men had probably been falling at her feet most of her life, and although he knew that not one of them could have loved her any more than he did, he was determined to do the right thing. She really didn't know him, and if she did, she might look at him differently. Added to that was the fact that, like it or not, she was a married woman, and until that mess was cleared up, Jack was not going to add to her confusion by putting himself in the middle of it. Still, when she looked at him like she was now, it almost paralyzed him, and he felt as if he were under some sort of magic spell.

"Jack," she said, taking her eyes from his but still standing so close that he could smell the perfume of her hair, "today Blake said something when we were alone in camp. He called you the famous Jack Brooks like he knew you before." Then, looking back into his eyes, she added "Do you know what he meant?"

He wouldn't—no, he couldn't—lie to her, but he wasn't sure how to proceed now that she had asked him directly. Slowly he took her hand, and they resumed their walk down to the river.

"For one thing," he began, "the only famous Jack Brooks was my father. He was considered an outlaw by some, mostly by what was considered the US government at the time. He and a small group of men would rob the government stores and transports."

They came to the river, and Annie seated herself on a rock next to a little eddy. "What would they steal?" she asked, looking at him frankly.

"Mostly food, but sometimes guns and ammo. This went on for nearly twenty years, and for whatever reason, he was never caught. Some people thought it was because the government just didn't have the manpower to track him down, but I think it was because everywhere he went, people loved him. Did you ever hear the old story of Robin Hood?"

Annie nodded.

"Well, that's how I like to picture him in my mind. Anyway, eventually he gained such a following that I think the government was afraid of an uprising. So they hunted him down and hung him." Jack skipped the part about how they caught him—he was not ready to reveal those events to Annie just now.

Annie guessed there was more to the story, but she didn't press him. Instead, she reached out and took his hand. "And what about you, Jack? Do you also rob from the rich and give to the poor?"

Jack chuckled. "No, I'm no hero. But I have been in my share of fights, most of them over territory or cattle; some were more personal—none were very pretty."

Annie pressed his hand. "Have you killed a lot of men?"

And there it was: the one question he had been dreading all along. He sighed. She had been looking down at his big hands; now she looked up suddenly and could see the cloud that seemed to have come over his face. Without so much as a pause, she stood and faced him. Leaning over slightly as he was still seated on the rock, she took his face in both hands and looked deep into his gray eyes.

"I know who you really are, Jack Brooks," she said. "I told you once that I knew you were the one. I'm not even sure exactly what that means, but I do know that as long as you're with me, I feel safe, and I trust you with all my heart."

For the second time in their short crazy time together, she kissed him on the lips. Jack felt himself give in as he was powerless against his own emotions this time.

"Annie." His voice was husky. Pulling back only an inch from her parted lips, he said, "Annie, I love you."

Her expression didn't change, and when he kissed her again and held her close, she didn't resist.

When he released her, she just stood back and smiled. "You want to see a trick?" she asked, her eyes twinkling brightly.

Jack said nothing—he couldn't. He felt as if all of the strength had been drained out of him. He had bared his soul, had told her the truth—at least some of it—and she had reacted as if he had told her the coffee was ready. Now as he watched her, she stripped off her moccasins and was wading into the little pool of water that had been diverted from the river by a huge boulder.

"I've never shown anyone this," she was saying, "well, except Wolf." And she giggled a little.

Jack watched, speechless, as she stood in the water that came just to the top of her knees. She then placed both hands on top of the pool so that they barely touched the surface. What happened next snapped Jack out of his trance and brought him to his feet. First the water began to swirl in different directions, as if the current couldn't make up its mind which path it wanted to follow. Then, slowly it came to a boil—but it wasn't heat that had caused the water to come to life—it was fish! Even as he watched, one of the smaller ones leapt from the water and splashed down between Annie's knees. With an effort, he lifted his eyes from the pool and looked into her face. She was smiling at him, and her eyes seemed almost to glow as she reached down with both hands and scooped one of the larger fish out onto the bank. Two more times she did this, and still the water continued to swirl and bubble. There had to be hundreds of them swimming around her in a pool no larger than an old bathtub. She then raised her hands from the water and as suddenly as they came, they retreated in every direction, as though someone had opened an invisible cage and set them all free. Annie stepped out of the water and looked up at Jack.

He was terribly pale—too pale—and for a moment she thought he might fall over. He was staring at the fish on the bank. He closed his eyes then reopened them as if part of his mind was convinced that they weren't really there. He turned to Annie, who had come up beside him.

"They're already dead," he said flatly.

"Yes," she replied. "That's the strange part about it."

Jack, incredulous, turned to her and barked, a little too sharply: "*That's* the strange part about it?!"

Annie stepped back from him a little, her eyes searching his face. "Jack," she started, "you don't understand."

Jack laughed cynically. "You're right about that. I really don't!"

Now he saw something in her face that he never expected to see—it was shame. She was embarrassed, but more than that it was mistrust.

Suddenly she turned, scooped up her moccasins, and ran back toward the camp.

Jack's mind was in such a whirl that he didn't even call out to her. After a minute he walked over to the fish lying on the bank. Picking up the largest of the three, he realized that although it was dead, it was still cold, as if it had just come out of the river. "What just happened here?" he thought.

He walked over and looked into the small pool. It was clear and shallow. He could see all the way to the bottom, but he saw no fish; detected no movement. Looking back toward the camp, his mind flashed a picture of Annie's face just as she had looked before she ran away. All at once he saw the truth of it, and he was ashamed. He had shared something about himself, something deeply personal, so she in turn had tried to do the same. In her own way, she was giving him a part of herself that she had dared not share with another living soul, and he had reacted like a madman. He had no idea how she had pulled off her little trick with the fish; probably he never would. But what of it! She had asked no explanation of him. Instead, when he didn't reply to her question about how many men he had killed, she had kissed him and told him that she trusted him above all else—and look how he had repaid her. Hurriedly, Jack scooped up the fish and started back to camp.

He came upon her about a hundred feet from the river. She was sitting on the ground with her back to an old poplar tree. Wolf was lying next to her and she was stroking his thick fur. Jack sat down cross-legged in front of her.

"Annie, I'm sorry." What else could he say?

For a minute she continued to look down at Wolf. She wasn't crying, but she had been. Then she sighed and looked up at him. "I shouldn't have expected you to understand, Jack," she said, with a sharp laugh. "I don't even understand. I have always known that I was different, but there is no one that can tell me why. Maybe my mother could have explained, but she is gone except in my dreams. You say you love me, Jack, but how can you? I saw your face back there: you were scared! You were frightened because you didn't understand. Well, I don't understand either. Sometimes it feels like I don't even know who I am."

Then, just as Annie had done only moments before, Jack took her face in his hands and said, "I know who you are, Annie Fuller. I too have had dreams, and you are the very manifestation of all of them. I do love you. I always will, and nothing or nobody, not even your less-than-conventional way of catching trout"—and here she smiled in spite of herself—"will ever change that. Please forgive me. I was just startled."

For a moment she didn't reply; then, still smiling, she looked up into Jack's eyes and kissed him again.

"Well, this is my lucky day: two kisses," he said. She giggled as he helped her to her feet.

The next few days were mostly uneventful, and the small band even began to fall into a routine. They would travel from sunup till dusk, following the river as much as they could, and then camp for the night. Blake figured they were making excellent time and said that if the weather held, they should be there within another ten to twelve days. As for food, there always seemed to be an abundance of small game around them wherever they camped, and although it was late in the year for such things, Annie always seemed to find some wild plants to supplement their diet.

Six days after they had set out from their little camp on the river, they came to a small marsh that had to be skirted. As they traveled east along its banks, they came upon a young moose mired in the mud up to its knees. Behind it and just out of reach, four huge timber wolves were trying to get at it. Blake expressed the opinion that it sure would be nice to have a steak for dinner instead of porcupine or rabbit. Silently, Jack agreed with him, but Annie was dead set against it.

"We could never carry the whole thing with us," she said. "Besides, we are not going hungry, and I refuse to take a life just so we can have something different for dinner."

"Would you leave it for the wolves, Little Mother?" Jacob asked, probably thinking of steak himself.

"No!" she said, flashing her eyes in his direction.

He would still call her "Little Mother" from time to time, and Annie hated it.

"We will help it!" she exclaimed.

With Wolf beside her, she started off toward the huge animal. In an instant Jack was beside her, smiling.

"So did you just plan on asking the wolves nicely if they would go hunt something else?"

Annie looked up at him with laughter in her eyes and said, "Something like that."

Wolf was walking slightly ahead. His posture was stiff, and as they approached the other wolves, the hair on the back of his neck seemed to stand up. The wolves saw them approaching but seemed uncertain of this new enemy.

What happened next only Jack and possibly Jacob understood. Annie stopped, with Jack slightly behind her and to the right, in case he had to fire on these animals. Wolf walked forward stiff legged, approaching the largest of the pack. The others seemed to cower around behind this one, which was nearly as big as Wolf himself. Jack could see that they were going through a formal introduction with Wolf, but their eyes kept darting back to Annie as she stood a few feet behind him. Suddenly the leader, who had been almost nose to nose with Wolf, lowered his head just as Wolf had done that first day Jack had met him. All at once the four of them slunk back into the timber, their tails between their legs.

Annie, not missing a beat, turned her attention to the moose.

"Jack," she said, "can you get the lead rope from the pack on the gray?"

Jack hurried back to Blake, who was sitting astride the big horse. He knew what she had in mind and he didn't want her getting trampled by the huge animal in its panic to escape. He told Blake to secure one end of the rope to his saddle horn.

Sudden understanding dawned on Blake's face, and he said, "Aw, you gotta be kidding me."

"Just do it," Jack retorted and started to play out the other end of the rope toward the frightened young moose. Annie took that end from him, and Jack started to protest, but she just flashed her eyes at him.

"It won't be as afraid of me, Jack."

His mind turned back to the incident with the fish as she started out into the stagnant water. "Ok," he said, "but the minute I sense you're in danger, I'm gonna shoot that animal and come in after you. Understand?"

She appeared not to even hear him as she inched her way toward the huge moose. She didn't speak to it as she did sometimes with Wolf. She only inched slowly, closer and closer to the animal. Finally she was near enough to touch it, and from where Jack stood, she looked like a small child standing next to it. She then placed one hand on its neck, and with the other she managed to toss the lead rope over its back. She was standing in water nearly to her waist and she had to reach her hand underneath the animal's belly to grab the end. Every muscle in Jack's body tensed as she almost disappeared underneath the water. Then she had it, and she managed to tie off a pretty good knot. She started back to the shore as slowly and deliberately as she had gone in. It was harder getting out, and Jack saw her struggling against the muck that threatened to suck her down. She stopped, looked down at her legs, and then looked back to him.

He saw fear in her eyes, but she spoke calmly. "Jack, I think I'm stuck."

Almost imperceptibly, she began to sink. Jack started toward her, holding onto the rope. Up until now the moose had been fairly calm, but the minute that Jack entered the water, it began to thrash water and mud in every direction. The rope slackened, and Jack yelled for Annie to grab it as he pulled the Colt out of its holster. He intended to shoot the rope as soon as Annie had hold of it, severing it between her and the moose. She could tie it around herself, and Blake could drag her out. But Annie interpreted his action differently and, grabbing the rope with both hands, pulled with all her strength, swinging herself up between him and the panicked moose.

Jack yelled for Blake to pull, and for a fraction of a second as the rope became taught, Annie's whole body came out of the water as she clung to the rope with both hands. Something gave, and the moose came free and almost stumbled. Thrashing and snorting, it headed for the bank with Annie close behind it. Jack saw that Annie had let go and was free of the mud, so he yelled to Blake to let go of the rope, thinking that the minute they hit the bank, the frightened animal would bolt for the trees.

Then the most amazing thing happened: the minute it felt the sturdy ground underneath its hooves, it stopped! Slowly it turned, faced the girl, and lowered its head, panting as she came out of the water and walked straight toward it. Annie reached up and rested her hand on its nose, then took a small knife from her jacket pocket. Jack and Blake stood, open mouthed and gaping, as slowly she bent down and severed the rope. For a full minute, nobody moved. Jack heard Blake swear under his breath, and the spell was broken. Annie turned calmly and walked back toward Jack, her eyes sparkling with delight.

"Well," he said, still staring at the moose as it began once again to graze on the grass at the edge of the marsh, "that could have gone better."

Annie stopped in front of him and he looked down at her. "Oh Jack," she said smiling up at him, "I have nothing to fear from the animals; it's people that scare me." For the next two hours, the young moose followed them north, prompting Blake to make the comment: "It's amazing how these dumb animals will follow her anywhere!"

To which Jacob, who was normally so stoic, replied, "Yes, and we three dumb animals are no exception!"

For the next three days, they continued on until they came to the Great Bear River that ran between Great Bear Lake and the Mackenzie. They had all become tired and moody, so Annie tried to lift their spirits.

"We are almost there!" she exclaimed. "I know the way from here."

The next day they passed through Norman Wells, but the town, or settlement, had long since been abandoned. That night they camped less than twenty miles from Fort Good Hope. The snow had been falling lightly all day, so they had built a couple small shelters with branches and pine boughs to keep it off of them when they slept. Now Jack was sure that they would make it. He felt some excitement at the thought of finally coming to the end of their journey, but Blake was in a bad mood and went to the smaller shelter and laid down. Annie also seemed down and retired early to her tent, leaving himself and Jacob alone in the larger lean-to on the other side of the fire. The snow was now falling in huge flakes, but thankfully there was no wind, so it wasn't unpleasant. Jack was glad that he finally had a little time to speak with his old friend alone. He had been meaning to get the man alone ever since he had stumbled onto their camp and now he wanted to pick his brain.

"So," he said, more in jest than anything else, "who was the friend you were meeting on the river?"

Jacob puffed slowly on his long pipe. "I suppose it was you," he said, never looking up from the fire.

"Ahh," Jack said, feeling that he had caught the old medicine man in a lie. "But you said the Great Spirit hadn't sent you this time."

Jacob slowly tapped out the ashes from his pipe on a rock beside the fire and sighed, as if he were trying as hard as he could to be patient with an unruly student. "No," he said, in his usual quiet voice. "I said, 'The Great Spirit didn't send me to find *you*' this time."

Jack started. "It's funny how everyone automatically assumes that the whole universe revolves around them," he thought. "So the Great Spirit sent you to Annie, then?" he asked aloud, still more joking than serious.

Jacob continued to stare into the fire, and Jack knew that any further attempts to draw him out would be fruitless; he seemed to have offended him somehow. Now the snow seemed to fall so thick that he couldn't even see the tent at the edge of the little clearing. For the first time since he left the cabin, Jack felt entirely alone. He looked around for Wolf, but he too was out of sight. "Probably out on one of his all-night hunting forays," Jack thought. He was just about to pull his coat over him and tell Jacob good night when he heard the old tracker speak—the words chilled him to the bone.

"When she sleeps, the snow flies," Jacob continued to stare into the fire, and for a moment Jack wasn't sure if it was him or Jacob that had spoken. Finally, he asked, "Jacob, why do you call her Little Mother?"

Jacob continued to stare at the fire for a moment longer and then looked over at Jack, as if he were waking from a dream. "Because she reminds me of a dream I once had," he replied, smiling his ghostly smile. "And if I am right, I am not the only one who has had this dream."

For a moment Jack continued to look at him through the thickly falling snow, then Jacob pulled his old cover over his shoulder and went to sleep. Jack slept badly that night. He seemed to wake up every hour. Finally, just as the stars were fading from the sky, he decided to give up entirely.

The snow had stopped, but there was at least three inches of the white stuff covering the ground. He looked toward the tent and could just make out Wolf's dark shape lying in front of it. Both Blake and Jacob were still asleep, so he stoked the fire and sat close to it, pulling his coat tighter around him.

"Today is the day," he thought. They would make it to Annie's home. But then what? He and Jacob were strangers; how would they be received? Would her father welcome them or try and send them away once his daughter was returned to him? He wasn't afraid, just curious as to how things would play out. He wondered how far away Boris and his men were. Could they have already made it back? He didn't think so, but these were all unknowns, so he turned his thoughts to Annie.

Who was she really? He knew her back story; she had told him. And he was sure that she was incapable of lying. But it was possible that she had left a lot of things out and that he didn't know half the truth. He was fairly certain that this was so, yet he found that it really didn't matter to him much. He loved her. Somewhere deep inside him a voice whispered: "I've always loved her and would give my life for her if it is required to keep her safe." He just wished he knew why. Since the first time he had seen her, it had seemed that unknown forces had been at work. It was as if his will had not been entirely his own. Was it possible that he, Jacob, and even Blake were just pawns in some larger game that none of them understood? It sure was beginning to feel that way, at least to him. This morning the feeling was stronger than ever that he was in for a great fight and that it would possibly be his last. He was sure that Annie would never purposefully hurt him, but she may have unknowingly led them all to their death.

He heard stirring from the tent, but he didn't turn. Annie quietly came up behind him and placed one small hand on his shoulder.

Kneeling, she whispered, so as not to wake the others: "You're up early."

"Yeah, I guess I'm a little nervous about meeting your father," he whispered in return.

"You! The famous Jack Brooks, nervous?" She mocked as she used her hands to shake out her glorious locks. "Well, don't worry, he's gonna love you. If there is anything my father admires, it's courage, and that's something you have more than is good for you. That first day when you met Wolf, I saw it, and when you came after me in Boris's camp; I have often wondered if anything scares you,."

"Yeah, there is at least one thing," he said, turning to look at her for the first time. For a moment she just studied his face. He was so serious, and when he looked this way, it made her regret that she had ever brought him into this mess. He loved her, and if he had been Blake or Andre or even her father, that would have been ok. She loved her father, and the other two had been mostly just a nuisance. But the fact was that Jack was an innocent bystander—she had dragged him into her world. Every man that she had ever known had loved her in one way or another, but Jack was the first one that hadn't expected anything in return. He had never asked her how she felt about him; he had never questioned her motives, and that had made her nervous. It was because of this she had opened up to him, shown him things that no one, except maybe her father, had suspected, because, well— she trusted him implicitly. He was the boy that she had dreamed of as a small girl: the dark man with no face; the strong man; the guardian. He was the one that she had waited for all these years. Although she hadn't told him of these dreams, he seemed to know it, and he had lived up to the image that her dream had shown her. Jack Brooks was no white knight riding in at the end of the story to save the day—he was her hero. But instinctively, Annie knew that all heroes need a cause.

She knew—or she thought she knew—what he was about to say as he looked at her with those dark-gray eyes; so right at that moment, she resolved to tell him anything he wanted to know.

She expected him to proclaim his love and ask of hers, but he surprised her as he had done numerous times before by saying: "Annie, why am I here? Why did you say that you knew I was the one?"

For a moment she was too startled to reply. She turned her gaze to the fire, saying simply: "I've dreamed of you my whole life, Jack."

Neither of them had noticed that Jacob had awakened and was staring at them from his sleeping roll.

"Dreamed of me, personally?" he asked.

"Yes," she replied. "You, personally. I always kind of expected that you would just show up one day."

Then he asked the question, or at least a form of it, that she had been expecting all along. "Annie, what am I to you?"

"I…" she started and then paused. "Jack, I don't know for sure."

By now the sun had peeked its head over the horizon, and they could hear Blake stirring in his bedroll.

Slowly Annie stood and looked down at Jack. "In time," she said, "I hope you will understand what you are to me." Quietly she walked back to the little tent.

Blake had rolled over but now fell to snoring. It always seemed that just as Annie was on the verge of telling him something important, there would be some sort of interruption, and now Jack was more frustrated than ever. He never showed anger, but as he thought no one was watching, he pounded the heel of his boot in the ground and cursed under his breath.

Suddenly Jacob's voice cut the still morning air, quiet but clear. "She can't return your love—at least not the way that you want her to."

Startled, Jack said almost angrily, "And why not, oh great and wise medicine man?" He regretted his words and his tone almost the minute he spoke, but Jacob seemed not to even notice.

"Because," he went on more calmly than ever, "*she* can belong to no *one*."

Jack was in no mood for Jacob's voodoo, and he said coldly: "A man just needs to know where he stands before he puts his neck on the line."

It wasn't one of his prouder statements, but there it was—he couldn't take it back. Jacob didn't even stir from his sleeping roll and his face was cold and calm; Jack wanted to punch it.

But his next words stayed with Jack until the day he died. "Jack," he said, speaking in that low sad voice that he had heard so many times before. "She can belong to no *one*, because she belongs to *everyone*."

Two hours later they were on their way, Jack and Annie riding the black and white, Blake and Jacob on the gray. They made good time, and by midafternoon Annie was sure that they would be home by sunset. They had lost the river, but now Blake, who had taken the lead, was guiding them by landmarks. Just as the autumn sun was getting ready to set in the west, they topped a rise, and Jack held his breath.

It was the country he had dreamed of—not just a close facsimile, but exactly, down to the finest detail. Throughout his journey he had entertained thoughts that he had somehow been guided, either by his sister, or Annie, or the Great Spirit that Jacob was always raving about, but he never really believed it until he came to this rise. It was his dream! The dream from his sister's house after she had died. He literally gasped as he saw dream become reality and spurred the horse into a run, leaving Blake and Jacob behind. Annie was laughing wildly as they came down the slope, but as they approached the large house in the center of a huge valley, she became quiet.

The front door of the huge dwelling opened, revealing a long porch. Annie asked him to stop short of the dooryard. Turning in the saddle so that Jack could make out every inch of her profile, she said, "I do love you, Jack. You must know that before we go in. I love you." And leaning back, she kissed him on the cheek.

The light from the open door was blotted out by the huge figure of a man; his voice was low and gruff. "Who's there?" He asked.

Annie replied joyously, "Me, Daddy. It's Annie."

# CHAPTER 11

David Fuller sat thoughtfully in a huge chair, listening to his daughter's story. She was holding nothing back. She had started with how Andre had proclaimed their union in front of all of his people. Jack listened attentively as he had never heard that part of the story and found nothing in it to convince him that it was a real marriage. There had been a preacher, someone named Chance, but from Annie's account, even he had been threatened into service. She then began telling about their first meeting, and Jack's mind began to wander.

They were seated in what Annie had called the living room, and Jack, who had never seen a house this big, much less sat in one, was impressed. There were a few pieces of old furniture, antiques that had been patched and repaired over the long years, but the majority of the room was furnished with new stuff that had obviously been made here. The craftsmanship was exquisite. A huge stone fireplace was centered in the wall directly opposite him. It was framed on both sides with shelving that looked relatively new. On these shelves were various knickknacks, some made of what looked like real glass, and a few battered books. The floor of the space looked like oak, covered here and there with exquisitely woven rugs of high quality. A great bearskin, almost as big as the one he had given Annie, lay on the floor in front of the fireplace. Everywhere his eyes fell, there was something new to take in, and he wondered how Annie's father had acquired so many fine things.

The object that stood out the most to Jack was the portrait above the fireplace. At first glance he thought it was Annie herself, but closer inspection told him that it must be her mother. The resemblance was there for sure—the woman in the portrait seemed to have the same glow about the eyes and mischievous smile that Annie got when she thought he was being too serious. She also had Annie's black hair. It was shorter and, Jack thought, not quite as full. He listened for a moment. Annie was at the point in her story when she had placed the first note in the old stump. Could it be that it had only been a few short weeks since he first saw her sitting in the meadow near his cabin? To Jack it seemed like he had known her forever, and everything that had happened before she came along was just a dream. Jack eyes fell on Annie and her father. They were sitting close together on an old sofa and the man seemed to be hanging on every word.

When they had first arrived, Annie had flown into her father's arms, and he had smothered her with kisses, saying, "Oh my girl, oh my little angel has come home!" When he finally set her back on her feet, Jack had been coming up the porch steps. She held her hand out to him, saying, "Daddy, this is Jack Brooks. I would have never made it home without him."

Jack thought he noticed a change in the big man at the mention of his name, but it had been only for a moment, and it had been dark on the big porch. The two men shook hands and Annie was all smiles as she looked from one to the other. Jacob was introduced, and after shaking hands with him just as warmly, he noticed Blake still standing in the dooryard.

Annie's father looked a little surprised by Blake's presence in their little party, but he shook it off quickly, saying, "Glad to have you back in one piece, Blake. See to the horses, will you? We can talk in the morning."

Jack saw a momentary look of resentment in Blake's dark eyes when he turned away swiftly, taking the tired animals with him. Jacob then excused himself, asking if he could set up a small camp in the woods just to the left of the house. Annie's father had replied that he was more than welcome to stay inside the house but could do as he wished, as long as he didn't camp too close to the village as the people were wary of outsiders. Jacob nodded and, tipping his old hat to Jack, started off toward the trees.

So, it was just Jack and Annie that were led into the big house. Annie was telling how Jack had single-handedly taken her out of Boris's camp. The big man was looking at him speculatively, glancing now and then at the revolver strapped to his hip. He thought it was probably impolite of him not to remove it before coming in the house, but it had been so long since he had been called on to remember his manners that he had simply forgotten. Annie continued her story, telling how he had been shot and how Blake had come to the rescue in the nick of time, leaving out the part about her pushing him and saving his life. She skimmed over the last part of their journey, saying little about Jacob and his mysterious appearance and ending with, "Then we came straight here."

Annie's father leaned back and stared at him for so long that Jack began to feel uncomfortable. He was about to suggest that he should probably camp outside with Jacob when the big man stood and came forward. Jack stood also, not knowing exactly what to expect. He noticed that his eyes were misty, and when he spoke, his voice sounded choked. "It would seem that I owe you a great debt, Mr. Brooks." Reaching for Jack's hand, which he held firmly but warmly, he said: "If there is anything I can do to repay your kindness to my daughter, all you need to do is ask. You are welcome here as long as you wish to stay."

"Thank you, Mr. Fuller, but I did no more than anyone else would have done had they known her for more than a minute."

David laughed heartily and put his arm on Jack's shoulder. "Maybe so, but I doubt that anyone else could have pulled it off. Boris and his men are dangerous, and have no doubt that, had they caught you, they would have killed you on sight."

Jack didn't reply to this, thinking to himself that if it came down to it, Boris might find him a little harder to deal with than your average settler.

This also seemed to dawn on Annie's father, and he added, "But it's possible they might have had their hands full with you, Mr. Brooks."

"Just Jack will be fine," he replied.

The big man smiled at this, told Jack that he must call him David, and that he was sure that they would become great friends. Turning to Annie he said, "Now, I'm sure that you are both tired and hungry after your long journey. I think I best find Blake tonight and thank him personally for his help in this matter." He started toward the door, saying, "I'll have Kitchi show you to your room." Pausing in the doorway, he said to Jack, "We can talk more over breakfast, say around seven thirty?" Jack nodded and David went out.

When he had gone, Jack turned to Annie, who still sat on the sofa. She looked tired; evidently reliving the events of the last month had taken something out of her. She was staring at the portrait over the fireplace with a far-off, almost vacant look in her eyes. He wanted to take her in his arms, but something held him back. He was only able to ask if she was glad to be home. The sound of his voice brought her out of her reverie, and she stood quickly, saying, "Oh yes, very glad." To Jack's surprise she walked straight past him, saying, "Where is Kitchi?" and was out the door before he could say another word.

He was shown to a room by a young man with dark eyes and a ponytail. He didn't speak, and Jack found that he himself was too busy with his own thoughts to inquire of the boy. As his mind turned over the day's events, it kept returning to Annie's last words to him before she ran to her father. She loved him; she had said it. But was it possible that she really felt the same way that he did, and if so, what next? Did he dare ask her to be his wife?

The room the young man led him into was as nice as the rest of the house, and for a moment he felt completely out of place. There was no fire, but the room was warm enough. Glancing around, his eye fell on two floor grates. Placing his hand over one of these, he felt warm air radiating from it. Then he noticed the lights: at least three of these were electric. Jack wondered again how this place, so civilized, could exist out here in the middle of the Canadian wilderness.

There was a light knock on the open door, and Jack turned to see Annie standing in the opening, holding a little tray with tea and corn muffins. She came in without asking and set it down on a low table next to the bed. "Thought you might need a little snack before you turned in," she said. Then, with no other word, she turned to go.

Jack wouldn't be put off twice. He caught her by the arm, not knowing exactly what he wanted to say, but determined to get her to explain her sudden indifference. "Annie, are you ok?" he asked after a short pause in which he rejected the more direct questions that leapt to his mind.

"I am better than ok," she said, smiling up at him. "Just tired."

He still held her wrist; he didn't want her to go. He wanted to hear her say those words again; he wanted to kiss her. But what he said was, "Annie, I was hoping we could talk for a minute."

She took him by both hands, and although she continued to smile, she said, "Get some sleep, Jack. Tomorrow I will show you around and you can ask me anything you want." Then she turned slowly and exited the room.

"Good night," he said finally, but she had already closed the door.

He looked around him again. The room was sparsely furnished, but the bed was comfortable, and after removing the heavy gun belt, he sat down on it. A line occurred to him, and he had to smile. It was an old saying he had heard his uncle use once or twice, probably pirated from some long-forgotten novel.

"If you can't have what you choose, choose what you have."

So he drank his tea and began to get ready for bed, but it was a long time before he dozed off. Even when he did, Annie's words were still replaying in his head: "I do love you, Jack."

He slept without dreaming, at least as far as he knew, and woke with a start to the sound of knocking on the heavy wooden door, followed by a gruff voice asking, "Coming to breakfast?" It was of course the man of the house, and he stumbled into his clothes.

He wished he could clean himself up a little before going down, but he saw no wash basin or water anywhere, so he had to content himself with combing his hair and tucking in his old shirt.

Once in the hall, all he needed to do was follow the smell of breakfast cooking and it brought him to a large and amply furnished kitchen. Pots and pans hung overhead and a large cookstove stood in the middle of the room. There was a sink with a hand pump on one wall and plenty of cabinet space. He saw his host sitting at a great mahogany table centered in what would have served well as a dining room but was actually just an extension of the kitchen. It struck him that the house that he had lived in with his mother and sister would have almost fit in this one room.

Jack approached the table, slowly taking everything in, and said, "Mornin', Mr. Fuller."

Annie's father looked up from his half-eaten breakfast and smiled. "I thought we had dispensed with such formalities last night, Jack." Gesturing to the seat opposite him, he asked, "Have you met Kitchi? He is Annie's stepbrother and our go-to man around here. He's also the best cook within eight hundred miles."

Jack nodded to the boy as he set a huge plate of food down in front of him.

"You wear that thing to bed?" David inquired, indicating the revolver at Jack's side.

Jack colored slightly and began to remove it, saying, "Sorry, it's a habit I can't seem to break."

As he started to set it down on the table, David asked, "May I?" and, before Jack could answer, had pulled the gun from its holster. "Forty-five, ain't it?" Jack nodded. "Awful heavy." David said, holding it out in front of him.

This action made Jack a little nervous, and he said without thinking, "Careful, sir; it's loaded."

David looked at him questioningly for a moment. Then, handing it back to Jack butt first, he chuckled. "Wouldn't be much good if it wasn't."

Jack admonished himself mentally—of course David knew as much about firearms as he did—what was he thinking? "Will Annie be joining us?" Jack inquired, searching for some common ground.

The problem was that he wasn't exactly sure where he stood here yet, and he felt as if he were being put on the spot. David only shrugged and said, "I doubt it. She left early this morning, as she often does." Then, seeing the alarm in Jack's face, he smiled and added, "Don't worry; she'll be back shortly. Besides, it gives us an opportunity to talk straight, if you get my meaning."

"I guess I do," Jack replied, trying to seem unconcerned. For a few minutes, neither of them spoke as both were concentrating on their breakfast.

Finally David pushed his plate aside and said almost apologetically, "I know who you are, Jack."

It was the same thing Annie had said to him only a few days earlier, and for a moment he was puzzled. But as he went on, Jack realized that this was more than just a feeling on David's part. He *had* heard of him!

"I saw your father in St. Louis, Jack," he started, "and I think I saw you also. But you weren't so imposing then. If I remember right, you were still clinging to your mother's skirts."

Jack felt the blood run to his face. "You were there?" he asked, his voice coming out in a whisper.

David sighed. "No, not in person, but I have good pictures. Perhaps you'd like to see them?"

"No," Jack said in an even voice. "I've seen them before."

"Yes, I'm sure you have," David acknowledged, looking into his coffee. "It's just that when I first saw you standing on my front porch, I felt a sense of dread, and I haven't been able to shake it. Don't get me wrong—I have nothing against you personally. I think what they did to your dad was a crime. It's just that—" Here he stopped, perhaps thinking he said to much.

But Jack knew exactly what the older man was driving at and finished the sentence for him. "It's just that you're worried I might hurt Annie, is that it?"

"No, not exactly," David said slowly. Then he seemed to decide on a different approach. Leaning across the table, he studied Jack for a moment before going on. "You must know," he said finally, "that your reputation precedes you, Jack."

Jack said nothing, but pushing his own plate aside, he stared back at the older man.

"I have heard," David continued, "from various sources that you have 'dispatched' thirty men all by yourself."

Still Jack said nothing. He was waiting for the other shoe to drop.

David, seeing that Jack wasn't going to dispute him, went on. "I have also heard that the government of the good ole USA—or at least what's left of it—has put a pretty hefty price on your head."

Jack stirred uncomfortably in his chair. He hadn't been confronted about his past in years, and as far as he knew, the government had given up on him or thought him dead. Most of the things that Annie's father was talking about had happened so long ago that it seemed like another life to Jack.

"Sir," he said finally, picking his words carefully. "I won't make excuses or try to justify anything you may have heard about my past. I will only say that I don't regret anything I have done. For me, it was a point of honor—mine as well as my father's. As for your daughter, please believe that I could never harm or allow anyone else to harm her in any way."

David must have gleaned something more from Jack's statement than was intended—either that or he knew more about the subject than he let on. A look of compassion took the place of concern, and leaning back in his chair, he smiled. "I'm sorry, Jack. I don't mean to bring up any bad memories. Just as Annie trusts you, I do also. But I think that as a father, I have a right to know a little bit about my future son-in-law."

This statement took Jack completely off guard, and he actually stammered a little as he said, "Oh no, sir! Um, I mean, you don't understand. I haven't, I mean, I wouldn't…"

Now David laughed out loud, and Jack, blushing to the roots of his hair, was about to protest further when David said, "Of course you wouldn't, son, but in matters such as these, you have no choice. She loves you, Jack. I could see it the minute you came through my front door. And take my word for it, whether or not it is in her power to give herself to one man remains to be seen, but under normal circumstances, what my Annie wants, my Annie gets."

Jack started to say something about Annie already being married but caught himself, not knowing exactly how to broach the subject of Andre with Annie's father. Luckily, Kitchi came back just then and took their plates, giving a moment's pause in the conversation. Jack was thinking he had better be careful on the subject of Annie—there seemed to be pitfalls everywhere. Still, he was beginning to feel more at ease around this man, so he was torn.

David seemed to read this somehow, and after a moment of uncomfortable silence on Jack's part, he said, "So what do you say, Jack? You tell me your story, and I'll tell you mine."

For a minute Jack looked down at the table. It wasn't that he was afraid or even ashamed to talk about his past, he just had spent a long time pushing those memories down, and now he wasn't sure were to begin.

Suddenly David got up and called to Kitchi, "Bring a pot of coffee to the library," and, motioning to Jack, headed off down the hall.

Jack followed, and presently they came to a small space at the back of the house. This room, Jack noticed, was in stark contrast to every other room that he had seen thus far—it was a mess.

David explained as he began to go through the drawers in an enormous desk, "I don't let anyone in here, and

I'm afraid I'm not a very good housekeeper. Please, have a seat, if you can find one."

Jack found an old chair upholstered in leather and sat down. David continued to rifle through the drawers until finally he seemed to find what he was looking for. He studied it for a moment and then crossed the room and handed it to Jack.

"Why don't you start here," he said and walked back behind the desk to sit down. Jack studied it. He had seen the newspaper with its caption "FAMED OUTLAW PUT TO DEATH!" a hundred times, but this copy had been framed and the picture was perfectly preserved.

"It used to hang on the wall right above were you're sitting, Jack. In my younger days, I took a great interest in politics in the US. Of course, that was back before the government there cut themselves off completely from the colonies. Back then there was free trade between the two, and newspapers were easily obtained. Consequently, I had heard much about your father.

"When I saw this picture, it struck me for the first time that he was a family man first and foremost. The look on his face always haunted me. You can see the pride he has in you and the love for your mother—it's as if he knows that his death is of no consequence as long as you're still alive."

Jack was still studying the picture and wondering at the impression that David had gotten from it. He personally had always hated it, and the only feeling he got from it was one of injustice.

Seeing that Jack wasn't ready to speak on the subject, David continued. "Well, at any rate, I didn't bring it out simply to relive old memories. You see, that photo wasn't always hidden away in my desk drawer. As I said, it used to hang on the wall right above your head there. Then one day, when she was about five years old, Annie climbed up on that very chair that you're sitting in and took it down. I remember it as if it happened only yesterday. She brought the picture to me and said, 'He looks so sad, Daddy!'

"I thought she was talking about your father, but she put her little finger on your face and said something that still gives me chills to this day. She was too young to be able to read, but just as if she had known you her whole life, she said. 'It's Jack, Daddy. Jack is my friend, and I don't like him to be sad.'"

The older Jack, the Jack that sat in the big chair across from Annie's father, had a sudden image flash into his brain, like a long-forgotten dream that had picked that very moment to reemerge. It was him and a little girl walking hand in hand through a forest, and the forest seemed to be on fire all around them.

Then the image or vision was gone, and David was saying, "I had always known that there was something, shall we say, 'different,' about Annie. But it wasn't until that day that I began to realize *how* different. Well, let me tell you, it scared me more than a little at first. I put that picture in a drawer, where it has been ever since. She never mentioned it again. Still, on more than one occasion, I heard her speaking to someone about her friend 'Jack' and how someday he would come and see her."

Jack looked up from the picture and met David's gaze as he said, "It always made me a little uneasy." Then, looking away suddenly, he shrugged his great shoulders and went on.

"Eventually, she seemed to grow out of her imaginary friend faze, and honestly I wasn't a bit sad to see you fade into her memory." Then, sighing deeply and glancing once again at Jack, he said in a voice that sounded almost melancholy: "And now you're here in the flesh. It seems almost preordained somehow."

Jack looked back at the picture. He had never really noticed his own face in it, even though he had seen it a hundred times. He had carried this article with him when he had gone east. On the nights when he couldn't sleep, he had studied his father's face, wondering what he was thinking. Now he noticed something new as Annie's father had put a new perspective on it: His father was looking at him, and the look on his face was one of triumph. He saw it now, as if after all this time, his eyes had finally been opened. His father was proud of him! From there he looked to his mother's face—there were no tears, but a look of defiance, as if she were the one about to be hanged. Was it possible that through all the years he had been wrong about his parents? His mother had always told him that his father had died for something he believed in, and Jack had foolishly believed it was some grand cause. Now David's words were forcing him to look at the photo in a different light. His father had died for something that he believed in, but it had nothing to do with politics. His father had died protecting what was most important to him: his family. A single tear rolled down Jack's face, and David seemed to find the contents of the desk fascinating.

When their eyes finally met, David asked, "So, Jack, are you a cold-blooded killer?"

Slowly Jack took a small pocket book from his jacket. From this he produced a battered newspaper clipping, the very same one that David had framed. As he unfolded it, another piece of paper fell out. It was the letter that his sister had given him the night she died—it was also the last letter his father had ever written to his mom, and Jack felt that it explained things better than he ever could. He advanced to the desk and handed it to David, who took it gingerly, never taking his eyes from Jack's face. After retrieving a pair of eyeglasses from the top drawer, he began to read out loud.

"Dearest,

I am writing once more to tell you that I am sorry, but if it is any consolation, this will be the last time that you will have to hear it. It's a poor defense to say that I did everything for you and the kids, but it is the only one I have. I must believe it's true, or else my life should seem wasted. Sometimes I think that things would have been better had I conformed and let things stand as they are—at least that way we could have been together. Who knows? Had we moved further west, we might have gone on our whole lives never to be bothered by this accursed government. Then I think of Jack and Mary, and I know in my heart that if we don't make a stand now, they will have it to do later.

Well, it's all water under the bridge now, and Lord knows we have been over this before. I guess you knew the score when you married a soldier, but please believe me when I say that I never meant to cause you any pain! It may have been selfish to want you for my own, knowing I could never give you the home and security that you deserve, but after all I am just a man, and I believed, at the time, that my love for you would be enough. Sweet Kate, if anyone has suffered it has been you, and now as the game is up, I see that more clearly than ever. It is in truth my only regret.

You must be stronger than ever now, honey, but if everything works out, you and the kids will be safe forever. They have found out about you—I don't know how, but they have—and you must move swiftly, or you will be caught. I have one last card up my sleeve and I intend to play it shortly. It should buy you some time. My brother Phil is already on his way to meet you. After that, you will be safe. If everything goes well, I should be able to follow you at the end of the month and then we will be together once and for all. My only wish is for you and the kids to finally be happy—nothing else matters now. Please know that I have always and will forever love you with all my heart. Whatever you hear about me in the future, remember this and believe it.

Forever yours,
J

PS I have enclosed a list of names—it is very important that Phil gets it. It may save his life someday."

David looked up from the letter and studied Jack so closely that he began to feel uncomfortable. Finally, he said, "Your uncle never got that list, did he?"

Jack looked down at his hands and, after a moment's pause, said, "She never got the chance to give it to him."

David leaned back in his chair and gestured for him to go on.

"Two days after receiving this letter, three men showed up at the house. They produced what they said was a warrant and tore the whole place apart."

Jack leaned back in his own chair, and as he told the story, it seemed to replay in vivid color in his mind.

His mother had pushed him and Mary into their own small room while the men began ransacking the house. Jack remembered how he had trembled with fear as he sat with his back against the bedroom door.

But Mary, who even at the tender age of twelve, had seemed like a grownup to Jack, had taken both of his hands and whispered: "Listen, Jack, they aren't going to hurt us; they just want some of Father's things." Then she had put her finger to her lips, indicating he should be quiet. She took him by the hand, and they slipped out of the room and down the hall. Their house at the time hadn't been very big, but there was a small foyer where people, upon entering, could take off their coats and boots. Above a small bench there had been an old mirror, directly opposite the kitchen door, reflecting the entire interior of the room. The problem was that if anyone happened to glance at it, they could also see whoever stood in the hall. Mary seemed unconcerned about the latter, and they both stood with their backs against the wall, watching the scene that played out in the kitchen.

Two of the men stood with their backs to the door. Jack saw his mother sitting at the table facing them. She looked so tired, and Jack had to fight the urge to run to her right then. Mary must have felt this because she tightened her grip on his small hand and once again put her finger to her lips.

The third man entered the picture, thrusting a photo in his mother's face and shouting, "How do you know this man!"

Jack saw her flinch slightly, and then in a calm voice, she said, "I don't. I told you all of these things were here when we moved in."

Suddenly the man's hand flashed out, striking his mother in the face, knocking her to the floor and out of his line of sight.

Even now, twenty some years later, Jack felt the anger surge up in him as he relived it.

Then the man had reached down and jerked his mother to her feet, and once again Jack could see her in the mirror. She was dazed. Jack could see the red mark on her face where the man had hit her. Then this bully grabbed her by both arms and, getting right in her face, whispered something only she could hear. This time she didn't flinch—instead, her features seemed to harden, a cold smile forming on her lips, and she spat directly into the man's face. Once again the man hit her, and this was more than Jack could take. Breaking from his sister's grip, he ran in and stood between the man and his mother, fists out in front of him. But the man had only laughed and grimaced. "Looks like the apple doesn't fall far from the tree."

Jack reclined in the comfortable chair and closed his eyes as he relived this hated moment from his childhood.

He sat forward and, looking David straight in the eye, said, "That man's name was Marcas McKay."

David blinked but showed little surprise at this revelation, so Jack went on. "The next morning, we were packed in a wagon and hauled back to St. Louis. Three days after we arrived, my father surrendered himself to the sheriff in Kansas City, who was a friend of his. The conditions of the surrender were that we should be set free and provided safe passage back home to Colorado. For reasons of her own, my mother insisted on staying for the execution and was even more insistent that I be with her—that's where that picture and article came from."

A hundred questions formed in David's mind but stopped just short of his lips. Finally, he asked, "And they never found the list of names that your father sent for his brother?"

Jack leaned back in the old chair once more and laughed. "No, and it turned out to be their biggest mistake. McKay and his men had ransacked the house, taking everything that could be considered evidence of our relation to the outlaw Jack Brooks. But for some reason they decided that my sister, Mary, was unimportant in the scheme of things. Maybe they thought she would be too much trouble, or that it simply wasn't worth hauling a young girl around.

"Anyway, at some point my mother was able to slip her this last letter from my father, and just before my mother died, she gave the list of names to me. The letter I never saw until my sister gave it to me just before she passed, roughly four years ago."

By now David was leaning over his desk, entranced by the tragedy that had befallen this young family. Finally, he said, "But your mother and sister had to know the consequences of giving you that list?"

Jack paused a moment, not sure how David would react to his next statement. Then he thought of Annie and all his doubts vanished. "My sister had what some might call intuition or...a sixth sense."

David smiled but said nothing.

"Anyway," Jack went on, "for as long as I can remember, she has been telling me about my 'destiny.' As I got older, I learned to just humor her, not really believing in any of it. It was one of these times that she gave me the list. I remember exactly what she said the day she handed it to me. She said, 'Take this, Jack. I have concluded that you will never find your future until you have done with your past.'"

He smiled at the memory, and David was getting ready with another barrage of questions when there was a short knock on the open door and Kitchi came in with the coffee. Jack was relieved. On one hand, he realized that David was asking these hard questions out of concern for his daughter, but at the same time, he felt as if he were being interrogated. Also Jack wasn't used to talking so much about himself, so as Kitchi poured the coffee, he took the opportunity to change the subject.

"Sir," he started, but David held up a finger and turned to the boy. "Thank you, Kitchi; that will be all for now. Will you let us know when Annie has returned from her walk?"

Kitchi said he would and went out.

"Sorry," he said, "I love that boy to death, but he's the biggest gossip in the house. Please continue, Jack."

"Sir," he started again, "can I ask you a question?"

David smiled. "I guess. I have been dominating the conversation. By all means Jack ask away, whatever I can tell you I will."

Jack thought for a moment, not quite sure what to ask first. Finally he said, "Annie says you have a cure for the walking sickness."

It wasn't what he most wanted to know, but he figured it was a good place to start. David surprised him by smiling as he leaned back in his chair and chuckled lightly. "Oh," he said, "I'm not laughing at you, Jack, and that is a good question—it's just that you seem to be starting at the end of the story. What do you really want to know?" Now Jack wished Annie would come in.

"I know," David said when Jack paused, "you're worried that you may be betraying some confidence between you and her. Admirable, but misplaced. I am pretty sure that there is nothing that you could tell me about Annie that would surprise me."

He took a sip of his coffee and hissed under his breath. "Too hot as usual." Then an idea seemed to occur to him, and he said, "Will you take a short walk with me? It will give this boiling mud time to cool down."

Without waiting for an answer, he stood and took an old jacket from a hook behind the desk, and Jack followed him down the hall and out the front door.

door, and Jack followed him inside. Two more lanterns were lit, and he realized that they were in a large workshop.

David turned to him, smiling. "I like to call this my laboratory. It's where I spend most of my time."

He chuckled a little to himself as if this were some private joke and asked: "Well, Jack, what do you think?"

Jack looked around. Something was funny here, but he couldn't quite put his finger on it. Slowly he walked the length of the room, observing its contents as he went. David remained silent, waiting to see if Jack would guess his secret. When he reached the far wall, Jack turned on his heel and then glanced at the older man, who seemed to have a mischievous gleam in his eyes. He started back toward the door, this time counting his steps in his head. Here he paused, then he took a spent cartridge from his jacket pocket and set it on the hardwood floor. Immediately it began to roll toward the back wall, picking up speed until it bounced off the leg of an old workbench and came to a halt. David's smile seemed to widen, but still he said nothing as Jack went over and picked up the brass casing. Then, he placed it on the workbench, but it didn't move. He gave it a little shove, but it only rolled a few inches and stopped.

"It's an optical illusion. The whole building slopes downward!"

"Yes!" David almost shouted and was about to continue when Jack interrupted him.

"Something else—there is more to this structure than just this room."

David could contain himself no longer, and he actually clapped his hands, exclaiming at the same time, "Oh, you're quick, Jack. I didn't expect you would notice that right away. What tipped you off?"

"Well, it was more of a feeling, really. On my first pass through the room, I was looking at the worktables and their contents, not paying much attention to the actual size of the room, and I almost walked right into the back wall. Something told me this was strange—it seemed like there should have been a lot more space, as if my subconscious had taken in the outside of the building, and it didn't match the inside."

Jack looked at the older man and blushed. He had come to rely quite a bit on his own intuition over the years, and mostly it had served him well, but he realized that it would probably sound almost superstitious to this learned man.

Yet David clapped his hands again and shouted excitedly, "Right! You're exactly right, my boy." It was as if Jack was his student and he had finally grasped the meaning of the universe.

Suddenly, light dawned on Jack's face, and he said almost in a whisper, "It's a decoy."

"Well," David began, "not entirely. This room has its uses. I like to tinker around in here. I don't know how much my daughter has told you about me and my little hobbies, but I sort of fancy myself an engineer of sorts. My passion is green energy. Do you know what that is, Jack?"

"I think so," Jack replied cautiously. "You mean like windmills and such?"

The twinkle returned to David's eyes as he said, "And such. But come, it's easier to show you than to try an explain."

He walked to the back wall and pushed lightly with the palm of his hand. A secret panel sprang open, revealing a sliding handle. David pulled it sideways, then stooping down and placing his hand under the wall, he said to Jack, "Shade your eyes a little; it will be bright in here."

Jack obeyed, and with a low grunt David pulled; the whole wall seemed to rise up before him.

Light streamed into the small room, and for a moment Jack was blinded, but his eyes adjusted quickly, and David hurried him forward, saying, "I don't like to leave this open too long. You never know who might happen by and look in."

Jack stepped forward while David grabbed a chain and, by pulling downward, slowly lowered the wall back into place. From this side Jack could see that it was nothing more than a huge door that slid upward into a recess in the wall, then he opened another panel on this side of the door and slid the latch back into place.

"There we are, nice and cozy," David said. "Welcome to our greenhouse."

Jack stared around him with awe. He had seen greenhouses before; his sister had even had one—but these were usually fragile, even temporary structures used mostly to germinate plants in the late winter or early spring to give them a head start on the short summer months. This was so far removed from anything Jack had ever seen or could even imagine that for a moment he felt as if he had slipped into the past and into one of the giant buildings of the long-dead cities. The whole ceiling was made of glass, and the late-morning sun was shining through brilliantly. The reason he hadn't noticed it from the outside was because most of the green house was level with the ground; although the trees had been cut back to let the sun in, the entire back of the structure was surrounded. It was at least forty degrees warmer in here and so humid that water droplets clung to everything. Everywhere you looked there were growing things; the very walls seemed to be made of plants. To his right was a row of five or six trees, their branches weighed down with what looked like oranges.

David noticed his gaze and said, "Ahh, yes, you have arrived just before harvest." Walking over to the nearest tree, he pulled one of the ripe ones off and tossed it to Jack, who almost missed it in his agitation. "Try one!" David exclaimed "They're exceptional—better than any you ever got in a market."

In fact, Jack hadn't even seen an orange in twenty years, much less tasted one. He was so stunned that he couldn't speak. In his hand was something that most people in this part of the world had never seen, and there were hundreds of them just waiting to be picked not five feet away.

"But how?" he whispered, feeling more and more like he was still asleep and having the most amazing dream of his life.

David seemed not to even notice his confusion and had already began to explain in a voice: slightly tinged with excitement "It's completely self-sufficient, heated by the sun, unlike the main house. You may have noticed the two turbines or windmills out behind the stables? I designed them myself, and they are what power the lights and electric furnace. The problem is, there is no way to store wind energy, although I have been experimenting with a battery of sorts." Here he paused, noticing for the first time the look of utter disbelief on the other's face. "Jack," he said, smiling and putting a hand on the younger man's shoulder. "I know this must seem so strange to you. In my excitement I fear I have done just what I warned you about: starting at the end of the story. You asked me if I had a cure for the plague, and the answer is yes—but it's much more than that!"

Now he gripped Jack by both shoulders, his eyes fixed directly on his face. They seemed to glow with an excitement he could barely contain. "What I possess—my little secret if you will—may someday have the potential to cure not just people, but the entire planet!"

Now David turned, and he paced up and down like a preacher about to give a sermon. "Jack," he started, "you have lived your whole life in the US. What have you observed about the climate?"

Jack thought for a moment and then said, "It's getting hotter. The winters are shorter."

"Yes!" David exclaimed as if he knew what Jack would say before he said it. "But why?"

Jack only shook his head at this, so David said, "We'll come back to that. What about the people? Why is the population decreasing at such an alarming rate? Well, I guess they're all leaving, moving north to the colonies. They can't sustain a crop anymore because of the drought, and unless you live near a large river, you would starve. Yet here in my greenhouse and in my garden, plants are thriving. How do you explain it?"

For a moment Jack thought hard about something he had been turning over in his mind ever since he had arrived in the north. Finally, he thought he had it: "The climate has changed here also. Just as it has gotten warmer in the US, it has gotten warmer here." Then he added, "That's probably why people are thriving in the colonies."

David sat down on a short bench and rested his keen gaze on Jack. "You're right, but you're only half right. The colonies are enjoying a brief period of prosperity, but it can't last. According to my research, they will also be gone within the next one to two hundred years."

Jack stared incredulously. "Gone? You mean abandoned?"

"Yes." David sighed. "Unable to sustain life."

"But that soon?" Jack managed to say, thinking of all the abandoned farms he had passed on his trek eastward.

"Yes, that soon," David replied, standing and putting a hand on Jack's shoulder. Then he smiled and, raising his arms, said, "That's where my little experiment comes in."

Jack looked around. "Have you found a secret? Something nobody else has thought of?"

"Yes, or maybe I have found something nobody dreamed existed." David gave him a second to digest this and then once again grasped Jack by the shoulders, "Our world is dying, Jack. It's happened before, but in a normal cycle—or should I say, if past cycles are any indication—we should be on the verge of a mini-ice age. History shows that mankind could survive that catastrophe, but somehow this time, the cycle has been broken. The earth isn't cooling but continuing to get warmer—and at an alarming rate. Combine this with the plague, and the relatively low birth rate, I believe it could be the end of us as a species.

"Maybe that isn't such a bad thing—the Lord knows that we have been deplorable housekeepers. But what I have here, what I have discovered right under my nose, could change all that. What I possess could literally convert the planet back to the way it was five hundred years ago!" Jack just stared at the older man, stunned into silence.

"Don't you see? This greenhouse is like a nursery that may well be the beginning of a whole new world!"

These last three words had an effect on Jack like getting hit with ice water. How many times in his relatively short life had he heard men talk about a whole new world? A better world? Sometimes it was the world of their ancestors; sometimes it was a man-made utopia in which the government provided for all its people. Jack was no visionary, but he knew well that this type of thinking was what had brought mankind to the brink in the first place; it was this type of thinking that his father had died fighting against.

David seemed to detect this change in his demeanor, and slowly he released Jack's arms and stood back, looking almost embarrassed.

"Well," he said, at last glancing sideways at Jack, "sometimes I do get carried away on the subject."

Jack smiled. He did like this man; there was nothing arrogant in him. He had no visions of world domination—if anything, he seemed to have a touch of that same naivety that was so prevalent in his daughter.

"So, what is it?" Jack inquired, trying to bring the conversation back to the present.

"What is what?" David asked as he had recovered himself. He was leading Jack back to the huge door/wall and was trying for the first time to seem indifferent.

"Your little secret," Jack said. "What is it?"

David stopped his hand on the door latch and, turning his head, he said slyly, "Why Jack, I was sure you could have guessed it by now." With one motion he threw the huge door open, and there, silhouetted by the light coming through the small door of the shop, stood Annie.

# CHAPTER 12

"I thought I might find you here," Annie said, walking forward and taking her father's hands. "So, Jack, has Daddy shown you his little project?"

Jack glanced at David, who didn't show any signs of agitation.

"Yes, we have been to the greenhouse," he said.

"Didn't I tell you he knew everything?" she said, turning her face to Jack.

A nod was all he could manage; his mind seemed to have momentarily left him. David leaned down, kissed her on the cheek, and inquired: "Where have you been hiding yourself this morning, little girl?"

"Well, I went down to the village to see some friends, but on my way back, I ran into Jacob. I invited him to dinner tonight."

Jack thought this a little odd, seeing that up to this point, Annie had done her best to avoid the man—but he said nothing.

David, however, said that he thought it a splendid idea and that he would invite Blake as well in order to get their perspective on her little adventure into the south.

It was a sunny day and the temperature had risen enough to melt some of the snow. Arriving at dusk as he had, Jack had gotten only a vague impression of the property, enough to know that it was the place he had dreamed about, but that was all. Now, in the broad daylight of morning, he could make out at least five different structures. One, Jack knew, was the barn. Another seemed to be a smaller version of the main house. The building that they were walking toward was a wide, short structure, the back half of which seemed to disappear into the trees, making it virtually unapproachable from any direction save the front. A low fence had been constructed around the front of the building; its obvious purpose was to keep out small animals and not people. David unlatched a little gate, and Jack saw the reason. They were standing in the fall remnants of a pretty good-sized garden. A stone path, about four feet wide, led the way from the gate to the front of the building, where it ended in front of a small wooden door with iron hinges and an iron bolt. This bolt was secured with the largest padlock that Jack had ever seen, and he had time to reflect as David produced the key from a ring in his coat pocket. It was funny that such strong hardware had been installed on what seemed like such a flimsy wooden door. The lock looked very old, but the key turned easily enough, and the huge lock sprang open. Before opening the door, David took a small lantern that was hanging on a hook beside it and struck a match.

"Very dark in here," he commented. "There are no windows in this building." David pushed open the little

David turned, secured the door, and taking Annie by the hand, started out of the workshop. Jack followed them, but he heard no more of the conversation.

His mind kept going back to what David had said. "It was Annie—she was his little secret!" Somehow, all of the amazing things that Jack had seen were tied to her. He was pretty sure that she didn't even realize it. If this was true, then it seemed to Jack that David was being unfair and almost cruel to his daughter. Was she to be just another scientific experiment to him? Surely not. He had seen the love for her in the older man's eyes. He couldn't make himself believe that David would ever intentionally hurt her. Still, he wondered if Annie had ever heard her father refer to her as "my little secret." Jack looked at the two figures walking about ten feet in front of him—they made a nice picture. Beside David, Annie looked more like a little girl than ever as she walked along, holding the big man's hand and laughing at something he had said. "How could there be any dark secret between these two?" he wondered. "And if there were, why would David let him in on it?" All the way back to the big house, Jack argued with himself.

As they reached the front porch, Annie turned and waited for him as her father continued into the house. "Will you take a walk with me, Jack? It's such a beautiful day; I thought I could show you the rest of place."

"I'd like that," he said, taking her arm in his they headed off toward the stables. "I've been thinking a lot about what you said last night, you know, when we first got here."

"Yes, I know," she said. "It wasn't fair of me to leave you…hanging like that, but sometimes my heart speaks when it should be silent."

Jack looked down at her and she met his eyes. She saw the concern in them and smiled as she continued. "However, as much as I wish it would be silent sometimes, it always speaks the truth."

To Jack it was as if a weight had been lifted from his shoulders, and it showed perceptibly. Still, he wasn't sure how to proceed, and for a moment they walked on in silence. As they reached the stables, Annie endeavored to help him.

"The truth is, Jack," she said, turning to face him, "everything happened so fast. From the time we first met until arriving here, we have practically been running for our lives. Everything was happening in a rush, and although you have begun to know me, there is still a lot you don't know."

"I know all I need to know," he interrupted, but she put a finger to his lips, saying: "Let me finish."

They entered the building and Annie walked over to the little black-and-white who nuzzled her warmly. "I'm not trying to play down any feelings that we have for each other, Jack. In truth, although you don't yet realize it, we have known of each other long before we met in person."

She paused, waiting to see if he would dispute this, but when he said nothing she went on. "Anyway, now that I'm home and safe with you in the same house, I don't feel as…rushed. Do you understand?"

He thought he did, but true to his nature, he waited for her to tell him. "We have time now, Jack—time to get to know each other. And time for you to learn to accept some things that, right now, might still be hard for you to understand."

"You mean your...abilities?" he said, thinking this was the wrong word but unable to think of a better.

Smiling at him she said, "See there? You're not even sure how to talk about it."

"Show me how, then," he said. "I want to understand; I want to be a part of your world."

"Oh Jack, you already are, but it's best that you take it in gradually and not all at once. Remember how you felt when you saw me throw the fish from the river?" Before he could answer, she went on. "There was nothing wonderful about that; it wasn't magic—yet you were afraid. I saw it in your eyes, but I knew that if I gave you time, you would try and understand."

"I am trying, Annie, but what does any of this have to do with our feelings for each other? You must know how I feel about you...and last night."

"Last night I told you the truth, Jack! I do love you, and nothing can change that. So let's just enjoy it, and in the meantime try and remember the little girl, your friend that would sometimes come to you in your dreams at night."

Jack's eyes grew large, and he stared agape at her as she smiled and nodded her head. "Yes, it was me, Jack."

There was a slight noise, like a twig snapping behind him, and Jack whirled around, the Colt fairly jumping into his hand. Annie gasped, and Blake, who had been listening to their whole conversation from his hiding place in the last stall, stepped out into view.

Holding his hands up and slightly out in front of him, he said, "Careful with that thing, Jack."

Annie, who had some inkling of Jack's ability but had never actually seen him in action, stood dumbstruck, unable to speak. Jack didn't notice this as he had his back to her, still training the gun on Blake's chest.

He said, "I am always careful. What were you doing back there?"

Blake lowered his hands and answered cautiously, "I work here, Jack."

He knew there was more to it than this, but thinking it was the wrong time to confront him with Annie standing behind him, Jack holstered the gun.

Blake smiled and turned to go, but Jack checked him, saying: "A little friendly advice."

Blake didn't turn, but he paused in the doorway, looking up at the sky. Jack continued, "I'm probably the last person in the world you would want to sneak up on."

"I'll keep that in mind," Blake said as he walked off, chuckling to himself.

Turning back to Annie, he was surprised to see her staring at the old revolver, her eyes even larger than normal. She didn't seem to be breathing. Jack took a tentative step toward her, and she seemed to flinch. Her eyes moved slowly to his face and her voice came out in a whisper.

"Jack?"

"Annie, what…?"

"How?" she started again, and then, looking back at the holster with the big J. B. stenciled on the side, asked: "Is it alive?"

Suddenly he understood, and it was his turn to smile. He had seen similar reactions before, but very few people who had seen him draw had lived to tell about it. Annie, whose only experience with firearms was limited to their use in bringing down game, was naturally affected by an action that he had learned to take for granted. It occurred to him that she might be feeling to a lesser degree the way he had the day he saw her catch the fish.

Taking her slowly by the hand, he said, "I guess you're not the only one with a few tricks up her sleeve."

For a few seconds, she continued to stare at him, not understanding. Then she relaxed, laughing nervously at the irony of the situation.

The rest of the morning was spent showing him the grounds around the old homestead, introducing him to people that lived and worked there. They ended up in the Cree village, which was situated less than a quarter mile northeast of the house. Jack had been in native villages before, but there was something different about this one. More than prosperous, it thrived, and he saw no sickness or hunger. In fact, everyone Annie introduced him to—which must have been most of them—seemed happy and healthy. When they first arrived, a group of children had run up to them, gathering around Annie, saying one word over and over: "Matisoon! Matisoon!"

When Jack asked her what it meant, she just shrugged her shoulders and said, "It's just the children's pet name for me."

It was late in the afternoon when they started back to the house, and as they approached it, Jack had a thought.

"Annie, what has changed your attitude toward Jacob?"

"What do you mean?"

"I mean, when we were traveling, you barely gave him the time of day, and this morning you invite him to dinner."

"Oh, I don't know. It's not that I don't like him; it's just that sometimes when he looks at me, I get uncomfortable—it's like he's looking through me into my soul. And I don't like him calling me Little Mother! But when I came upon him this morning, he looked so sad, and it came to me that I had probably been too hard on him."

"You say he looked sad?"

"Well yes, in a way, but that was just part of what made me look at him differently. I came into his camp completely by accident, and he was sitting with his back to me. So I was just going to pass by when guess who greeted me?" Jack looked at her questioningly. "Wolf! He has been staying with Jacob since we got here. Anyway, we talked for a few minutes about nothing important, and I asked him to come to dinner. He seemed pleased that I invited him and said he was sorry if he had caused me any worry. Then I started off expecting Wolf to follow as he always does, but when I looked back, I saw that he had laid down beside Jacob. I thought, 'Well, if Wolf can trust him, so should I.'"

Jack laughed. "You think Wolf is a better judge of character than you are?"

"Well…he likes you," she replied, pushing him playfully.

"Yeah, but if you remember, the first time we met he wanted to rip my throat out."

"I may have let him do it too had I known then how much you were going to tease me," she said, smiling mischievously.

Suddenly he caught her up and, holding her close, said, "Too bad. Then I would have never been able to do this." He kissed her tenderly then slowly let her slip back to the ground.

That evening as they sat down to dinner, one guest was mysteriously absent. David had looked everywhere that afternoon for Blake but had been unable to find him. "It's so strange," he said more to himself than anyone in particular. "He seems to have left the country entirely."

Jack and Annie exchanged a look, but neither spoke.

So David asked if they had seen anything of him on their tour of the compound. Jack glanced again at Annie, who only shrugged her shoulders and said, "I think he was down at the stables when we went by earlier."

"Huh, very strange," David repeated but showed no desire to pursue the subject further.

The food wasn't fancy, but it was cooked to perfection, and Jack congratulated Kitchi more than once on his culinary skills. David meanwhile was engaged in finding out more about Jacob, and "his people." Jacob, stoic as usual, was doing his best to respond to his questions in short, vague sentences, glancing nervously at Jack now and then for help. But Jack, who was half amused at Jacob's discomfort, waited until the meal was nearly over to let him off the hook. He did this by bringing up a subject that he knew was near and dear to David's heart—namely, his greenhouse.

Jack said, "I was really impressed by your greenhouse today. I've seen smaller ones, but they were just temporary structures. Yours looks as if it has been there for a hundred years."

At this statement Annie smiled and rolled her eyes at her brother, who immediately stood and began clearing the dishes. Annie also stood and said she would get the coffee and dessert.

This sudden exodus by his children only made David chuckle, and turning to Jack he said, "It would seem that my own family has had their fill of their dinner, as well as this subject. It is fortunate for me, however, that you two gentlemen haven't known me long enough to be bored with my sermons."

Sometimes David's way of talking gave you the idea he was talking down to you, and Jack could see that it made Jacob a little uncomfortable. But as he went on, his speech lost its haughty tone, and both he and Jacob were somewhat taken aback by what he had to say.

He began by describing the variety of plants that he had accumulated over the years and how he had come by them. It seemed that most could be found in the colonies, but some he had imported from other countries.

This highly interested Jack, who asked, "You mean from the US?"

"Most of them." David said, stroking his beard and looking up at the ceiling. "But at least two came all the way from the UK."

"You mean from England?" Jack asked, hoping he didn't sound as stupid as he felt.

David answered his question with one of his own. Folding his big arms over his chest, he eyed the two men gravely before asking: "What do you know of the old world, boys?"

Jack thought for a moment. "Just stories I've heard from my mother and uncle, plus what I have seen in some of the old cities."

"And what have you seen?" David asked, looking sharply at Jack.

"Well, not much really. Most of them were crumbling into dust, and it can be dangerous to walk about in them. Nobody lives in them; some people even believe they're haunted."

David chuckled. "And so they are," he said. "But do you know how it all came about? The end of that world, I mean."

"Well, my uncle always said it was the sun that killed the cities and that when the people left them, they became infected with the plague."

"Vague," David interjected, "but not entirely untrue. You see, the cities and the people who lived in them were highly dependent on the technology of the time. It's true enough that this aspect, of their world, or at least part of it, was destroyed by what are called 'coronal mass ejections,' though that in itself would have only been a temporary setback. You see these 'CMEs' were only one factor in a series of events that led us to where we are today. Long before the sun put an end to technology, the earth itself had been going through some major changes. The main concern was that the planet seemed to be warming at an alarming rate—not that it was happening overnight, but it was happening. There was a big debate at the time as to whether human beings, with all of their technology, were the cause of this 'global warming.' Well, they never were able to come to an agreement on the matter, and after the sun spat out its lethal dose of cosmic rays, they had more pressing things to worry about.

"Back then there were nearly seven billion people on the planet, boys. Can you imagine—seven billion?! Shoot, there were over three hundred million in the US alone."

Jack tried to wrap his brain around these figures. He knew what a million was all right, but the word was usually used to imply some idea of the infinite, as in, "There must be a million stars out tonight." He couldn't even fathom three hundred million, and the word billion had no meaning at all to him.

"Surely the plague couldn't have killed them all," he said. "And what about us? We are still here, and healthy babies are born every day. Was it the walking sickness?"

"Ah…the plague," David said. "That is a subject of great controversy, even today. You see, the plague you speak of, the one that started in the US a few years after the sun flares, was a very different thing to what we call the 'walking sickness' today. But I will tell you more of that in its turn. The original plague, or the 'black death' as it was called at the time, was simple enough to understand—it had even happened before. It was caused simply by the living conditions in the great cities. The medicine at the time was fairly effective at curing it, at least in healthy people. But either because of their inability to survive outside their technological bubble or their almost total dependence on the government, millions of people perished without any knowledge of why."

"But what about the rest of the world?" Jack wanted to know. "Could something like that affect the whole planet?"

"I suppose under some circumstances it could have," David went on. "But it didn't, because as I said, it was caused mostly by the unsanitary conditions in the big cities. I'm sure that there were, and still are, people that live in places, like remote regions of Africa, that were entirely unaffected by it. How it spread so quickly through Europe and Asia is where the controversy comes in. Back in the early twenty-first century, the United States was really the only superpower left in the world and had pretty much appointed itself as the world's police force. The result was that they became very unpopular; they had many enemies. Terrorism around the world was rampant, and some governments, especially in the Middle

East, began to fold in on themselves. Radical groups were taking over, and it was all that the American government could do to protect their own people. So when the first sun flare hit, there were some that believed that it was just another act of terrorism, even though there had been a few good men that had been warning of the impending cataclysm for years. Anyway, to make a long story short, when everything started to collapse, the US government—which by the way, had already begun to fracture—felt threatened on all fronts. It was rumored that a certain faction of the government took the notion that if the great and powerful United States of America were to fall, it should take as many of its enemies as possible down with them. So either by accident or design, a new kind of plague began to circulate, and this one went global."

Jack and Jacob had been enthralled in this story, and the latter hadn't spoken for the last ten minutes, but now he said thoughtfully: "You mean the walking sickness."

"Exactly!" David exclaimed. You see walking sickness is a completely different animal from the normal plague outbreaks in the past, and what I can tell you about it is mostly conjecture on my part—a guess, if you will. First, I'm convinced it was created in a laboratory somewhere and probably in a hurry considering how it has mutated over the years. Second, I think it must originally have been an airborne virus or maybe it was introduced into the water supply—it doesn't really matter at this point. Suffice it to say that the original version only killed about a quarter of the population; either some people were immune or they just weren't infected in the first place. From what I gather there was a period of about two years when it seemed to vanish completely, then it came back with a vengeance—only it had mutated into what we have today. Again, I'm only speculating, but my best guess based on what little research I've done is that it's become part of the human genome. I read somewhere that up to eight percent of our DNA consists of remnants of ancient viruses."

"This is all way over my head," Jack said. He was beginning to understand why Annie had left in such a hurry.

"In a nutshell," David went on, "human beings are all pretty much built the same. Still, some people are more susceptive to illnesses such as cancer or the flu, and as I believe now the walking sickness—all because of a very small variation in our basic make up." For about a minute, nobody said anything. Jack for one was more puzzled than ever—if what David was saying was true, how could it ever be cured? Finally David broke the silence, saying: "At any rate, after it all went to hell in a handbasket, I'm sure there were attempts in all countries to shore up their losses, but you must remember—not just the US but the entire civilized world had been highly dependent on technology for everything, from making coffee to running their war machines. Add to this the civil unrest caused by illness and famine in many of these countries, and any outside threats became secondary. Over the next hundred or so years, some governments closed up shop entirely, while others, like in the US, seemed to totter almost on the brink."

Jack was looking down into his empty cup, trying to digest everything that David had said, when something occurred to him. "But how do you know all this? And what about this place? You have managed to retain some of that technology. What of things like coffee and canned goods? These things must have come from someplace, with the ability to produce them on a large scale. Plus, even the settlement down in Fort Simpson had ammo for my thirty-thirty. If I remember correctly, they even had a sort of mail service."

"It's true," David went on, hardly waiting for Jack to finish his statement. "Things are still quite civilized in some regions of North America, but for the most part these regions are above the forty-ninth parallel—that is to say, in what was once Canada. For all intents and purposes, the United States has no governing body. The last vestiges of that were snuffed out with one bullet."

Here he paused, studying Jack's face for any reaction, but seeing nothing to make him feel he had hit a nerve, he continued. "Even if that shot had never been fired, it was inevitable that the government would have become…unnecessary, shall we say?"

Jack made no comment on the subject, so David only said, "Well, I for one say good riddance to bad rubbish! As for who has been driving the carriage for the last four years, I don't know. Maybe someone picked up the reins, but information has been sporadic at best. You probably know more about that than I do, Jack."

"No, not really. When I left Denver, there was still a community there. But the mail had stopped running, and a lot of people were packing up and moving north."

"Yes, that seems to be the trend," David said. At that point, Annie and Kitchi came in with pie and coffee.

As Annie poured him a cup, he asked, "But if the US has stopped producing things, where do you get your own supplies? Like Annie's jacket, for instance."

"My jacket came from the colonies last spring." Then, turning to her father, she said, "It was a birthday present along with my bracelet." She held it out for Jack to see.

Jack smiled at her and said, "It's very pretty."

He directed his next question to her. "But how is it that the colonies have the resources and the people to produce such things?"

Annie sat down beside him and asked, "Have you never been there, Jack?"

"I haven't. You see, when I came north, I had the vague idea of going there first, but I came up through what my map said was Alberta. If I understand correctly, the colonies are a good deal east of there."

"Yes, they are in what used to be called Ontario. Isn't that right, Daddy?"

David's attention had been temporarily drawn from world events to the huge piece of pie that Kitchi had set before him, but he shrugged and managed to say between bites, "Yes, for the most part."

For a few moments, the talk was suspended entirely as they all turned their attention to dessert. Jack savored every bite of his pie, which turned out to be apple—it was the first he had tasted since leaving his uncle's ranch. When he had finished, he turned to Kitchi and complimented him on it.

"Oh, I don't bake," he said, "unless you count biscuits. Annie made this herself."

Annie smiled at his half-questing, half-teasing look and said, "Yes, Jack, I can cook something other than rabbit stew and fish."

This statement produced a playful argument between brother and sister over who was more adept in the kitchen, which was only interrupted by Jacob inquiring where they got the apples.

This brought David back into the conversation. "Ah yes, Jacob—you haven't had the privilege of seeing our greenhouse; perhaps tomorrow I could give you a tour. Your friend Jack here was very impressed."

Jacob thanked him and said he would very much like to see it himself, which brought Jack's mind back to what they had been previously discussing.

Addressing David he said, "You mentioned England—are there still a lot of people in Europe?"

David took his last bite of pie and studied Jack over his coffee before he answered.

"There is one government that has managed to survive and even thrive at times over the last two hundred years. You see, shortly after the plague broke out in Europe, jolly old England reverted to its original monarchy—how or why, I don't know. But what it came down to was that this monarchy, instead of fighting to hang on to the old technology, had the foresight to put aside what they lost and began almost immediately to use the tools they had left. By doing this they were able to preserve their infrastructure, at least to a degree. This gave people hope, and to put it simply, they were able to unite the populace. As a result, they adapted more quickly than the rest of the world. Oh I'm sure it wasn't easy, and it most assuredly didn't happen overnight, but somehow they managed to hold things together. They have railroads and steamships just as they did in the late nineteenth century and they are self-sufficient. It's only been in my lifetime that they have ventured out of their own country. When they did, they found need for their goods and services, as well as trade, in the colonies. I suspect the United States would have done the same if they had been united under one system. But as we know, that didn't happen; instead, the government tried to rein the people in, confiscate their firearms, and generally pin them down. America was ripe for civil war even before the catastrophe. It was a societal problem. The populace had become too dependent on their leaders." David sighed and looked down at his coffee. "Someone once said, 'A democracy is only as strong as its weakest link.' You see, a democratic society is a great idea as long as its people tend to it. But once that society becomes complacent, starts…relying on the government to take care of them, they usually end up paying for it with their freedoms. It's happened before. Ancient Greece comes to mind as one example, but that's just one old man's opin- ion. Anyway, to sum it up, not all of America's citizenry felt this way. Some—a minority, it turns out—were fed up with the situation and rebelled. The result, as you know, was the War of the States, which as far as I know is still going on to this day in one form or another. Your own father, Jack, was one of these 'freedom fighters.'"

Jack stared at the older man for a moment and then, shaking his head, said, "No, my father only wished to protect what was his. He and his gang were considered outlaws."

"Well," David interjected, chuckling a little at these words, "Aren't all people who would stand up to tyranny considered 'outlaws' by the government they oppose?"

Jack said nothing. His mind whirled with these new ideas that David had introduced, and he wished for a little time to put them all in order. Annie came to the rescue.

Standing, she held out her hand to Jack and said, "I believe I'll be going to bed now. I got up too early this morning."

Then, kissing her father's cheek, she retired to her own room. Jacob also stood, saying he would return in the morning to see David's greenhouse. He let himself out and started toward his own camp, much troubled by some of the things he had heard.

Kitchi yawned loudly, but instead of bidding him good night, David asked the boy if he would brew more coffee and bring it down to his office. Then, turning to Jack, he said, "Will you join me for a smoke?"

Jack, who knew he wouldn't be able to sleep and did not want to do anything to upset his host, followed the older man down the hall to his sanctuary.

Taking the opportunity to stretch his legs, Jack strolled around the office, looking at nothing in particular. He noticed that David had hung the old newspaper clipping back up on the wall over the leather chair and stopped to look at it.

David came up behind him and, placing a hand on his shoulder, said, "Good and evil are not always so discernible in these situations, Jack. When you shot Judge Marcus back in Missouri…"

Jack spun on him, looking straight into his eyes with something like wonder.

"You knew?" he whispered, his breath coming out in a gasp.

"I told you, Jack, I have followed your and your father's careers closely."

"But you never said anything to Annie about it? About me?"

"Why would I? The better question would be, 'Why have I kept tabs on you and your father's doings for all these years?'"

He raised his eyebrows, and Jack saw that he was surprised that he hadn't asked this question before.

"Well?" Jack said, raising his own eyebrows in response.

"Well?" David sighed. "It's like I said before, deep down somehow I knew that one day our paths would cross, and we would be united in a common cause—a joint venture, so to speak, that must inevitably take place at some point." He turned and started back to his chair, beckoning Jack to follow.

Sitting down behind the huge desk, he smiled and said, "Bear with me a little longer, my boy, and the amazing David will prophesize about your future. But first, there is one last thing I would like to clear up on the matter of your father."

Jack said nothing but looked at David intently. Part of him wished to talk about anything else, but David continued. "Your father didn't realize it, just as you don't even now, but he was probably the last man left in the country capable of reuniting the states. He was very popular, and people would follow him. Just before he died, it was estimated that the Brooks gang alone had over three hundred members, and wherever he went, people sheltered him. Did you know that he was considered to be one of the most influential people in the country at the time of his death?"

Jack was astounded and he said, " by who" his eyes never leaving David's. "By his own government, for one. Why do you think they wanted him dead? After he was caught, thousands of people marched on the capitol, and I believe that with one word from the man himself, there would have been an uprising, and the government would have been overthrown. But for some reason—a reason he took to his grave, I'm afraid—he did everything in his power to avert it, and he paid the price with his life."

Jack thought he knew the reason, but he couldn't bring himself to state it just then.

"Well, that's all I will say on the matter as I see it upsets you, but I didn't want you going through life thinking that your father was a mere train robber or gangster. He was a good man whom I believe could have been great had he not been betrayed by some of those closest to him."

David took two cigars from a box on his desk and handed one to Jack. Then, leaning back in his chair, he said, "Now let us come to the heart of the matter and, I suspect, the answers to a lot of those troubling questions knocking around in that head of yours, Jack."

Kitchi shuffled in with the coffee and then excused himself, saying, "Don't keep the poor man up too late, father."

When he was gone, David resumed, "Remember what I said about the earth and how it seemed to be warming at an alarming rate?"

"Yes, but you also said that it was being caused by technology," Jack put in.

"No, I said there was a debate as to whether human beings and the technology of the twentieth century were causing it. The other side of the argument was, and still is, that earth's changes run in cycles and that this is just another in the long history of the planet. The problem with that theory, if it is true, is that by now the earth should be cooling—in fact it should be on the verge, as I told you before, of a mini ice age."

Jack could tell by the pause that David expected some kind of reaction to this statement, but he wasn't quite sure where the older man was going with this, so he remained silent.

David went on, obviously a little impatient at Jack's complacent attitude. "You see, the earth is very old—over four and a half billion years old, as a matter of fact. And during that time, it has gone from a frozen ice ball to a tropical rainforest and nearly back again, even before us humans inhabited it. But even during our short time here, there have been radical climate changes, hot to cold and back again. You might be interested to know that there was a mini ice age about a thousand years ago that probably had a hand in a plague, the first 'black death' that hit Europe hard in the mid-1300s."

Jack really wasn't interested, but he hoped that this was leading to something, so he tried to be patient.

"Anyway," David went on, "our problem now is that the earth isn't cooling—or at least I believe it isn't, and that could be a problem for the whole human race. The very last problem!"

# CHAPTER 13

The two men had talked—or rather David had talked, and Jack had listened—until nearly one in the morning. As a result, Jack, who was normally an early riser, found that the sun was well up when he finally rolled out of bed. Scratching his head, he tried to remember something of what David had said in that last couple of hours before they parted. But his mind, by that time, had been dull and full of his own thoughts, so David had only commanded half his attention. He remembered something about the wheat belt and the corn belt; something also about a climate shift that David said accounted for the drought in the US. Well, he was sure he would have the opportunity to hear it all again—once David got going on one of these subjects, there was no stopping him.

Looking around he noticed that this morning someone had placed a basin of water on the small table and there was a towel hanging on the back of a chair. He knew it had to have been Kitchi's handiwork. He had always prided himself on his own cleanliness, and it dawned on him that he had not had the chance to wash up yesterday. So he gave himself a sponge bath and put on the best shirt of the three he currently owned. As for pants, there was nothing to be done about that—he only had the one pair. He had been in the process of making another when his cabin had been burnt to the ground, along with everything inside it. "Maybe Annie has some buckskin lying around, or maybe we could go hunting later this afternoon, and I could get my own."

Thinking these pleasant thoughts, he hurried down the stairs to find her. There was no one in the kitchen. Apparently, he had missed breakfast, but he saw there was coffee on the stove and a few pieces of cold meat on a plate. Attached to the plate was a yellow piece of paper, and Jack couldn't help but smile as he read it: "Here's your breakfast, sleepy head. If you decide to get up today, I might let you take me riding."

Taking his coffee, he went out on the porch. There was a slight chill but nothing like it should have been at this time of year. Setting his cup on the rail, he walked down the steps. Glancing toward the stables, he wondered if Annie was already there. He didn't wonder long, however, as the next moment he heard her light step on the porch behind him.

"Thanks for the coffee," he said, his back still to her.

He heard her laugh and as he turned to face her, she said, "It is just impossible to sneak up on you!"

She stood on the second step, which brought her small figure roughly up to his own height. He stopped at the bottom of the landing, and their eyes met. She seemed to be studying him again, searching his soul—

something Jack still couldn't get used to. He loathed to take his eyes from hers.

Finally she said, "Would you take a ride with me? There is something I want to show you."

Jack nodded and held out his hand to her.

They started off toward the stables, Jack looking down at her from time to time but not speaking. He noticed that she was dressed much the same as she had been the first time he saw her, with the exception of the leather leggings under her dress. He momentarily wondered if they should grab some warmer clothes, just in case.

As if reading his mind, she said, "We won't be going far." Then looking up at him, she added, "We'll be back before supper."

They found the two horses in good shape but restless. They moved about nervously in their stalls, and Jack realized that these particular horses had probably never seen the inside of a barn. When Annie approached the little black-and-white, it calmed down immediately and tried to nuzzle her hair, which made her giggle.

Jack smiled. "How could anyone not love this woman?" he thought.

It was short work to get them saddled, and within half an hour, they were riding side by side across the big clearing toward the river. At first they rode in silence, both busy with their own thoughts, then Wolf passed them at a trot.

Annie shouted to him, "And just where have you been all morning, mister?!"

Wolf stopped and turned to her, shame faced, and she laughed, saying, "Ok, I can see you're busy—off with you."

But he didn't go far; instead, he seemed to content himself with staying just ahead of them, occasionally putting his nose in the air and then trotting off again. They watched him for awhile, Annie with that far-off look that sometimes came into her eyes. Then, as if awakening from a dream, she turned to Jack and said, "Did you say something?"

"No, I was just wondering what you were daydreaming about," he said, smiling but not looking over at her.

"Oh, don't pay any attention to me, Jack. Sometimes I'm just off in my own little world."

Jack turned to her, smiling, and said, "Ah, well, you'll have to take me with you sometime."

"I am," she replied sweetly. But there wasn't any humor in her eyes as she said it. "Did you and my father have a nice talk?" she asked, changing the subject. "I hope he didn't keep you up too late."

"Not at all," he replied. "Actually, I found what he had to say quite interesting."

Annie smiled and patted her horse. "Sometimes he can get carried away when it comes to his little experiments."

This was hitting close to the mark, and Jack wondered if David had told her about their conversations the day before.

"Do you help out? In the greenhouse, I mean." He was trying to sound only mildly interested.

For a moment she gave him a fixed look, then she faced forward and said, "Oh yes, I personally helped to plant everything in there. Once a month I apply a special plant food that he has invented." She paused a moment and then, smiling to herself, added, "Daddy doesn't like to get his hands dirty."

They had reached a narrow valley bordered on one side by the forest and the other by a huge rock outcropping. It looked to be at least a mile long and a hundred yards wide.

Suddenly, Annie stood in the saddle and, turning to Jack, said: "Race you to the end!"

Without another word she put her heel to the little horse and was off like a shot. Jack was taken off guard, and by the time he had caught up with her, she had passed into the forest and was winding along a small path that cut through the trees with Wolf right at her heels. She had slowed to a walk. Jack was catching up to her and they could hear the river not far away. They had gone only a short way when suddenly the trees opened up on a small circular clearing hemmed all around by dense forest. Mysteriously, Wolf melted back into the trees. Annie dismounted and turned to him; she was flushed and a little out of breath from their race.

"Do you know where we are?" she asked, her eyes bright with excitement.

"No," he said, his own eyes never leaving her face.

"This is where I was born."

For a moment he continued to stare down at her, entranced once again by her beauty. "It comes from inside her," he thought. Then with great effort he dropped his gaze and slid from the saddle. At first Jack noticed nothing special about the place. To his left he could just make out the bank of the river. The trees, mostly spruce, seemed to grow especially thick right here and formed an almost perfect circle. Then, for the first time, Jack noticed a behemoth of a tree. He wasn't sure how he had missed it before, as he had ridden right past it.

Slowly he walked toward it, and Annie was saying, "Isn't it wonderful?"

Jack could have thought of more appropriate words to describe it, like creepy or strange, but he held his tongue. Most of the trees surrounding the little clearing ranged in height from about twenty to thirty feet—but this tree was at least twice that and probably twenty feet in diameter. But that wasn't the strangest part! This was no spruce. As a matter of fact, Jack couldn't tell what it was. The whole trunk of the massive thing seemed to twist as it shot upward, as if at some point it had tried to turn itself completely around. The branches, which began to jut out just above its smaller cousins, made a canopy over the entire area. Jack imagined that in the summer, when it had all of its leaves, it would almost completely block out the sun. Kneeling, he picked up a handful of these leaves. They were huge, almost as big as his hand. They had all turned various shades of red, depending on their extent of decay. The floor of the clearing was completely carpeted with them to the depth of nearly an inch. Slowly he reached out and placed the palm of his hand against the mighty trunk, only to draw it back suddenly. It was warm! Annie had come up beside him, taking his arm and putting it around her shoulders.

Jack continued to stare at the monstrosity, but he asked, "What kind of tree is this?"

"I don't know. I have never seen another like it, but the native people won't come near it. They say it has been here forever and can never die."

"And you were born here?" Jack asked.

"Yes, and my mother died here, almost right where we are standing."

Jack unconsciously took a step backward, and Annie laughed. "She's not buried here."

"Let's walk down to the river; I bet the horses are thirsty."

As they approached the river, Jack noticed a little eddy not much different than the one in which Annie had shown him her little fishing trick.

Smiling to himself he asked, "Is this where you learned to fish?"

Annie turned and, giving him a little smirk, said, "Yes, and I can teach you how to do it if you have the patience, Mr. Smarty Pants."

For the first time in a long time, Jack laughed out loud. "Maybe later," he said. "I'm still trying to get over your ugly little tree back there."

Leaving her horse to drink in the little pool, she turned and walked toward him. Mischief in her eyes, she suggested, "You shouldn't talk about her like that, Jack. She might be angry with you!"

For only an instant, Jack thought she was serious, then she smiled, put her arms on his broad shoulders, and looked up into his gray eyes. "I'd hate to have to cut her down."

He was beginning to feel a little uncomfortable—this was a side of Annie that he had never seen and he wasn't sure he liked it. Her body language was different and her voice even seemed deeper, huskier. Every movement was purposeful, even sultry. Dragging his eyes from hers, he looked up at the sky. The day had become a dull, heavy gray, and he hadn't even noticed.

"How long had they been out here?" he wondered. "Hours? Days?"

He felt tired as if he could sleep for a week, and Annie still clung to him.

He managed to say, "I don't think anyone could cut down that monstrosity."

His voice sounded different, as if it came from inside a tunnel. He was looking down at her again, and now he felt something close to panic. Her eyes were wide dark-blue pools and he was drowning in them. Then, standing on her toes, she kissed him. Jack was too dazed to do anything but kiss her back. A fleeting thought crossed his mind: "She's draining my energy!"

"You know, Jack," she was saying, "we don't have to go back. We could stay here forever. Just you and I. Wouldn't you like that? I would belong to you and nobody else. Isn't that what you want?"

He heard his own reply come in a whisper: "Yes." And he saw her smile.

He felt that if she let go of him, he would simply fall over, and somewhere deep in the recesses of his fading consciousness, he heard Jacob saying, "She can belong to no one, Jack!"

With a supreme effort, he managed to look away, and although his body still felt so heavy, his mind seemed to clear a little. It was getting dark. Looking up again he saw that the clouds had begun to turn from gray to black. Then something seemed to snap in his mind, like the sound of a far-off rifle shot.

He managed to say, "No, a storm's coming. We have to hurry back."

Annie released him, but when she stood back for just an instant, he thought he saw a look of anger pass over her delicate features—it was gone as fast as it came, like a bolt of lightning. She turned to look at the river, and he could see that her hair was wet. He was starting to feel like himself again, and he realized that while they had been standing there for who only knows how long, a fine mist had enveloped the whole forest. They're clothes were starting to get wet, and the temperature seemed to have dropped by ten degrees!

"Annie," he said trying to keep his voice steady, "we have to go back. A storm is coming. We're already wet and we have no dry clothes."

Something was terribly wrong here—there was some danger that he couldn't see, and every nerve in his body seemed to be screaming, *"Run!"* At first she didn't appear to have heard him, and then slowly she turned. Her eyes had a vacant look that alarmed him even more.

She spoke in the same husky voice. "Nothing can harm us here, Jack. Stay with me." Then she spoke the three words that Jack always loved to hear: "I love you."

She was standing right before him again, and he felt his strength waver, but now he was on his guard.

"Don't you want me, Jack?" she said, her voice rising to a pleading tone.

Jack placed his hands on her shoulders and shook her lightly, saying, "Annie, snap out of it."

Like a flash, the anger returned. "You want to possess me, don't you? Just like everyone else! You can't live without me. Isn't that right?"

She had drawn close to him again, a mask of pure hatred on her face. Her breath, normally so sweet, was rancid like rotted leaves as she hissed, "C'mon Jack, take me. Take me right here!"

He slapped her—not a light tap either. He slapped her good. For a moment her eyes blazed again and her small frame seemed to convulse; for a moment every muscle became taught. Then she fainted. If Jack hadn't been there, she would have fallen to the forest floor, but he caught her lightly. Snow began to fall all around them as he carried her to the horses. Somehow he managed to get a foot in the stirrup and hoist them both up on the gray. Moving slowly and making sure the smaller horse was following, he started out of the clearing. The very air seemed electrified, and as he passed the huge tree, it felt as if an invisible barrier had grown up in front of him. The wind began to howl, and before he reached the grassy meadow, the snow was falling in sheets. Jack had been in the north for almost four years, and he was quite aware how fast a storm could blow in, but this seemed almost supernatural. Pulling his hat down to shield his eyes, he leaned over the small figure in front of him so as to protect her from the worst of it. The snow seemed to come from every direction, and despite doing everything he could, they were both beginning to be covered by it—neither of them had been dressed for a blizzard. He plowed on, but he knew they couldn't stay out here in the open much longer; he wasn't even sure he was going in the right direction. Within twenty minutes of leaving the small clearing, there were over two inches of snow on the ground, and Jack realized he had no idea which way he was headed.

He began to turn in the direction of the tree line when suddenly the horse reared. Jack was taken totally off guard, and both he and Annie were thrown to the ground. Both animals bolted and within seconds had disappeared into the blinding snow; he was bewildered at the sudden action of the horse, but he found he was unhurt. Immediately he went to Annie, who had fallen only a few feet away and took her in his arms. He could see nothing beyond a few feet, but slowly he stood and walked in the direction he thought the forest must be. It was their only chance! With Annie still cradled in his arms, he plowed on, head down, his hands becoming numb and his face being stung by the wind-driven snow. It seemed that he had been walking forever, without a tree in sight. Still he kept moving, because to stop meant the end for both of them. It was then that a voice seemed to come to him from out of the blizzard. He stopped, head still down, and listened.

"Jack, Jack—this way!" It was faint and barely audible over the wind, but…"Jack!"

Now he looked up in the direction he thought the voice was coming from. About twenty feet ahead and slightly to his right, he could just make out a shadow plunging through the storm. He called out, "Here! Over here!" But the figure seemed to be moving away from him. Jack started after it, wondering if he were just imagining things. Just when he thought he had lost it, the dark figure reappeared and it seemed to be beckoning him forward with its arms.

"Hurry, Jack! Almost there!" were the words he seemed to hear above the storm. Lowering his head, he walked faster, listening for the voice to direct him, but he heard it no more. He was still looking down when he realized that he was no longer plowing through snow— he was walking on dirt; looking around he saw that he had made it to the trees.

"It stopped snowing," he thought.

But that was impossible. Then turning around he understood: He saw that he had somehow stumbled into the perfect wind break. Behind him, the way he had come, the storm still raged on. On the other three sides, he was surrounded by solid rock, while above him snow swirled in every direction. He looked around for his mysterious savior, but there was no one there.

"All in my head," he thought.

Jack was weak and his mind seemed to be temporarily out of service. He was moving now more on instinct than anything else.

He looked down at the girl who lay limp in his arms and fell to his knees. Her lips had already begun to take on a bluish tint. Putting his ear against them, he thought he detected her breathing, but it was shallow—he had to get her warm and out of the damp clothes right away. Looking around he noticed a slight depression under one of the big boulders. He staggered to his feet, hoping that it would be deep enough to serve as shelter. It was a small opening, but once he had dug out the leaves and twigs that had accumulated inside, he was able to put Annie far enough under that she was sheltered entirely from the elements.

There were a few items that Jack always had on his person: his .45 was one, but it was of little use to them right now; the other was a small fire-making kit. It contained matches when he could get them and a small piece of flint just in case he couldn't. By now his hands were stiff from the cold, but he managed to pull these items from his pocket, hoping they had remained dry. There were three matchsticks left, but they seemed ok—if only he could find some dry wood. There had been a few small pieces under the rock where he had placed Annie, and using some dead pine needles from the same place as kindling, he managed to start a small fire with his second match. Then, walking around the enclosure, he gathered the driest pieces he could find and set them close to the small blaze. This done, he took his knife and cut pine boughs. By placing these against the boulder, he was actually able to make a small enclosure that sheltered them and the fire to some extent.

Now he turned his attention to Annie. He had made the fire as close to the opening as he could, hoping to warm the inside of the little den. It seemed to be working, but not fast enough. Both of them were still soaking wet, and by now the temperature was below freezing. Taking off his own jacket, he hung it as close to the fire as he dared and began to remove Annie's moccasins and leggings. Her dress was fairly dry, being made of deerskin, so he went to work massaging her hands and feet, which had also started to turn blue. For thirty minutes he did this, only stopping to put another piece of wood on the fire. Finally, he saw that the bluish tint was leaving her lips, and her breathing seemed more regular. He took down his jacket, which had become quite warm, if not entirely dry, from its place near the fire. He wrapped it around her legs and feet, then he hung her clothes in its place. There wasn't much else he could do for her.

They were so unprepared for this sudden storm. Once again, he cursed his own stupidity for going off without at least warmer clothes and a little food. Assuming he had gone in the right direction, they couldn't be more than a mile from the little village. He looked out through the trees. The snow was falling harder than ever, but at least the wind seemed to be dying down. He could try to make it back, but the thought of leaving Annie out here by herself made him shiver all over. For the first time, he took stock of himself and realized that he was still soaked; his feet felt like blocks of ice. No, they would have to stay here and hope the storm would blow itself out before the snow got too deep. He didn't hold much hope for this—the sky was still dark and he had no idea how late in the day it was. They would probably be out here all night and he needed to prepare for that. Looking back at Annie, he was relieved to see that the color had come back to her face and she seemed to be sleeping easily.

"When she sleeps, the snow flies," came drifting through his mind, and he shivered again. "Get it together, Jack." First he needed to find more wood—if the fire went out, they were done.

Finding the wood wasn't the problem—finding dry wood was. Now that the wind had died, the snow was falling straight down and was beginning to cover the floor of their little enclosure. Still he gathered what he could and cut a few more long branches from a large spruce to use on the makeshift shelter. Just when he was about to remove his own boots and warm his poor frozen feet, the miracle happened.

At least it seemed like a miracle at the time. He had just sat down near the fire and was placing the driest piece of wood onto the little blaze when a huge buck stepped out of the trees, not twenty paces to his right. He was too startled at first to even move. How many times had he wished to come across an animal like this when he had been out hunting? Sometimes he would go weeks without seeing so much as a track, yet this one had walked right into their camp! Later he would tell himself that the animal had been disoriented by the storm and had simply wandered in to get out of the worst of it, not sensing danger until it was too late—but what happened next he could never quite explain. As good a shot as he was, Jack would not, in the best of circumstances, be able to bring down a huge deer with a pistol. For one, his hands were numb; to draw quickly was out of the question. Still, he reached down and eased the .45 out of the holster, still holding the piece of wood in his left hand. As quiet as he was, the deer still detected the movement and turned its great head in his direction. If he would have fired just then, things would have turned out much differently, but his better instincts took over, and he realized that it would have been a waste of a bullet. He fully expected it to bound off the minute it saw him—incredibly, it did just the opposite. Slowly it took two steps toward him and stopped again. Still, Jack didn't fire; it was too surreal. He found the whole thing unexplainable. In the end he was so entranced that he probably would have let the animal walk right up and lie down by the fire if he hadn't heard a small voice whisper directly behind him.

"Shoot it, Jack!"

He fired. The deer jumped almost straight up and then fell dead where it had stood. Turning, he saw that Annie was awake. She had curled into the fetal position and had covered her entire body with his jacket. He laughed incredulously as she smiled wanly up at him. He felt once again that everything was right with the world.

# CHAPTER 14

Roughly twenty miles south and west of where Jack and Annie were fighting for their very lives, a solitary figure stood looking out a small window at the coming storm. He wasn't an especially imposing figure: average height, average build, and in fact, if you saw him in a crowd, your eyes might just pass right over him. But if you ever had the misfortune of actually meeting him face to face, you weren't likely to forget it—there was something about him that was almost unearthly, as if he were more spirit than flesh and blood. He had dark hair, which he kept tied neatly in a short ponytail, and dark eyes that stood out in stark relief against his pale face. One moment you might guess him to be middle aged, the next in his early twenties—even a simple change of expression seemed to transform him into a completely different person, as if there were multiple people inhabiting the same body. Yet for all of this, Andre was not without his attractions. For one thing he was highly intelligent. Having been educated in the colonies, he had a pretty good grasp of the world he lived in, both past and present. But probably his best attribute was his ability to remain completely calm in every situation. He never acted out of fear or anger. Where most men would lash out, Andre took time to reflect on the bigger picture; this was why people were willing to follow him, and that's exactly what he was doing now as he stared out the little window at the conglomeration of canvas tents and shanties: looking at the big picture.

It was his new bride that was the center of the problem, he thought. But how did she really fit into his plan? What he wanted was the cure for the plague and that blasted greenhouse. His initial plan that the father could be gotten to through the daughter had backfired—she had run away.

She was back now, but she seemed to regard their union with contempt and had even come home with some American. All of this Blake had told him yesterday when he had come over to the camp in a huff. It had taken Andre a good hour and a bottle of whisky to calm him down. The old man had dismissed him and treated him like a hired hand. This was Blake's complaint, and even though Andre could have pointed out that that was exactly what he was, he didn't. It was through Blake that he had learned about the goings-on over at the compound in the first place. So instead, he sympathized, he listened, and he consoled. The drunker Blake got, the more he realized that this Andre fellow was really the only friend he had in the world. He had been more than happy to tell him everything that had happened on their journey back to the house, and about how he had come upon Jack and Annie in the barn acting all lovey-dovey.

Andre played his part of the sympathetic friend admirably. Consequently, he knew almost as much about Jack Brooks as Annie's own father. For the first time, the little twitch had appeared over Andre's left eye. It wasn't that he feared this newcomer; he knew that he had enough firepower right under his feet to level David's whole compound—and with the return of Boris and the rest of the men this morning, he was sure he would have no trouble getting his little wifey back. No, these were not big problems; the real problem was getting David to cooperate. As smart as he was, he knew that if he simply killed the lot of them, all of the old man's little projects would be useless.

The storm was really getting bad. He could barely make out the camp not fifty feet away. "They must be freezing," he thought briefly, but he felt no concern. There were nearly a hundred of them out there—men, women, and children. For the life of him, he couldn't remember why he had brought them along in the first place. Some vague notion of safety in numbers, he supposed. Not that these people would be of any use to him in a fight—half of them had nearly died on the way here. If it hadn't been for David and the girl, they would probably be dead now, and part of him wished they were. They were always demanding something of him, and when it came right down to it, they were more of a liability than an asset. Well, what could he do? In the long run, it didn't matter. He would probably keep the ones that could prove their worth and get rid of the rest. "After all, who cares about them?"

Turning back to the little desk, he had a sudden thought. "Annie! Annie cares about them." And from what he had seen, the feeling was mutual. Taking a bottle and glass from his top drawer, he poured himself a drink before returning to the window. "Maybe these people will come in handy after all," he thought as he tried to make out the tent that was closest to the cabin. He could see nothing now—the storm was here in all its fury and it was a total whiteout. In his mind, though, everything had become perfectly clear.

# CHAPTER 15

The snow continued to fall throughout the night. Jack cleaned and skinned the huge deer. After procuring enough meat to get them through a couple days, he dragged the rest of the carcass as far from the camp as he could manage in the deep snow. He returned to find Annie completely dressed again in her now dry clothes and sitting close to the fire. He dropped his bundle and went to her.

"Are you ok?" he asked, not sure if she had fully recovered her old self.

"I am now," she said, smiling up at him, a slight tremor in her voice.

"You're still cold," he said and took up the huge deerskin, meaning to clean the inside the best he could before giving it to her as a blanket.

"I can do that," she said, taking out her pocketknife. "Please, I need to help somehow."

Jack handed it over and went about making them something to eat. Cutting off a hefty piece of venison, he placed it on a spit. He picked up a small piece of wood and, using the tip of his knife, began to hollow out a circle in the center.

Annie had been watching him and curiously asked, "What are you making?"

"Well, we won't go hungry," he replied, "thanks to either God or blind luck. Plus there is plenty of snow to melt if we get thirsty, but we need something to melt it in."

He showed her the makeshift cup and she laughed. "Jack, you're amazing! You think of everything!"

"Not really," he said. "If I had I would have brought one of the antlers back. It would have worked better and I wouldn't be ruining my best knife."

Neither of them had spoken about the incident that had brought them here; Jack was just happy to have her back to her old self—still, he wondered how much of it she remembered.

Finally he said, "Storm sure blew in in a hurry."

"Yes," she agreed, not looking up from her work. "Don't think I ever saw anything like it."

Jack paused for a moment and studied her. She seemed to be purposefully avoiding looking at him. Her hair had fallen down over her face, and she seemed intent only on her work.

"Annie," he said after a moment's silence.

Slowly she raised her head, and Jack could see that her eyes were full of tears ready to spill out at the slightest word from him.

"Well," he said, turning his attention back to the piece of wood, "I couldn't be happier about the situation. I've finally got you all to myself for awhile."

For the next hour, he talked about trivial things: his home and the people there; places he had been and things he had seen. Eventually Annie's mood seemed to lighten, but by the time they had finished eating and had tried out the homemade cup, she seemed exhausted. Finally she admitted that she was still a little tired might rest for awhile.

"Sure," he said, trying to hide the concern in his voice. He covered her with the deerskin and built up the fire. She was asleep almost immediately and Jack sat alone in front of the fire. The snow fell more lightly now, and looking straight up, he could even see a few stars glinting through the clouds.

Everything was really going to be ok, he thought, even though five short hours ago, he was sure they wouldn't live to see another day. Come to think of it, that was how it had been ever since he had first seen Annie in the little meadow near his cabin—one minute peril, the next minute bliss. He wondered if it would always be that way with her. Not that it mattered—he knew that as long as he had a breath left in him, he would be by her side, come what may. His thoughts turned to something she had said in her trance or whatever it was.

"You want to possess me, don't you, Jack? Just like everyone else."

He knew on some level that it hadn't been her talking, but he also realized that there was some truth in what she said—everyone that came into contact with her seemed to either worship her or covet her. Was he any different? He wasn't sure. What he did know was that he would take his own life before he caused her one bit of grief. Still, you could make the argument that he had done his share of worshiping over the last few weeks; the thought of it made him blush. Was her power over him that great? Before Annie, most women had tended to avoid him, and the ones that didn't would describe him as aloof or even cold; never had he professed his love. It wasn't in his nature to be overly affectionate, yet he had been fawning over Annie like a schoolboy with his first crush.

Part of his mind protested this by saying, "She hasn't exactly pushed you away, and who kissed who first?" Well, whatever came of it, he felt that his first priority was to protect her. But from what? Everyone? Everything? There were times when she seemed so vulnerable, like now; at other times she seemed to be beyond his protection.

Slowly a thought began to surface in his already overtaxed brain. "There are some things that not even you can protect her from." This thought didn't feel like his own, and for a moment he had a vision of that awful tree standing in the clearing by the river as a shiver ran through his entire frame.

Quietly he heard Annie say, "Jack, you can crawl in beside me—if you're cold, I mean."

Jack turned to her, wondering how long she had been watching him. "It is warmer under here, and there is no harm in sharing body heat."

"No, of course not," Jack stammered; then, placing another piece of wood on the fire, he crawled in beside her, putting his arms around her shoulders.

They both lay silent for a moment, and then Annie spoke. "It wasn't me, Jack—down by the river, I mean. It wasn't me that said those awful things. It was her!"

"Who?" he asked almost automatically.

"I'm not sure." she continued. "Before today she has only come to me in my dreams, but this was different. It was like she was inside my head controlling my actions but not my thoughts. I could see everything as if I was watching from inside myself, but I was powerless to stop."

Jack stirred uncomfortably. "I'm sorry I slapped you, Annie."

"Jack," she said, rolling over to face him. "I told you it wasn't me."

She kissed him lightly and laid her head on his chest. Soon she was breathing heavily, and Jack knew she had gone to sleep. It was a long time before he finally dozed off.

It seemed like only a moment later he was awake, but he realized it had been hours when he noticed the fire was almost burned out. Annie still lay against him, her head on his chest. He knew he needed to stoke the fire yet couldn't bring himself to leave her side. Without really realizing what he was doing, he tightened his arms around her and kissed the top of her head. She stirred and with eyes still closed smiled up at him.

"Morning," she whispered, nuzzling closer to him. "Did you sleep?"

"Yes, but the fire is going out, so I need to get up."

"Ok," she said sleepily and rolled over as Jack slipped out of the little nest.

The morning air was cold and tiny ice crystals floated through the air. Jack walked out of the little rock enclosure that had been their salvation to find that although the snow was deep in places, the wind had blown most of it out of the clearing. He felt that if it was just himself out here, he could probably make it back to the house, but Annie wasn't dressed to walk two miles in subfreezing temperatures. He was pretty sure he could carry her, as light as she was, but the possibility was there that it may start to snow again. The chances of them finding another shelter along the way were pretty slim. On the other hand, they couldn't stay here indefinitely. His hands were already starting to freeze, so he took one last look around the clearing and started back to camp. Annie was awake but still huddled under the deerskin; only her wan face showed out at him.

"Did you find the horses?" she asked as he came toward the fire and squatted down.

Jack hadn't even been thinking about the horses—surely they were dead or dying, but he didn't say this to Annie.

"Oh, I'm sure they headed for home as fast as their legs could take them."

"Somebody will come looking for us," she said, pulling the fur tighter around her small shoulders.

Jack knew this was true, but he wasn't sure how long it would be. If the weather didn't hold, whoever came would be in more danger than they were. As he thought this, he glanced up at the sky and noticed that it was turning gray again. His eyes fell back to Annie, but she seemed to have gone back to sleep. He busied himself with fortifying the shelter. By midday it was snowing again; this time there was no wind and the snow fell in huge heavy flakes straight down, covering the ground right up to their little enclave. Jack would have liked to work some more on the deerskin, fearing it might start to rot, but Annie hadn't stirred, and he wasn't sure if he should wake her. Finally he went to work, making them a small meal and melting some snow, thinking that she would have to wake up at least long enough to eat something.

When he did wake her, she only drank a little water and refused to eat anything, saying, "I'm just so tired, Jack. I'm sure I will feel better tomorrow."

With that she rolled over and was almost immediately asleep. Something was wrong. In the short time that he had known Annie, she had never slept more than five or six hours at a time. In fact she had almost always been the first one in camp to stir—except once. Jack had been sitting close to the fire and gnawing on a piece of venison when it occurred to him that there had been one other time when she had slept in so long that he finally had to rouse her. It had been the night that she had that strange dream and Wolf had saved her from sleepwalking right into the river. The next morning, she had been hard to awaken and had in fact been drowsy the whole day. Eventually that night she had seemed to snap out of it; the rest of the journey she had been fine. Maybe these dreams or trances sapped her energy somehow. He went back to his supper, thinking he had solved at least one riddle about the girl who lay behind him. When he was done eating, he built up the fire and crawled into the little den next to her. thinking, "She'll be her old self in the morning."

But she was worse. He had gotten up, and after building the fire once again, he had gone out to find more wood that he could dry out. The snow had stopped sometime in the night but had left at least another foot on the ground. Jack found himself having to dig out some of the dead branches as he walked along. In the process he managed to scare up two snow hares and, if his hands hadn't been so cold, could have brought them both down. As it was, he did manage to cripple one, and he was glad to have something new to offer Annie for breakfast. As he struggled back to camp with his arms full of firewood, he held his prize out in front of him. He knew that the shots would have awakened her, and feeling a sense of pride in the fact that he was taking such good care of her, he was anticipating his reward—her beautiful smile—that would be all for him.

As the camp came into view, he saw that she still hadn't stirred, and an uneasiness settled over him. He came into the shelter, making as much noise as possible and dropped the wood on the ground before the fire. Still no movement came from under the cover. Jack felt the blood run out of his face and slowly he knelt and pulled back the deer skin. Her face was still hidden under her black tresses, but he could see that she was breathing, so he shook her lightly.

"Annie?" No response. "Annie!" he said, shaking her harder.

He was relieved when she pulled her hair back and looked up at him through sleepy eyes. "Jack, what is it? Has somebody come?"

"No, but I thought you might be hungry."

As an afterthought he pointed at the hare and said, "I got some breakfast."

At this she did manage a little smile, but she still only seemed half awake. "Sure, Jack," she said, already pulling the cover back over her. "Let me know when it's ready."

Within a few seconds, she was once again breathing heavily, leaving him to prepare breakfast, more worried than ever.

By the time night set in, Jack's uneasiness had turned to fear—there was something seriously wrong. He knew he would have to act soon, or Annie would die.

He had managed to get her to eat a little and drink some water. She had almost fallen asleep during the meal. She had laid back down and Jack had to shake her again.

"Annie, what's wrong?" he asked, his voice rising almost to panic.

She opened her eyes just enough to see him. "I'm just tired, Jack," she said in an irritated little girl voice that reminded him too much of his sister in the last stages of her sickness.

"Annie," he started again, but she interrupted him this time and spoke as if she were talking in her sleep. "I need to get away, Jack. I just need to get away." Then she fell instantly asleep again.

He pondered over this statement. "Get away?" He knew that sometimes people would take to their beds for days when they were sick or depressed. Was that what she had meant? Was she just trying to escape her troubles through sleep? For the thousandth time, he wondered how well he really knew her. He wished her father were here; he would know if this was a common occurrence for her. But the more he thought about it, the more he doubted it. His mind kept returning to the day after her sleepwalking incident. He could remember that as the day went on, she seemed to get better and better, so by the time they had camped that night, nearly twenty miles away, she had been perfectly fine, even joking as they got ready for bed that she had gotten enough sleep for a week. Was that it? When she had said that she needed to get away, had that been her subconsciously trying to tell him that she needed to get away from here, from this spot?

"No," he thought, light dawning in his mind—not this spot. Suddenly he began to think of their progress from the little clearing and that awful tree. In that storm he had lost his way, but as near as he could figure, they couldn't have come more than a quarter of a mile. It was at least another two back to the house. Could it be that she was still under some influence that he didn't understand? That she was trying to tell him that she needed to put more distance between herself and that influence? His former self would have dismissed this thought entirely, but Annie had changed him somehow; had shown him things that he could not explain. In a way she had opened his mind, and as much as the old Jack fought against the idea, the new Jack was fairly sure that he had hit the nail on the head. But how? He couldn't just carry her away; they would both die of exposure. Maybe he could go for help and leave her here—yet deep down he knew that he couldn't do that. Something told him that if he left her here under this rock, he would never find her again. Finally he made up his mind that if she wasn't any better by morning, he would carry her home. "After all," he thought as he laid down next to her on that third night, "it would be better to die with her than to live without her."

# CHAPTER 16

Jack lay awake throughout the night, thinking about the almost suicidal mission he was about to undertake, among other things. For instance, why had no one come looking for them? Surely there were dog teams in the little village, and he would have thought that Annie's father would be almost frantic by now. At first he thought that maybe the storm had prevented them, but yesterday, although it had snowed heavily, a dog sled could have traversed the distance in less than an hour. He supposed it was possible that no one had any idea where to search, but he knew they had been seen riding out toward the east.

As far as his own plans went, there really wasn't much he could do to prepare, and he was restless to be doing something. The sun had been rising later and later, and finally Jack felt that sun or no sun, he could lie there no longer, so he got up and walked out into the darkness. It was bitterly cold and he had a hunch that the temperature wouldn't rise above freezing for many a month now. As he came to the clearing, he noticed that the snow was beginning to fall once more, very lightly now, but he knew how fast that could change. He hurried back to the camp and began putting together what few items that they had. He cut the small rabbit skin in to two halves and used them to line the toes of his boots, but he realized that other than the deerskin, there was really nothing here that could be of help to him—even the little cup he had carved would be of little value on the move, and if he were really going to do this, he intended to keep moving until he dropped. Kneeling down beside Annie, he hoped that she might be at least a little better, but this time she wouldn't wake, and her breathing seemed shallow.

Once again he glanced around and saw there was nothing left to do. So, wrapping the cover as tightly as he could around her small body, he scooped her up as if she weighed no more than a house cat and started off toward the clearing. An hour later found him still fairly strong, but his hands and feet were beginning to get numb. He had tried to keep his hands under the cover, using Annie's body heat to warm them. The rabbit skin had managed to keep his toes fairly dry, but plunging through almost a foot of snow for over an hour had had its effect. The futility of the effort was starting to come home to him. Turning he saw his own trail fading out behind him but only for about a hundred feet; after that it was lost. So he went on—what else was there to do? He could make out the trees at the far end of the little valley, but they never seemed to get any closer. Lifting a corner of the deerskin, he looked down at the sleeping girl in his arms and actually smiled.

"Well," he said, "here we are. I've finally got you all to myself, and all you want to do is sleep."

He chuckled, but he didn't like the sound of it; he covered her face again and resumed his talk.

"You know," he said, as he trudged along, "it occurs to me now that your idea about going to the US wasn't such a bad idea after all. I haven't really told you much about my home, but I'm sure you would love it there."

He continued on this way for another half an hour, walking slowly and talking to the lifeless form in his aching arms. Occasionally he would laugh when he would remember something funny, and then he would forget what he was saying. Finally he reached the end of the valley—he had been walking for nearly two hours. Although he didn't know it, he had come only a little more than a mile. He was on the brink of exhaustion, and frostbite was beginning to set in around his toes. When he reached the trees, he turned again to look at his trail, but it was gone. It had been snowing pretty hard for at least the last twenty minutes and it had covered his tracks. Now he walked through the trees, not even really sure what direction he was going.

Suddenly he stopped and turned his head slightly.

"Did you hear that?" he asked the girl. "Sounded like a wolf!"

Standing completely still, he listened, but the sound didn't repeat itself.

"Maybe…just a little rest is what I need," he said, looking down at the form under the cover, and with that he sat down, placing his back against one of the trees, his precious bundle still in his arms.

"I've been meaning to ask you about that," he said. "Wolf, I mean. I thought he went everywhere with you."

There was, of course, no answer to this, but once again he thought he heard the far-off howl of a lone wolf. "Maybe he finally found himself a girlfriend," he mused.

He was almost done in, but for the last hour Jack had been pretty much indifferent to the situation, not really feeling or sensing anything. His feet had continued to move long after his mind could direct them. Although he didn't realize it, he was closer to death's door than he had ever been—pushing on it, in fact. So when he sat down against the spruce, it wasn't only to take a short rest; it was the only thing he could do. His legs would no longer support him. Had you asked him how he felt, he would have replied cheerfully, "Me? Oh, I'm fine; never better," and would have gone on talking to Annie as if they were sitting in a warm kitchen drinking coffee. The fact was, hypothermia had set in, and although he really did feel fine, he was far from it. His core body heat had dropped, and he had frostbite on his right foot. His face was raw from the blowing snow and his lips were cracked and swollen; most men would have fallen down dead by now—yet somehow, he lived on.

Once again he was sure he heard something and became completely still, even holding his breath, but nothing came to his ears. There was only the silent snow as it fell through the trees, slowly covering his outstretched legs.

"Speaking of girlfriends," he went on, "you know I never really had one."

Reacting as if Annie had protested this astounding fact, he said, "No, really! Oh sure, I know what you're thinking: A big handsome man like me never had a girlfriend? Hard to believe, right?"

He croaked out a laugh and smiled up at the sky. Then he looked down at the deerskin that was now almost completely covered in snow and closed his eyes.

He yawned, as his voice took on a sleepy quality, and said, "It's true enough, though. So I was wondering, you know after all this is over, how you would feel about being my first?"

He was about to add that she didn't have to tell him now, that she could think about it, when he heard the noise again. There was no doubt about it this time—not a lone wolf howl, more like the barking of a dog or dogs. Once again he held his breath and listened. It came again, closer than before. Raising his head slowly, he forced open his heavy lids and gazed dully through eyes that were nearly snow blind at the edge of the trees. There he could just make out the fuzzy outline of a lone wolf and behind that a larger outline. A dog sled and loud barking came to his ears. As these forms came on, so did the reality of his situation like a punch to the stomach—he realized that he could no longer feel his feet. All at once every muscle in his body seemed to scream at him. Suddenly he thought of Annie: he couldn't remember the last time he had checked on her. With trembling hands he brushed away the snow from the blanket and uncovered her face. What he saw brought a gladness to his heart that he had never felt before, and his body seemed to be warming from the inside out. She was awake and she was smiling. As he gazed into that beautiful face, he felt his own goofy smile spread across his cracked and swollen lips.

In a voice that was no more than a whisper, she said one sentence. Although sleds were pulling up right in front of them with men and dogs making an enormous racket, all Jack heard was, "Yes, Jack, I'll be you girl-friend."

Jack was still looking down into Annie's upturned face when Wolf, followed closely by David, bounded up and stood on Jack's outstretched legs. He licked Jack's face once and then sniffed at the deerskin covering that, although frozen stiff, had long since began to rot. He pawed at it as if he had some reversion to it being so close to his mistress. He whined once and sat back on his haunches. Jack found it humorous and began to laugh as David squatted down in front of him.

First he looked to Annie, but when he saw she was awake and smiling, he said to Jack, "Well, you're in a pretty fair mood for a man on the brink of death."

"Far from it," Jack replied. "As a matter of fact, I feel like I could carry her all the way back!"

The two men stared at each other for a moment, a world of meaning in their eyes. David then turned to bark some orders.

"No, don't bother making camp. We are less than a mile from the house. Bundle them on my sled."

Looking down at his daughter, he said, "We'll be home in time for supper."

The preparations were made, but when David bent to pick up his daughter, she amazed everyone by standing on her own and then offering to help Jack; as for himself he was surprised to find that he couldn't even get to his knees, and two burly men had to carry him.

Three quarters of an hour later, they pulled up in front of the big house. Jack noticed that the storm had left a lot less snow here and the sun was actually melting it in some places. How could there be such a drastic change in the temperature only a mile from where they had been found? He had little time to speculate on the matter as once again he was carried, but instead of taking him to his room, Annie insisted he be carried directly to her own, where she said she could better take care of him. Mentally he felt fine and started to protest, but Annie held one small finger against his lips and said, "Doctor's orders." So they carried him to the bed and set him down on the edge.

Annie turned to him and in a stern voice said, "Don't move. I'll be back in a minute." Suddenly he was alone. Jack looked around—this was the first time he had been in Annie's room.

It seemed small compared to the other rooms in the house, but that could have been because the bed took up almost half of it. Jack studied it for a moment. It was a huge canopied thing, draped with sheer curtains of some material Jack had never seen. He touched one of these and said to himself, "Silk?" The posts resembled nothing more than four trees growing right out of the floor that had been stained and varnished to a high sheen. He saw that sitting here on the edge, his feet dangled a good six inches from the ground, and he thought, "Annie must have to get a running start just to get into it."

He could hear her somewhere down the hall giving orders, and he smiled as he glanced around the rest of the room. He saw at once that he needn't have been worried about his own housekeeping. It wasn't that the room was dirty; there didn't seem to be a speck of dust anywhere. No, the best way to describe Annie's room was cluttered. Straight in front of him against the far wall was a dressing table with a mirror and a small chair, the top of which was completely covered with small boxes, hairbrushes, and other things that Jack knew only as girly stuff. On the same wall as the headboard, there was a window draped with thick, dark curtains. A rocking chair stood in the corner with various pieces of clothing flung over its back haphazardly; a foot stool with a few books stacked on it made up the rest of the furniture. Turning slightly to look behind him, he saw another curtain and guessed that this was her closet. Then he noticed a photograph tucked into one corner of the dressing table mirror and was straining his eyes to get a better look when Kitchi came in. He was carrying a basket, which he set down in front of the bed.

Closing the door he said, "We need to get you out of your clothes."

Jack didn't argue, but he found it nearly impossible to do on his own; his feet felt like blocks of ice and he could barely lift his legs. With Kitchi's help he managed to get undressed and into a large robe just as Annie, with two men that he had never seen before, came in carrying buckets of water. Annie went to the curtain that Jack assumed covered her closet and pulled it back, revealing an old clawfoot bathtub. The men poured the water into the tub. Annie then directed them to place Jack into it.

He started to protest, but Annie was already speaking to him. "Listen, Jack," she said earnestly, "you're just to sit in the tub. Don't move around, and don't touch any part of your feet, do you understand?"

Jack nodded. He was already starting to get a tingling sensation in his toes and he had an idea of what was coming.

"Drink some of this," she said and handed him a glass of liquid that smelled predominately of whiskey.

He paused and then, looking into her eyes, drank it off in one gulp.

"Good," she said as the two big men picked him up and carried him to the bath. The water wasn't as warm as he expected it would be. He felt a slight shock when his bare skin touched it, but he settled down, and the curtain was pulled. There was a commotion of buckets clanging and men talking. The door closed, and Jack thought that he was once again alone in the room.

Then Annie spoke from the other side of the curtain. "How do you feel?"

"Like a man in love," he replied and smiled to himself.

"Be serious, Jack," she demanded, and her voice seemed to quaver a little.

"Well, my legs and arms feel heavy, and there is some pain in my toes."

"What color are they?" she wanted to know.

Jack knew she was worried about frostbite, and he didn't like being the cause of her anxiety.

"They look ok," he said, noticing that they were mostly yellow except the little toe on his left foot, which was almost black. "I'm gonna lose that one," he thought, but even this couldn't darken his spirits.

Annie was ok, and she had practically given him her hand today.

"Jack, tell the truth, or I will come in and look for myself!"

By now his toes were really starting to hurt and he could feel the beginning of cramps in his calves.

"Annie," he started and then paused, not knowing exactly how to proceed.

"Jack, can you feel your toes yet?"

Through the curtain he could see her silhouette. She was kneeling and her head was down.

He began again, "Today when we were in the forest, I said some things."

"You were delirious, Jack!"

"Maybe," he said, "but do you remember what I asked you?"

There was a pause, and then, barely audibly, she said, "I remember."

Suddenly the urge to see her face, to look into her eyes, was overwhelming. With a supreme effort, he hoisted himself out of the tub and pulled on the huge robe. Through the curtain he saw her rise to her feet, and as they stood there with only the flimsy piece of cloth between them, he said, "I was wrong. I don't want you to be my girlfriend."

"Jack, you don't have to explain," she started, but he interrupted her midsentence.

"I want you to be my wife."

Pushing the curtain aside, he looked down into her shining eyes and whispered, "Annie, will you marry me?"

A single tear rolled down her cheek, but she made no effort to wipe it away. Her lips trembled, and more tears began to fall. But through the tears, she smiled and said, "Yes, Jack, I will be your wife."

If he had been stronger, he would have grabbed her up and held her, but it had taken all his remaining strength just to stand—now he was afraid he would fall over. Somehow, he managed to make it to the bed with Annie's help. As she leaned over him, he kissed her and told her he loved her again.

Slowly they parted, and Annie said, "I want to make you better, Jack, but I don't want to scare you."

"You already have," he protested as she shook her head.

Leaning close to him she said, "Remember the fish?" He nodded. "Well, I don't ever want to see that look in your eyes again, Jack, understand?"

He understood. Smiling up at her, he calmly lay back on the bed.

First she took his hands and examined the fingers. Then, folding his arms over his chest, she kissed him lightly and said, "You must be very still."

For a moment she just stood there beside the bed with her eyes closed. Slowly and gingerly, she took his right foot in both hands. By now both feet had begun to throb, yet the minute she touched him, the pain subsided and was replaced by an odd tingling. Jack saw, or thought he saw, a faint blue light issuing from Annie's fingers. When she laid his foot back on the bed, the pain was completely gone.

He was about to speak, but, as if she were reading his mind, she said, "Shhhh, Jack, you must be quiet now."

Picking up his left foot, she began again, only pausing slightly when she came to the blackened toe. Here her hand hovered for a moment, and Jack looked into her face. Her eyes were closed, and her head was tilted slightly to one side as if she were listening to some far-off sound. Looking down, Jack saw that all the hair on his legs were standing up and the very air seemed to shimmer. Finally she placed his foot back on the bed and stood back. Her eyes had that same far-off look that he had seen so many times before. Without realizing what he was doing, he swung off the bed and grabbed her by the shoulders.

Slowly she smiled up at him and asked, "Better?"

For a second, he didn't understand the question. Then, looking down at his feet, he saw that they were completely healed. They were red as if they had been soaking in hot water, but the frostbite was completely gone. What's more, the cramps in his legs had subsided, and although he felt slightly fatigued, he had no problem standing on his own. He looked at Annie, who was smiling up at him, and said with awe in his voice: "I'm cured. You cured me!"

She put her hands over her mouth and giggled.

Jack said, "But how, Annie? Where does this come from?"

"From love," she said simply. "It's the power of love, Jack." And she giggled again.

# CHAPTER 17

J ack walked on his own power back to his room, still
wearing the huge robe and nothing else. Kitchi had
taken his clothes and he didn't exactly have an extensive wardrobe to draw from, but this was just a passing
thought as he traversed the hallway that led to the guest
room. Part of his mind kept marveling at how well he
felt and the fact that only thirty minutes ago he had been
practically an invalid—even this and the strange way
in which Annie had healed him were only secondary in
his conscious mind. The whole experience seemed like
a dream in which he could only remember small details.
The main thought that kept circling lazily around his
brain like a bumble bee circling a spring flower was,
*"She said yes!"* Upon reaching his room, he found Kitchi
already there. A wash basin had been set on the dresser
with soap and water and he was laying out some sort of
clothing on the bed. Jack didn't want to startle him and
was about to utter a polite cough to get his attention
when he turned and said as calmly as if Jack had been
in the room with him the whole time, "This is a suit
of clothes that father bought me a couple of years ago.

They are a little too baggy for me and the pants won't stay up, so I never wore them. I thought they might fit you as we are nearly the same height."

Jack looked over the clothing and, holding the blue cotton shirt up to his shoulders, asked, "What do you think?"

Kitchi examined him a moment and said, "Yes, I think they will fit nicely. Father said that he thought you might be feeling better and to tell you that we will be eating in about an hour, if you were up to joining us at the table."

"Yes," Jack replied, smiling. "I feel very well, as a matter of fact, and I have something I need to discuss with him anyway."

He thought he caught a gleam in Kitchi's eye, and as he turned to go, he said, "Yes, Mr. Brooks, I will let him know."

Jack was curious about this man, so he said, "No, wait a minute, would you? We haven't really had any time to talk."

Kitchi turned, eyebrows raised, and Jack pointed to the only chair in the room and said, "Sit with me while I get ready."

Kitchi looked hesitant for a moment, but Jack's smile won him over, and he shrugged and took the seat.

"Annie calls you her brother," Jack began as he looked through his things for a small razor.

"Yes, and I call her my sister, although of course not by birth."

"So, David—I mean Mr. Fuller—adopted you then?" Jack continued.

"Not exactly. You see, I was born with the sickness, and back then, back before Father found a cure, babies born with the plague were…" Here he paused, not wanting Jack to get the wrong impression.

But Jack turned and, looking him straight in the eye, said matter-of-factly: "They were put to death, right?"

"Right," Kitchi replied a little hesitantly.

"That is a pretty common practice down in the states," Jack said. "Although there are some that think it inhumane and are trying to put a stop to it. Anyway, go on; I really am interested."

Kitchi went on, a little relieved that Jack seemed to understand the situation. "Well, before she died, Mrs. Fuller was quite active in the village and much loved—almost as much as her daughter is today. She was considered among the people a good nurse and midwife. So, she was present at nearly all the births. When I was born, she was there. The clearest sign that a baby has the sickness, you know, is the constant crying and refusal to take the breast."

To this Jack just nodded; he had seen it before.

"Well, I showed both signs, and Mrs. Fuller knew what was to be my fate. So, she told my mother and father, who were out of their minds with grief, that she would 'take care of me' humanely and make sure I had a proper burial. Well, of course she had no intention of ending my life but was prepared to make me as comfortable as she could until I passed. Less than a year later, my mother died, and my father walked off into the woods, and nobody ever saw him again. For some reason I lived on, and although I couldn't speak and needed almost constant care, I kept on living right into my eighth year. By then the lady Mrs. Fuller had been dead for six. Her husband, who loved whatever she loved, continued to care for me—as a matter of fact, he says that I am the reason that he worked so long and hard to develop his cure."

Jack had been in the process of shaving his face in a small mirror when something in Kitchi's voice made him turn and look at him. He was staring across the room at nothing in particular, and when he spoke, his voice was low and soft. "I remember it like it was only yesterday. There were maybe a dozen people standing around the big front porch, all looking toward my father as he told them that he had finally found it and that they would all be better very shortly. I had been sitting in an old rocker just behind him. Most of the time I was confused and didn't even realize what I was doing, but some days everything was clear, and I could understand what was going on around me, even if I couldn't find the words to express myself; this was one of those days. I remember Father took one small capsule from a jar and, calling Sister to him, whispered something in her ear. She was so young, but she looked up at Father with such understanding and love that she seemed much older than me. Then, taking the capsule from him, she came to me and took my hand. I tell you, Mr. Brooks, never before and never since have I loved anyone more than

I did that little girl. Still holding my hand, she placed the capsule between my lips and said, 'Eat it up, Kitchi; it will make you all better.' So I did and it was sweet; most medicines are bitter, and you have to drink lots of water to get them down," he said, turning to look at Jack, "but not this."

By now Jack was mesmerized and stood staring at Kitchi, razor in hand and face only half shaved.

"Then what?" Jack prompted impatiently.

"Then what!" Kitchi said, and a huge grin spread across his face. "I was cured! Not gradually, but right then and there. You see, as I said, I had good days where I could understand what was going on around me, but I had never spoken, never been able to make my mouth form the words—it was as if that part of my brain that controlled speech had been left out of me. But when Annie, that little six-year-old Annie, took me by both hands and said, 'What do you say, Brother?' Something seemed to pop in my head like a blue bolt of lightning! Then, clear as day and with tears running down my face, I spoke my first words: 'Thank you.' Let me tell you, at those words, the people on the porch knelt in unison and sent praises to heaven."

Suddenly, understanding exploded in Jack's brain, and he almost shouted: "And Annie, did she give the pills to all of the people herself?"

"Well, yes!" Kitchi said, surprised at Jack's excitement. "She always has. Father says it makes people feel more at ease if she does it."

"Ha! I'm sure," Jack exclaimed a little too urgently.

Kitchi was beginning to look a little uneasy and Jack saw that he was getting ready to bolt.

"I mean," he said, lowering his voice and turning back to the mirror, "that's an incredible story. So do people still come to receive this cure from your father?"

"Well, no. The plague has been completely wiped out in the village, and until Andre and his people showed up, none have come this far north."

"Tell me about Andre."

At the mention of this name, Kitchi nearly spat. "He is a vile man who takes what he wants without asking."

"Like your sister?" Jack interjected, wiping his cleanly shaven face with a towel. He turned to look at the young man.

Kitchi looked back at him blankly for a moment, then seeming to realize he had said too much, he stood up and walked toward the door. "We probably should be getting on to dinner," he said upon reaching the hall. "When it comes to food, my father is a very impatient man." Then he was gone, leaving Jack to get ready by himself.

The clothes turned out to be a pretty good fit; the sleeves of the shirt were a little short, but he found that if he left off the jacket that was too tight in the shoulders and rolled them up to the elbow, it looked all right. It was the pants that impressed him most—they were made of denim and fit him perfectly. Jack hadn't worn anything but animal skins for as long as he could remember, and the soft cloth felt light and comfortable against his skin. The only mirror he had was his small shaving glass, which made it impossible for him to see the entire picture. Still, he thought he looked fairly presentable. "I could use a haircut," he observed, noticing the way his hair was starting to curl up on his shoulders, but that would have to wait. Taking one more look to make sure he had done a sufficient job with the razor, he put down the mirror and went out.

As he entered the dining room, the first person he saw was Kitchi. He was setting out a huge plate of some sort of meat and nodded to Jack when he saw him.

David came in behind him and clapped him on the shoulder, saying, "Well, you're looking well, Jack. I see our girl has fixed you right up."

"Yes, sir," Jack replied as David took his seat at the head of the table.

He was wondering to himself how this big man, who seemed to have no ill will toward anyone, could have been using his own daughter, or at least her gifts, for his own purpose—and as far as Jack knew, without her knowledge. He made up his mind that when he talked to David privately later, he would find out his motives once and for all, for her sake. He was just thinking that he had quite a few questions for Annie's father when he heard a light step behind him. Turning around he saw her standing in the huge doorway, and my goodness—had she ever looked so beautiful?! He had often asked himself this question during their trek north, but outwardly she had always been the same in her buckskin dress and denim jacket. Her hair, although she had always taken great care with it, had always been down and only adorned now and then with an occasional feather or ribbon. Tonight, as she stood framed in the entryway like some glorious painting come to life, there was no sign of the girl in buckskin; this was not David's little Annie—this was Jack's Annie; this was a woman. The dress was strapless, emerald green, and flowed almost to the floor, showing just the tips of little white shoes. Her hair had been pinned back behind her ears and fell in long dark ringlets down her back. Around her neck she wore a gold cross with a loop at the top, and on her wrist was the gold bracelet, the only remnant of the girl he first met in the little meadow by his cabin. The room was dead silent.

Then Kitchi gasped and from behind him David echoed Jack's own thoughts in a subdued voice. "My little Annie is no more."

Jack himself said nothing. He was a statue, a dumb thing with no ability to speak or even move from the spot. Then Annie stepped toward him and took his hand, thus breaking the spell. As long as he lived, he never forgot that moment—for that's all it was: just one moment in a life filled with moments. Even if he lived to be a hundred, that memory, that moment, that mental picture of *his* beloved Annie, would be just as vivid and wonderful as it had been on that night, that night of their engagement so many years ago.

# CHAPTER 18

A s for the dinner, Jack thought it was the finest he ever had, and not just because of the food. After the initial shock of seeing Annie in her "girl clothes," as Kitchi called them, everyone settled down, and the mood was a happy one. The meat turned out to be caribou; it was so tender you could cut it with a fork. Besides the meat there were mashed potatoes with gravy and fresh asparagus, something Jack had never tasted and couldn't seem to get enough of. Between mouthfuls David gave a colorful account of their search for Jack and Annie. It seemed that Jacob had been the one to sound the alarm even before the storm hit, coming to the house and telling David in his cryptic way that someone should start after them. Then he had disappeared, and no one had seen him since.

Jack felt a chill run down his spine, and the memory of the shadow man that had led them to the rock enclosure suddenly leapt into his mind. Could Jacob have been out there with them somehow? He soon dismissed this thought, knowing that he could never have come so far so fast.

David said, "It wasn't until the horses had come in, bringing the full brunt of the storm with them, that I started to get really worried. We had to round up a search party, and not even the natives would venture out until the worst of it had blown over. Funny thing, though," I couldn't find Blake. I thought maybe he could help me rouse some of the men, but when I went to his bunk to look for him, he was gone, and nobody seemed to remember the last time they had seen him. Anyway, once we finally got under way, Wolf showed up and we began a search of the whole valley and the surrounding woods—not even old Wolf could pick up a scent. Strange really—we must have gone right by your camp that first day. We should have found you."

Jack didn't find it strange at all. He had a feeling they could have searched until they were old men and never find the spot where he and Annie had camped. Right away part of his brain protested. That's nonsense he thought, and realized dimly that this was the old Jack talking, the Jack before Annie, and he was glad that he wasn't gone entirely.

"We probably never would have found you if you hadn't moved when you did," David was saying. "We were on our way back and in pretty low spirits, when Wolf seemed to lose his mind. He kept heading off the teams; even crippled one lead dog when he wouldn't turn. Then he took to howling and sniffing the air like he does. We dumb humans finally got the idea—after that he led us right to you."

Jack and Annie smiled at each other, having both experienced this behavior in Wolf before.

David asked him to tell their side of the story. Jack gave him an abbreviated version, leaving out everything that happened down by the river. For this, Annie gave him a grateful look.

After that, the conversation turned to less serious matters, and Annie as well as her older brother joined in, telling stories of their childhood together and some of the mischief they had gotten into. To Jack, who had lost both of his parents as well as his only sister, the scene made him a little melancholy—then it came to him that this was to be his family, and he began to look at them in a new light. Was he home? Was this to be the place where he finally settled down? The idea was a pleasant one. After all, wasn't this the place he had dreamed of? What had his sister said, that he would find a great treasure? Was Annie herself—or maybe this almost magical place where she lived—the treasure his sister was talking about? It sure made sense. As far as he knew, there wasn't another place on the planet like it, and he was sure there was no one in the world like Annie. But if this were true, he thought, sooner or later people would find out about it—about her. Andre and his people already had and look what had happened. Maybe that was why his sister had sent him: to protect it; to protect Annie. Looking around the table, he took in each person separately. Did any of them realize what they had here? They were all so happy, smiling and laughing. Didn't they realize that all of this could be taken away in an instant?

Annie looked over at him and must have seen something in his eyes, because her laughter died out slowly. Smiling her best smile, she said, "Why so serious, Jack? This is a time to be happy."

Everyone was looking at him now and he felt a little uncomfortable. He managed to smile and said, "This is just so nice. I don't want it to end."

At these words Annie took his hand and said, "Jack, don't you see? This is just the beginning."

David raised his glass and exhorted, "Here, here! To many happy times to come."

Jack raised his own glass, but somewhere in the back of his mind the old Jack whispered: "Not yet; not quite yet."

When dinner was over, David said, "Annie, why don't you show Jack around? Kitchi and I will clean up the dishes." Turning to Jack he said, "We can talk later; just come find me. I'll probably be in my study."

Jack nodded as Annie took his arm and led him into the hall. They started their tour upstairs, walking past the guest room, which was on the far end of the long hallway, to a narrow door just opposite his.

"You know what this is, Jack?"

"A bedroom, I guess; maybe Kitchi's, though I never heard him go in there."

"No, Kitchi's and Daddy's rooms are both downstairs. This," she said, throwing open the door, "used to be a bathroom with a working toilet. For reasons of his own, my grandfather tore it out along with all the plumbing. Daddy says he was probably worried about disease or something. Anyway, when I was about sixteen, he had the old bathtub taken out and put in my room, and we turned this into a clothes closet."

Jack looked in. It was dark, but he could see lots of dresses on hangers and mostly women's clothes. "These were my mother's; it's where I got this." She spun around in her dress, showing it off. "Some of them are falling apart, but we just can't seem to get rid of any of them. When I was little, I used to hide in here, and sometimes I would fall asleep and dream of her."

She closed the door and they continued down the hall. There were three more rooms on that level, but two of them were empty and mostly unfurnished. Annie's room was at the opposite end of the hall from his, and they had to pass it to get to the staircase. As they did, Jack glanced in, but Annie showed no intention of going in. Something caught his eye, however, and he stopped her.

"Annie," he asked, "who is the picture of, the one on your mirror?"

She laughed. "I thought you had maybe seen it when you were in here before."

"Yes, I noticed it, but I was too far away to make out who it is."

"That's funny," she said as she walked over to the little vanity. Carefully, so as not to tear it, she removed it from the mirror, saying, "You would think you could recognize yourself even from a distance." She handed him the picture, and he looked it over.

It was him all right—younger by six or seven years for sure, but him just the same. "I don't understand," he said, handing the picture back.

She tucked it back into the corner of the mirror frame and turned, taking his hand. As they walked back down the stairs, she said, "Up until about two years ago, my father would get newspapers from different places in the shipment we receive every fall. I found that picture in one of the papers."

Jack cringed a little. "What did the paper say about me?"

They were entering the big living room now, and she went to the huge fireplace and stood looking at the portrait of her mother. With her back to him, she said, "I don't know; I didn't read it."

Jack stared at her back. Standing there in front of the fireplace perfectly still, looking up at the portrait with her black hair flowing in loose curls down her back, she looked like a child playing dress-up. She sighed audibly and said, "I wish my mother were here. She would have loved you, Jack." Turning to look at him, she said, "And you would have loved her." She crossed to the couch and sat down, patting the seat beside her. "Sit with me, Jack."

They sat together on a sofa that looked as old as the house itself. "Are you worried about talking to my father?" she asked.

"Not about us getting married," he answered.

"Then what is it, Jack? You seem worried about something. You're not having second thoughts, are you?"

Jack looked at her, awestruck at such a statement. "Oh Annie, never have I loved anyone the way I love you, and tonight—my goodness, when I saw you! That dress and your eyes." He was stammering and he knew it, but he had to make her understand once and for all. Catching his breath, he started again. "Remember back at the cabin when I asked you if you were real and not just a dream or a figment of my imagination?"

"I remember. I told you I was real."

"Yes, but every now and then, I see you, and I have to pinch myself. It's as if my mind is still not convinced that I'm here with you in this wonderful place."

"Why, Jack? Why is it so hard to believe?"

"Because nothing is this good! Nothing in this hard world is even close to this good!" He got down on one knee so that he could face her and took her hand. "Annie, sometimes I wonder if you and your family realize what you have here. Do any of you know what it's like out in the real world?"

"Well, Jack, I guess I don't really. I'm sure Daddy does. He's been so many places."

"But does he understand," Jack went on urgently, "how precious this all is? How precious you are?"

"I don't follow you, Jack. Are you saying that we should be worried about…the outside world."

Jack nodded and said, "That's exactly what I'm saying. Take this man Andre, for instance. He is part of that world, and you know how evil he is."

For a moment she made no reply; folding her hands in her lap, she looked down at them. Jack was about to break the silence, fearing he had hurt her somehow, when she looked up at him, smiling, and said, "Yes, Jack, you're right about Andre. But you are also from that world, and I would trust you with my very life. I love you, Jack, and no one, not a hundred Andres, can ever take that away. There is nothing special about this place, Jack; you are mistaken about that. It's the people that make it special, and now that you're a part of it, I know that nothing from the cold world that you speak of can harm me. I told you that I dreamed of you, but it's more than that—I've known you since we were both little, and truth be told, even before that. Although you pretend not to remember, you've known me. I knew that someday you would come—and here you are. I tell you this now because you have asked me to marry you. I could have told you all this that first day in the meadow, and it would have been just as true." She took his face in her hands and said, "I *am* a real woman, and although I know others might see me as something more, I need you to see through all of that. Accept me as I am."

She still held his face in her hands, their lips only inches apart. Jack could have easily kissed her, thereby dropping the current subject forever, but some part of him couldn't let it go at that.

So instead, he said, "Who are you really, Annie? Please, I must know."

She sighed. Dropping her hands and leaning back against the old cushion. "I don't even know myself yet, Jack. I probably will someday, and part of me hopes that day is a long way off, because when I know…when we know…I fear…"

She paused, her eyes resting on the portrait over the fireplace.

"What, Annie? What is it you are afraid of?"

There were no tears in her eyes when she spoke and there seemed to be a tone of resignation in her voice. "I fear that you will have to let me go, Jack."

"No!" he exclaimed, coming to his feet. "Never!"

"Jack!" she pleaded, leaning toward him.

But he was having none of it. "No, Annie. I refuse to accept that you are some plaything that Andre or your father can use for their own purpose! I won't stand for it. Don't you see? I can't let you go, not now that I finally have you!"

He realized too late what he was saying. He flushed red and turned away from her to hide his feelings. This was so unlike him and he stood with his back to her, not knowing how to take it back. He expected her to be angry, maybe even leave the room. Instead, he felt her small hand on his shoulder.

She said, "Look at me, Jack."

He turned, surprised that she wasn't angry.

A calm sort of understanding had come into her eyes as she said, "Would you be my keeper then, Jack?"

What could he do? He had already said as much and he was furious at himself for letting his emotions run over.

Annie just shook her head slowly and said, "I don't believe that for a minute. 'Cause if I did, I could have never returned your love. Be happy in the present, Jack, and let the future take care of itself." She kissed him tenderly, and then, turning to go, she said lightly, "Now go ask my father for my hand before I change *my* mind."

He watched her pass out into the hall, his heart so full of love and his mind so full of doubt. "Let her go?" he said to himself. "I'll die first!"

As he walked down the hall to David's office, he thought, "Well, she's right about one thing. There is no sense in looking for trouble." He found David leaning back in his desk chair and smoking a cigar. He looked content, and when Jack came in, he didn't bother getting up.

"Pull up a chair, Jack. Smoke?"

"That sounds good, but first there is something I need to ask you, sir."

David took his feet off the desk and leaned forward. "It's like that, is it?" he chided, grinning around his own cigar.

"Yes, I'm afraid so," Jack replied. The two men stared at each other across the desk for a few seconds, both knowing what was coming.

Finally, David broke the silence. "By all means, Jack, let's get the formalities out of the way, then we can get down to business."

Jack cleared his throat. "Mr. Fuller…sir, I would like to ask for your daughter's hand in marriage."

He wasn't sure what he expected, but he knew that David wasn't surprised.

He said, "Well, Jack, did you ask her?"

"Of course."

"And? What did she say?"

"She said yes!" Jack exclaimed, a little surprised at this line of questioning.

"Well then, I guess it's a done deal."

And with that he stood, extending his hand to Jack over the old desk. As their hands met, Jack had a momentary feeling of dread, as if he had just been handed the keys to a kingdom that was on the brink of destruction.

It was gone in a flash as David smiled and said, "Welcome to the family, son. Now, how 'bout that cee-gar."

They sat and smoked in silence, each having so much to say but neither knowing how to start. Finally David, being naturally the more talkative of the two, began. "Well, Jack, now that you have her, what are you gonna do with her?"

"Well, sir," Jack began, and David cut him off.

"Jack, please—from now on it's David or Dad. I won't answer to anything else."

Jack felt the heat rise to blush his cheeks; it was gonna take him a little time to get used to his new family.

"Well, David, I know how much everyone here loves her, and I am sure that she would be happiest right where she is."

"How 'bout you, Jack? Could you be happy here so far from your own family and friends?"

"I could be happy wherever she is, and I have had kind of a plan in the back of my head that eventually I might bring my aunt and uncle here."

He watched David's face as he said this and the man didn't disappoint him. Smiling, he said, "Of course, Jack. I wouldn't have it any other way."

Jack felt a little more than relief at this statement and was encouraged to go on. "But there is more to it than that," he said, still a little embarrassed by his new association with the old man. "You see, I have dreamed of this place more than once, and the more I am around Annie the more I feel as if..." He didn't know exactly how to finish the statement, but David came to the rescue.

"Like you were meant to be here all along," he said, gazing at Jack through a thick cloud of smoke.

Jack smiled. He thought that David's ability to see straight through him fell short only of Annie's. "Anyway, what I really am trying to say is that if I am to stay—I mean if *we* are to stay—I want to earn my keep."

He thought David might show some surprise or a least a little skepticism at this statement, but he just put his feet back up on his desk and took a long draw on the cigar. He seemed to be collecting his thoughts, and after a moment, he said, "I'm not a young man anymore, Jack. I'll be sixty-one this June, and the hard truth is I won't be around forever. Before you showed up, I spent many a restless night wondering what was to come of the place when I'm gone. Oh, I know that Annie is more than capable of taking care of things in her own way, but it's a lot bigger job than you would think, and she really has no interest in my research. As for Kitchi, he just doesn't have the ambition to take on so much. As I've said, part of me knew that you would show up some day;

heaven only knows Annie has told me enough times. To be honest with you, I always felt a sense of dread when I thought of it. But now that you're really here, in the flesh, I find myself a little relieved. You see, I know what you're capable of, Jack, and I pity the man that crosses you. On the other hand, I know something about your past as well as your father's, and I am confident that you will always try to do what's right. But the main reason I trust you so much and am willing to hand over my greatest treasure so easily"—the significance of the word "treasure" was not lost on Jack—"is that *she* trusts you."

He chuckled a little as he went on. "As for you earning your keep, as you put it, I'm sure we can find something for you to do around here, if that's your only worry. My question to you is, do you really know who you're marrying, Jack?"

Jack knew what he was referring to, and he figured this would be a good time to bring up some of his concerns. "Well, I have seen some things…and I know she's…different, but somehow that makes me love her all the more."

David chuckled again. "Jack, don't fool yourself into thinking you have seen even a quarter of what she is capable of—not even she knows what she is capable of."

"Do you?" Jack asked, not sure where his future father-in-law was going with this.

"Not for sure," he said. "But I have some suspicions."

Before Jack could ask what they might be, David got up and went to the huge bookcase. He looked through several volumes before he found what he wanted. After placing it open in front of Jack, he returned to his place behind the desk. The book was very old, and some of the print was so faded that he couldn't make it out, but what he could read he read out loud.

"Demeter: In ancient Greek religion and myth, Demeter is the goddess of the harvest who presided over grains and the fertility of the earth." The rest of the paragraph was too faded to read, but as he scanned the page, he came upon another line that got his attention. "Demeter's epithets show her many religious functions. She was called the Corn Mother who blesses the harvesters. Some cults interpreted her as 'Mother Earth.'"

Looking up from the book, he said, "You're not saying that Annie is this Demeter come to life, I hope."

"No, not exactly, but throughout history there are similar myths that are essentially the same even across cultures. The Hebrews had Asherah, which is Semitic, meaning mother goddess. The Egyptians had Isis and her sister Nephthys. I've even heard some of the native children call Annie 'Matisoon,' which means simply 'giver of life.'"

Jack recognized the word as the one the children had called her the other day, then he recalled how Jacob always called her "Little Mother" and how she hated it. Jack leaned back in his chair, a look of concern on his face. David let these ideas sink in. Finally, Jack said, "Even if any of this comes close to the truth, Annie is her own person. She still has free will."

David folded his hands on top of the desk and looked at Jack with real compassion. "Does she, son? I fear that this is one question that cannot be answered this early in the game."

This statement frustrated Jack and his anger flared momentarily. "This isn't a game," he said evenly. "We are talking about a real woman and your daughter, not some goddess come to life. Have you spoken to her about these things? Have you told her that it's her and not your miracle pill that cures the plague?"

Jack realized he might be overreacting, but he had held these questions in check, and now that he had started, he was determined to have some answers.

"While we're on the subject," he continued, leaning forward in his chair, "what about your little science experiment, out in the shed? Tell me, David, what are you experimenting with? The plant life or Annie?"

He was still leaning forward, looking the older man straight in the eye—now he knew that he had crossed the line, but when it came to Annie, his heart always seemed to override his brain. He also felt that now that she was to be his wife, he had the right to know certain things.

For a moment David continued to look at him with that same look of grief and compassion. Jack began to feel uncomfortable.

Finally, he said, "I can see that you love her very much, Jack, and I am glad of that. But don't think for one moment that my love for her isn't just as strong. I have watched her grow from a quiet little girl into the woman you saw tonight, and it hasn't been easy. Put yourself in my place for a moment. Imagine walking out on the front porch and finding your two-year-old playing with grizzly cubs while their mother stood watching only a few feet away.

"When she was six, one of her best friends drowned in the river. Two days later nearly a hundred-yard stretch of it froze solid in the July heat, causing a major flood downstream when it suddenly thawed. These are just a couple of examples and not the worst of it. What have you seen here in the short time you've known her?" He continued. "A few parlor tricks? What if I were to tell you I have personally seen her control the weather?"

Suddenly Jack felt very small compared to David, and a thought came to him as he sat contemplating Annie as a child.

"There was a fire, wasn't there?" he asked finally, looking at David with a new respect.

For the first time since he had met him, David looked shocked, but he only nodded silently, and then, speaking like a man in a dream, he said: "She was about eight years old, I guess. She had wandered off again, and everyone in the village was looking for her. It was me that found her about a quarter mile south of here. I heard her crying, and when I finally saw her, I noticed that she was standing over a fawn that had been partially trapped under a fallen tree. She was trying to push the massive thing off of it, and my heart went out to her. I stood completely still for a moment. I could see that the animal's back was broken. I guess I was thinking about what I would say to console her, then in one swift motion, she stood straight up and pointed at the sky." David looked down at his hands for a moment, then, glancing sideways at

Jack, he said, "Have you ever heard the expression 'a bolt right out of the blue,' Jack?"

He could only nod his head as David went on. "One bolt of lightning came, seemingly out of a clear blue sky. It hit the fallen tree just above where the fawn lay pinned, but she must have underestimated her own power—either that or she simply hadn't learned to control it, because the tree was vaporized along with the fawn. It left a crater in the ground twenty feet in diameter. Of course, I didn't find this out until later when I went back and looked at the spot."

David fell back in his chair and relit his cigar.

Jack looked at him with wide eyes and said, "And she herself was unhurt?"

"Not a scratch," David replied. "But I, who had been standing twenty yards behind her, was hit with a full concussion! It threw me ten feet into a rock outcropping, bruising my back pretty bad. I found out later that one of my eardrums had burst. The strangest thing, though, was the hundreds of little splinters, some of which penetrated my clothes and stuck in my skin. The fire started slowly, but by the time I came to my senses, it had nearly encircled her as she stood there shrieking at the sky. Somehow, I managed to carry her out before the whole forest went up. It burned over a thousand acres before a hard rain came and put it out—whether the rain was also her doing or not, I don't know. I do remember, however, that for days afterward she kept saying, 'It's not my fault, Daddy,' and 'I didn't mean to.' We never talked about it after. It seemed that she had made up her mind that nothing like that would ever happen again, and it hasn't. See, I was like you, Jack. Do you know why I never discussed these things with her? Because I was in denial also, hoping that as she grew, she would put aside these strange powers of hers, or that they would somehow fade away, like a child's imaginary friend. It hasn't happened, though. If anything, her power has grown stronger, and every day she becomes more aware of it. The thing is, Annie has led a very sheltered life here, Jack—everything she loves is here; she has known very little heartache. I guess what I'm trying to point out is, if she can bring lightning out of the sky and cause a huge fire over the death of a forest creature, what might she be capable of in defending someone she has given her heart and soul to? I tell you, Jack, it's a bigger responsibility than you're willing to admit."

Jack stood and walked over to the one window in the room. Looking out into the dark night, he asked, "Why her? What is the purpose of these so-called powers?" Turning again to David, who had also risen, he said, "She doesn't seem inclined to use them. From what I have seen, these things seem to happen without her even noticing." David yawned and stretched, saying at the same time, "It's like when you draw your revolver." He saw that Jack didn't understand the analogy, so he went on. "Annie told me just the other day that it was almost unnatural how fast you could draw. Yet to you it's the most natural thing in the world. Although your gift, if you want to call it that, was probably partially inherited, you have also had years to practice it. *You* have been honing your talent since you were a young boy. *You* were mentored by someone who probably shared it, or at least knew the mechanics of it. But who is there to mentor Annie? Who in this whole world shares her talents and can guide her in their uses? As for the question of their purpose—well, I will give you my theory if you want it. I'm not sure you will like it. Just know this, Jack: I am not your enemy. I have done my best to give Annie a good life to this point. Now you have come to me asking permission to take over this task. Yes, I call it a task, because although I am sure that she will give you great joy, I also know firsthand that she can bring great sorrow to those who love her most."

Jack thought this over for a moment. Sitting himself back down, he looked over at David, who, although tired, seemed to regard him with a patience that was almost irritating. He took a moment to compose himself, and then he said something he was sure that David couldn't refute.

"It doesn't matter."

David did look surprised by the statement, but all he said was, "I don't think I understand."

"It doesn't matter," Jack repeated, shrugging his shoulders. "You're right, I don't know Annie the way you do. To be honest with you and myself, I think I loved her the first time I saw her. I knew nothing of her gifts, or 'powers' as you call them, and I don't love her either more or less because of them. In fact, I wish for her sake that she knew nothing of them herself, though I can't see any reason why she would need a mentor as you say. Why invite trouble? If these things happen naturally, I will learn to live with them, just as she will have to learn to live with certain things about me. You saw her tonight—she is no longer a little girl. She is in fact a full-grown, beautiful, intelligent woman who is more than capable of making her own decisions in these matters. You have done an excellent job of raising her and protecting her, and I have nothing but respect for you myself. But sir, you must see that it is time to let her be whoever she wants to be, not what you, I, or anyone else thinks she should be."

This was a long speech for Jack, but he felt that David needed to know that he would no longer stand by and let anyone—not even her father—use her for their own benefit.

David understood; in a way he was relieved. He said, "You're right, of course. I have spent so much time pursuing the secret that I have forgotten about the girl. Well, starting tomorrow, that all ends. I will tell her everything, then I will turn her care over to you, Jack. But I think it my duty to add one more piece of advice.

"I think—no wait, scratch that—I *believe* that this gift of Annie's is much more than the ability to perform a few tricks or even to cure the plague. I truly believe that she has the power, somewhere inside her tiny frame, to save the world. To...cure the planet, if you will; set it back on its normal cycle maybe. No, don't shake your head until you hear me out."

David stood, and to Jack it seemed that the man had aged ten years in the last ten minutes. "Jack," he said, coming around the desk and taking him by the shoulders, "who she wants to be, as you so eloquently put it, may have very little to do with who she really is."

After this statement, both men grew silent. They were plainly talked out, and when Kitchi poked his head in and said, "I'll be going to bed now, Father, unless you need me." David replied, "Yes, Kitchi, I guess we are all a little tired." Before the boy could turn to go, David checked him. "Um, Kitchi, before you go, come in here for a moment, would you?"

The boy obeyed and David went to a small cabinet next to the fireplace from which he produced three stout glasses and a bottle of some sort of whiskey.

"I've been saving this for a special occasion," he said, as he broke the seal and poured a generous amount into all three glasses. Then to Kitchi he said, "I want you to shake hands with your new brother-in-law."

Kitchi grasped Jack's hand and welcomed him to the family, then David passed around the glasses, raised his, and said: "To Jack and Annie. May all of their dreams, past, present, and future, come true."

# CHAPTER 19

J ack came awake slowly, wincing slightly at the dull throb in his head. He was lying on his side; cracking one eye open, he saw that some kind soul had placed a pitcher of water and a glass on the nightstand next to his bed. He swung his legs over the side, vowing that he would never drink whiskey again, and gulped some water straight out of the pitcher. Looking down he saw that he was still dressed in his clothes from the night before, then it all started to come back to him.

After David's toast, Kitchi had made one, and Jack, not wanting to be outdone, had also toasted his new family. After that came a series of toasts to Annie herself, and by the time they were done, the bottle was almost gone. It had been a long time since he had tasted the strong stuff. He remembered swaying a little as he climbed the stairs to his room and had a vague idea that he and David had carried Kitchi to his room, but he couldn't remember when or if David had even made it to his. This was why he never drank, he thought. It dulled his wits. But last night he had felt safe—and besides, how could he have refused his soon-to-be father-in-law? The water seemed to help, so he drank some more, pouring it into the glass this time. Through a crack in the curtains, a dim light shone into the room, and he wondered what time it was. There was an old clock that was still fairly accurate in the family room but nothing here to tell him whether it was dusk or dawn. Not a sound issued from the hall—or anywhere else in the house for that matter. He had a feeling he was the first one up. Maybe a little fresh air would do him good. So, taking another long drink from the glass, he smoothed back his hair with his hands and made his way out into the hall. He saw that Annie's door was open and felt a slight pang of guilt; he hoped she didn't know about their little party last night. Instead of going to her room, he slipped silently down the stairs and into the family room. The old clock said nine, but he was so disoriented that he wasn't sure if it was p.m. or a.m. He was about to make his way to the kitchen to put on the coffee when he heard Annie's voice coming from the front porch.

Annie had risen early as she normally did and gone down to the kitchen to make breakfast. She was surprised to find her father already there but not surprised to see him nursing a hangover. Silently, she went about making her cure while her father sat at the table with his head in his hands. When she had it done, she sat down across from him.

"I take it you boys had a long night," she said, pushing a glass of green-colored liquid toward him.

David, who had been through this ritual before, said nothing but downed the concoction in three great gulps.

Annie smiled. "Good boy." Taking the glass to the sink, she poured herself a cup of coffee and sat back down.

"I hope you didn't get him too drunk," she scolded, as David began to recover himself.

"You needn't worry about your fiancé, doll. He can hold his own."

Annie's eyes lit up. "So, he talked to you then?"

David smiled and took her hands across the table. "Yes, we talked. It's just like you always said: 'He's the one all right!'"

Taking his huge hand in both of her small ones, she kissed it and said, "I told you, Daddy. I always told you he would come."

David told her a little of what had passed between him and Jack the night before. Feeling better, he excused himself to clean up a little. Annie got the old glass pitcher down and filled it with water; Jack would need it when he woke up. She tiptoed into his room, but when she saw him sprawled on the bed and snoring loudly, she couldn't suppress a giggle. Setting the water on the nightstand, she stood back to study her man. "Well, he sure doesn't look like the famous Jack Brooks now," she thought and turned to go. Something caught her eye, though—something sticking out from under the bed. Kneeling down she fished it out; it was Jack's .45 still in the holster. She studied it, then looked up at the man on the bed. A feeling of uneasiness came over her. She didn't know where it was coming from. She wasn't clairvoyant, not even by the farthest stretch of the imagination, but she had always had the most vivid dreams—not just when she was sleeping, either. Sometimes she daydreamed. And it was in these dreams and lucid meditations that she had first met Jack Brooks. As she looked at him now, a line came to her from an old song her father used to sing: "Do I wait for you, or do you wait for me, and will you always be, only in my dreams?"

How long had she known him? Six weeks? Six years? Deep down she thought she knew the answer to this question. As she slowly stood, she whispered, "Six thousand."

If anyone had been observing her, they would have seen a blueish halo form around her raven hair. In his sleep Jack stirred restlessly, and Annie brought herself back to the moment. He is really here, she thought, and I am to be his bride. This thought, which brought her a momentary feeling of bliss followed by an almost inexorable feeling of dread, made her want to run from the room. Looking at him now, unarmed and deep in a sleep that was no doubt brought on by the festivities of the previous night, he seemed vulnerable for the first time since they had met in the small meadow. She thought, "I cannot hurt him, and I won't!" Then, turning her face to the ceiling of the small room, she said in a whisper, "I only want to be a woman—to be his wife!"

The answer came swiftly, not in a thought or a whisper, but in a voice loud and clear in her head: "He is only a man. Take him if you wish, but he is of no consequence!"

Annie lowered her head and, as if in prayer, said aloud, "But I love him!"

Silently, almost stealthily, she pushed the big revolver back under the bed and left the room. As she descended the stairs, she tried to put her finger on the trouble. What was it about the old revolver that had unhinged her? She tried to picture it again as it lay on the floor under the bed, but she could only see it in her mind's eye, the way it looked when he was wearing it. She paused for a moment on the last step and a thought had begun to form in her mind. "Because he's always wearing it!" But this was silly—Jack was Jack with or without his gun.

To this the voice replied: "It is the source of his power. He has yet to prove what he is without it, and with it he is no more than a hired killer."

"Not true," she whispered. "The power is inside him—I know it."

The tears were very close. As she reached the hall, her thoughts were interrupted by a loud knock at the front door, startling her out of her trance. Wiping her eyes with the palm of her hands, she started toward the door. It was probably Blake or one of the men coming to see her father on business. She was just getting ready to open it when the voice in her head nearly screamed, *"Stop!"*

For half a minute, her hand hesitated just above the latch. When the voice didn't repeat its warning, she tried to tell herself she was being silly and reached again for the latch. Then her father was there asking who it was and she backed away, letting him answer it.

David stepped out onto the porch and pulled the door shut before Annie could follow. It was Andre that had knocked, yet as David looked around the dooryard, he saw that he had his whole gang with him. He took them all in and, turning to Andre, said, "And what can I do for you this fine morning?"

Andre smiled amiably and said, "I was hoping to speak to your daughter."

"I'm afraid that won't be possible. It seems that you have put her in an awkward position, and she no longer wants anything to do with you."

"Oh?" Andre replied in that same smooth voice. "I hadn't heard."

"Yes," David went on, his voice stern and unaffected. "It seems that there was something about a forced wedding that was almost instantly annulled."

"I see," said Andre, stroking his short beard and stepping imperceptibly closer to the door that he knew separated him from Annie. But when he saw that the big man meant to make a stand, he relaxed against the railing of the porch and said casually, "And by whose authority was it annulled?"

David, who was a good six inches taller than Andre and twice as broad in the shoulders, crossed his arms. Taking a step forward, he said, "I suppose the same authority that saw her married against her will."

Andre, to his credit, didn't flinch. He only raised his eyebrows and said, "Against her will? I don't remember her protesting to the union." Turning to Boris, who stood fidgeting in the dooryard, he said, "Boris, do you recall the young lady having any objections?"

Boris's "No, sir" was barely audible, and he only glanced sideways at David when he spoke.

"Nevertheless," David went on, "she doesn't love you, Andre. She never would have married you if she hadn't been concerned for my safety."

Andre looked up at the old house almost nonchalantly. There didn't seem to be anyone else stirring inside, but one couldn't be sure. After a moment's thought, he turned back to David and said, "Well, I am not the sort of man that would force a young lady into anything. If she had just told me how she felt, I would have never gone ahead with the ceremony. But she is young, and perhaps my intentions were misunderstood."

David didn't move, but he chuckled a little as he said, "Perhaps."

For a moment David thought that this might actually be the end of it, so he said, "Well, if there is nothing else I can do for you…"

But Andre wasn't finished. "Actually," he said as David turned toward the door, "there is another reason for my visit." Then, sitting himself down on the porch railing and looking as humble as he could, he said, "It's my people; they are sick again. Some new virus, I'm afraid. We have done all we could for them, and I'm worried that some of the younger ones might not live through it."

Suddenly the front door came open, and Annie, who had been listening to every word, stepped out onto the porch behind her father.

"Annie, go back in the house!" David whispered.

But she closed the door behind her, saying a little impatiently, "Father, the little ones!"

Andre's smile began to widen as she came forward, and he had to force himself to look dejected. "Yes," he said before David could interrupt, "they are very ill. They run high fevers and there are ugly red spots on some of them. Listen, Annie, your father tells me that I have misinterpreted your feelings for me. Perhaps I was overzealous. You see, I was so taken by you—I want to apologize for any misunderstanding on the matter." Annie knew this for what it was: a ploy to smooth things out with her father but basically a load of crap. But how could she not help if people were sick?

Looking up at her again he said, "Of course I would never hold you to a promise that you feel was made under duress. I would understand if you would prefer not to see me anymore, but I beg of you, don't let that stand in the way of helping these poor people."

Andre stood, a look of genuine concern on his face as he went on, "Won't you come with us and see what you can do? I assure you my intentions are good. I will have one of my men escort you back home this evening."

Lowering his eyes to her feet, he said solemnly, "You needn't have to see me at all, if it's your wish."

He looked so sincere and had been so convincing, but Annie knew better than to fall for it. She found that she was no longer afraid of him—too much had happened and she had changed somehow. "Of course I'll come" she said, before David could stop her. She would have gone with him that very moment had her father not intervened.

Taking Annie by the hand, he said to Andre, "We will both come, but I need to put some things together first. Sounds like it could be measles, and you can't be too careful when it comes to infectious diseases."

Annie turned to her father to protest, but before she could utter a word, Jack stepped out on the porch to say, "There's no need for you to trouble yourself, Mr. Fuller. I'll bring her over first thing in the morning."

At the sound of his voice, Annie flinched, and her father squeezed her hand almost painfully. Andre, who knew very well who the newcomer was, didn't bat an eye. Addressing Annie and her father, he said, "And who do we have here? Another hired hand?"

Before David could answer, Jack stepped forward. Putting one hand on the big man's shoulder he said, "More like an old friend of the family."

Andre's eyes met Jack's, and you could have cut the tension with a knife. He smiled his best smile and said, "Well, any friend of the Fullers is a friend of mine, Mr....? Sorry, I didn't catch your name."

Jack felt the muscles in David's shoulders contract as he said in a cold yet almost indifferent tone of voice: "I didn't give it."

For what seemed an eternity, no one else spoke. The two younger men stood within a few feet of each other, eyes locked in combat yet both smiling easily as if they were old friends sharing a private joke.

David broke the silence in a voice that sounded much calmer than he really felt: "We will all be out tomorrow morning first thing—that's the best I can do."

Andre saw that this was David's last word on the subject. He realized that, short of storming the place, he was out of options.

"Very well," he said, addressing David but still looking at Jack. "Tomorrow morning we will expect you."

David could have let it go at that, but he was still angry, and as he watched Andre descending the steps, he shuddered to think what could have happened if Annie had answered the door alone. So, when Andre got to the dooryard, David said, "Next time you have business with me you needn't bring your henchmen. I'm sure we can work things out man to man."

Andre turned, smiling his best smile. "Oh yes, about that—you see, I've heard there is some dangerous outlaw lurking about." Turning his eyes once more on Jack, he added with a laugh, "One can never be too careful, you know."

As soon as the men started to ride away, Annie whirled around to face her father and said, "Daddy, we must hurry. If it is measles, some may be dying as we speak!"

David said nothing but hugged her to him, realizing just how close he had come to losing her for good. It was Jack alone that answered her entreaty. He was standing at the edge of the porch with his back to them as he watched the riders disappear into the trees. He spoke in a quiet, clear voice that sounded almost sad. "I don't think you can do anything this time, Annie. You'd better leave this one up to me."

It took some time to convince Annie that Andre's story had probably been a ruse to get her back to his camp alone; that it would be safer if she stayed behind until the two men could assess the situation. Finally she was appeased by the promise that if the people really were sick, Jack would come back for her.

The rest of the day was spent preparing for their journey. Jack wanted more firepower, so David showed him a small room that was hidden under a trapdoor in the kitchen. Here were dozens of rifles, a few handguns, and all the ammo he could wish for. Jack selected a .38 caliber revolver and a .30-30 rifle that was almost a replica of the one that Blake had taken from his cabin. Unfortunately, there were no bullets for the .45, though David assured him that he could get some by next summer. Smiling at the joke, he counted out what he had left in the loops of his holster. "Seventeen," he said with a sigh, to which the older man replied with a grin. "Then you get the first seventeen, and I'll get the rest with my scatter gun."

David had armed himself only with an old shotgun that had been sawed off so close to the wooden stock that it made it almost useless except at close range. Jack commented on this, but David only smiled and said, "I would have to be close; my eyes aren't what they used to be."

As for the rest of the preparations, David said he would take care of them, and he urged Jack to go and talk to Annie.

"She seems awfully down about being left behind," he commented as they came up from the gun cellar. "Try and cheer her up a little." But before he found Annie, there was one other piece of business that he needed to take care of.

He found Jacob on the porch. Smiling, Jack said, "How is it that you always manage to show up just when I need you?"

Jacob smiled back and started to say, "The Great—" Jack interrupted him, saying, "Yes, yes, the Great Spirit; I know. You really need to get out more and meet new people—*live* people."

Jacob grunted and, looking out across the dooryard, said in his matter-of-fact tone, "There is a group of men camped just inside those trees at the back of the house."

"Andre's men?" Jack inquired thoughtfully.

"Could be. They're not from the village and they're well-armed."

Jack thought about it and finally said, "Tomorrow morning me and David are going to ride out to Andre's camp. Maybe these men were left behind to storm the house once we were gone."

Jacob nodded his assent, adding, "Maybe you ought to put off your trip for a day or two."

Jack thought it over a minute and then, shaking his head, said, "I've got a better idea."

He found Annie in the kitchen. At first she didn't even notice him, and it wasn't until he sat down across from her at the big table that she looked up. Her eyes had a dull, glossy look, and for a moment Jack was alarmed.

"What is it?" he asked, taking her hand.

"Nothing. Everything. I don't know—*something*," she said, and at the same time she pounded her little fist on the table. "This morning I came into your room before you woke up."

"Yeah, I've been meaning to apologize for that," he interrupted. "Your dad—"

"No, Jack, it's not that!"

Standing, she walked over to the sink and looked out the small window.

"Annie, what's wrong?"

For a moment she stood there, her back to him, her fingers drumming the countertop. Suddenly she turned.

"It's all wrong! Do you remember when we were little?"

Jack said nothing, but his eyes had a puzzled, far-off look in them.

"In our dreams. Don't you remember?" she persisted. "Please, Jack, I need to know that you remember!"

She wasn't sure why this was so important, but ever since this morning when she had seen him lying on his bed, the big revolver tossed carelessly aside, she had felt vaguely uneasy. As the morning wore on, it became more and more important to connect the Jack from her dreams to the one passed out in the upstairs bedroom. She stared at him wide eyed, waiting...

He continued to stare vacantly into space; then slowly his eyes seemed to widen, and he said softly, "Yes," then a little louder, "Yes, I do remember something—a fire!"

She grasped at this, and in a voice that was almost pleading, she said, "You were my hero. You were my knight in shining armor! You led me through the fire. You said, 'If I made it, I could kill it.' Do you remember, Jack?"

It came on him in a rush—the dream that had been only a vague memory suddenly projected itself full force and in living color on his mind.

They had been standing in the forest hand in hand. He must have been about fourteen years old and she only seven or eight. All around them the forest burned, and creatures big and small were running past them, some literally on fire. Looking down at his little friend, he had seen the fear in her eyes—not for herself, but for him.

"You were so little," he managed to say, but the mental picture never wavered.

"You said, 'It's too big! It's too late. I can't stop it now!' And what did you say, Jack?" she asked, her voice suddenly far away. "What did you tell me?!"

He paused, waiting for the memory to catch up. In his mind's eye, he saw himself kneel down so that he was on eye level with the little girl. He saw himself take both of her hands in his and say, "When she smiles, the sun shines. When she cries, it rains. When she sleeps, the snow flies. When she wakes, it's spring." Together they repeat the rhyme over and over, and as they do, she begins to cry. They are both crying, but they stand transfixed, the inferno raging around them, holding each other's hands. The next moment it's raining—not a gradual buildup of drops here and there, but a sudden downpour. They are both still crying, yet they're also smiling, because the fire is sputtering, and the flames are shrinking.

This memory flitted through his mind in a matter of seconds, and as the picture began to fade, Jack looked from the little girl only to find the grown woman standing before him in her own kitchen, the tears flowing slowly down her pale cheeks.

"When she cries, it rains," he says finally as he takes her hand in his.

For a moment Annie didn't move. But her eyes, which had seemed so dull only minutes before, seemed to light up the entire room as she said, "Oh Jack, you haven't forgotten! And now perhaps, if you will only let yourself, you may begin to remember other things; things buried deep down inside your very soul."

For a moment Jack stood dazed, staring into those glowing pools of light. He felt as if he *could* remember other things: other places, other times, other Annies— and yes, even other Jacks! The room seemed to spin out of focus and he caught short glimpses of other rooms; different landscapes; and a huge ship where Annie stood on the bow, gazing out at a vast ocean. The ocean wavered into a desert, and she stood in the doorway of an ancient monolith in a flowing gown that billowed out behind her like the sail of a ship. These pictures passed through Jack's mind in seconds. A blue light had seemed to surround him on every side—but it was too much too soon, and Jack's mind repulsed these visions. Annie had done a lot to expand it in the last few months, but it was still too closed to realize these things. Slowly that light began to fade, and it was once again just Annie—his Annie, standing before him in the huge kitchen. She was smiling up at him, but he felt like he was missing something important; his brain struggled to regain it. Annie saw the puzzled look in his eyes and knew what it meant.

Taking both of his hands in hers, she whispered, "It's ok, Jack. Go slowly. It will all come back to you in time." And she let herself be folded into his strong embrace.

The rest of the day, Annie and Jack sat in the kitchen talking about dreams and their childhood, generally getting to know each other better. To Jack it felt like he was waking from a long sleep and everything was being revealed; to Annie it was confirmation that she had been right about him all along. Suffice it to say that the time passed quickly, and before either of them knew it, the sun was going down. By now they had moved from the kitchen to the front porch, but neither could recall how or when.

They sat close, Annie leaning on his shoulder, his arm wrapped around her slim waist.

"Jack?" she mused, the playfulness returning to her voice. "When did you first love me?"

He was going to say—or at least the first thing that came to his lips was—"The first time I saw you." He paused. A strange thought came into his head, and before he could check it, he whispered: "Annie, I think I've loved you forever."

# CHAPTER 20

"I'm going," Jack announced, throwing his saddle over the gray's back. "This is the last obstacle between us. For all I know, this is the reason I have come here to your home—it's my destiny."

Annie shook her head vigorously, her dark hair finally coming to rest on her shoulders. "No, Jack. He is unimportant; I am not afraid of him."

"Annie, he has your father. Would you just leave him to die?"

"It's not my father he wants, Jack. He'll be back, and when he comes, we will deal with him here!"

They hadn't even noticed that David was gone until after breakfast—even then they hadn't been worried until they had found the note. Annie had found it when she had gone in to tidy up her father's room.

It was a long, rambling note but the gist of it was: "We have your father. If you want him back, you will come alone to my camp." It wasn't the note itself that had driven Jack into a rage, but the way it was signed: "Your loving husband, Andre."

Well, he intended to reply in person, and no one, Annie included, was going to stop him. The horse was ready and Jack turned to Annie.

"Listen, I want you to stay near the house. The other night Jacob and I found a group of Andre's men camped not far from here. I have told Kitchi to round up some men, and when I return, I may have company, so don't show your face under any circumstances!"

"But Jack!" She pleaded.

"Annie, listen to me. We have had little time to get to know each other, but after yesterday I almost feel like we have known each other forever. Probably nothing will come of my going to Andre's camp, but you must know: This is what I do. It's the only thing I've ever done well and I'm very good at it. So let me do my part, and when it's over, we will be together—me, you, Kitchi, and our father."

Annie stepped back from the horse as Jack mounted. She had to admit that she was touched by the way Jack had so intimately referred to her father as "our father," but something deep inside was still telling her that this was all wrong somehow.

Reaching out to touch his boot, she said, "What about yesterday? Everything we talked about? Don't you see, Jack? It's not your gun I need; it's you—it's always been you!"

He hesitated, looked up at the graying sky, saying the one thing he couldn't tell her the day before. "Listen, Annie. I've never been what you might call a deep thinker; belief in anything I couldn't lay my hands on has always come hard to me. I sometimes think that I have only survived as long as I have by acting first and asking why afterward. Then I met you. You have changed me somehow—made me more alive, made me question things that I have always taken for granted. In most ways I thank you for that, but I'm a slow learner, and right now I need to do the only thing I know how to do—the only thing I've ever been good at!"

For a moment she only stared up at him, taking him in just as he was in that moment, and for the first time since she met him in the meadow, she saw only the gunslinger; yet this didn't frighten her because *she* knew, even if he didn't, that this was only one part of what made the whole man—a very small part.

She took a step back and, looking directly into his gray eyes, said simply: "I could stop you if I wanted."

It wasn't meant to be a threat and it wasn't taken as one.

Jack only smiled down at her, saying, "No, I don't think you could. Anyone else maybe, but not me."

With a suddenness that startled her, he turned and galloped toward the trees. Annie was left standing by the stable, not knowing what to do next. A wet nose nuzzled her hand, and she looked down to find Wolf watching Jack's progress intently.

"Go with him, Wolf," she said suddenly.

As if he had only been waiting for a word from her, he was off at a dead run to catch up with the horse and rider.

Jack rode out like a shot, but not because he felt there was any need to hurry to Andre's camp. He figured that if they had meant to kill David, he was already dead. The real reason he was in such a hurry to leave was that he knew that on some points, Annie was right. Still, he wasn't about to stand around and let another man—particularly this man—dictate his actions. He had no misgivings about riding into Andre's camp alone. One thing he had always been sure of was his ability to stand up to anyone in a fair fight. His honor was at stake here, and although he didn't expect Annie to understand, he did expect her to let him defend himself—because when it came down to it, it wasn't just about Andre's claim on the woman he loved: it was the fact that Andre refused to acknowledge him at all that really stuck in Jack's craw. Well, he would introduce himself formally, and when it was done, only one of them would still be left to claim Annie's hand.

This thought had a calming effect on him. He realized now that he was racing across the plain like a man pursued. The gray was panting and snorting as they reached the edge of the trees; Jack slowed him down to a walk. "Three months ago," he thought, "I wouldn't have been so scatterbrained." But three months ago he hadn't known Annie. He had gone about a hundred yards into the trees when he came upon a small brook, so he stopped to let the horse drink.

He was only about a quarter of a mile from the house, yet the very air seemed different here. Jack looked around and listened. There were no sounds here: no squirrel chatter, no bird song...just silence. He felt as if he were being watched; the hair stood up on the back of his neck.

The gray became suddenly agitated, stepping back from the creek, swishing its tail and trying to turn back. Jack managed to hold him steady, but he too felt a sudden urge to return to the house.

Something was wrong here—not just with these woods but with this whole expedition. A thought kept trying to invade his mind; something about treasure. He pushed it away with some difficulty. Slipping from the saddle he tried to reassure the horse by patting him on the neck and talking in a low, soothing voice. It was silly, of course, these premonitions—it showed how big of an affect Annie had on him. The gray was still spooked, so he decided to walk for awhile. He led the animal through the densest part of the forest. They hadn't gone half a mile when the uneasy feeling seemed to pass. Once again he could hear the birds and forest creatures going about their business.

Jack reckoned that Andre's camp was only about two miles from Annie's house, and he had already come about half that distance. He half expected to encounter a guard of some sort any time. He had no plan—his only thought was to reach the camp and confront Andre. Even in his haste, he realized that they would never just let him stroll in unmolested.

Finally he came to a rise that looked down on an almost circular plain surrounded by forest. On one side, tucked up against the trees, were two hastily built cabins facing a small tent city. He could detect no movement. There were a few fires still smoldering in front of the tents, but other than these, the place looked completely deserted. He started his descent, meaning to circle and come around behind the cabins. He realized that they might expect this, but it was better than coming in from the front, which would make him an easy target for anyone in the tents. When he got within one hundred feet of the cabin, he stopped, tied the horse to a fallen tree, and proceeded on foot.

He had begun to think that the place really was deserted when he detected a slight movement just to the right of the larger cabin. Instinctively, Jack fell to the ground, the .45 already in his hand. Not daring to even breathe, his eyes riveted to the spot where he had detected the movement, and he waited. Perhaps a minute passed; nothing happened. Then Jack's sharp eyes made out the barrel of a gun and just the edge of an old hat—they were expecting him! As he watched, the man moved back and was once more entirely concealed. He knew that where there was one sentry, there had to be more. He dared not move until he could discern the other hiding spots; this was made harder by the fact that the rear of the building was mostly concealed by scrub brush that any number of men could be hiding in. Plus there were no windows on this side, which meant that he would have to enter from the front if he got that far. Minutes passed, and Jack was beginning to realize that in his hurry to get to Andre and possibly save David, he had trapped himself. It was a miracle that he hadn't been detected and shot outright. He couldn't turn back the way he came, and he couldn't go forward without exposing himself.

Just then, he saw a slight movement in the bushes on the left side of the cabin. "There's number two," he thought, but it brought him little satisfaction. If anything, it made things worse as it put him almost directly in the middle of these two men. It was a desperate situation, and he had just about made up his mind that his only option was to fake surrender and then rely on his speed to gun the two down when they moved from cover. The only problem was that these were probably not the only two out there. Well, there was nothing to be done about that—he figured his chances were fifty-fifty, whereas trying to shoot it out with them from his scanty hiding place was considerably less.

He was just getting ready to call out when two things happened. First, two gunshots rang out from inside the cabin. The man in the bushes stood up suddenly. Jack fired automatically, and the man fell before he could take a step. The second thing that happened Jack didn't understand until later—the other man had turned and Jack caught just a glimpse of him as he started for the front of the building. There came a sharp roar, followed by a loud scream and another shot. After this, all was silent. Thinking that at that very moment his father-in-law could be in a struggle for his life, Jack threw caution to the winds and ran toward the building. Coming around the front, he was brought up short by what he saw: two men standing in front of the door, another lying dead in the dooryard. Standing over him, teeth bared, was Wolf! They hadn't noticed him—in fact, they both looked frozen to the spot.

Jack heard one say in a shaky voice, "It can't be real. It's too big!"

The other replied, "Shoot it quick, before it gets us too."

Jack put a bullet in both, then flattened himself against the wall of the cabin. Still, Wolf did not move. His eyes had shifted though to something inside the door. Jack realized that if he didn't act fast, Wolf would probably be shot.

Inspiration struck, and Jack called out, "In the cabin—you may as well surrender. We have the place surrounded."

No answer. Wolf had stopped growling, but his eyes remained riveted to the same spot. Jack looked out at the tent city; it was obviously deserted. The thought from earlier flashed through his mind: "I've been fooled!"

He found he was sweating, even though it couldn't be more than thirty degrees outside. He tried again. "Come on out," he said. "We won't shoot."

The answer that came chilled Jack's blood. Suddenly he realized the extent of his blunder—it wasn't David's voice that came from the cabin, but Jack recognized it just the same.

It was Blake, and he said simply: "No one left here to shoot."

This was followed by a snorting sort of chuckle and a fit of coughing. Slowly Jack made his way to the door and peeked in. Two men lay on the floor; there was blood everywhere. One body was lying crosswise in the door, the hilt of a knife sticking out of his chest. Half of the blade, the part that had come out his back, lay broken beside him. Another lay, half concealed, behind a small desk, his throat cut from ear to ear. An old pistol was still clutched in his right hand. Blake sat in an old rickety chair behind the small desk, smiling.

"Where's David?" Jack asked, pointing the gun at Blake's head.

"Not here," he replied. "Never was here." He chuckled lightly, which led to another coughing fit. When he looked up again, Jack noticed a trickle of blood at the corner of his mouth. Wiping it away, Blake nodded to the man with his throat cut and said, "Jerk shot me after he was already dead. I thought I could get the drop on them. They ain't from Andre's gang; just a bunch of old men from the colony. I guess they was considered expendable. Andre left me here with them to take care of you. But the more I got to thinking about it, I began to realize that I had been duped also. I guess he thought he could kill two birds with one stone. Part of me was convinced that you wouldn't be stupid enough to fall for it, so when I saw my chance, I took it."

Jack holstered the .45 and said, "It's a good thing you moved when you did, or I'd be as dead as these by now."

Blake managed to stand, enabling Jack to see for the first time the bloodstain that was blooming out on the front of his shirt.

"How'd we both get so stupid?" he said, swaying a little. "No, don't answer that; I know how. It's that little girl that's done it, and now we're both as good as dead."

"Well, I ain't dead yet," Jack replied, and he turned to leave the cabin.

Blake checked him. "Wait!" he said, his voice lower now that all the humor had died out of it. "I ain't dead quite yet either. Do you have any idea what kind of firepower you're up against?"

Jack hesitated, but he wasn't really listening to Blake; his mind was working over the fastest way back to Annie.

Blake continued, "Let me go with you. If nothing else, I might be able to draw their attention while you get the girl out."

Jack looked back to the blood on Blake's shirt. "How bad is it?" he asked.

"Well, it ain't good. If we could stop the bleeding for awhile I think I could ride." Blake told his story while Jack examined his wound. "Andre had said that he really wanted nothing to do with the girl. It was the cure for the plague and the rest of David's little secret experiments, that's what he was really after. Once he got that, he said I could do whatever I wanted with her."

Jack tensed at these words and squeezed Blake's shoulder.

"Ow!" he cried out. "Careful! Besides, you got me all wrong, Jack. My intentions were as honorable as yours. I love her, too—

or I thought I did. At least I had a powerful urge to have her to myself. Somehow I had it in my head that if I could get her away from here, away from you, she would learn to love me back. I was also pretty sure that your days were numbered. I knew that if she were to stay here, she would be in constant danger from Andre and his men."

Jack had finished his examination and looked into Blake's eyes. "And how do you feel about her now?" he asked.

Blake stared back, suddenly smiled, and shrugged his good shoulder. "I'm as good as dead already. If you mean to go back and take on those men alone, so are you. So, what does it matter?"

# CHAPTER 21

Annie stood alone in the great room at the front of the house. When Jack left, she had come back to her own room. Removing her moccasins, she laid down on the bed, feeling as if she could sleep forever. It had always been this way with her—when she was under great stress, she slept. Upon awakening, everything would be better, and she could almost believe she had been dreaming, but this time sleep wouldn't come. She kept wondering about her father's fate. She tried not to think about it because it sent her into a crying fit. It was impossible to shut out the feeling of dread that had come over her. Eventually, wearily, she had gotten up. Not even bothering to put her moccasins back on, she had come down here to watch and wait.

It was her fault—all her fault! Because of her the two men she loved more than anything, more than life itself, were in mortal danger.

"If not already dead," the voice whispered.

Annie sighed deeply. Not that it mattered—*they* were coming, the bad men. And this time, no one, not even Jack, would be able to stop them.

In her mind the voice said, "You can!"

This internal voice had been with her almost constantly for the last few days. Whether it was her own thoughts or someone else's that kept invading her head, she didn't know. At this point she just wished it would shut up and leave her alone. She walked to the far end of the room and looked out the window. To her left she could see her father's workshop backed up against the trees. To the right she could just make out the corner of the barn and stables, about a hundred yards from the great house. Directly in front of her, the wide valley stretched away to the west. She could see all the way to the tree line on the farther side. The whole place seemed deserted. Straining her eyes, she tried to make out the smallest movement, but everything seemed unnaturally still. "They *are* coming!" she thought.

Immediately the voice corrected her: "They're already here."

Turning angrily from the window, she shouted at the empty room: "*Shut up! Shut up! Shut up! Can't you see that I am all alone here?*"

"You are never alone, child," replied the voice. It seemed sad, almost melancholy. She was facing the fireplace, where the portrait of her mother had hung above the mantel since before she was born. Her eyes were drawn to the face and she studied it as if for the first time. Her mother had been a beautiful woman, and this picture surely brought out her best features. In it she was smiling, and her eyes seemed to glow with laughter, as if she had been told some funny secret and was doing her best not to let it out.

"Oh, Mother," she said out loud. "If only you were here."

How many times had she thought this over the years? Hundreds? Thousands? When she was four and had skinned her knee on the porch steps; when she was nine and her father had scolded her for riding to the river with some of the boys from the village, leaving her crying and confused in this very room; or when she was thirteen and one of those same boys had told her that he loved her—these were some of the times when a mother was needed in a young girl's life, and Annie had had her for none. Only this portrait and a few photographs were all that remained to comfort her, and she *had* found comfort in them—many a night she had sat here and stared at the portrait as her father read or talked of his day. There were times when it actually seemed to speak to her. Today, though, it was mute. Annie looked at it with a feeling, somewhat like resentment, for the first time.

Out loud she said, "You weren't here for me, Momma."

The inner voice that seemed to pester her on every other subject had no reply. Slowly she became aware of a sound coming from just outside the front door. It was a light tapping, one that she had heard many times before. Running to the door, she threw it open. Before the open door sat Wolf, his tongue lolling out and panting as if he had been at a dead run.

"Wolf!" she cried and threw her arms around his shaggy neck.

After a moment she stood, looked around, and asked absently: "Wolf, where's Jack?"

However, Wolf only whined and lay down on the porch in front of her. She started toward the steps, meaning to have a look around the place, but Wolf stood and barred her way. Something was wrong. Inside the house she had been distracted, but now she felt it in every fiber of her being. For a moment she stood completely still, not knowing exactly what to do next. Unexpectedly a hand was clasped over her mouth and she was being dragged back into the house. Wolf made no move to help her. Instead he simply followed her and her attacker through the front door.

Closing the door with his foot, he whispered close into her ear: "Shhhh, Little Mother, it's me."

She barely had time to even put up a struggle, and now that she heard Jacob's familiar voice, she became very still. Slowly he released her, once again urging her to be quiet by putting his finger to her lips. Without another word he led her down the hall into the kitchen.

Turning he said, "The whole place is surrounded."

A chill ran down Annie's spine, causing her to shiver involuntarily. Jacob saw this and smiled down into her upturned face.

He said, "Don't fret, Little Mother. Jack anticipated this, so there are friends about also."

Annie stiffened. "Jack? Is Jack here?" she asked almost desperately.

"No, not him," Jacob replied honestly. "But I'm sure he'll be along. No, it's some of the men from the village. About twenty, I think. When I told them that you were in trouble, the whole place wanted to come. I didn't think it wise to put too many in harm's way."

Annie studied Jacob's face—there was something he wasn't telling her; something he was struggling to keep from her.

It came to her suddenly, and she asked, "My father?"

Jacob faltered a little, but he managed to meet her eyes as he said, "He's here, and he is all right. But what we have to worry about right now is keeping you safe. "

Before she could reply, he turned. Looking about the room, he said, "Take me to where your father keeps the weapons."

She led him to the kitchen and removed a small rug from in front of the table to reveal the trapdoor. Jacob pulled it open and stared into the darkness. Annie had taken an old lantern from a nearby shelf and lit it with matches she found in a desk drawer. As she handed it to him, a footfall was heard in the hall. Suddenly Kitchi entered the room, looking haggard and with a small cut across his forehead.

Annie ran to him, kissing him gently on the cheek, saying, "Oh! Kitchi you're hurt."

"Not bad, Sis." Turning to Jacob, he said, "They're coming—looks like the whole village."

All three crept back into the front room to peer out the window. It was the same window she had been looking through only twenty minutes earlier—same workshop, same barn, same long valley. Coming out of the trees as if in some mass exodus, they came: not just Andre's thugs, but the whole camp. Annie felt before she saw that they were coming not as an army, but as refugees. These people had no idea what they were walking into, and her heart went out to them. For a moment she stared as if in a trance. There were hundreds of them—men, women, and children. She knew that none of them knew of the conflict that they were walking into. Jacob stood close beside her.

Turning to him, she said, "They'll be slaughtered! Our own people will mow them down!"

Jacob had guessed this also, but his only thought was how to keep Annie safe. His last order, given to a young man from the village, was "Defend the house from all outsiders."

Their men were in a precarious position. Due to the lack of cover and the fact that Andre's men had already surrounded the house, Jacob had left them all in the woods behind the workshop, in hopes that if there was a rush on the house, they could come up from behind and ambush them. He realized now that they were between the enemy and the enemy's camp. If they shot down their leader, would they riot? If they did, then surely their small force would be overwhelmed.

Well, it was too late now to speculate; his one job— his only purpose—was to keep the girl safe. Gritting his teeth, he took her by the elbow and led her back to the kitchen. Pulling up the trap door, he turned to her and said, "You best get below, Little Mother, until it's safe." Then, as an afterthought, he added, "It's what Jack wanted."

Up until now Annie had let herself be led. She seemed to be in a daze and everything was happening too quickly, but at the sound of Jacob's calm voice calling her "Little Mother" once again, she came out of it.

Turning on him suddenly, she said, "I will not hide in the cellar while hundreds of people die because of me! I will fight. And if you call me 'Little Mother' one more time, I will take you down first!"

Turning to Kitchi, who had followed them in, she said, "Go down in the cellar and pick four good rifles and as much ammo as you can carry. Place one rifle with ammunition at each window in the front room. Do not fire one round unless you hear from me personally. Do you understand?"

Kitchi, who had been taking orders from Annie since she was able to talk, didn't hesitate.

Rounding on Jacob, she said, "Now you. Figure out a way to get a message to those men behind the shop that they are, under no circumstances, to fire on those innocent people!"

Before Jacob could so much as utter a word in protest, she pushed past him and started for the front door. Her intention was to walk out on the front porch and call them all out to confront Andre once and for all. "Olly olly oxen free; come out come out, wherever you are!" But as she passed the largest of the windows in the front room, something caught her eye.

Almost simultaneously the voice in her head cried out: "Stop!"

Slowly she walked closer to the window. The people from Andre's camp were closer now; she could make out individual faces. What had caught her eye, though, and what held it now was a lone rider—and he rode a pale horse.

# CHAPTER 22

Blake's horse stood exactly where he had left him—this was their first lucky break. As Jack helped Blake into the saddle, he noticed their second. Leaning against a post, so close to the horse that it was amazing the animal hadn't knocked it over into the high weeds—then truly all would have been lost—was Jack's own .30-30.

"Can you shoot?" he asked Blake, eyeing him skeptically.

"Fair," Blake replied, wincing as he threw his leg over the horse.

He was obviously in a lot of pain and Jack was beginning to have his doubts about him even making it back to the house. For the first time since he had entered the cabin, he noticed Wolf—an idea occurred to him.

Calling the animal over, he kneeled down. Taking his shaggy head in both hands, he looked straight into his blue eyes that seemed so much like Annie's.

Speaking softly, he said, "Our girl's in trouble, boy, and you can get to her much faster than we can."

Wolf responded by licking his face lightly. Standing up, he said in a louder, more commanding voice, "Go to her, Wolf. Go to Annie!" But the huge creature was already off at a dead run even before his mistress's name had passed Jack's lips.

They found Jack's own horse right where he had left him. Instead of going back the way he had come in, they took the easier path across the valley. They were soon winding their way through the forest that separated Andre's camp from everything he loved. This was a pretty extensive forest with several small streams and a few large clearings, one of which he had passed within two hundred yards of earlier. They were almost at the very spot where Jack had paused when he came in. Yes, here was the brook where the horse had drunk—and here came the same uneasy feeling. Pulling up, he motioned for Blake to stop also. Slowly he dismounted and once again walked the horse. All of his senses were on high alert; nothing stirred. Jack was just getting ready to climb back on the gray when his keen eye caught a slight movement just ahead and to the right. Without even seeming to move, Jack drew his gun and fired. There was a muffled cry, and four men broke cover, two from the very spot that Jack had fired at. The other two Jack only saw from the corner of his eye as they were to his left and slightly behind him.

"On the left," he said in a voice so calm and even that he might have been commenting on the weather. But Blake needed no prompting—he, too, had felt something was wrong. Although he was injured and not as quick as he normally would be, he managed to raise the rifle and fire at the closest of the two, even as Jack spoke. The first man went down slowly, firing his pistol at nothing in particular. The second one ducked behind a tree and began taking pot shots at Jack, who seemed to be completely ignoring him.

With an exclamation of "Darned fool!" Blake dismounted, took careful aim at the tree where the shooter was hiding, and waited for the man to peek his head out one more time.

As for Jack, from the moment the first shot rang out, he knew that these men weren't trained killers. First of all, the spot that they had picked for the ambush gave him and Blake the advantage. Secondly, they had been impatient. If they had remained hidden for just a few more seconds, they could have had him and Blake in a crossfire and they would be dead by now. It was a rookie mistake, and Jack had neither the time nor the patience to deal with amateurs right now. Instead of ducking for cover, he went straight at the two, emerging from the brush. Bullets whizzed by him, one so close he actually felt the wind of it, but he walked on unconcerned. When he came to within fifty feet of them, he fired. The man on the left, who was coming at him at almost a dead run, fell dead, his heart exploding in his chest. The other had stopped to take better aim. Even as his comrade fell, he pulled the trigger. At this range he could hardly have missed, and for a split second, Jack's life actually hung in the balance—but fate was with him on this day, and instead of the loud report both men expected, there was only a dry click. The gun was empty. Slowly, Jack raised the .45, meaning to put a bullet right between the unlucky man's eyes.

He paused. In the heat of battle, Jack had paid little attention to what these men looked like. He knew instinctively that to hesitate in a gunfight meant certain death; now he saw the truth for the first time. With the pistol still trained on the other's forehead, he glanced at the body that lay a few yards in front of him, and a shudder ran down his spine. They were just kids! The dead one might be about sixteen and the one in his sights even younger. Just as it was coming home to him that he was still pointing his gun at a helpless child, he heard the .30-30 go off again. Blake had managed to get his man. At first glance Jack thought it was the boy that had been killed, because the moment the rifle went off, he fainted dead away.

The two men looked around them, expecting to see reinforcements coming out of the trees. All was silent, though. Blake stood with some effort and walked toward where Jack was kneeling over the body of the young boy. Blake hadn't witnessed the scene between him and Jack, so when the kid started to move, he lowered the rifle on him. "Wait!" Jack hissed, trying to keep his voice down. Turning to the kid, who was just beginning to come to, he placed his finger over his lips, indicating he should be very quiet. He stood and whispered to Blake: "Watch him. I'll be right back."

He slipped silently into the forest. He was looking for the first man, the one he had taken the first snap shot at.

He was sure he had hit him, but chances were he was only wounded and might even now be rallying the troops. These fears proved unfounded, however—he found his man right where he felled him behind some scrub brush. This man was not much older than the one that Blake was guarding. He was about to move on when he saw the young man's head move slightly—he was still alive. Jack kneeled down and the boy opened his eyes, looking Jack full in the face. His lips moved and Jack strained to hear him speak. The only sound Jack could hear was a low whistling coming from deep in his chest. Jack knew from experience what that whistling sound meant: the kid had been shot through the lung, and nothing, not even Annie, could save him now.

Jack had killed many men in his career—although not half as many as he was credited for—and he had even been beside some of them as they took their last breath. For the first time in his life, as he knelt beside this young kid who should have had his whole life ahead of him, he wished that his aim hadn't been true.

A trickle of blood was beginning to run from the boy's mouth. He was trying to speak again, so Jack leaned over, placing his ear close to the young man's lips. He spoke three words. When Jack heard them, he uttered a low groan. Slowly Jack stood and looked around him. The ground behind the scrub had been trampled by many feet. He saw that a path had been worn down heading off to the north. They had probably been watching in shifts, changing people every morning and every night, but they weren't camped here. Cautiously he worked the back trail and had gone no more than 150 yards when the smell of smoke came to his nostrils. Fifty more feet, and he heard voices. Finally, coming to a small clearing, he saw them: Andre's whole camp. For a few minutes, Jack watched them silently. For the most part, they looked haggard, starving, and just plain worn out. They were making no effort to conceal themselves, and it suddenly struck Jack that they were probably left here to die.

Once again that young man's final words came back to him: "Not my fault."

"No, son," he thought sadly, "not your fault. Not theirs either."

Blake waited for what seemed like an eternity for Jack to return. He was pretty sure he was slowly dying, and the slowly part was no consolation. He didn't particularly want to do it here. Besides, before he died, he had a score to settle with Andre, and he meant to take him with him if he got the chance. Finally he saw Jack coming back in a different direction from the way he had left. He was carrying something, and as he drew nearer, Blake saw that it was a dead boy.

When he got close enough, Blake whispered, "Any more live ones?"

Jack nodded and, throwing the body over the saddle of the gray, said in an authoritative tone, "You from the camp out there in the clearing?"

The boy surprised him by nodding. "We was lookouts. Our orders were that if anyone was traveling west, we should just let them pass, but if they was traveling east, we was to kill them."

"Hmm. And what about the rest of the people? Do they also have orders to kill anyone that happens by?" Jack asked sarcastically as he synched the rope that would hold the dead boy down.

"No. No, they don't know nothin'," the boy said hurriedly. "Look, mister, they're unarmed and mostly just hungry. They were all told to wait where they are and someone would come back for them. We are all moving to a better camp. Andre says there's plenty of game to eat and houses to sleep in. He says that nobody will go hungry anymore or die of the sickness."

During this speech, Jack had been watching the kid closely, and Jack felt that he really believed what he was saying. Jack also felt that he must choose his words carefully.

"That sounds nice," he said looking up at Blake. "Is there anybody already living in this place that might object to your people invading their home?"

The boy shook his head vigorously. "Oh no!" he said emphatically. "Andre says it is only an old man and his daughter. She is Andre's new bride, and we have been invited to come live with them in their valley."

"So why have you all been left out here in the woods?" Jack knew the answer to this, but he wanted to hear what excuse Andre had given.

"He said that if we all just showed up at once, we might frighten them. So he was going to speak to them first and find out where we would be setting up our new camp. "

Jack had been squatting over the boy, almost cross-examining him; suddenly he stood up and turned to Blake.

"Yep, he's one of them all right." Returning his gaze to the youngster, he remarked, "I'm surprised he didn't recognize you right away!"

Blake knew better than to say anything, but his eyes were saying, "What in the world are you talking about?"

The kid, however, had much to say, and he almost immediately began to relate the story of his sad but eventful young life.

His name was Kara, and he belonged to a clan or group of people called Cossacks. They—his people, that is—had originally come from Juno, Alaska, where Andre had been some sort of mayor or governor. They had survived there for years before Andre came along, but the last two winters had taken their toll and the plague had wiped out half of the town. Last spring Andre had gone on an expedition and he had found an old army base. He and his men had returned with a lot of weapons and a story. He called all the people together and announced that he had found them a new home that was free of the plague. He said there they would live like kings and have as much food as they could eat.

Looking down as if he were trying to bury the memory, he sighed and said, "That summer we crossed the mountains, and a lot of people died, either from starvation or the walking sickness." His face brightened as he said, "But finally they had come here and met the lady. She was an angel on earth and had come among the people as if she were no better than a common person. She cured the sick and gave food to the starving. Shoot, before long we all recovered, and it was like the miracles in the black book that Chance reads to us. But then she left, and Andre told us that we would only have to wait a little longer before we could stay with her and her father permanently. Some of the people got restless, and if it wouldn't have been for the guns and Andre's men, they might have snuck away.

"Then one day a couple of months ago, the girl had come back to our camp with her father. She was so beautiful and she had a cure for everything—some people that were almost dead, she gave them a special pill and they got better in one day!

"Everyone loved her. So, when Andre announced that she was to become his wife, the whole camp showed up for the ceremony." Here Kara paused and asked Jack timidly, "Have you seen her?"

Jack only nodded, not wanting to reveal too much to this young man.

The boy nodded back, and looking up at the sky, he said, "I think she's the most beautiful girl on earth!"

During Kara's narrative they had drawn closer to the camp, and as they approached it, Jack thought that if all of these people felt about Annie as Kara did, he might be able to swing them over to his side—but he would have to be careful.

Leaning close to Blake, he whispered, "Some of these people have probably seen you. Just act as if I'm in charge. If they ask any questions, refer to me."

Blake nodded, but under his breath he said, "I hope you know what you're doing." So far the young boy hadn't thought to question Jack on any of his claims, but as they entered the camp, he noticed a group of men that were huddled around one particular fire turn to scrutinize him. "Here we go," he thought. He realized that even though they seemed to be unarmed, if his plan failed, he and Blake would be overwhelmed just by the sheer number of people. Jack was leading the horse with the dead boy on it. As he approached the men around the fire, he noticed how they kept glancing down at the Colt on his hip.

Stepping up to the fire, he said, "Which one of you gentlemen are in charge here?"

At first no one spoke, and their eyes darted suspiciously from Blake to the gun on his hip. Jack was conscious of a tightening of the whole camp and he realized that he was past the point of no return—even if he wanted to, he couldn't shoot his way out of this crowd.

Blake, who had been walking right beside him and trying not to wince, asked, "What are you going to tell them?"

Jack glanced around him. These people were ragged; they were tired; they were hungry—and if he was right, which he prayed he was, they were fed up.

Looking straight at Blake and speaking in a voice that everyone could hear, he said, "The truth, of course!"

There was one man that Jack had set his eyes on the minute they had come into the inner circle. He was possibly in his late forties or early fifties. He was a tall man, and Jack thought that if he hadn't been so worn away by hunger, he would have been a formidable man. It was his eyes that had attracted his attention. He had a look of defiance that made him stand out from the rest of the sheep around him. So, turning to him, he unbuckled his gun belt and handed him his only means of defense. At first the man didn't stir, only looked at him questioningly.

"Take it," Jack said. "If I speak anything but the truth in your eyes, you can shoot me with it."

Returning to the packhorse, laden with its burden, he said, "Whose son is this?"

No one stirred, but presently a man, who had stood stoically as Jack walked by, came forward. With a sneer he cut the lashings with his Buck knife and pulled the corpse to the ground, dragging him almost fiercely away from the man who had killed him.

Jack only nodded, trying his best not to betray any emotion whatsoever. He turned and faced the old man again, still holding out the gun belt. The man took the belt and, glancing at Blake, said, "I know all of Andre's men." Looking around to Jack again, he finished: "You ain't one of them."

"No," Jack replied. "I'm not. I won't lie to you. I bring you your dead and a message."

Now up to this point, Jack had been operating on a hunch, combined with what the young boy Kara had told him. So by handing the old man his gun, he was truly taking the first leap of faith he had ever taken in his life—and it was big. He was literally putting his life, Annie's life, and—if only he had known it at the time—the life of every man, woman, and child on the planet in the hand of one old man.

Rotating around, Jack addressed the whole crowd. "You've all been fooled and I believe you have been left here to starve." The people, who had been mostly silent until now, set up a general murmur, and Jack didn't much care for the sound of it. Gradually the murmur died out, and Jack realized that they were all looking to the man with his gun, who had raised his hand.

He spoke in a quiet but firm voice: "I guess we'll hear what the man has to say."

Jack paused and took time to look around him before he spoke. He had always been a quiet man and hated speaking in front of a large group—this was without a doubt the largest group he had ever faced. He focused his attention back to the older man, who looked at him with raised eyebrows as if to say, "Ok, speak your piece."

Jack took a deep breath and played his ace.

"You have all seen the girl that Andre claims for his wife."

Again that low murmur ran through the crowd, but this time Jack noticed more than a few nods of assent, so he was encouraged to go on.

"I am here to tell you—and those that have been close to her will know I speak the truth—that she is in fact no one's wife." Here Jack paused, wanting to have complete silence before he continued. He had it.

"Those of you that have spoken with her and been close to her know that she is different. You may have noticed that despite her young age, she has a great gift for healing the sick."

More nods of assent, so Jack pressed on. "I also have noticed these...talents...and much more—so much more in fact that I believe she may someday save us all!"

Here there was an audible gasp and the voice of the old man cut in just in time with his question. "But who is she?"

Jack looked directly into the older man's eyes for a moment. Had he gone too far? He wasn't sure. His question seemed sincere enough, but he knew that if someone had come to him with this story six months ago, he would have chalked them up as a lunatic. That said, however, these people were sick, hungry, and almost devoid of hope—maybe they were ready to believe in anything that could bring that hope back.

He had been silent for so long that the crowd had become restless, so the old man repeated his question.

"Well, stranger. Who is this girl that you put so much faith in?"

These words decided him, and still looking directly into the other man's eyes, he said simply: "She is...Nature's Child."

The crowd now erupted. Some of them obviously objected to this claim, but they were the minority. Most of them were nodding their heads and saying things like, "It's true. I've seen her heal the sick," or "She is uncommonly beautiful."

Then a voice came from the crowd, a little louder than the rest. "How do you know this? Who are you?"

Jack contemplated. He was being as honest as he could be with these poor people—shouldn't it follow that he be just as honest with himself? It was time to lay all of his cards on the table.

"I am…" he began, then for no reason he could understand, tears welled up in his eyes. Even Blake, who had been listening with as much attention as the rest of them, seemed to choke a little.

"I am her guardian, and I come to you now to tell you that I cannot do it alone! I have come to you because she is in grave danger from the very man that has led you here to your destruction."

Now Jack saw that he was losing them, but they weren't angry or even uncertain. No—now they were only frightened. How could they hope to stand up to Andre and all his firepower? Even if they believed in Annie, they knew nothing of him. He realized that they needed proof that he wouldn't abandon them as Andre had. But he wasn't Annie—he could not create a miracle.

Jack was out of ideas and his eyes met the old man's, who still held his gun belt in one hand. He could see that he would receive no help from this quarter. His whole countenance seemed to say, "See what I'm up against?" Just as Jack began to think that he had made the biggest mistake of his life, to his great surprise, it was Blake that came to the rescue.

"Wait, Jack," he heard him say. "This man speaks the truth! Some of you know me; I have been one of Andre's men. I also have been taken in by him. I also have loved the girl that has come among you, and I can tell you that she only wanted to help you. She never wanted to be Andre's bride and she can still help you if only you will help her! This man here," and he pointed to Jack, "he is telling you the truth. He has come a long way to save her and now he must surely fail—unless you help him."

For a moment there was complete silence.

Then the old man spoke for the first time since Jack had started his narrative. He expressed the feelings of the whole group by saying, "But how can we help? We are starved and beaten down. We have hardly any weapons—and even if we did, Andre's men are trained killers. They're armed with machine guns and who knows what else. They would just mow us down!"

Jack felt that he had them now; he knew that one wrong word could turn them away. Facing the speaker, he addressed him personally yet spoke loud enough for everyone to hear. "One thing that Andre told you is true—there is a place for you all here and there is a cure for the plague! What he didn't tell you was that she alone holds that power, and he means to possess it for himself. He means to leave you out here or worse, to send back his henchmen to finish you off!"

Jack let this sink in for a moment, and then he added: "I was no different than you three months ago. I was just trying to get by in a world that seems to me to be dying away—I had no direction; surviving day to day was my only goal in life. Then I met her, and she made me believe in something more. Now, I can't guarantee that some of you won't get hurt or even die—I can't even say for sure that we will be successful. But as for myself, I would rather go down fighting for something I believe in than wait around for someone to save me. I may very well be killed myself, though in the long run that would be of little consequence. She is the only thing that matters now. I truly believe that if she dies, we all perish. Her fate is our fate!"

This last line made more of an impression than Jack could have hoped for.

The old man stepped forward to hand Jack back his gun, saying, "Stranger, we are tired, hungry, and mostly just weary of life. I for one am sure that if we were to come with you, we would be of little help."

He had them, and he thought with a little help from above they could still prevail. Jack looked the older man in the eyes and said, "You need not fight *with* me, just not *against* me. There is such a thing as strength in numbers, and with you all behind me, I think we can make a pretty good show of it."

It took less time than Jack could have hoped to get them all moving. The old man, whose name Jack found out was Chance, had gotten things organized pretty quickly—the fact that these people really didn't have anything much to carry helped to expedite their departure. Still, with over a hundred people in tow, he realized that it could be another hour before they reached the compound. He rode in front, Blake beside him, and he started to notice that the man was sagging more and more in the saddle.

"You know," he said, trying to sound indifferent, "Annie can probably help you if we make it through this."

Blake snorted his laugh, then winced. He meant to make one of his patented smart aleck comments, but seeing the sincerity on Jack's face, he stopped short.

"Yeah," he said finally. "I'm counting on it."

"You know," Jack went on, "it could have been you she fell in love with."

Blake managed to straighten up in the saddle at this comment, but he shook his head saying, "No, it was always you, even before I came along. Don't get me wrong—I would still gladly cut your throat if I thought she would turn to me, but I know now that that is impossible. I just want my chance at Andre."

"You'll get it," Jack replied, and in his heart, he wondered if this was true.

More to change the subject than anything else, Blake asked, "So what's the plan?"

Jack smiled. "There is no plan," he said.

Blake grunted and then, sitting up a little straighter in the saddle, said, "Good. Seems like every time there is a plan, something goes wrong with it."

After a while Jack dropped back to talk to Chance, who was walking along wearily, almost at the back of the group. When he saw Jack, he gave him a sideways glance. Jack could read the question in his eyes.

"Not much further," Jack reassured him.

"It's a good thing," he replied. "I don't know how much further we can go."

Jack climbed down from the horse, feeling a little twinge of guilt that he was riding while the rest of them were forced to walk.

After a few moments, Chance asked Blake's question. "So what's the plan?

"The plan," Jack started, with an easiness that he didn't feel, "is that we get you folks to the house and get some food in you. You all look about half starved."

Chance laughed bitterly. "So what about Andre? If what you say is true, I don't think he is going to be exactly happy to see us."

"You just leave him to me," Jack said, smiling. "All you need to worry about is this last mile."

This statement seemed to stir some emotion in the old man because he stopped and turned to look at Jack. For a minute he just studied Jack's face as if looking for any trace of deception. Finally he turned and started walking again, saying in a choked voice, "I hope you're right, stranger. Cause that's about all I have left in me."

Jack's heart went out to the man, and he felt that no matter what happened, he would do what he could for these people.

They walked in silence for awhile, until Jack realized they were getting close to their destination. Turning to Chance, he said, "I need to go back up front, but if you can ride, I will leave you the horse."

Chance surprised Jack by shaking his head, saying, "You're our fearless leader. You go on ahead. We'll be along as fast as we can."

Jack walked his horse slowly back to the front of the group. As he went, he tried to offer words of encouragement; his words, at best, brought only nods of assent. They were so beaten down that they almost didn't seem to care where they were going. Jack felt anger beginning to well up inside him. "What kind of monster would drive a people almost to their death, just to satisfy his own personal needs?" Jack had come across plenty of selfish people in his life. He had encountered men drunk with power and men who would kill you for a piece of silver. But *never* had he seen such a blatant disregard for human life on this scale. Chance had said that they had left their home 500 strong. Now what was left? Maybe 120 starving, ragtag refugees. There weren't many children, but Jack had noticed one little boy, maybe eight or nine, trudging along beside his mother. His eyes were wide and vacant; they stared out of a dirty face that was gaunt and thin, but as he passed him, he had looked up and smiled. This simple act had the effect of adding fuel to a fire, and Jack set his jaw. His eyes seemed to grow darker as he threw his leg over the saddle and trotted back to where Blake rode on doggedly.

They halted as they neared the end of the forest, waiting for the stragglers to catch up. Jack had a feeling that the woods were being watched, and he wanted to make as big a show as he could when they entered the valley. This was not Annie's Jack—this was the old Jack; this was the Jack that had ridden his horse into a courtroom in Missouri and gunned down Judge Marcus—this Jack was a cold killer! Turning to Blake, he said, "We'll ride straight to the house. We'll go slow. But if I get ahead, stay with these people. If anyone tries to harm them, or prevent them from coming, kill them!"

Blake only nodded, but he thought to himself that he was glad he wasn't in Andre's boots—what he had seen in Jack's steely eyes had been nothing short of murder.

Jack rode a little ahead and turned as the people entered the valley behind him. Raising his voice so that he could be heard by all, he said, "Stay together and follow me." On a whim he added: "You're almost home!"

This statement seemed to give them encouragement, and Jack noticed, with some satisfaction, that they seemed to walk a little faster and with more confidence.

# CHAPTER 23

Andre felt he was prepared for anything they could throw at him, but he had left nothing to chance. If worse came to worst, he had an ace in the hole, so to speak. They had arrived at the house just before noon, easily surrounding it and taking up their positions as they waited for some sign of life. He had been informed by his own men that Annie's boyfriend had ridden out toward his own camp that morning. Well, he had expected as much—with any luck, that particular obstacle had already been eliminated. The house was silent; he was beginning to think that it was deserted when from his hiding place near the rear of the house he saw that blasted wolf lope into the dooryard. After sniffing the air, he walked cautiously up to the front door. Boris, who was beside him, raised his rifle. Just as he was about to put a bullet into the animal, the door flew open and Annie herself came out onto the porch. Andre was thinking fast—was it possible that in their haste to save Annie's father, her friends had made the ultimate blunder and left her alone in the big house? If this was so, then Blake was in for it—not that he cared what happened to Blake; still, he could scarcely believe his own luck.

Annie had leaned down and thrown her arms around the animal. She stood up, and it seemed that she would walk right into his trap! But the darned animal stood in her way—he wouldn't let her pass! Just as he was about to shoot the wolf himself, a man, one that he had never seen before, came up from behind Annie and dragged her back into the house. The wolf followed but didn't show any alarm; this all happened so fast that he had no time to act. Leaning back against the side of the house, Andre contemplated this new development. Boris was whispering something in his ear, but he waved him off. He needed to think! Why was he hesitating? The gunfighter was gone. Even if there were men in the house, surely with the firepower he was carrying, he could overwhelm them. Still, he couldn't very well just blow up the house with his young bride still inside. Contrary to what he had told Blake, she was what he really desired, and with her came real power.

Before he could decide, a man came around the back of the house, and Boris in his nervous state nearly shot him! It was one of their own scouts, and what he had to say was very interesting; it seemed that a small group of men from the village were amassed in the woods behind the workshop. "Ah ha! So, this is their game." They meant to trap him between the woods and the house—they somehow knew he was here.

It came to him suddenly, so he gave his orders to the scout, who slunk back the way he had come.

"What will we do?" Boris was whining. "We will be caught in a crossfire."

"Calm yourself," Andre replied sharply. "Be patient for once in your miserable life." This had the effect of a dash of cold water on him, and Boris fell silent. Two minutes passed, then five. Boris was just opening his mouth to ask what they were waiting for when suddenly a loud explosion followed by a sheet of flame erupted in the woods where the villagers were hiding.

Turning to Boris, Andre smiled and said, "That's our cue."

Taking the lead, he started toward the house, calling out, "All of you men—follow me."

As he came around the front of the house, he could see that the woods behind the workshop were on fire, but a heavy snow was falling and he knew it would soon be extinguished. He could hear men shouting and a few cries of pain coming from that direction. He directed a few men toward the area with orders to finish off whoever was left; he didn't think there would be many. He turned to the house and was about to speak when a bullet ripped through his left arm. Cursing, he fell to his knees as his own men opened up on the house. Boris emptied the whole magazine in the old machine gun with one burst, almost taking out some of their own men who had hit the ground after the initial shot. Taking cover behind the steps of the front porch, he waited as the people in the house returned fire. Vaguely he was aware of shots being fired from behind the workshop. He recognized the rat-a-tat of the machine gun and the AKs that his own people carried. He could also hear the boom of a shotgun, and he knew that his men carried none of these weapons. This was getting out of hand fast, and he knew that he needed to regain control.

"Cease fire!" he yelled. "Cease fire, you idiots!"

Slowly the firing ceased with the exception of an occasional burst from the woods; now Andre could make himself heard.

"Annie!" he yelled, no answer.

"Annie!" he tried again. "People are getting killed. I know that this is not what you want!"

Still no answer.

"The house is completely surrounded. You and your friends can't escape. Just come out and we will talk. There is no reason for anyone else to get hurt," he lied.

He waited, but still there was no reply. He was beginning to get impatient. His arm was throbbing where the bullet had grazed him, and he wasn't at all sure that Annie hadn't been hit in the melee.

Finally, he yelled, "Your boyfriend's dead, Annie." His anger getting the best of him, he went on: "And many more will die if you don't throw out your guns and come out this minute!" Now the silence was complete; there were no more shots came from the forest and he was just about to order his men to storm the house when Annie's sweet voice cut through the still air.

"You're wrong."

Andre shook his head. "What?" he shouted, the anger now apparent in his voice.

"I said you're wrong—Jack isn't dead."

Andre chuckled. "Oh, but he is, Annie. Not by my hand, but by Blake's."

"You're still wrong," Annie said, again her voice maddeningly calm.

For a moment nobody said anything. Andre stood and, composing himself the best he could, walked by himself to the middle of the dooryard. Here he turned and faced the house, holding his arms out to show he was unarmed. Andre was no coward, and he knew that Annie would never let them shoot an unarmed man. In a calm voice, he addressed the front of the house.

"Annie, I didn't come here to fight with you. I only wish to be honest with you, my wife. My people are almost all dead. The rest lay dying, and this man who would steal you away from me is dead back at my camp."

Annie stepped in front of a window that had been shattered in the fight. She looked down at him calmly, and Andre smiled up at her. In that same sweet voice, she said, "I am not sure where you are getting your information, Andre, but I assure you, you are wrong on all accounts. I never consented to be your wife, and as for Jack and your poor desolate people...well, I think you'd better take a look behind you."

For a moment he didn't move at all, just stood there staring up at her. In an instant she vanished from the window. Slowly, he turned to look behind him; what he saw shocked him more than anything else could have. The smile lingered on his face and then a change came over him. Something inside him snapped. He dug his fingernails into his palm, drawing blood. He jumped up and down in the dooryard, stamping down the snow and generally throwing a hissy fit. Coming toward him, not more than a hundred yards away, were his people. Leading them, as if he were some sort of demented messiah, was Jack freaking Brooks. They came slowly enough that Andre had time to almost wear himself out before they had come another ten yards.

Finally, he managed to gain a little control of himself and shouted, "The big gun! Bring me the big gun!"

There was a shuffling behind him as a man appeared, carrying the rocket launcher, followed by Boris, who looked as if he were about to bolt. The man who had brought it had fired it before and had become fairly accurate with the weapon. Had Andre been calm and in his right mind, he might have directed this young man to fire into the group, killing dozens and maybe even Jack in the process. But he wasn't in his right mind, and he snatched the weapon from the man as soon as it was loaded, aiming it directly at the man on the horse. The weapon went off. The rocket went wild and over the heads of the whole group, landing way beyond them, blowing up dirt and snow but nothing else—this was the last straw. Throwing the weapon to the ground, he proceeded to jump up and down on it until he tripped and fell into the snow—he began to laugh wildly. The men that were left had gathered around him and were staring wildly at their fearless leader as he threw his little temper tantrum. There were twenty-seven of them, including Boris.

As Boris helped him up, he managed to say more calmly to the men who had gathered around him: "Kill them! Kill them all!"

Facing Boris, he said, "I think it's time that we presented my wife with her wedding present."

With that the two men walked off toward the barn.

Of the fifty men that Andre had counted among his force, ten of these had gone off into the woods to finish off whoever was left after the rocket had gone off. Although two men had been killed, most of that small rag tag group from the village had suffered no more than minor injuries—these were brave men and devoted to Annie. So, although they had never witnessed anything like it before, the explosion hadn't weakened their resolve. There were just over thirty-five of them, and although Andre's men had been better armed, they had rushed them, easily overwhelming them. They only lost one more man in the process. After killing all but three of them, whom they promptly tied up, they hunkered down and waited for orders from the house.

In the house they had no way of knowing how the battle was going in the woods. Jacob was of the opinion that their people had either been wiped out or fled. Annie was afraid he was right, and if she hadn't seen Jack alive, well, and leading Andre's people, she might have surrendered herself, in order to avert any more bloodshed. Kitchi kept saying that if they could just stay calm until Jack actually got here, everything would be ok—after all, he wouldn't be coming so slowly and so openly if he didn't have some sort of plan. It was Kitchi who had upset the apple cart. He had seen Andre step into the open and suddenly it came to him that if he killed him, the rest would just melt away. So he had taken his shot, but he had never fired this particular rifle before. The shot was off, and he only grazed the man. What followed left them no chance of returning fire. It seemed like every window exploded at once. Bullets cut through the front door, breaking lamps and splintering furniture.

Jack had no plan. He had the vague idea that there was strength in numbers, but he also knew that Andre would probably not hesitate to kill his own people. Then the woods behind the workshop exploded, and he pulled up short. For a moment he waited, unsure of what had happened and unaware of anything going on in the house. He saw a single man step out into the dooryard, and he suddenly felt the urge to hurry. He knew this man was addressing the people in the house, but from this distance he could hear nothing. Snow was beginning to fall heavier, making it hard to make out anything except shapes. Had Annie seen him? He wasn't sure. He hoped so, thinking that if she knew he was there, it would prevent her from doing anything rash. Suddenly a single shot rang out, and Jack saw the man go down, then begin to drag himself toward the house. In response, there was a barrage of bullets. Jack could restrain himself no longer.

Turning to Blake, he said, "Give me the rifle; I'm going ahead. Bring them as fast as you can."

# CHAPTER 24

Annie stared out the front window. The snow was falling so thick now that she could no longer see the group approaching the house. Inexplicably, Andre and Boris had run off, but the remainder of his men stood guard in the dooryard, facing away from the house. The windows had all been blown out, so she could hear everything going on outside. The men didn't speak, but she could hear the sounds of shuffling boots and guns being cocked. The snow was piling up on the porch; some was even making its way into the front room where she stood. Suddenly everything was dead quiet and she became aware of the biting cold air against her skin—that was when she heard the sound. At first she wasn't sure what it could be, but she noticed that Andre's men had heard it also and had brought their guns up, ready to fire at anything that would come out of the snow curtain. Annie looked around her. At the other window, Kitchi was crouched with his rifle; he, too, seemed ready to shoot the first thing he saw. Beside her was Jacob.

Even as she realized what the sound was, he said, "He comes for you, Little Mother...God have mercy on their souls."

Out of the blizzard, not fifty feet away, a lone rider appeared, first as a shadow. The machine guns barked, but they were soon cut down and the rider came on. Annie strained her eyes when suddenly everything seemed to clear. The snow pushed back, making a sort of stage of the area directly in front of the house. She could see Jack! He had the pistol in one hand and the rifle in the other. Every time he fired, men went down, yet he rode on unscathed, almost as if the snow itself provided a shield from the bullets that flew around him.

# CHAPTER 25

There were six bullets in the .45, seven in the .30-30. Jack knew he needed to make every shot count, which he did. His last shot took a young man holding an axe right between his eyes, and he let the rifle slip from his hand. He had no thought now but to make it into the house. The men continued to fall before him, and he realized that someone was helping him. Fifty feet from the front door he pulled up, astonished at what he saw. Andre's men, the ten or so that were left, had thrown down their guns and were surrendering. Jack realized that he still held the Colt in his hand, but he knew that it was empty. A tremendous cheer rang out to his left, and he realized his own good fortune—the men from the village had come through. When they had seen Jack's heroic charge on the house, they had backed him. Now as Andre's men abandoned their guns and knelt down in the snow, they cheered heartily.

He saw her now, looking through the shattered front window. For a moment, her eyes met his, and Jack felt more than saw the message she was sending in those deep-blue pools. They shifted to the right and Jack saw them change. He started to turn in the saddle, but before he could turn all the way, he heard a loud report. He and the gray fell to the ground. The gray neighed and struggled to regain its feet. Two more shots came in quick succession. Finally, it lay still. The world seemed to swim in front of his eyes and he felt water run into one. He brushed it away, but his hand came back red. "Shot," he thought disjointedly. He heard Andre call out Annie's name and he struggled to regain his feet. Unfortunately the huge horse had died practically on top of him, so he was pinned to the ground.

Annie had witnessed the whole thing from her position at the window. She had seen Jack ride in, guns blazing. She had seen the people from the village emerge from the woods, forcing Andre's men to lay down their guns—but she had also seen something that no one else had. Behind Jack and slightly to his right there were three men under the poplar—two on foot and the other on horseback. Annie recognized all of them immediately. One was Andre. He seemed to be holding a horse's bridle. The second was Boris, and the third the one on the horse's back was her father. The snow was still coming down hard as ever, but for a moment it seemed to blow away from the little scene, and she could see clearly that he had been blindfolded and his hands were tied behind his back. Around his neck was a sturdy rope that had been thrown over a branch about fifteen feet off the ground. He was to be hanged right in front of her!

She gasped. Jacob, who was standing next to her, cursed for the first time since she had known him. She was about to cry out to him when she saw Boris raise his rifle and take aim at Jack. Before a sound could escape her lips, the rifle went off. Both Jack and the horse went to the ground. She jumped, but still no sound escaped her trembling lips. Jacob suddenly left her, but she hardly noticed. Her eyes were riveted on the horse as it struggled to stand. She took a step closer to the broken window, straining her eyes, trying to make out its rider. Two more shots rang out and then all was still—all of this happened within a matter of seconds. As Annie was searching in vain for a sign that Jack was still alive, she heard Andre call out to her.

"He's dead, Annie."

She was in shock. "Dead?" She thought. "Jack, dead."

Part of her protested as she continued to stare at the big animal lying not twenty feet from where she stood. There was no movement, and where the horse and rider had fallen, the snow was already getting deep enough to cover them.

"He really is dead this time, girl." This was the voice in her head, come back to haunt her.

"No," Annie whispered, the tears already forming in her deep-blue eyes.

"Yes!" the voice replied, more insistent this time. "But your father isn't! You can still save him!"

"No!" Annie protested a little louder, sounding like a spoiled little girl that wasn't getting her way. "No, I can't, and I don't care anymore!"

"Yes, you do," the voice continued, and it had taken on a softer tone. "Look inside yourself, girl, and I will help you."

Annie said only two more words as the tears streamed down her cheeks. "I'm scared!"

"Don't be afraid, child." This time the voice seemed to be all around her and not just in her head. "Don't be afraid—Mother's here."

Again Andre called out to her. "Please, Annie, there has been enough bloodshed today. Look, I have brought your father home. All I want in return is what is rightfully mine—all I want is you."

There was no answer to this, and Andre became impatient. He fairly screamed, "You are my wife and you will obey me! We were united before God and everyone in the camp. I demand you come to me at once!"

Kitchi, who had been crouched beside the other window the whole time, watched as a change came over his sister. He had seen it many times before, the trancelike state; the talking to herself, almost as if she were sleepwalking. He saw her shiver as if a sudden chill had enveloped her whole body. She turned and looked straight at him and he saw that this was no longer his little sister—this was something terrible and beautiful at the same time. Her dark hair shimmered and seemed to blow back of its own accord. And her eyes! They weren't just deep blue anymore—they were like two blue candles that lit up the whole room. It was as if her very soul was trying to escape through them. Then she did something that seemed even more terrible than anything he had seen so far. She smiled at him, and he felt, only for an instant, that terrible power that he could never understand and never wanted to. He shrank from her, and for a moment her expression changed to one of anger. Kitchi trembled violently, thinking that she would surely kill him on the spot. Then Andre yelled something about her being his wife, and slowly she turned toward the front of the house. Now the blue light seemed to envelope her whole body as she became very still.

In a clear voice that sounded nothing like her own, she said: "Coming, dear."

# CHAPTER 26

Jack's wounds weren't as bad as they appeared. He hadn't been shot, but when the horse had fallen underneath him, he had struck his head on a protruding rock, then the horse had fallen on his leg, spraining his ankle. Other than that he just had a few bumps and bruises. Still, the head wound was nothing to laugh at; he had lost quite a bit of blood. He felt as if he were in that half-waking state between dreamland and reality. He was cold and he thought that he had forgotten to shut the window before he went to bed, and now the snow was coming right into the cabin. His blanket had been pushed down to the end of the bed, and half-consciously he reached down to retrieve it. Instead his hand came in contact with wet hair. Slowly he opened one eye. His head ached like he had drank too much whiskey the night before, and his other eye seemed glued shut. He felt someone's hand on his shoulder, so he turned to look, but this just made everything blurry. He heard his name spoken right next to his ear and vaguely recognized the voice. He tried to put a face to it, and slowly it came to him.

"Jacob," he croaked, his own voice seeming to come from far away.

"I'm here, Jack," was the reply. "You're going to be ok."

Jack looked out of his one open eye, asking: "How did I get outside?"

"Shhh," Jacob said and began to rub his face and head with snow.

Finally Jack was able to open both of his eyes, and he was about to ask again how he had gotten outside in the snow when he heard Annie say as clear as a bell in the growing silence: "Coming, dear."

Immediately he was brought back to the present. He struggled to pull himself out from under the dead horse. With Jacob's help he finally managed to free himself and they fell back, both of them panting. He glanced to his right, taking in the scene underneath the old poplar. His first instinct was to grab for the revolver, which had fallen under the horse also.

Jacob whispered in his ear, "Shhh, there is nothing we can do to help her."

Jack hadn't looked toward the house, so now he turned his head so violently toward it that the world began to swim again. He almost fainted.

"Easy, Jack," Jacob said, bracing him up. "She will be ok."

For a moment, Jack stared at the old medicine man like he was crazy, but Jacob's attention was fixed on the house, so slowly he turned his own gaze back in that direction. Later when Jack was lying in a cozy bed, warm and healed of his wounds, he couldn't be sure how much of the scene that followed was real and how much was brought on by the head wound. At first nothing seemed alive inside the old house; there was no movement at all. Unconsciously his eyes became riveted on the front door, then slowly it began to open, a soft blue light flooded out of the house, and *she* stepped out on the porch.

There was an audible gasp from everyone in the dooryard as Annie stepped into their view. Her glowing eyes glanced at the source of this new sound, bathing them all in blue light, but these people seemed not to interest her, and she slowly turned toward the three men under the tree—that's when all hell broke loose.

The snow that had been falling so thick that at times it was hard to see even ten feet in front of you suddenly turned to rain. Lightning flashed silently inside a dense fog that seemed to hover just fifty feet above their heads. Stranger yet, the rain was almost warm, and as it fell the snow began to melt and turn to slush. Everyone, including Jack, was struck dumb by this phenomenon, and all eyes were glued to the small figure as she descended the porch steps. On the last step, she paused for a moment, her whole figure enveloped in soft blue light, then she stepped off the porch and a new development occurred that brought the natives to their knees.

As her bare feet touched the earth, wildflowers seemed to spring up all around and beneath them, only to die almost instantly as she moved on. This effect made it look as if she were walking on a carpet of flowers that was withering, dying, and starting to decay in her wake.

Jacob remarked later that it was as if they were living their whole life within just a few seconds, just to serve her. At first it seemed as if she had just stepped out for a leisurely stroll with no real destination in mind; then slowly, almost reluctantly, she bent her path toward the tree where her father sat on the horse, waiting to be executed.

Jack looked at the three men there, huddled under the tree, and found three different emotions projected in their faces. Boris stood in wide-eyed terror, trembling all over as he watched the little apparition advancing toward them. Annie's father, who was unable to actually see his daughter because of the thick bandanna that had been tied over his eyes, sat listening intently to every sound, and he must have gleaned something of what was happening because he seemed to say, "lord help us all" or something close to it. Then his attention was drawn to Andre, who in his madness, had stretched out both arms and screamed: "Yes, come to me, Annie!"

She had walked maybe half the distance between the house and the tree when the sound of his voice seemed to stop her in her tracks. For a moment she stood completely still as the warm, almost springlike rain fell around her and the wildflowers sprang up between her toes, then she cocked her head slightly as if she were listening to someone only she could hear. Smiling her sweetest smile, she knelt down and plucked a rose that had no business growing this far north at any time of the year.

This proved to be too much for Boris, who was at heart a God-fearing man, and he bolted toward the barn.

He had gone maybe thirty yards when Annie raised one delicate hand and without even glancing in that direction, pointed toward the structure. Suddenly it erupted as if there had been too much pressure inside; to his horror, Jack saw a miniature tornado emerge from the wreckage. Boris had seen it also, but it was too late. He turned to his left, but with the swiftness of a cobra, the tiny twister struck out and swallowed him. Then it began spitting him out one limb at a time, his head rolling almost to Andre's feet. Annie seemed not to notice any of this as she continued her slow, terrible walk.

She had come to within ten feet of her father and would-be husband when Andre shouted: "Stop! Annie, I *will* kill him!"

It flashed through Jack's mind that at this point Andre's threats were useless, but he saw that the man was quite insane and even though he had yelled for her to stop, his arms were still extended toward her, beckoning her to come on.

She did stop, however, and for a few seconds the whole universe seemed to stop with her. No one spoke or even moved. The rain still came down but had become lighter and was beginning to turn cold. Annie raised one delicate arm and pointed not at Andre or the accursed tree that her father was to be hung on, but straight up at the sky.

For maybe ten seconds, nothing happened—no one moved or even seemed to be breathing. Andre was standing with his arms still outstretched to receive her, and David was smiling atop the horse, which, although wide eyed, wasn't even twitching. They all looked like statues carved by some demented sculptor. Suddenly, without any warning, a bolt of lightning shot out of the low clouds, lighting up the whole world, followed almost instantly by a clap of thunder that shook the very ground and brought most of the bystanders to their knees. It blinded Jack, and for a few moments he was unable to see even his own hand before his face.

Slowly his burning eyes began to distinguish shapes, and the first thing he saw was that the tree was on fire. As they began to focus a little better, he noticed that the whole thing had been cleaved in two. David himself now sat in the mud, seemingly unhurt. The rope was still around his neck, but the severed end lay burning on the ground, and the horse that he had been sitting on was sprinting blindly toward the forest. Andre was on his knees before the small glowing figure that used to be Annie, holding his head and screaming over and over: "I loved you!" Slowly, almost tenderly, she reached down and took his hand. As he groped for her, like a drowning man, he began to sob uncontrollably. Annie spoke, but her voice was unnatural, almost otherworldly.

She said: "I am here."

Andre was still on his knees, but he managed to raise his head, and Jack saw that his eyes had been burnt completely away and he searched through blank sockets, his face raised up to her. She seemed not to notice this deformity as she bent close enough for him to feel her breath on his burnt skin. This breath of air seemed to have a soothing effect on Andre, and he seemed almost to smile as he said softly: "I really do love you."

Once again, the universe stood still, and Jack saw that the blue light still flickered in her eyes and danced around her body like electricity.

Annie began to speak but in a voice that was terrible—it seemed to come not from her lips but from the very air around them. Her words were strange and unfamiliar. "Dear little man, you have always loved me when you think I am beautiful and bountiful, yet you will curse me when I am not. Since time unremembered you have taken what you needed, leaving death and petulance behind. Still, I have always been here, cleaning up your mess behind you.

"For I am a patient mother and a loving mother. I have scolded you, but to no avail. I have punished you to no avail. Still, you mistreat and abuse all that I hold sacred. If you truly love me, why are you continually trying to hurt me?"

She didn't wait for an answer but continued. "Now it is time to rest, for me as well as you. When I awaken, things will be as they were before you came here. Will you also awake?"

Here she tilted her head to one side as if she were contemplating the matter. Leaning even closer to the blinded man, she said, "Well, that is not for me to decide."

There was a moment's pause, as if she were giving Andre his chance to repent of his many sins. But he could neither hear nor see anything and instead of humbling himself in front of this terrible creature who had condemned him to eternal sleep, he screamed into her face, spraying blood and spit into it: *"You belong to me!"*

Annie—or the thing that used to be Annie—didn't flinch, even though their faces were only inches apart. Instead she giggled, and in that instant, she was just Annie again as she said, "No, silly. Don't you get it? It's you who belongs to me," and she kissed him lightly on the forehead.

The moment her lips touched him, two things happened. First the rain stopped—not gradually, as if after a spring storm, but all at once; as though someone had turned off a huge tap above the low, dense fog. Then the temperature dropped so abruptly that everything began to freeze. It seemed to start exactly where Annie's lips had touched Andre's forehead, slowly spreading down the full length of his body, transforming him into a living ice sculpture. From there it picked up speed to spread over the damp earth toward the place where Jack was sitting. Pandemonium broke loose. People were scattering in every direction, running in horror from the advancing ice sheet that seemed to radiate out in every direction.

Jack did not run. His eyes had never left the small creature who still stooped over the frozen form underneath the decimated poplar. Slowly and painfully, he rose to his feet. The ice had reached him now and he raised his hands to ward off an icy breeze that seemed to blow through his very soul. Instead of freezing him solid, though, as it had Andre, the ice simply passed under him, welding his boots to the spot. He saw that the same thing had happened to Jacob. Nor was the dead horse flash frozen, either. It occurred to Jack that only the things Annie had actually touched had frozen and the only thing she was in physical contact with now was the bare earth.

Jack looked up to see that Annie had straightened up. She was still staring down at the frozen man and she was weeping. He called her name, but she seemed not to hear. He tried to free his boots from the ice, but it was no use. He called to her again, and still, she didn't move. Less than forty feet separated them and he knew she could hear him, yet she continued to block him out. Somehow, he had to break through whatever power held her. It was Jacob who came up with the solution.

He had sat back down on the ice and was unlacing his frozen moccasins. "She can't hear you, Jack—or if she can, she can't answer. It's not Annie we are dealing with here."

Jack got the idea, but how to address this person he wasn't sure. Following Jacob's example, he began unlacing his own boots, his mind racing furiously. What exactly was this entity? He had a vague idea, but then what was Annie to it? Finally, he had his feet free of the boots, and frantically he stood in his stockinged feet on the ice.

"Mother!" he called. This word produced a slight effect as the woman turned her head to glance at him. Its eyes blazed for a moment, then it turned away again.

"Mother!" he called again and added as an afterthought: "Let her go or I will be forced to kill you!"

This got her attention and he heard Jacob exclaim behind him: "Oh, Jack!"

She turned to face him and smiled that awful smile, then she addressed him by name. "Well, well, Jack. And I thought you to be one of the more intelligent of your species." Before he could reply, she raised one hand toward him and said, "Come here, Jack."

It felt as if some giant hand had clasped him around the neck and suddenly he was sliding across the ice on his knees. He came to a stop directly in front of her, but although she had lowered her arm, that invisible hand still seemed to hold him so he could neither stand or move.

Her whole body seemed to be humming with some electric current as she said: "So Jack, even you who have treated me with reverence your whole life and worshiped at my alter; you who only a few short hours ago were professing your undying love for me just as this fool has done." She pointed to the ice sculpture that used to be Andre. "Even you," she went on, "would see me destroyed?"

His first impulse was to say, "I love you, Annie. I could never hurt you." For now that he was this close, he could see it was Annie after all, at least in the flesh. Fortunately, out of the corner of his eye, he caught a glimpse of the last man who had professed his love for her, and he checked himself. "This isn't Annie," he thought again.

A voice that sounded suspiciously like his sister whispered, "Yes, Jack, but who is Annie to her?"

Light dawned in Jack's eyes as he looked straight into that terrible, yet somehow still beautiful face and said gently, almost tenderly, "I have worshiped you, Mother, and I have protected you when I could—that is what I intend to do even now."

Jack felt the invisible hand loosen slightly and she laughed in his face. "I need no protector, Jack. There is nothing on earth that escapes my power. No, Jack, it's this girl that you wish to save, not me! Besides, there is nothing to save me from."

Now Jack was at a loss. He glanced at David, who had been listening to every word, but for the first time since Jack had met him, he had nothing to say. Then, like a flash, something did come to him—something David had told him about his daughter that Jack had dismissed at the time. Now those words came back to him in a flood, and it was as if a light had been turned on inside his overtaxed brain. He had said, "I truly believe that she has the power somewhere inside her tiny frame to save the world, to...cure the planet, if you will." Suddenly Jack knew—he understood everything! Bracing himself for the final battle, he summoned all his remaining will-power and pushed back against that invisible force that held him. He managed to get to his feet. She looked a little startled and actually took a step back.

"You are wrong," Jack said, looking straight into those glowing blue pools that could at any moment flash out and turn him to cinders. "I can save you from yourself!" Then bracing himself for this final fight, Jack pushed back even harder and said:

"Who is this girl of flesh and blood? If not your own child, then at least your prodigy?"

"All things of this earth are my offspring," she said a little indifferently.

But Jack saw that the blue light had retreated into a delicate garland that encircled her head. "Yes," Jack went on, "but you did not create her, and she *is* special. You saw that the night she was born. She is *your* last hope as well as ours; that is why you preserved her. You are dying, Mother, and this time there is nothing you can do to stop it! But I believe that she can, and now you would destroy her as well as yourself before she has even had her chance!"

Once again, her eyes blazed out, and Jack felt the invisible hand tighten as he was lifted nearly off the ground. Still, he managed to whisper: "I tell you, Mother, that there is one even more powerful than yourself that has created her, and not even you dare question his motives." Then, just when he thought she would snap his neck like a twig, she suddenly and completely released him.

He fell to one knee before her, rubbing his sore throat, and looked up at her, ready to fight on if he had to. But there was no fight left in her, it seemed. She only sighed and said in a voice that sounded beyond weary, "You are right, Jack, on all points. I am dying, as you put it, although I tell you, nothing really dies." Here she shook her head and sighed once more, and Jack could almost believe it was Annie saying, "But I have neither the time nor the patience to try to explain these things.

"The night this girl was born, I saw something in those eyes that I had seen before, something familiar, and for the first time in a millennium, I felt hope! Oh, her father can speculate all he wishes about her name or true identity. Call her Demeter, or Isis—these were both priestesses and worshipers of mine at one time, but names are not important. She is even older than these. If I were to give her a name, it would be Eve or even Lillyth, as she was my first protector, *my* guardian if you will have it. So, I preserved her as you put it, and I would have saved the mother as well if it had been in my power.

"I have never been a vengeful mother. I don't kill for the sake of killing, but as you also have said, it is not my place to interfere with providence. Anyway, the mother was already gone to where I don't know, but I do know she lives on somewhere. These things I tell you, Jack, because just like you, I fear that unknown abyss and would save myself if I thought there was a way. You ask me to give her a chance, and although I know that you ask for your own selfish reasons, I will give it to her. Perchance she is all we think she is—and maybe it's me that is being selfish—but like you, I wish to live! However, heed my words, Jack: just as her father in this life has warned you already, I, her mother, her true mother, would warn you also. You may take her to be your wife, and she will, I'm sure, bring you great happiness—but beware of your own feelings. You cannot afford to be self-serving in this matter, because she belongs to all of us. If you hold her hostage with the power of your own selfish love as you have done before, we are all lost."

The blue light had completely retreated now, leaving only a slight glow in Annie's deep-blue eyes. Then she looked around for the first time at the destruction she had left in her path. She showed no remorse as she said, "One last thing, Jack." And thankfully it was only Annie's clear sweet voice that he heard. "I will always be with her. For whoever created her created me also. We are eternally linked in some way that not even I understand. Remember that, Jack, because she too serves one higher than me, and not even your love for her can alter her destiny."

With that she was gone. Her last words sent a chill up Jack's spine that had nothing to do with the cold ice he was standing on.

# CHAPTER 27

Jack stood on the front porch of the big house, surveying the landscape around him. It had been over a week since that awful scene had played out, not fifty feet from where he stood, but very little had changed. Andre was gone—Annie had insisted that they bury him right away. Unfortunately, when they had tried to free his body from the ice, it had simply shattered into little pieces. Mercifully, Annie hadn't been there to witness that. Jack had seen to it, and what remained of him was packed into a makeshift coffin and nailed securely shut. When he was lying in his own bed or talking and laughing with David across the big kitchen table, he could almost believe that it had all been a bad dream—then his hand would steal to the burn on his neck just below the jawline, and the reality of it would set in. When Annie had first seen this mark, she had turned from him in shame, for there was no doubt that the burn was the exact size and shape of her own little hand. But Jack had raised her face to his and kissed her forehead, his eyes telling her what his words could not. They never spoke of it. After that, he did what he could to keep the burn hidden from her, and it was already starting to fade.

However, once you left the confines of the house and stared out at the devastation that Annie had left in her wake, there was no way of denying or ignoring the facts—for as far as the eye could see, the earth was locked in a sheet of ice nearly three inches thick. In some ways it resembled a huge frozen lake—that is, until your eyes fell on some rock or shrub that appeared to be floating on the surface. As for the old poplar, that had been cleaved nearly in two. One side had fallen completely over, and some of the remaining branches were locked in the ice, but the other half had simply leaned toward the house, pointing at it like some huge accusing finger. Beyond this unworldly apparition and a little to his right, he could just make out what was left of the barn and stables. It wasn't much—just a few posts sticking out of the ice at odd angles and one wall leaning outward at such an angle that it seemed to defy the laws of gravity.

The one piece of good news was that miraculously, hardly anyone on their side had been killed. The people from Andre's camp that had been so slow in their pilgrimage to the house had shown surprising agility and swiftness in their retreat. It had taken him and David nearly two hours to round them up and get them back to the village. As for the native people who had so valiantly fought off the men behind the workshop, only two had died. Jack thought this a miracle in itself, considering the overwhelming firepower of Andre's men. The casualties on that side had been a lot worse: of the fifty or so men that had been Andre's army, thirty-two had died, including Boris; two more lay dying in the house. Annie wasn't optimistic, even though she had done everything in her power to save them. She had one other patient, however, that she had saved, and now that he was feeling better, it was all Annie could do to keep him confined to his bed. Blake had not turned tail and run with the rest of the group but had fainted either from loss of blood or sheer terror. They had carried him into the house, and with Jack's help, Annie had cauterized the wound, bandaging him up the best she could. At first she didn't have much hope, saying, "I'm afraid he's lost too much blood." However, the following morning she found him sitting up in the bed and asking for whiskey. Presently he was being his old annoying self again, and Annie was almost fed up with him.

"I've told him a hundred times," she complained, "that he needs to remain as still as possible, lest he reopen the wound. But he won't listen to me." She stomped her little foot as she declared this, and Jack had to suppress a smile that he knew would only vex her more. "Plus, he's rude!" she went on. "If I were a big strong man like you, Mr. Brooks, I surely wouldn't let anyone talk to my future wife that way!"

Now Jack had to put his hand to his mouth to cover his grin. He cleared his throat and spoke as seriously as he could, "I'll have a talk with him, dear."

With that she had stormed off, muttering something about men in general. She was scarcely out of earshot before Jack's laughter escaped him.

He did have a talk with Blake and, to his surprise, found him quite changed from the man that had tried to kill him. When he entered the room, Blake lay on his back, staring up at the ceiling, a scowl on his face. The moment he saw Jack, he smiled and held out his hand. Jack took it, and they shook warmly.

Jack pulled up a chair, saying, "Look Blake, I know you're impatient to be up and about, but Annie is only trying to do what's best for you."

Blake laid back and went back to scowling at the ceiling. "I know it!" He griped. "But there is something important I need to take care of back at the old camp!"

"It can't be that pressing," Jack replied. "And to tell you the truth, I don't know how you would get there even if you were heathy. Have you had a chance to look out the window?"

"Are you kidding?" Blake snapped, turning his head to look at Jack. "That little tyrant won't let me out of this accursed bed for a moment. Look! She's even brought a bucket for me to pee in. She treats me like a little boy, and I won't stand for it much longer!"

Jack broke out in laughter again. He couldn't remember a time in his life when he had laughed so easily as he had the last couple of days; he supposed it had a lot to do with the great sense of relief he felt at having the woman he loved safe and by his side.

He could see, though, that Blake was not laughing, and whatever it was that was bothering him was serious, at least to him. Reaching into his pocket, Jack produced a couple of cigars. Handing one to Blake, he said, "I could go for you," he offered, "providing I could find a way across the ice without breaking my fool neck."

Blake eyed him warily for a moment, dragging deeply on the cigar. Eventually, seeming to make up his mind, he propped himself up on one elbow and asked, "Do you think it's possible that us two can trust each other now? I mean, now that things have come out the way they have?"

Jack looked into the big man's eyes and without any hesitation assured him, "As far as I know, I have never given you any reason not to trust me."

Blake continued to stare into Jack's face for a long moment, and then he nodded slightly, saying, "No. No, I guess not." Lying back against the pillow, he ruminated, "The truth is what's back at that camp—at least part of what's there—could be as important to you as it is to me."

Later as Jack stood on the porch looking out at the devastation, his mind turned to the problem of traversing the ice and getting back to the old camp as soon as he could. The remainder of Andre's men had been simply disarmed and let go. Most of them had family among the people, and Jack had assumed that they had just followed them into the village—but if any of them knew what Blake knew, they might have started back already.

Annie came out onto the porch behind him. He put one arm around her shoulders.

"It's awful," she said remorsefully, looking out at the old tree and shuddering involuntarily.

"It will melt," Jack said to console her. Smiling down at her, he suggested, "We could go ice skating!"

She smacked him lightly on the shoulder and reprimanded, "Seriously, Jack, I wish I could make it go away. I should be able to!"

Jack knew that she had tried, but any remnant of the power that had caused the devastation seemed to have dissolved with her anger.

"Annie, I have to go out to Andre's old camp tomorrow," he said abruptly. He knew that she would object or want to come with him, and he could think of no way of breaking it to her gently.

She continued to stare straight ahead, not saying a word, until he began to think she hadn't heard him. Then she sighed deeply and, turning to him, said, "Ok, Jack, but promise me something."

"Anything," Jack said, surprised at the calmness in her voice.

"Promise me that whatever you find there, you will destroy it. Don't bring anything back with you."

Jack started. Had Blake talked to her about this? "Annie," he began as she put one finger to his lips, looked him straight in the eye, and said, "Promise me, Jack."

He was taken so much by surprise that, scarcely recognizing his own voice, he vowed, "I promise."

He left early before anyone was awake. He hoped to make it to the old camp that night, leaving him all day tomorrow to take care of his business. Annie had effectively thrown a wrench in his plans, and now he wasn't exactly sure what his business would be. The first hour he had struggled across the ice. Twice he slipped and fell, but as the sun rose, he noticed that there were white patches of snow here and there, which seemed to indicate bare patches of earth. By the time he reached the tree line, the ice was completely gone, and he was able to jog along at a fairly rapid pace—this had sent a feeling of relief through him that he scarcely wanted to admit. Part of him had been almost sure that Annie had managed to freeze the entire earth solid. He laughed at the thought now, at his own foolishness. By midday he found himself less than a mile from his destination, so he sat down on an old stump to have some lunch.

As he ate his sandwich of bread with venison, he took in the forest around him. He felt good; he felt almost at peace—this was the world that was meant for him; this was his natural element. When was the last time he had been by himself without a care, just him and nature? He found that he could almost remember nothing of his life before Annie. How long had he known her? It seemed as if she had always been there somehow, yet he knew that he had lived an entirely different life before her. Suddenly and unexpectedly a feeling of homesickness hit him. He wondered what his old uncle Phil was doing right at this moment. Did they think him dead? What of his nieces and nephews, some nearly grown? A feeling of sudden guilt overcame him as he thought of the drought that had come to the valley the year he left. He would go back, he thought, and if need be, he would bring them here before next winter. This resolution eased his mind, and tucking the remains of the sandwich in his pocket, he stood to go. That's when he heard the gunshots—not just a stray shot here and there, but a whole barrage of gunfire. Somewhere near the old camp, a war had started!

He ran through the woods but not haphazardly. He knew from past experience the lay of the land, and he didn't want to approach the camp from the front. He was searching for the same rise that he had come to the last time he was here, and finally he spotted it. Running to the summit, he fell on his stomach, out of breath, and peeked over the edge. The scene before him was the last thing he expected to see—the solitary cabin and the stable were engulfed in flame. There was no sign of human life, but Jack saw two deer racing up the slope behind it, and he could still hear an occasional gunshot coming from inside its burning walls. "Surely," he thought, "no one could still be living in that hell." Even as he thought this, another shot rang out. He saw a figure emerge from the doorway, and he seemed to be carrying something. The figure staggered out of the flames and fell down the steps.

This was enough for Jack, who had never expected to find all this chaos in a deserted camp. He sprang over the hill and descended the summit, sliding down the last few feet and hitting the level ground at a dead run. He approached the burning cabin cautiously. The gunfire had ceased, and as he got closer, he saw that the man who had emerged from the flames had risen to his knees and appeared to be trying to bury another in snow. He sprinted the last few feet while understanding dawned in his face: the man lying in the snow had been on fire and the other had been trying to put him out. As Jack came upon them, they both turned to look. Jack was startled to see that one of them, the one who had been on fire, was none other than his old friend Chance.

For a moment the older man stared at Jack as if he were seeing a ghost. He then turned toward the burning cabin and, patting his companion on the shoulder, said, "I'm ok. Only my clothes have been burned." Jack too turned toward the cabin, and as he did another gunshot rang out from within.

"We had better move off," he said, so the three of them made their way slowly toward the trees. The gunfire had entirely ceased by now and the only sound was the light crackling of the fire as the cabin continued to burn. It had started to snow lightly. With the help of the younger man, whom Jack recognized as one of Andre's guard, they went to work on a makeshift shelter. It didn't take the two long to set up the small camp, and soon they were all three sitting around a small fire, drinking strong coffee and smoking. The younger man, whom Chance had introduced as his nephew Cody, was a dark-haired giant with deep-set eyes and huge arms that seemed on the verge of bursting through the sleeves of the old jacket he wore. His size made him seem intimidating, but Jack saw when they shook hands that he was still just a kid. His polite deference to Chance as well as himself eased Jack's mind as to his motives. The burning of the cabin and destruction of the weapons it held had been entirely Chance's doing, but how had the old man known about them? Did he also know of the old chest that Blake had told him was under the floorboards? Jack decided to keep his mouth shut about this, at least for the time being.

It was the old man that broke the silence when he said, "Fighting between men must end."

Jack said nothing but gave the old man an inquiring look.

"I have often thought that we humans were slowly dying away, that our time of ruling this earth was close to an end. Yet after what I witnessed a week ago when all three of us stood in the dooryard of the great house, I knew it for sure."

"I'm not sure I follow," Jack interjected, and Chance heaved a sigh.

"This world has grown old before its time, much like me," he said, smiling slightly. "Every child has heard the story of how the sun reached out and destroyed the old cities—but that was just the beginning of the end, you see. Since then, we have all been trying to get back what we lost. We've been trying to rebuild a world that we knew nothing about, and for what purpose? I have seen a great deal in my life, Jack. I have lived through war and famine. I have seen railroads built, only to lie dormant, their rails rusting into dust. Whole countries have been abandoned because the land dried up, and the people moved on. Every year there are fewer and fewer people, and the less of us there are, the more we fight over what's left. Remember what the girl said to Andre? 'Now it is time to rest—for me as well as you.'"

Here Chance looked into Jack's eyes and said, "You may have stopped her from destroying us that day, but the being from whom she draws her power still exists. She will draw on it again someday."

Jack could only repeat what he had said before: "Maybe she will use that power to save us."

Chance shrugged his shoulders. "What's to save? She made it very clear that she is here to save the planet, not the inhabitants."

Jack thought about it a moment before replying, "Doesn't the planet include humans?"

Chance chuckled to himself and replied, "You're a glass half-full kind of guy, aren't you Jack? I mean, why would she want to save us?"

"If I remember my Bible stories correctly, weren't we supposed to be the guardians of the earth in the first place? Maybe she needs us as much as we need her."

None of them wanted to spend any more time than they had to at the old camp, so it was decided that they would rest for a few hours and then start home. Chance had curled up beside the fire and gone to sleep almost immediately.

Jack turned to the younger man and said, "I'm gonna go take a look around."

He half expected Cody to question him or offer to go with him, but he simply nodded his head and went on staring into the fire. The snow had pretty much stopped, but it was still overcast. As Jack approached the cabin, he saw that the only thing left of the fire was a few glowing embers here and there. It was hard to make out much of anything in the darkness, and since he had only been in the cabin once, he wasn't sure he could even find the trapdoor that Blake had told him about. The front of the little structure was still standing, but as Jack stepped up on the porch, he felt it sway slightly under him. Cautiously, he stepped across the threshold. He noticed that the porch and the front wall were really the only things left of the building. He could see now there had been a break in the clouds, and a shaft of moonlight partially lit the burned floorboards. The desk was still there, sort of, but when he went to push it out of the way, it crumbled to pieces. Feeling with his fingers, he managed to find the small hole that Blake had mentioned. Hooking his index finger inside, he pulled up. The door came up so easily that he nearly flung it across the room. The box was there and Jack extracted it. After fumbling with the catch for a moment, he managed to get it open.

It was all there, just as Blake had said it was. Jack ran his fingers through the cold coins. He held one up to the light and smiled to himself. Well, Blake would have it. He had no use for it. Jack had really only been concerned with the store of guns that had been left behind. These, Jack was sure, had been all but destroyed. Remembering his promise to Annie, he took the box out to the forest and hid it in an old log.

He rejoined the other two, finding them anxious to start back. "Anything left?" Chance asked as he approached the fire.

"Not much." Digging into his coat pocket he produced ten or twelve coins, which he handed to the older man. "Found these in the desk," he said, "Thought you and your nephew might like a souvenir."

Chance smiled, but he gave them all over to Cody, saying, "Not me, though. I don't want nothing else to do with this godforsaken place."

# CHAPTER 28

J ack sat at the kitchen table drinking coffee. It had been three months since his trip to Andre's old camp. It was early morning, and no one was up but him. He had always been an early riser; he liked having this time to himself. They had been so busy lately, and it was really the only time he had to collect his thoughts. They had managed to clear some paths through the ice, so people were able to pass back and forth between the house and the village. It had been unseasonably warm the past week, and a lot of it had already begun to melt.

He smiled as he remembered Annie's relief at this, "Oh Jack, I was afraid it would never go away!"

As for himself, he knew that it would melt eventually—he was just glad to see it happening, if for no other reason than her peace of mind. Every morning he would find her staring out at the huge ice sheet, the tears either running down her cheeks or clouding her eyes, and although he would try to assure her, she couldn't get it out of her head that she had done some permanent damage.

One morning she had turned to him, sobbing, and said: "Never again, Jack!"

He knew what she meant. He knew that after her first few attempts to use her power to melt the ice, she had given up and had sworn to herself and him that she would never use it again.

He had taken her face between his hands and whispered softly, "I don't think it's that easy, love. I think it is part of you, and if it's part of you, then it can't be a bad thing."

The village had absorbed Andre's people without a hitch. Jack thought, for probably the hundredth time now, how amazing it was that the human race could still come together in a crisis. Most of these people, emaciated as they were, had fully recovered under the care of the native people as a result of Annie's constant forays among them. She had gone down there every day, in all kinds of weather. She was a nurse and a doctor to these people, taking to them her little bag filled with herbs, fresh fruit, and vegetables that had been grown in the lab behind the workshop. The lab, as Jack had learned to call it, had been unaffected by the catastrophe and continued to produce its bounty, under David's watchful eye. But Jack knew that as much as Annie protested that she would never use her power, the plants there continued to thrive because of her. For all of her doctoring down at the village, Jack was confident that it was really just her mere presence that had brought the sick and forlorn people back to life. At first they had been frightened by her presence among them, but it didn't take long for that fear to turn to something like awe—they worshipped her. When Jack had accompanied her yesterday, he had seen how the children had run out to meet her, gathering around her, all talking at once. Their parents were more reserved, but they would look at her with shining eyes and a sort of wonder as she came among them.

Then there were the new people—the new people were the ones that had begun showing up about a month ago. They seemed to trickle in every day, by twos and threes; or sometimes a group of eight or ten would show up and set up camp. Jack thought that if it kept up like this, they would have a regular town bigger than Fort Simpson by next winter—how they heard of this place and why they were coming, Jack at first had written off to the regular migration north that had been going on for years.

Then one day he had met a family of four coming toward the house. He told them where they could find the village, but the father had said they had already been there and found it quite inviting. For a moment they all just stood there awkwardly. Jack was about to ask if he could help them in some other way when the little boy, who couldn't have been more than six or seven, blurted out: "Where's the Little Mother?"

Jack startled. "This must be Jacob's work," he thought. After telling the family where they could find Annie, he went to search him out.

"I have met no one today," was his answer to Jack's somewhat irritable inquiry. "Besides," he went on, "she is usually there to meet the new people when they come into the village."

Jack knew this was true and he wrote it off to idle gossip, yet he couldn't shake the feeling that this family had known about Annie and that it was because of her that they had come.

The main problem they were up against was how to feed so many. The village itself had always been self-sufficient, but it was getting harder to supply meat for the growing population. Jack himself had taken on this problem, and with the help of Blake, who had recovered fully by now, they had managed to kill quite a bit of game—although they had to travel further and further away to find it. They usually made these trips by dog sled and would sometimes be out two or three days at a time. As a result they had become pretty close, as men often do who have come through a battle together.

Jack still wasn't sure if he would trust him with his life, but ever since he had come back and told him where he could find his gold, Blake had treated him with a new respect. He was coming to Jack instead of David when he had a question. David himself had put all his efforts into restoring the house and barn—with the help of his remaining cowboys, they had gotten a lot done, considering the circumstances.

He was just getting up to refill his cup when he heard the front door open and Blake's heavy tread coming down the hall. He came into the kitchen just as Jack sat down, two full cups on the table. He was grinning from ear to ear. In his hands he carried the box that Jack had placed in the old log.

Setting it on the table, he said, "My goodness, Jack! Do you have any idea how much is here?"

"Not a clue," Jack said, leaning back in his chair and lighting his pipe.

Blake sat down across from him and in a conspiratorial whisper said, "Nearly four hundred Canadian eagles."

"Jack!" he exclaimed. Leaning closer, he added, "We're rich!"

Jack smiled easily and said, "No, you're rich."

"Aw Jack, I wouldn't feel right not sharing—after all, you're the one who risked his neck to get it."

Jack looked down at the box, which Blake had set reverently on the table and thought: "I could by a new rifle or a ring for Annie." He was turning these things over in his mind when he heard the floorboard creak lightly. Annie herself appeared in the doorway. For a moment she paused, her eyes meeting his. She smiled her best smile and went to the cupboard for her own cup.

Jack turned again to Blake. "You keep it," he said.

Annie came over, setting down her coffee, fell into his lap, and kissed him.

Blake grinned, picked up the box, stood up, and said, "You sure, Jack?"

"Yeah," he answered, not taking his eyes off of the beautiful face only inches from his own. "You keep your treasure, Blake. I've already found mine."

# THE END

# AFTERWORD

Jack stood on the small rise, looking down at the skyline. Even in the few years since he had last seen it, it had altered considerably. It seemed to have shrunk and there were a few less buildings blocking out the horizon. In another hundred years, he thought there would be nothing left of the old city. Indeed, if the climate wasn't so dry, it might have fallen already. "Well," he thought, "it was no great loss." Maybe it would be better when all remnants of the old world were buried in the dust.

He heard Annie's light step behind him, and he turned, smiling. She was wearing the heavy coat that they had bought in Fort Simpson, because although it was nearly June, the mornings were still cold out here in the high desert. He saw also that she had replaced her leggings with the denim jeans that they had bought in the same place. She had tucked them down into her old moccasins. Wolf was wandering aimlessly behind her, sniffing at every shrub he came to. Jack wondered again at the devotion of the animal.

Two days after that final scene at the old house, Wolf had disappeared, and for weeks nothing was heard of him. One morning he and Annie had ridden out to that monstrosity of a tree where Annie had been born. He and her father had both protested—Jack, for one, having had quite enough of the supernatural for awhile—but Annie had insisted, saying she wanted to see if anything had changed. Jack didn't understand why she thought anything would have changed, but he scarcely let her out of his sight those days after coming so close to losing her. They approached the spot silently, almost reverently. Annie was impatient, reaching the clearing before him.

Suddenly he heard her exclaim: "Oh Jack! Have you ever seen anything so wonderful?"

He dismounted and walked the last few yards, and as he came upon the old tree, his breath caught in his throat. The tree was there, but the only resemblance to the tree Jack had seen before was its sheer size. Gone were the bare branches—they were now covered with huge green leaves, millions of them. Each leaf was as big as Jack's hand. They blotted out the twisting, gnarled trunk, down to within twenty feet of the ground. But that wasn't all—at its base, some sort of vine with small white flowers blooming from it every six inches or so had grown up and encircled the trunk all the way to the lowest branch. This would have been a stunning sight to behold, even in the middle of August, but it was only the end of February, when all the plants and flowers still lay dormant under two feet of snow. Annie approached it slowly. Turning toward him, she laid her hand lightly on the tree.

"It's a tree of life," she murmured, smiling at him. For just a moment, blue light seemed to run down her arm and into her face—but it had only been a moment. When Annie withdrew her hand, still smiling, it was gone.

Later, Jack wasn't sure it had happened at all. He told himself, for his own good, that it was probably just a trick of the light. The trip back was proving to be a somber one—Annie seemed to be lost in her own thoughts, and once or twice he had caught her wiping away a tear from one pale cheek. They had just reentered the forest on the far side of the valley, not far from where he had collapsed with Annie in his arms only a few months before, when they heard a short yip, just to their right. Annie brightened almost instantly and dismounted, combing the ground with wide eyes. Then the sound came again: "Yip, yip."

Annie walked forward and, climbing up on a slanting rock, lay down to peer over the edge. Motioning with one hand for him to join her, she put one finger over her lips, telling him to come quietly. He lay beside her and looked down—what he saw was two wolf pups! He turned to look at Annie, not daring to speak. She seemed not to have any reservations; both pups were looking up at her. She turned to Jack, smiling her best smile.

"Their mother must be out hunting," she said.

Jack was about to suggest that they had best leave before she got back when he glimpsed a low shadow slinking through the woods toward them. "Too late," he said, his hand going to the butt of the revolver.

Annie's hand covered his as their eyes met.

"Fine," he said, "but we had better go."

They both turned at the same time and Jack nearly leapt out of his skin—behind them, not two feet away, his paws planted on the very rock they were lying on, stood Wolf himself.

Jack cursed and Annie gave him a disapproving glance. She threw her arms around Wolf's shaggy neck, exclaiming: "Wolf, you're a daddy!"

It wasn't until a few weeks later that they realized that Wolf had become more than just a daddy. David had been out hunting with a few people from the village when he had spotted a good-size wolf pack running an old moose straight at them. His first thought was to shoot the thing for himself—he had even taken a bead on it when a large wolf bolted from the scrub and pinned it to the ground. There was no mistaking it: Wolf had become the leader of the pack. David's eyes gleamed with delight as he told of how the big fellow had taken down the moose all by himself. Jack had glanced at Annie with some apprehension. How would she take losing her old friend?

He was surprised when she had smiled in spite of the tears that threatened to spill over her cheeks to say, "Wolf has his own family to look out for now—and so do you, Jack!

Then a strange thing had happened on the very day that they were to depart on their journey back to Jack's home. Jack had already mounted his horse, a fine animal that had been David's favorite that he had given to Jack as a wedding gift. Annie was giving her brother a final hug goodbye, and David himself was standing by for his turn when suddenly Wolf bounded up and sat at her feet. He just sat there, looking up at her as if to say: "You weren't gonna leave without me, were you?" Everyone had a good laugh, which was good considering you could have cut the tension with a knife. Although they had promised to return with Jack's people as soon as they possibly could, it was hard to part with their friends and family here. That evening as they were making camp, Jack had questioned her about Wolf's reappearance.

"It's strange," she said, "the only way an alpha male would ever abandon the pack is if he were challenged and beaten by another alpha."

Both of them found this highly unlikely—Wolf was by far the largest timber wolf Jack had ever seen. Annie turned to him eyes wide and gasped. "Unless...Oh Jack, you don't think..."

Jack took her hand in his, "What, Annie?"

"Unless his mate died!"

She looked so concerned. Any little thing seemed to set her off these days, and Jack had been doing everything in his power to make her life as carefree as possible. Jack took her in his arms, not knowing exactly what to say to comfort her. Then something dawned on him.

"You know, Annie," he began, "I didn't think much of it at the time, but those pups were pretty big."

She took a step back from his embrace and looked up at him questioningly. He put his hands in his pockets, looking a little embarrassed. "It's just that it seems kind of impossible that Wolf could have been following us all over the place and still had enough time to start a family."

Light dawned in her eyes. "Of course!" she said. "I just assumed that they were big like their father, but maybe Wolf was just a surrogate!"

"You're right," he went on. "Could be the real father was killed and Wolf was just taking his place until he could get them established in a pack."

Annie thought about it for a minute, then looking over at the animal in question, who appeared to be hanging on every word, said: "I don't know, Jack; that seems unlikely. For one thing, wolves seldom leave their mates on purpose. Even if she weren't his mate, it would mean that Wolf adopted a family, challenged the head of the pack, became their leader, then one night just up and left them to fight it out."

"Or," he said, smiling a little sardonically, "maybe he let another dominant male take over."

For a moment she just stood there, staring at the ground, her dark hair falling over her shoulders. He was just reaching out to touch it when she looked up suddenly, her blue eyes looking straight into his.

Putting both hands on her hips and cocking her head she asked, "Jack Brooks, are you trying to get me to believe that Wolf intentionally threw a fight just so he could come back to me?"

"Why not? I know I would," he said, his smile faltering a little.

For a moment she just stood there, hands on her hips, brow furrowed, eyes round and questioning, when suddenly her face lit up and she began to laugh. At the same time she launched herself at him and he caught her easily in his arms. Their lips met and all of the humor went out of the moment.

# TO BE CONTINUED...